**Books by Jessica S. Olson
available from Inkyard Press**

Sing Me Forgotten

SING
ME
FORGOTTEN

JESSICA S. OLSON

Recycling programs
for this product may
not exist in your area.

ISBN-13: 978-1-335-14794-3

Sing Me Forgotten

This edition published by arrangement with Harlequin Books S.A.

For questions and comments about the quality of this book, please contact us at
CustomerService@Harlequin.com.

Inkyard Press
22 Adelaide St. West, 40th Floor
Toronto, Ontario M5H 4E3, Canada
www.InkyardPress.com

Printed in U.S.A.

For Jon.

You wrangle kids, you keep the peanut butter stocked, and you don't bat an eye when I ask you how best to stab a person with a shard of glass.

You're the real dream, and this book wouldn't exist without you.

CHAPTER
ONE

I am a shadow. A shimmer of black satin. A wraith in the dark.

Music soars above the audience to where I hide behind a marble cherub near the Channe Opera House's domed ceiling. The lead soprano's vibrato trembles in the air, and my eyes fall shut as her music sends her memories rippling across the inside of my eyelids in shades of gray. The images are fuzzy and the emotions distant, but if I surrender myself to them, I can almost forget what I am for a moment.

Every night when the curtains rise and lights engulf the stage, when the seats fill with whispering patrons and the air shivers with the strum of strings, I glimpse the world outside—a world I've never seen with my eyes but know better than the beat of my heart because I've experienced it through a thousand different pasts.

The lead soprano's memories pull me in, and for a moment I am her, dashing out onto a stage bathed in golden light and sending my voice to fill the theater. The audience watches me dance, and though I cannot see their expressions from the soprano's vantage point, I imagine their eyes glassy with tears as my song plunges into their souls and strums along their heartstrings with slow, practiced grace. Their faces shine, their gazes riveted on my beauty. I raise my hand to my own cheek where I can all but feel the warmth of the spotlight.

But instead of smooth skin, my fingertips slip against my mask. I jolt my hand away, hissing, and relinquish my hold on her past.

My attention flicks to the premium box where Cyril Bardin meets my gaze. *You're too visible, Isda*, his eyes say.

I shrink into the shadows as applause smatters like raindrops below, not nearly enthusiastic enough to ensure adequate ticket sales. It seems the soprano, though nearly flawless in her performance, was not enough to make up for the rest of the abysmal cast.

Luckily, I'm very good at my job.

The clapping peters out as Cyril strides onto the stage. The performers line up behind him, tugging at their costumes and adjusting their wigs as discreetly as they can. Where their smiles pull across lips tight with too much makeup and wrinkle in tired, powdery lines around their eyes, Cyril's is charming, as always, accentuated by a regal, high forehead, paper-white hair, and a clean-shaven jaw. He gestures to the crowd with twinkling eyes. "Merci, my illustrious guests." His voice booms out to bounce back from the far walls. "It has been truly a pleasure to entertain you tonight."

Without thinking, I reach for the pendant at my throat and twist its chain around my fingers as anticipation bubbles like champagne in my stomach.

"Now before I bid you au revoir, it is time once again for the Channe Opera House's age-old tradition of having the audience join our performers in a special rendition of the Vaureillean classic, 'La Chanson des Rêves.'" Cyril turns to the orchestra at his feet and nods. "Maestro."

The conductor cues up the strings, then climbs onto the stage at Cyril's side and raises his baton. As one, the audience launches into the familiar tune.

The skin on my left ankle bone prickles—the place where I once carved the Manipulation Mark that enables me to harness my magic. The scar has since faded and been scraped away by clumsy tumbles down the stairs, but the ability that carving it gave me is still just as strong any time voices fill the air with music. My power purrs to life in my chest, reaching out toward each voice, yearning for the memories that live in them. I scan the faces quickly, letting images and emotions trickle through me one after the other, a burbling current of sights and sounds and smells.

When people sing, I see their memories, starting with the newest. If I want to, I can comb backward through time, sifting through the liquid swirl of moments in their minds as though rippling my fingers through water in a creek.

It is only in these moments that I truly feel alive. Where the world has forced me to hide, hated me for my power, tried to kill me for what I am, I have found my purpose in surrounding myself with its music and holding the memories of its people in my hands. They don't know I'm there, churning through their minds among their secrets and darkest moments, but I know. And no matter how many nights I've spent up here tucked away in the shadows, the thrill of finally having some measure of power over them sends tingles straight through every nerve of my body.

This is my performance, the only one I am allowed. I may not be able to stand on a stage and hypnotize them with my voice, but in this small way, I am just as much a part of the production as the dancers and singers.

I slip into each audience member's recollection of the performance like a ballerina into her spotlight, skipping from one mind to the next, easing away any negative emotions I find there and replacing them with positivity. Once the tone is right, I move on to erasing the moment where the lead tenor's voice cracked on that high G and eliminating the instant when one of the backup dancers tripped as she twirled across center stage.

I whisper-sing along with "La Chanson des Rêves" as I work, the words so familiar they fall off my tongue as easily as breathing. The chorus is my favorite part.

> *Who was the monster, the man or Les Trois,*
> *In Time's unstoppable tread?*
> *Was it the terrible queens, the world's guillotines,*
> *Who bathed Vaureille in red?*
>
> *Or was it the man with love in his heart,*
> *Innocent and brave though he seemed,*
> *Who unsheathed a blade, their hearts he betrayed*
> *As he ended their lives while they dreamed?*

I work quickly. With nearly two thousand seats in the theater, it is impossible for me to modify every person's recollection of tonight's performance, but I don't need to tamper with them all. If I can do the majority before the song ends and my connection breaks, it should be enough to encourage positive reviews, repeat ticket sales, and season pass popularity.

The orchestra strums out the final refrain, the audience falls silent, and the images vanish from my mind.

I twirl my pendant's chain around my pinky as a grin spreads across my lips.

The air fills with the rustle of patrons making their way to the exits, and I survey their expressions as they tug on gloves and babble enthusiastically to one another, dressed in silks and tuxedos, adorned with pearls and top hats. Their cheeks glow with the flush of excitement. Their arms wave emphatically as they speak. Their hands dig into their purses for the glimmering coins that will buy them tickets to return.

Cyril catches my eye from the stage. He does not smile—

that would be too obvious—but the creases in his cheeks deepen in approval.

I nod, chest heaving slightly from the expense of power, and settle back to wait for the opera house to empty.

Only once the workers have cleaned away the litter from the seats, extinguished the lanterns, and packed off for home, do I emerge from behind the stone cherub on the ceiling. I drop silently through the trapdoor that only Cyril and I know about and land like a cat in the upper hallways of the opera house.

The grand, palatial building cradles me in its dark depths as I make my way to the main floor, across the shimmering tile of the lobby, and toward Cyril's office in the east wing. The faint scent of smoke curls lazily in the air as the newly extinguished candelabras stretch their arms toward the high ceilings in the shadows.

My skirts *shush-shush-shush* across the floor, the only sound to break the silence. I breathe easily. Now that the lights are out and the people are gone, there is no risk of being seen, no risk of having someone catch sight of my mask and wonder at what it hides, no risk of being discovered and sent to my death.

Stars glitter in the windows as I pass, and I pause for a moment to lean on a windowsill, undo the latch, and push the pane wide. Crisp, autumn air brushes against my neck and ruffles the raven feathers attached to my mask. I drink in the taste of approaching autumn, the crumbly musk of orange-red leaves, the slight chill on the edge of the breeze.

The grayish glow of gaslights carves shadows along the maze of cobbled streets outside. A horse nickers nearby, and the scrape of carriage wheels chafes at the wind.

What would it be like to walk along those streets? What

would my footsteps sound like if I were to stride over those cobblestones? What would the air feel like on my bare face?

I know the city of Channe better than anyone. I've seen every inch of it, from the lavish homes up on the hill to the sooty district of the factory workers to the west. I've explored it through the eyes of bakers and councilmen and cabbies alike—anyone with enough money in their pockets to afford a night at the opera.

But to actually see it *myself*? Not in flimsy, black-and-white memories where the sensations have been dulled and the emotions siphoned away by the passage of time, but there in the middle of it all? To really experience it? I lean against the window frame as constellations sparkle like jewels in a sky of black velvet.

Laughter draws my gaze to the street corner. The soprano whose memories I viewed earlier climbs into the dark recesses of a cab, followed by one of the lead dancers.

My jaw stiffens.

As much as I love their music and the memories I see in it, I cannot help but resent every last one of them. The performers, the dancers, even the patrons. They, all of them, play a role in making simply existing dangerous for me. It is they who would shriek at the sight of my face, they who sneer at the mention of gravoirs, they who have carefully constructed a society in which I am not welcome.

It is because of them that the world will never hear my voice.

I pull the window shut and, instead of heading upstairs to Cyril's office like I'm supposed to, I turn and reenter the empty theater.

It is silent as a tomb, the watchful dark a cold caress as I make my way to the stage, mount the stairs, and stride to its center. I turn and face the gilded, plush seats.

The chandelier and theater lights have long been extinguished, and the room is full of shadows. I pretend each one is a patron like those in the soprano's memory. They watch me with rapture, their brows raised in awe. They sit forward in their seats, holding their breath, waiting for my next song.

I tip my head back and close my eyes, imagining the gentle hum of a bow sliding along the strings of a violin, ushering in the opening notes of my aria.

But as I inhale and open my mouth to sing, a soft ballad strokes along the shell of my ear.

I stop. Hold my breath. Turn my head toward the sound.

The quiver of a faraway voice slides through a melody I don't recognize. A man's voice. A rich tenor that glides from note to note with the smoothness of melting butter.

I should ignore it, exit the theater, and mount the stairs to Cyril's office. I should stay far away from whoever is singing in the dark.

But my body shifts toward the music, drinking it in, letting it shiver into my ears and roll down my spine as I make my way back up the aisle and into the hall. My pace is slow at first, but it quickens as I get nearer. What kinds of memories might I see in his refrain? What new parts of the world might I discover?

His voice is snow the day after a frigid night, its surface smooth as glass and sparkling like diamonds. It is the bright fire of autumn transforming the world into a kaleidoscope of burning reds and golds. It is the soft caress of darkness, welcoming and accepting and constant.

Everything in me stills. The thrum of excitement in my pulse eases; my lungs cease their in-and-out movement; even my heartbeat slows. His vibrato sweeps from note to note, pulling me with it.

When I reach the end of the hallway, his memories crash into me all at once with the force of a thousand tons of stone.

I stumble backward against the wall and grasp the foliage carved there so tightly pain stabs into the pads of my fingers.

Where every other memory I've seen has been a faraway wisp of grays and muted glows, his are achingly vibrant, full of color and vivid sunlight.

They swirl through me, a rainbow of emotions and hues sweeping me along like the tide of a monstrous river. Instead of dropping into his most recent memory, I plunge backward in his mind, spinning past echoes of laughter and flashes of music, too enthralled by the deluge of feelings to settle on any one memory and instead letting them all wash through me, a sparkling cascade of life.

My body tingles, sparking like lightning as though I've come alive for the first time in my seventeen years. As I hurtle through the images, one face jumps out, and I stop. Stare.

She's a small girl—maybe six years old—crowned in dark hair that looks so real I swear I could reach out and let its silkiness trail across my palm. With a bright blue ribbon tied at the crown of her head and a lacy periwinkle nightgown clinging to her petite frame, she could be any other child in the world.

But my body goes rigid when I see her. The blood drains to my feet, and I sway where I stand. My hands dart for my pendant, clutching it so hard its ridges cut through the flesh of my palm.

This girl could be any other child in the world but for her face.

Her face is like mine.

My knees buckle, and I crash into a nearby candelabra. It topples, clanging like a gong against the tile.

The tenor's voice breaks off, and the memory vanishes. I scramble upright, heart thundering, sweat making my hair stick to the nape of my neck.

"Hello?" the tenor calls.

I back up several paces, staring horrified at the candelabra at my feet.

And then I run.

Visions of the night of my birth when I was dropped into a well and left to drown engulf me as I lift my skirts and bolt around another corner. As a gravoir, a supposed memory-twisting monster, it is impossible for me to forget a single moment of my existence. But the memory of the cold water, the burn in my chest, and the grip of Cyril's hands as he dragged me back out and whisked me to safety has never felt more real or immediate to me than it does now as I flee for my life.

For if that tenor catches me, if he removes my mask and sees what I am, the death that has stalked me since that frigid, wet night will finally claim me.

CHAPTER TWO

The tenor's footfalls trail me, echoing against the ceiling and statues until it seems as though he is everywhere at once. I slam one foot in front of the other and pray to the God of Memory to hide me away where this man will never find me.

I careen around a staircase and skid to a halt in front of Cyril. His hair glows like a white halo in the starlight, and his lips pull tight into a line as his eyes flick from my face to the hallway behind me. With a grimace, he grips my elbow and steers me into a deep alcove in the wall before sweeping forward to meet the tenor.

"Monsieur Rodin," Cyril says, his voice quiet and tense as the tenor comes around the corner. "What on earth are you running for?"

"I'm sorry." The tenor slows to a stop but dodges a look past Cyril's shoulder to the hallway where I am hidden. I press my back against the wall, praying my black dress stays obscured in the shadows and the crystals I've sewn into my mask don't glitter.

The mysterious tenor is a boy around my age. He wears threadbare clothing and a cap atop a mop of dark hair that hangs across his eyes and tangles in his eyelashes. "I saw someone," he says as his chest heaves in and out from our chase. "It could have been a thief."

Cyril chuckles. "It was probably the Opera Ghost."

"Opera Ghost, monsieur?"

"Oui. They say there's a phantom that haunts these hallways at night, though no one has ever been able to prove its existence."

The boy frowns, glancing past Cyril again. "That was no ghost. Whoever it was knocked over a candelabra."

"My dear Monsieur Rodin. Emeric, was it?"

"Oui, monsieur."

"Emeric. I make rounds every evening at eleven. If there are any thieves on the loose, I will no doubt find them." Cyril crosses long, thin arms across his chest. "Now, unless I am much mistaken, I thought I made it clear when I hired you this morning that you were to mop the third floor corridor by ten o'clock."

"Oui, monsieur, I was just finishing up."

Cyril pulls a polished watch from his breast pocket. "And here it is nearly ten thirty."

Emeric nods and drops his gaze to the floor. "Oui, monsieur. I'm sorry, monsieur."

"I suggest you get to it." Cyril pats the tenor's shoulder. Emeric flinches at the touch, and in his sudden movement, something flashes at his throat. I squint to get a better look.

Through a small opening in the collar of his shirt, a blue stone peeks from the gap between his collarbones, strung on a thick, leather cord. It is clear and bright as a summer sky, and I tighten my grip on my own necklace to keep from gasping at its luster.

Emeric shifts again, and the stone disappears from view.

"Don't you worry about the thief or the Opera Ghost or whatever it was you might have seen," Cyril continues. "I run a tight ship around here. Nothing gets past me."

Emeric frowns, and his thick brows furrow as though he's not quite convinced, but he nods and takes off at a lope back the way he came.

I find myself leaning out of the alcove to watch his departure, eyes tracing the sharp angles of his broad shoulders and the steady stride of his long legs.

Once the boy has disappeared and the sounds of his footfalls have faded, Cyril speaks but does not turn. "Isda?"

I swallow, releasing my pendant and tucking it back into the neckline of my dress. My hand smarts where the corners of the trinket jabbed into my skin. Though my blood still surges thick with the excitement of all I saw in Emeric's memories— the colors, the light, that gravoir girl—I force my breathing to slow. "I'm so sorry, Cyril. It was an accident. I—"

Cyril turns tired eyes on me. "We cannot afford accidents, Izzy. You must be more careful."

I nod, cheeks burning under my mask. "I know. I got distracted."

He sighs, then gestures toward the stairs. "Shall we?"

Gathering my skirts in a sweaty grip, I follow him up to the fourth floor and down the hall to the ornate oak door of his office. He shoves a large metal key into the lock, scrapes it sideways, and eases the door inward. The room exhales a cold puff of air into my face. I trail inside behind Cyril and begin lighting the lanterns on the wall as he crosses to the open window to pull it shut and latch it tight.

Usually, Cyril is all abuzz at our nightly postperformance meetings, jabbering about ticket sales and the amount of money earned and the enthusiasm of the guests as they bid him their goodbyes. Tonight, however, he avoids my eyes, rearranging the items on his desk like they've personally affronted him, his jaw clenching and unclenching so forcefully I'm afraid it might crack.

The lanterns' orange light illuminates thousands of books

crammed into every spare corner of the wall-to-wall shelving. Golden titles wink their cursive script from worn-out spines. A framed map of our city, Channe, and another one of our country, Vaureille, stand propped against the back set of shelves. Golden vials of memory elixir line every spare space alongside piles of elegant fountain pens and playbills from past shows.

My breath stills, as it always does, when I catch sight of the small statue Cyril keeps on the shelf behind his desk.

It is a depiction of Les Trois, the three terrible gravoirs spoken of only in whispers. The three women who once bathed Vaureille's streets in blood and taught the world to fear people like me. To kill us.

I tear my gaze from their disfigured faces and bared teeth as I take my place in the wooden chair across the desk from Cyril, a chair I've sat in so many times it curves like it was built to nestle along the contours of my spine. Knotting my hands in my lap, I stare intently at the floor, ignoring the way the eyes of Les Trois seem to bore into my forehead, and wait for Cyril to say something. Anything.

"I'll try to be more discreet," I reassure him. "I won't let it happen again."

He plucks a book from the shelf, studies its cover, and places it on his desk, careful not to rattle the array of vials standing in neat little rows in one corner. Gripping the cover between his slender hands, he grimaces at its title for a long moment before raising his gaze to mine.

The gray-blue of his eyes swims with emotions I know so well on him I could put them to music. Disappointment pulls their corners tight. Frustration smolders in the set of his brow—so low his lashes quiver against its ridge. But his fear is the strongest; it ripples in the color of his irises as though a stone has been dropped there and the worry has grown into a tide. I could compose an entire concerto exploring that look with tentative quarter notes and underlying bass beats.

I rise, cross to the table, and place my hand lightly over one of his, never once blinking, never once dropping his stare. "I'm all right, Cyril. He didn't see me. He doesn't know what I am."

"You're certain?" His voice is barely a whisper.

"Oui. I'm safe."

As we silently regard each other, I can almost hear an echo of his voice reading methodically through the poem at the end of my favorite fairy tale, *Charlotte and the Mirror of Forgotten Things*, and the way the tired quiver of each syllable lulled my tiny, five-year-old body into slumber. *When Charlotte looked in the mirror, she saw a great many things*, he murmured more times than I could ever count. *A bone, a bauble, a book, a barrel of berries picked last spring...*

"It's all right." I reassure him with a squeeze of my hand.

Cyril blows out a breath, jaw working, and then, finally, nods. "You cannot let your guard down, Isda. Not ever." His voice lowers. "I'm sure I don't need to remind you that carelessness could cost you your life."

I shake my head. "You don't."

"Good. Because losing you would—" He swallows and pinches the bridge of his nose. "It would ruin me." He drops his hand and settles his palm over my knuckles as the corners of his mouth tick upward. "Besides, you've made yourself pretty indispensable to me with your memory modification prowess. I don't know if the opera house could manage without you."

I chuckle. "I'm glad I've been helpful."

He searches my face with gentle eyes. "But does it fulfill you? I wish as much as you do that you didn't have to hide, that you could be a bigger part of the shows. Heaven knows you're a better vocalist than any I have ever hired."

A blush warms my cheeks. "It is enough for me."

He cocks his head, sensing the tremulous lie. We both know that nothing but being on that stage will ever be enough for me.

I lean closer to him and meet his gaze. "It is more than any other gravoir has had a chance for, and for that I will be forever grateful."

"Promise me you'll be more careful."

I nod. "It won't happen again."

He holds my stare for a long moment, then releases his grip on my hand, taking his place in the high-backed leather chair behind his desk. His expression relaxes. "Now. Other than what happened with the Rodin boy, I'd say you did quite well tonight. The audience seemed in great spirits after 'La Chanson des Rêves.'"

I perch on the edge of my seat, not even bothering to keep the excitement out of my voice. "I was able to erase that moment where the tenor's voice cracked from the memories of at least three-quarters of them."

Cyril's lips curve into a pleased grin. "You are getting faster. You keep this up, and we'll sell out every seat in the place for *Le Berger* in a few months."

"Selling out *that* show shouldn't be too difficult."

Cyril plucks one of the vials of memory elixir from his desk and rolls it along his palm. "It has historically been a crowd favorite, that's true."

The vial in his hand is identical to every other vial I've ever seen, and yet I find myself mesmerized by the sight of it. Barely the length of the pad of the thumb, the spiraling fendoir symbol carved into its surface is so tiny it almost looks like nothing more than a chip in the glass. The memory elixir inside glimmers gold, and as it slides back and forth when Cyril turns it over, I marvel at how the memories I see in the minds of the people who visit the theater could come from such a simple yet elegant substance.

It's too bad fendoirs—the ones who extract the elixir from people's minds—are not allowed into the opera house. Otherwise I might have been able to get into one's mind and see what it must be like to do such magic. To siphon away human memory's base form—the pure essence of remembering, ready to be sold to the highest bidder who can then drink and use it to compound their own ability to recall the past.

Does the elixir of Emeric Rodin's memories look different from everyone else's? I imagine it to be a dazzling thing, shining with every color fathomable and somehow full of music.

"Have you held auditions for *Le Berger*'s lead tenor role yet?" I ask absently, hypnotized as Cyril transfers the vial thoughtlessly from hand to hand.

"Oui. This morning." He tosses it up in the air, then catches it and points its cork at the door behind me. "That boy showed up asking to be considered. Never a day of training in his life."

I frown. "I heard him singing. That's why I was distracted. His voice—"

"Doesn't matter if he has a nice voice. Critics can spot an untrained performer within the first three notes of the opening number." Cyril slides the vial back into its place among the others and steeples his hands in front of his chin, regarding me with a thoughtful expression. "I offered him the janitor job instead. Perhaps if he spends enough time mingling with the right sort of people, he'll work his way up to be something of consequence someday. And I'll pay him handsomely, so if he's smart about his finances, I daresay he may one day be able to afford a tutor."

"I suppose…" But it still seems a pity Cyril never let the boy sing for him. Just remembering Emeric's voice now sends a thrill of gooseflesh down my arms.

"Speaking of *Le Berger*…" Cyril's eyes sparkle, and a tiny smile plays at the corners of his mouth. He reaches into his suit jacket and retrieves a stack of papers bound together by golden thread. "You'll never guess who was in the audience tonight."

"Who?" My eyes are sharp on the papers in his hand. Though only the back of the stack is visible, the thickness of it and the way it is bound together make it look as though it might be a set of sheet music.

The grin steals wide over his mouth as he flips the booklet around for me to see the cover. Gold lettering betrays it as a special edition printing of the organ arrangements of the music from *Le Berger*. "André Forbin."

"No!" I squeal, leaping to my feet. "Where was he sitting?"

"Box seat below mine." Cyril holds the music out, and I snatch it from him and flip open to the front page where Forbin's regal signature loops in elegant black ink below where it lists him as the opera's main composer. "I discovered the sheet music when I was visiting Chanterre last week. I know you already have the organ arrangement, but when I saw this was a special edition, I couldn't resist."

I run shaking fingertips over the music notes, stark midnight against the pristine white of the parchment, barely daring to breathe or blink.

Cyril's voice goes soft. "Well? Do you like it?"

I launch myself at him, flinging my arms around his neck. "I love it!"

He chuckles and pats my curls. When he releases the embrace, I clutch the music to my chest and sit back down in my chair, barely able to keep myself from bouncing.

"If only *you* could play the lead soprano in *Le Berger*. You have the perfect range for it," he muses as he returns to his own seat.

"Thank you." The words are sour on their way out, and I purse my lips. Because he's right. I *do* have the perfect range for it.

Just not the perfect face.

He sighs, tugging a slender folder from the shelf and flipping through its pages.

"Any trouble lately for the Council?" I survey the rows of record books on the shelves behind his desk. Cyril spends his days working on the King's Council of Channe and has done so for as long as I can remember. His wealth and influence in the city have made him a very prominent member of the governing body.

"Hmm? Oh, no." He rummages in his drawer for a fountain pen and scratches a few words on one of the pages. "Usual things. Keeping the Memoryless from getting out of hand in the streets, checking in on the fendoirs in their Maisons des Souvenirs to make sure they're behaving, things like that." He heaves a great sigh and looks sideways at me. "You know, one day soon I will be more than a simple clerk on that council." He pauses a moment, rubbing a thumb across the tip of his smooth chin.

"What is it?" I ask.

He slides both hands flat against the desktop. "It's just… LeRoux. The Head of the Council of Channe. He's so careless. He keeps terrible records, and he does not take seriously the danger brewing within our city."

"What do you mean?"

"The fendoirs are planning something." Cyril's eyes dart to the window, and he grimaces. "I see them congregating in the streets, whispering together. LeRoux is too soft with them. Gives them too much freedom. He forgets our history, what happened last time we let them roam like this."

My eyes dart to the statue of Les Trois, and I shudder. "Do you really think it could happen again? Even without gravoirs?"

"Fendoirs pose their own risks, though you're right, it would not necessarily be as terrible as last time right away. But the longer we turn a blind eye to the subtle insurgencies, the greater the threat becomes," Cyril says. "I've expressed my concerns, but LeRoux never listens. He is putting us all at risk. If he isn't stopped soon, we'll all suffer for it."

"It's that bad?" My eyebrows rise.

Cyril mops a hand over his face. "I sincerely hope I'm wrong." He stares down at his files, but his gaze is far away.

"You'll figure something out."

He smiles. "I always do. Now, off to bed with you. I've got a lot to get done before I can go home."

"I'll leave you to it, then." I make my way to the door, nearly knocking over a wooden globe on my way.

Cyril chuckles. "Careful, chérie. That was a gift from the King."

"Right. Sorry." I steady the globe before tugging the door open. With one foot in the hallway, I look back over my shoulder. "Thank you for the music, Cyril."

He lifts his eyes from the file he's writing in and nods, fond wrinkles crinkling around his mouth. "Of course, my Izzy. Of course."

I pull the door shut, then shuffle along the hallway, around a bend, and down flight after flight of stairs. Deeper and deeper I plunge into the belly of the opera house, where lustrous hallways adorned with gilded angels give way to stone and cobwebs, where the air grows cold and quiet, where brilliance transforms into the quiet mystery of nighttime and solitude.

CHAPTER THREE

The catacombs deep beneath the opera house are my domain. In them, I fall into the sweet, accepting embrace of darkness and the unassuming simplicity of silence and secrets.

I slip through the tunnel that leads to the empty crypt I've claimed as my own and strike a match to light the array of candlesticks that adorn every corner and surface of my room. Flickering firelight makes facets in the stone walls and ceiling sparkle like a lace of orange, winking stars. It illuminates the bed in the corner draped with a duvet the color of red wine and the ornate shelves crammed with songbooks and massive stacks of loose sheet music.

In the center of it all stands my organ. I move toward it, running my hand along its smooth, carved edges and its shining metal pipes. Cyril had it brought in for me when I was six years old, and other than him, this organ is my oldest and dearest friend.

The allure of its keyboards pulls me around, and I take my place on the bench. Shoving aside the composition I was working on earlier today, I set the new *Le Berger* music in its place and study it for a moment. My gaze follows the climb of the sixteenth notes up the staff where they trill for a beat before tumbling back to the bottom. I trace my pinky finger along the artistic flourish of the treble clef.

I don't need to read the sheet music to play the pieces from *Le Berger*; I've had the whole score memorized for years. My fingers go right to their positions for the opening aria, but before I dive into the familiar right-hand ascending scale that ushers in the beginning bass tones, I pause.

The memory of Emeric's voice is still there in my inner ear, curling its way quietly, languidly into my head and down the hollow of my throat to the place where my heart triple-beats the rhythm of his melody.

My hands slide upward into a new position.

I exhale.

And play.

The music comes from somewhere deep inside, like a gentle beast awakening. My fingers speed one over the other, dancing across the keys, skipping along sharps and flats like a stone along the ripples of a pond. The balls of my feet depress the pedals, filling the chamber with a rich sound, thick and slippery and deep as molasses against the stone walls.

My piece begins as an echo of Emeric's, but soon it transforms into a rush of the emotions I felt in his past. Love. Safety. Hope. As I trail out sixteenth notes as high as the warbling of birdsong, I pause.

Silence.

Emeric's embarrassed, apologetic grin fills my mind. His deep dimples. His dark hair trailing shadows in his eyes.

I drag my hands to the left and let the resonant, booming notes there roll, somber and dark as a ballad of the night.

It is only when my fingers slip from the keys that I realize my arms are shaking. I open my eyes, pull my mask off to scrub my fists across my gnarled cheeks, and blink when they come away wet.

I stare down at the glitter of tears on my knuckles.

What has this janitor done?

All my life, I've longed for the world outside. To be one of the opera performers who come and go as they please. I've glimpsed family dinners around beautiful wooden tables, springtime walks in Channe's city parks, the adoration of a lover's eyes just before a kiss.

But never until tonight have I seen it with such clarity, in full color, so sharp and detailed that the memories feel like they are my own. Never before have I grasped what living could truly be like.

Now the world outside pulls at me, begging for me to join it, to breathe it in, to taste it.

Tears continue to film across my vision as I turn my mask over in my hands. This mask was meant to hide my face from that world out there, keep the secret of what I am a bit harder to unravel. Cyril had it made especially for me by taking my measurements himself on my sixteenth birthday last year and sending them off to an artisan in the north. When it arrived, it was a plain, black thing that covered me from forehead to chin, ear to ear. I added the embellishments, the tiny crystals that encircle the eyes and lips, the beads swirling in filigrees of sparkle across the cheekbones, the raven feathers around the eyes.

With a mask like this, I am almost beautiful.

I trace a finger lightly along one of the feathers.

Keeping my promise to Cyril means I cannot go looking for the janitor boy.

But I don't have a choice.

For though the harsh world out there would destroy both Cyril and me if I am discovered, one thing has become so clear it rings straight through my bones and into my soul: I have to find Emeric Rodin again. I have to hear him sing.

For now that I have tasted the world hidden in the lushness of his voice, my chest churns with a hunger deeper than

I have ever known. A craving that has taken hold of every part of me. A need rooted in the cracks of my core.

But it isn't only the vividness of his memories.

That little gravoir girl with the smile on her lips and the sunshine in her hair... I have to learn more about her.

Gravoirs are killed at birth, executed as soon as their monstrosity is discovered and ascertained by the authorities as worse than the markings of a fendoir. I was lucky that Cyril saved me from that fate, but who pulled that little girl from the water? How is she living in a world of open skies and smiles and blue hair ribbons?

Is a life like that—a maskless, free life—possible for someone like me?

If I can figure out how she's achieved it, I may finally be able to stand on a stage like the one far above me, and not just when the patrons are gone and the lights are out. Maybe there's something that Emeric's memories of this girl could teach me...some way for me to finally have the spotlight and the backup symphony and the awestruck audience.

I glance upward, as though I can see past the stone ceiling all the way to Cyril's office.

He asked me to be careful, and I gave him my word that I would. But Emeric's memories hold in them the possibility of not only stepping outside the opera house but *living* in that wide world out there. Finally breaking free from the society that has chained me to the shadows. Performing on a stage. *Affecting* people with my music.

I can't just crouch back into the corners and hide anymore.

Cyril, for as much as he loves me, has never felt what I have at the hands of this hateful world. If he had, he would understand.

Emeric's voice echoes in my mind. I close my eyes, letting my skin shiver with pleasure, and grip my pendant in my fist.

Cyril doesn't have to find out.

CHAPTER
FOUR

I sit at my perch the following evening, grasping the cherub's meaty stone calf with one hand and knotting my finger in the chain of my pendant with the other. I try to lose myself in the memories of the singers onstage, but the images there suddenly seem so dull, so lifeless, so distant after what I experienced in Emeric's mind. And, now that I've seen the colors of *his* past, the grayscale memories I've already viewed dozens of times from the same cast I've been watching for months no longer thrill me the way they did before. I find myself scanning the audience and peering into the faces of ushers in the doorways, looking for that suntanned skin and pair of dimples that haunted my dreams last night.

When the performance ends and Cyril takes the stage to begin "La Chanson des Rêves," I snap to attention.

Focus, Isda.

Tamping down the adrenaline sparking like fire in my veins, I peer between the cherub's knees into the faces of the patrons below. They open their mouths and begin to sing.

Their memories do not assault me the way Emeric's did. They tug lazily at my power, a half-hearted prickle along the place where the Manipulation Mark used to be on my left ankle. I sigh and grip onto that feeling, propelling my mind into their memories and beginning my work.

If I'm going to be able to listen to Emeric sing again without Cyril finding out, I'll need to do my job just as well as any other night. Cyril is an observant man. If anything is out of the ordinary, he'll know I'm up to something.

Channeling everything Cyril has ever taught me about keeping my emotions in control, I breathe deeply through my nose and barrel through the sea of memories below me.

When the song reaches its finale, every audience member is smiling.

With sweat slicking the back of my neck and my chest heaving, I slouch against the curve of where the wall meets the ceiling, twirling a stray bit of hair around my thumb, and wait for the opera house to empty and the lights to go out.

An eternity has passed by the time I've deemed it safe to slip through my trapdoor, and my nerves are so raw I feel as though I might explode out of my own skin. The simultaneous thrill of knowing I'm about to go looking for a boy I'm forbidden from seeing and the anxiety about the risk I'm taking in doing so have me quivering.

It takes every ounce of self-control I have not to run straight for the third floor where Emeric is supposed to mop the tile. I cannot allow him to see me this time. I need to be much more careful than I was last night—no getting lost in the memories and toppling into candelabras. I'll hide, listen, and watch, and no one will know.

I slow my pace and lift my skirts so they don't rustle against my legs. Keeping to the edge of the hallways and hugging the corners, I force my breathing to stay even and silent.

What if Emeric already finished mopping? What if I missed him, and he's already gone home for the night? What if he decides not to sing while he works this time?

As the panic of that thought seizes me, a muffled humming

trails from a few corridors away. I pause, gripping the nearest statue to steady the sudden quake in my legs as relief fills my whole body, and follow the lovely lilt of the pure tenor tone I've been hearing in my mind since last night.

Once I get within range of where my power can latch on to the music—this time I'm just down a short flight of stairs and around a small bend—I ease into the space behind a velvet chair and sink to the floor.

His memories surge bright and beautiful, pummeling against my power, trying to get in. The skin on my ankle thrums along to the beat of his song as I close my eyes and try to focus through the barrage of images. Plunging past the ones of earlier tonight, I swim backward through time, dipping my face into each scene long enough to search for the gravoir girl before pulling back out and continuing my search.

After a dozen memories, anxiety begins to knot in my chest. I haven't found her yet, and the realization of how long it might take to look through an entire lifetime of memories makes my blood run cold. I don't have that kind of time. Emeric could finish mopping and leave soon, and Cyril is expecting me in his office to talk over tonight's results. If I don't show up, he might worry and come looking for me.

I spin through the memories faster and faster, ignoring the way my stomach feels like it's being wrenched out through my throat every time I have to pull myself out of a particularly beautiful moment to move onto the next one.

Images blur past of a small apartment, a candy shop, a kind-looking man with curly, black hair and a plump, round belly. About a hundred nights spent sitting outside an opera house—though not Channe's opera house, I can tell that much. Dozens of coins being collected in a small wooden box and then later dumped out onto ticket counters. Emeric sitting enraptured, grasping the armrests of a plush theater seat and staring wide-eyed at performers on a stage, desire and need twining through his gut.

Clenching my fists, I tread backward faster and faster to Emeric's childhood, skipping whole years as I go. Scenes flash past of him serenading rows of homemade, hand-stitched toy animals in kitchen chairs, of him practicing dance combinations in a quaint bedroom, of him singing to a sweet little girl in a pale blue nightgown—

The memories vanish, and I gasp as though I've been plunged into ice-cold water. It takes me a moment to orient myself, to remember how to breathe, to get my vision to focus.

"Are you okay, mademoiselle?" a voice asks nearby.

I jolt sideways, smacking my head on the back of the chair. I leap to my feet, wincing, and scramble away from the shadow towering over me.

"I'm sorry. I didn't mean to startle you. It's just…you were huffing and puffing back there. I worried you were having some sort of fit." The figure leans forward, and a shaft of starlight slants across his face. He grins. Dimples deepen in his cheeks, and a turquoise stone glimmers at his throat.

The need to run surges hot in my blood, but my legs feel as though they're made of lead.

Emeric runs a hand through his hair and cocks his head.

Right. He's still waiting for a response.

The words stick in my throat. I open and close my mouth like a suffocating fish.

I've never spoken to anyone besides Cyril in my life. Never made eye contact or had a conversation.

"I—I'm perfectly well, merci." My voice comes out squeaky and high-pitched. I swallow, remembering Cyril's oft-repeated words, *If you aren't in control of your emotions, you aren't in control of anything.* Willing my heart to stop its feverish attack on the inside of my rib cage, I straighten my skirt. If I act too strange, this Emeric boy will suspect something's off. In order to stay alive, I need to prevent that at all costs. "For your information," I force out, "I was not having a fit. I was...resting."

"Ah. That makes so much more sense." He nods, white teeth flashing. "Because hyperventilating is a fantastic method for putting oneself at ease."

I blink. Is he...mocking me? "I'm sorry, who did you say you were?"

"Oh, how rude of me." He holds out his right hand for me to shake. "I'm Emeric Rodin. I was hired on as a janitor here yesterday. Never been a janitor before in my life, but my mother's favorite punishment for misbehavior was making me scrub our house from top to bottom, so I suppose I'm actually quite the expert when it comes to mopping and dusting things."

His hand hangs awkwardly in the air for another moment before he finally shoves both of his fists into his jacket pockets and leans casually against the wall.

"Uh...were you going to tell me your name, or am I supposed to guess?" he asks.

The starlight casts a bluish glow along his profile.

"Because," he goes on with a nervous chuckle, "I'm historically terrible at guessing games. I'd probably come up with something like 'Celeste,' and then you'd tell me that that was the name of your favorite aunt who died last week, and then I'd feel like an imbecile." He pauses, eyes widening. "Wait, you don't have a dead Aunt Celeste, do you? Or a deceased pet cat with that name?"

I purse my lips. Fear has clenched a fist so tight on my insides that my dinner is threatening to come back up. My gaze darts upward to where Cyril is waiting.

"I am deeply sorry if you know a dead Celeste," he goes on in a rush, cheeks darkening. "I told you I'm bad at this. But, see, I'm even worse with awkward silences, and you standing there not talking is making me quite nervous, so if you could just muster up the strength to say something, I'd appreciate it a whole lot."

I take a deep breath and force the terrified quiver out of my voice. "You talk too fast."

"Thank you," he says in a whoosh of an exhale. "Er—I mean, sorry. I do talk fast. My uncle tells me that a lot. Can't get me to shut up most of the time."

"I believe that."

He snorts. "Ouch."

My cheeks feel like they're on fire. "I'm sorry. I didn't mean… I just…" I wring my hands. I've talked to Cyril plenty of times. Why is having a conversation with this boy so absurdly difficult?

He smiles. "It's all right. And completely fair. I think I even passed out once because I was talking so much I forgot to breathe."

"Really?"

His chuckle is like music. "Maybe." He gives me a devil's grin. "So should I call you 'mademoiselle,' or have you got a name tucked somewhere behind that mask of yours?"

My stomach jolts at the mention of my mask, but I keep my hands soft against my skirt and my breathing as normal as I can. Perhaps he'll think me only a simple fendoir and not a gravoir. While fendoirs by law aren't allowed in any public places where people may sing, they are protected by the King of Vaureille due to their ability to extract memory elixir. Even though fendoir faces are nowhere near as misshapen as gravoir ones, they are required to wear masks when they go out in public. Granted, those masks aren't usually adorned with feathers and crystals—just simple silver bits of fabric to cover what the unmarked would rather not see—but hopefully this Rodin boy won't think too hard on that.

He's still waiting for my response, bouncing a little on his heels.

What harm could there be in his knowing my name? It's not like it's in a record book anywhere.

I clear my throat. "I'm Isda."

"Lovely name."

"Isn't it?" I say before I can help myself. I've always loved the name Cyril chose for me.

"All right, Isda...is there a reason you were crouching behind that chair?"

I brace my shoulders and lift my chin, trying to exude far more confidence than I feel. "I was listening to you sing, actually. You have a remarkable voice."

He rubs the back of his neck. "Uh...merci. It was just an old tune from my hometown. Nothing special."

"The song may not have been, but your voice was."

He darts a glance at me. "Awfully kind of you to say so."

"I wasn't being kind. Only honest."

"It was kind all the same."

I bite my lip, thoughts racing, the images of his memories still dancing like ghosts on the insides of my eyelids. I need some way to get this boy to sing for me—and sing for me a lot. If I'm ever going to be able to wade through seventeen years of memories, I'll need time. Time that will have to come from more than just stolen moments stalking him in hallways.

The vision of him from his childhood performing on a makeshift stage in front of an assortment of toys flashes across my mind. It's obvious he loves music. I waded through hundreds of glimpses of what looked like an obsession with the opera.

I think of Cyril's words from last night about Emeric coming here to audition for the winter show.

"You really deserve to be on the stage, not back here mopping floors. Have you ever considered auditioning?" I try to act casual even though my mind is whirring at top speed, weaving together the threads of an idea. An idea that goes against everything I promised Cyril last night about being careful. But if I succeed, it might be worth the risk.

He shrugs. "I have, but no one seems to want to even hear me sing before making up their minds about my abilities."

"Have you been professionally trained?"

"Do I look like the type of guy with enough money to afford something like that?" He gestures to his patched jacket.

"Without any training, no opera house is going to look twice at you. But, as it so happens, I am a very accomplished vocal teacher." I'm surprised at how easily the lie slips from my lips. I just hope he doesn't hear the edge of eagerness in my voice.

He raises one eyebrow. "You? You can't be old enough to—"

"It's not about age. It's about experience, and I have a lot of it. So what do you say? Would you like vocal instruction or not?"

"I can't pay you."

"Did I mention money?"

"If you're not in it for pay, then what are you in it for?"

For the way your memories make me feel alive. For the things I could learn from the gravoir girl in your past. For the chance to be free.

"If I can get a singer onto the stage here," I say, fabricating the lie as I go, "I can prove my worth as a—a vocal professional. Get the world to take me seriously."

"But..." He pauses awkwardly, running his hand through his hair once again. "But you're a fendoir, aren't you? Fendoirs aren't exactly allowed to work in musical professions, what with the risk of you extracting all our elixir or whatever."

"Don't you find it a little unfair that the only thing fendoirs are allowed to do is work in Maisons des Souvenirs?" I ask. "What if you were born with some talent, some ability that you hated doing, and you had a passion for something else—say, music? Should a person's whole life be defined by what their face looks like, some power they wish they could have been born without—" I drop my voice to a deep, intense whisper "—or some fate they never asked for, never wanted?"

After a long moment, he speaks, though when he does, the words are barely more than a murmur. "You're right. It's not fair."

"I'd like to teach you," I continue, never dropping his gaze. "Because your voice is remarkable, and it deserves to be heard."

Though his expression is intent, the faint furrow in one of his brows tells me he is still not entirely convinced. "Where would these lessons take place? And when?"

I swallow. The only possibility, the only place where we won't risk discovery, is in my crypt underground. Cyril hasn't come down there in years, and it's not likely he'll return anytime soon. But the idea of bringing someone into that place, that private, peaceful, intimate place, drops a stone in my gut.

Balling my fists around my skirt, I respond, "I live here in the opera house. Well, below the opera house. You'd come with me down there to study every night at midnight."

"Seems awfully...secretive. What if we simply asked Monsieur Bardin for a practice room somewhere during the day?"

Time is running out. My ears are trained on the ceiling above us, waiting for a creak, a click of heels, some sign that Cyril is coming to find me. "Cyril allows me to live here, to hide away from the fendoir profession as long as I promise not to meddle in anything or risk his reputation. I daresay he'd not love the prospect of me teaching voice lessons in broad daylight somewhere anyone could stumble upon us."

"Cyril?"

"Monsieur Bardin," I snap, annoyance flaring. Why is he asking so many questions? "He's an...old family friend."

Emeric's demeanor lightens. "Really? So you know him well?"

How much do I tell him? "I suppose he's more than a family friend. He's like a father to me."

Emeric's brows rise, and the corners of his mouth curve upward.

I glance past him toward the stairs, convinced I see Cyril's long, willowy shadow descending toward us. "I'm sorry, but I've got somewhere I need to be. Would you like the lessons or not?"

Emeric follows my gaze over his shoulder to the same empty staircase, but he no longer seems unconvinced. "As long as you promise not to steal any of my elixir during these lessons..."

"Really, Monsieur Rodin, you insult me."

He holds up his hands. "One can never be too careful when lovely, masked ladies are involved."

I start. Did he just call me *lovely*?

He holds out his hand again for me to shake. "When will we begin?"

I eye his hand for a moment before settling my own into his grip. The sensation of someone's skin against mine sends a jolt of panic through me. Panic—and something else. Something sweet, like the warm embrace of a bright cantata.

"Meet me at midnight in the front lobby," I release his hand, stride past him, and mount the stairs. Once I'm sure I'm out of his sight, I let out a steadying breath.

It worked. Emeric believed me, and in less than an hour, we'll meet again for our first lesson.

If I pull this off, I might actually end up like that gravoir in his memory: free.

CHAPTER FIVE

My meeting with Cyril is brief, and when we're through, I fly down the stairs to straighten things in my room. I stuff dresses and stockings under my bed and tug the duvet into a more presentable arrangement. Glancing at a small, silver-lined wooden clock on my nearest bookshelf, I groan. There are still dirty goblets on my night table, and crumpled pieces of parchment litter the floor from when the composition I was working on last week gave me trouble, but midnight is only a few minutes away.

I grab a dagger from a shelf and tuck it into my sash, then stuff a handkerchief into my pocket and sprint through the catacombs and up into the opera house.

Around the corner from the front lobby, I stop to straighten my mask and tug my corset into place. After waiting a few moments for my breathing to slow, I roll my shoulders and stride forward.

Emeric stands with his back to me in front of the main entrance, gazing out the window at Channe's peaked roofs and the black-blue sky beyond.

"Monsieur Rodin," I say, pausing halfway across the lobby.

"Emeric," he corrects without turning. "Doesn't the city

look remarkable at night? All the streetlights and the smoke from the chimneys?"

"I've always thought so."

He faces me, eyes as bright as the stars behind him. "Have you lived in Channe your whole life?"

I pull the handkerchief from my pocket. There's no time to chat—Cyril could pass by at any time. "We should get going. Blindfold yourself."

He snorts. "Definitely not."

I take a few steps forward, still holding it out for him. "It'll be...safer if you don't know the way."

"Safer?" He raises an eyebrow, but he's grinning in a lop-sided sort of way that deepens the dimple in his right cheek. "Forgive me if the idea of being unable to see while sneaking around a haunted opera house with a mysterious fendoir carrying a dagger doesn't make me feel 'safe.'"

I scowl. "Don't be ridiculous."

"Oh, I'm the ridiculous one?" He shakes his head, his smile widening into both cheeks.

"Put the blasted thing on."

"No."

I glare. "What if I say 'please'?"

"Gentility is always worth a shot."

I roll my eyes. "Please?"

"What a remarkable, polite little thing you are. But...still no."

I shove the handkerchief against his chest. "Are you always like this?"

"Like what?"

"Incorrigible. Irritating. Impossible."

"Yes." He laughs. "And, might I add, that was some impressive alliteration."

"Now I see why you're so good at mopping floors."

He squints. "What does mopping have to do with my best character traits?"

"You said your mother made you scrub things every time you were troublesome."

He throws back his head and lets out a laugh as bright and clear as church bells. "Touché!"

His laughter, though quiet, echoes against the tile and the walls. I cast a look over my shoulder, praying Cyril is either so consumed with work in his office that he doesn't hear it, or that he's already packed up and headed home for the night.

"Fine." I turn back to Emeric and snatch the handkerchief back. "Don't wear it." Spinning on my heel, I stalk off.

"Am I supposed to follow you, or…?"

I whirl. "Honestly, were you dropped on your head as a child?"

"I'd say that is a definite possibility. It would explain a lot."

I throw my hands in the air. "Yes, you're supposed to follow me."

"Right, glad that's all straightened out." He jogs to catch up. "Lead the way, Isda."

I freeze at the sound of my name. Though I've heard Cyril say it thousands of times, it's never sounded like *that*.

"Everything okay?" Emeric is watching me, curiosity crinkling the corners of his eyes.

"Yes. Perfect." I walk briskly down the corridor without bothering to check if he's coming.

We round a corner and come upon a floor-to-ceiling painting of Les Trois glaring at Saint Claudin as he swings for their throats with a shining, curved blade. A shiver prickles down my spine, and I avert my gaze from the contorted faces of the three gravoirs whose screams are forever immortalized in oils on this wall. I make to stomp right on past it, but Emeric halts. He stares intently at the image, his mouth twisted in a knot.

I follow his gaze to Les Trois. Marguerite is on the left, the tallest and fairest of the three, with hair so pale it's almost silver flowing like water along her willowy frame. Violet eyes sparkle in a frame of thick lashes as her mottled face pinches in fury.

Éloise is next. She is petite and round and fierce, her hair as red as mine and cropped short so that it flares like fire around her face.

And on the right is Rose. Hair black as ebony trails straight and silky to her bare feet. She is always the one who sends a chill straight into my bones with her long, spindly fingers and dagger teeth. The arch of her neck, the clench of her fists, the flush in her cheeks—her entire being exudes rage. But there is pain there, too. In her eyes. An ache, a longing, a betrayal. For it was she who loved Claudin, according to the legends. And it was she whose blood he spilled first when he killed Les Trois and became the savior of the world.

Emeric steps forward and runs a hand along their gowns, where brushstrokes of black paint swirl like smoke around their legs. His fingers trail upward to the blood dripping from dozens of marks carved into every inch of their exposed skin. I recognize the Manipulation Mark on their ankles—a straight line with a lightning bolt through it that resembles my old scar, the one that unlocked my ability to do my work every night for the opera house. The runes shine crimson from their forearms, their collarbones, their throats.

I've asked Cyril about the other gravoir marks many times. His answer has always been that they are too dangerous, too volatile, and that it was already risky enough teaching me to use the Manipulation Mark.

Yet, every time I pass this painting, I wonder what else I am capable of. What I could do with those other symbols.

But I'll never find out. If Cyril caught me with any of those runes carved into my skin… I shudder at the thought. His trust is one of the few things I have in this life.

A little voice in the back of my head whispers that I'm betraying Cyril now by bringing Emeric to my crypt and allowing him into my world.

This is different, I reassure myself. *I'll be careful. Nothing is going to happen.*

"We should go." My voice squeezes through the tight space in my throat. What if Emeric rethinks his assumption that I'm just a simple fendoir hiding from her destiny? What if he sees what I truly am in Rose's face?

He drops his hand and nods, but his eyes linger on Les Trois. "I've never seen a painting of them before. Most people don't even like to speak of them."

"Really?" I glance back at the image. There are dozens of similar depictions throughout the opera house, and Cyril keeps that small sculpture in his office. But now that Emeric mentions it, I guess I've never seen paintings of them in any of the memories I've witnessed.

"They're beautiful," Emeric says softly.

I stare at him. "What?"

He catches sight of my expression and laughs. "I mean, they're terrifying, too, of course. Don't misunderstand me. I'd probably soil my britches if I ever came across them in real life."

I snort. "Right. Uh…this way." I continue down the hall, and after a moment, he follows.

We walk in silence for a while. Only our footsteps and the trailing of my skirt on the ground make any sound. As I lead the way into a side stairwell that spirals down to the opera house's basement, Emeric says, "You never answered my question."

"Which question?"

"Have you lived in Channe your whole life?"

I trail my hand along the banister as we descend into blackness. There are no windows down here, but I know these stairs and hallways like I know my own heartbeat.

"Yes," I say simply. "Never been anywhere else."

"Never? Not even to Chanterre? It's less than a day's ride away."

"Not even to Chanterre."

He whistles, then stumbles and knocks me into the wall. "I'm sorry. I can't see a thing."

Of course. I dip a hand into a pocket and pull out the simple cigar lighter I use to light the candles in my room downstairs. I flick it on, and the tiny yellow flame illuminates Emeric's face.

"Better?" I hand it to him and resume my descent.

"Excellent."

The firelight behind me casts my shadow on the floor, long and unnatural. The feathers in my mask jut from my head like the horns of a demon, and my stomach prickles. I tear my gaze away as I lead Emeric past storage boxes and old costumes piled haphazardly in the basement to a large, gilded mirror on the wall in the far corner of the room.

We stand before it, the reflections of his face and my black mask wavering eerily in the lighter's glare. I press a hand to the cold glass and push. The mirror swings inward, revealing a set of steep stairs trailing downward. The icy, silent air of the world underground sends a familiar chill up my legs.

"You live down there?" Emeric holds the flame out into the opening, but its light does little to penetrate the blackness below.

"Are you scared?"

"You know, if I'm being completely honest with you..." He meets my gaze. "Yes."

"Don't be. I'm the scariest thing down there, and you don't seem to have a problem with me."

"Yet." He says it like it's a challenge. "After you, mademoiselle."

I move into the dark, and he follows close behind until we reach the bottom.

He surveys the granite tunnel, the cobwebs hanging from the ceiling, the damp floor beneath our feet. "Well, this is downright homey."

"Over here," I say, and he trails me through the tunnels, around sharp curves and down long ramps until we reach the catacombs.

Brown, crumbling bones line the walls, and massive crypt doors inscribed with old runes poke out among the femurs and skulls every few feet.

"Who were all these people?" Emeric inspects one of the skulls as we pass, his face so close his nose skims its jaw.

"They exhumed the remains in the cemeteries when Channe began to get too crowded a few decades back. Had to put them somewhere."

"So they decided to arrange them in artful patterns underground. Makes sense," Emeric muses as we reach my crypt. I shove the stone door aside and usher him through. The candles within are still lit from when I came down to clean earlier, and their soft glow seems to calm him. He puts out the lighter and hands it to me as he passes.

I breathe in slowly through my nose as my stomach claws its way to my throat.

I've brought a person into my room.

Emeric pauses and stares. "This is where you live?"

I bustle past him to the bookshelves against the far wall and thumb through a stack of papers there for some music. "Yes." I feign indifference, but the hackles on my neck rise as his gaze roves over my trinkets, my bed, my clothes. My organ.

Gritting my teeth so fiercely my temples ache, I pull out a few arias from well-known operas and turn back to Emeric. I catch sight of him inspecting the piping at one corner of my organ, and the blood drains from my hands.

"This is beautiful craftsmanship," he says.

"Don't touch it."

He blinks at me, his thumb poised on one of the thicker pipes. "What?"

"I said—" I stalk to his side and smack his hand away "—don't touch it."

"I'm sorry. I didn't mean to—"

"Are you familiar with any of these arias?" I shove the sheet music into his face, hands shaking, cheeks pulsing hot.

Maybe it was a mistake to bring him here. This is my world. These are my things. This is not a place for meddling hands or judgmental eyes.

Taking the papers from me, he thumbs through them. "Yes, more or less. I love this one from *Agathon*." He holds it up for me to see.

"We're going to sing through a few of these so I can get a sense of your range, ability, and control. So I understand better what I'm working with." I whisk them out of his hands and take my place on the organ's bench, fanning out the pages and steadying my breath.

He stands behind me, keeping his hands in his pockets. He is so close that if I leaned back a bit, I'd brush against him. I sit stock-straight and try not to think about the way his scent is curling around me, an aroma of vanilla and burnt sugar.

I place my hands on the keyboard as my eyes flit across the music, noting the key and time signatures. Emeric inhales behind me, and I launch into the opening aria of the opera *Agathon*.

When Emeric's voice fills my crypt, it takes everything in me to keep his memories at bay. If I am to pass as what I say I am, if I am going to be able to convince him that I am worthy of his time, I need to behave like nothing more than a vocal teacher now. He needs to trust that I have no ulterior motives. Which means I must focus on his technical ability— not on the beautiful images and soul-shattering emotions his voice sends into the deepest recesses of my heart.

Not to mention the fact that if I surrender myself to his memory tide now, I may never resurface.

As we flood the room with sound, my fear and nervousness at bringing him here melt away. The cascade of notes from my organ mingles with the rawness of his voice, and my skin cools.

His music was meant to be here.

When we finish the *Agathon* piece, we move on to another. Then another. The more I hear, the more I never want him to stop. Now that I'm paying attention to his voice instead of his memories, the injustice of it all makes my blood turn to ice.

Cyril never even let Emeric audition. He turned him away simply because he'd never been trained.

The world *deserves* to hear this. In all my years at the opera house, I have never known a voice meant to command a stage more than this one.

If I could listen to him every night for the rest of my life, this ache I've had to live with since birth, this thirst for the outside…all of that might finally fade. With a steady supply of his vivid memories, I wouldn't need any of my own. I could live *through* him. If he became an opera performer, I could spend my nights in his memories of the stage. The things I see in his mind feel so real, it would almost be like performing myself. Even if I am never able to learn anything about that gravoir during our lessons, if I can find a way to get him to stay here forever, to be hired on as a Channe Opera House salaried performer, I might have a chance at living a life that feels almost whole.

My fingers barrel across the keys in a sharp crescendo, and Emeric belts out an angelic falsetto that brings tears to my eyes.

I need to get him on that stage.

I slam into the final chord, and the tones vibrate in my stomach until I release the keys. The walls and ceiling hold on to the sound long after we've gone silent, trembling under the weight of his music.

CHAPTER
SIX

"Where," Emeric asks in a voice barely above a whisper, "did you learn to play like that?"

"I taught myself." I look over my shoulder. He stands mere inches from me, his chest heaving.

"How?"

I point to the rows of music books lining my walls. "Lots of reading. Lots of studying. Lots and lots of practice."

He makes the sign of the God of Memory by drawing the first two fingers of his right hand from his left temple to his right. "I've never heard anything like you."

"I could say the same about you." I tear my gaze from his and gather up the music. "Although you do need instruction on breathing techniques and a few other things. Your lower range could use some strengthening, but we'll fix that up with some practice." I make my way to the bookshelves to put the music in its place, then scan through some of my more technical books for scales and arpeggio drills. Emeric follows, glancing through the titles with me, though he keeps his hands respectfully in his pockets and off my things this time.

"First off." I yank down one book to flip through it. "You need to think about breathing more from your diaphragm. I could practically hear your shoulders rising when you inhaled. You'll get a much fuller, more supported sound if you fill your belly with air and push it out with the muscles in your abdomen."

I prattle on, telling him to hold his hands on his stomach when he sings to make sure he feels it balloon out with every breath and describing breathing exercises to strengthen the muscles.

"Do you wear all of these?" Emeric interrupts, and I whirl to see him no longer looking at the music books at all but instead staring at an array of masks on my shelf.

"Have you been paying attention to a word I've said?" I huff.

"Of course. Breathing and stuff. Do you wear all of these masks?" He points at one and offers me that maddening grin of his. When he catches sight of my glare, he holds up his hands. "You can't be angry with me. I'm not touching anything."

Heaving a dramatic sigh, I snap the book I was perusing shut, shove it under my arm with the others I've collected, and cross to his side. "Most of those are from when I was younger. They don't fit very well anymore." I touch the place where the one I'm wearing curves over my jaw. "This was specially made."

"Did whoever made it do the decorations, too? The crystals and the wingy things?" He fans his fingers out around his eyes and wiggles them.

I bite down a smile and shake my head. "No, I did the crystals and the...'wingy things.' Which, by the way, are called feathers."

"Feathers." He smiles so wide his dimples cut halfway up his cheeks. "Look at you, already teaching me stuff."

"Now are you going to stop snooping about so we can get on with the lesson?"

"Yes, I think I'm done with my snooping." He pauses, his attention snagging on something behind me. "Oh, wait. I lied. What are those?"

I follow him to the shelf where a multitude of things I've collected around the opera house over the years is displayed. Most of them are odds and ends I found in the theater after performances, things the patrons accidentally left behind: pocket watches, cigar lighters, a silk glove, an earring, a sketchbook, an embroidered lace handkerchief. Pieces of the outside world I can hold in my own two hands.

Emeric inspects them all, and my cheeks grow hotter and hotter with each passing second. He must think me a fool, hoarding these useless baubles as though they're worth something. I find my hand dipping into my neckline to pull out the pendant there, stroking its corners for comfort as I force myself to breathe easy.

He stops on an old brass memory snare—a little orb-shaped trinket superstitious people wear around their necks in hopes of remembering things that having their elixir drained has made them forget. It is certainly not the most ornate or expensive thing on the shelf, but he regards it with warmth. The God of Memory's symbol of protection—a simple circle within a larger diamond—has been engraved meticulously on one side.

"My mother had a memory snare like this one," he says softly. "Only hers was silver. She used to kiss it all the time. Several times a day, in fact. I remember once as a child asking her why she kissed it so much, and she told me that she did that whenever she was living in a moment she hoped never to forget."

I'm not sure what to say to him. Though memory snares are lovely sentiments, they're utterly useless. The mind has only a finite store of memory elixir—each person is born with seventeen years' worth of it. Once they come of age at seventeen, their bodies begin to repurpose the elixir used in their earliest memories to create new ones. But if they hit hard times and decide to sell their elixir for extra coin, that memory capacity shrinks.

The only way for people to make sure they never forget anything is to purchase enough memory elixir to last a lifetime. One can never have too much—once a person consumes enough to remember everything, the excess elixir serves to sharpen details, to keep the passage of time from dulling the sensations. The most brilliant minds in the world are the ones belonging to the wealthy—those who can afford millions of vials.

It's science. And while the memory snares are a beautiful thought, nothing can keep a memory from disappearing if a person runs out of the elixir necessary to hold it there.

I suppose this is one thing I have to be grateful for. Neither fendoirs nor gravoirs can have memory elixir extracted. I'll remember every moment of my life until the day I die.

"What is that?" Emeric points at my hand.

I glance down at the pendant in my fist. "Just something I found in a dressing room once."

"May I?" he asks, holding out a hand.

I pause, considering. I hardly know him, and I've exposed so much to him already. What might he do to me with the information he knows, the things he's seen tonight?

I look up into his face, searching for the promise of violence, the hatred Cyril's always told me the world harbors for creatures like me, the disgust I've been taught runs thick in their veins. But all I see is curiosity. And kindness.

With shaking hands and trembling heart, I lift the necklace over my head and drop it into his outstretched palm.

He brings the pendant close to his face, studying the little gold piece of jewelry with care. His gaze traces over its whimsical box shape, the lovely carvings around the outer edge, the scalloped top, the glass window on the front revealing a tiny, exquisitely rendered ballerina poised midtwirl within.

He pauses on the dancer, angling the charm back and forth in the light.

"I found it at the end of our performance season the year I turned five," I babble, feeling terribly exposed as he inspects it. This is the first time I've taken it off in years. "As a child, I used to look through that window and imagine myself as that little ballerina and the box around her as the opera house. I'd dream about what it would be like if I had a face like that, if I'd learned to dance. She has a pretty smile, doesn't she?"

I hate how my voice quavers, like the battering of a hummingbird's wings against the wires of a cage.

Emeric nods. "She is pretty. Then again, I've always had a thing for redheads." He catches my gaze and winks.

I step back, my whole body suddenly so hot I feel I might pass out. I adjust my mask, pushing the stray hairs that frame it behind my ears.

"It looks like there are hinges here," he muses. "Does it open?"

"Open?" I frown. "I don't think so."

"Don't these look like little hinges? They're small, but I'm almost certain that's what they are." He holds out the pendant for me to look.

I squint and shake my head. "Those look like part of the decorative engraving work."

He slides a nail along an invisible seam, pinning his tongue between his teeth. With a grunt, he grips either end of the pendant and pulls.

I lunge for it. "If you break that, I swear to Memory I'll murder—"

The pendant pops open. The little dancer's platform rises a few centimeters and twirls. A faint, tinkling melody plays as she spins.

I gape. "How did you—"

"Shhh." He presses a finger to his lips and closes his eyes.

The bell–like music trickles around the room, barely louder than an exhale, and yet its lovely song melts away the shaking in my hands, the fear in my heart. My own eyes fall shut, and I listen.

Emeric hums softly along, a countermelody that weaves among the notes.

"Do you know it?" I ask.

"It's an old southern Vaureillean lullaby," he says. "My mother used to sing it to me when I was small." He clears his throat and, when the melody repeats itself, begins to sing:

Meet me in the darkness,
Meet me in the night.
Meet me where the star-touched breeze
Whisks away the light.

For there under the canopy
Of a tall and silent tree
Midnight comes to life, my darling,
To guard our memories.

The shadows of yesteryear
Where dawn and afternoon fade
Keep our moments quiet waiting
In a whisper-worn glade.

As they rest in moonlight,
Angels sing them all to sleep.
So meet me in the darkness, darling,
Where past and present meet.

I hold my breath as his voice slides from word to word and keep the images of his past at bay, determined to hear every note. When the melody comes around again, I open my mouth and join in.

My perfect gravoir memory means I already know the lyrics by heart, so as I sing with him, I break off into a high soprano obbligato.

The cold, underground air around us shifts as our music intertwines on its breath. With my eyes closed, nothing exists but our voices and the chime of tiny bells.

We crescendo together, our duet rising until it fills the earth, until it bursts right through the mountains, taking wing on the breeze and swirling into the sky to shake the stars.

And for the first time, I feel free.

Emeric's voice slips its hold around mine, twining through me, threading its fingers in my countermelody, caressing its way through my vibrato, fitting in all the open places. Vowels entangle. Consonants undulate against each other.

I cannot breathe, cannot think. Everything is stars and colors and light. Sparks trail up and down my arms, and flickers dance under my skin.

We reach the last line as one, a final crash against a rocky shore dusted in moonlight.

My eyes fly open. We stare at each other, chests heaving. He's inches away, so close I can see every fleck of amber in his dark, dark eyes. Every shudder of those black lashes. Every quiver of his lower lip when he inhales.

I'm drunk on his burnt sugar scent, intoxicated by the heat billowing between us.

The pendant's tiny melody slows to a stop, and we are left in silence but for the rush of heavy breathing and the galloping roar of blood in my ears.

One of my clocks chimes the hour, and the sound sends a jolt through my limbs.

I can't be singing like this—*feeling* like this—with anyone. I'm a gravoir, a shadow in the underground world of the dead. I seize the pendant from Emeric's palm, ignoring the way the calluses on his fingers leave trails of lightning on my skin, and yank the necklace back over my head.

"You'd better go." I jam the music books I'd nearly forgotten I'd been holding against his chest.

"But—"

"Take these. Do the breathing techniques. Practice going into your lower registers."

"Wait."

"You remember the way out?" I all but sprint to the crypt's door to heave it open for him, fumbling in my pocket to retrieve the cigar lighter.

"Yes, but—"

"Fantastic." I shove him out into the catacombs and throw the lighter after him. "See you tomorrow night. Same time."

"Isda—"

I slide the door shut so hard dust poofs in the air. Pressing my back to the cold stone, I yank my mask off and wipe the sweat from my brow. My knees quake and then give way, and I crumple to the floor.

Before yesterday, the only life I'd ever lived was the one I stole in glimpses through the memories of the opera performers' songs. The only feelings I'd ever experienced were ones of longing and loneliness.

In just a few short hours, because of one heart-wrenching, soul-splitting, star-shaking voice, I'm unraveling, every piece of my symphony rearranging, rewriting itself in new, thunderous ways.

I take a slow, shaky breath, trying to remember how Cyril has always taught me to keep my sentiments under control. Inhale. Exhale. Focus on my center. Let the silence and stillness fill me.

But nothing is still or silent. The tiny music box necklace, which I stuffed back into my neckline, rests against my skin. The metal is warm, as though his hand is there pressing gently against the *thud-thud-thud* of my heart.

CHAPTER
SEVEN

The following night, I knock on Cyril's door for our after-performance meeting, surprisingly calm considering the fact that less than two hours remain until I'll see Emeric again for our second voice lesson.

Instead of shouting for me to enter, Cyril pulls the door open a crack. "I'll be just a moment," he calls back into the room before moving into the hallway with me and easing the door shut.

"Who's in there?" My voice quavers. Did Emeric tell someone about me? Is a member of the King's Council of Channe waiting in there to cart me away? I press my hands against my stomach and try to breathe through the iron fist that has clamped itself around my lungs.

"An experiment." Cyril's eyes sparkle.

I chew on the inside of my cheek and wait for him to continue. Cyril wouldn't be grinning giddily like that if we were in any danger.

"I've brought someone in to test a theory I have about your powers."

"What theory is that?"

"You told me you erased the moment when the tenor's voice cracked from people's minds, correct?"

"Oui."

He grips my shoulders and tilts his head closer to mine. "My theory is that if you are able to *manipulate* the emotions in a memory, and you are also able to *erase* things from the past, then it would stand to reason that perhaps you could *create* images of your own, as well."

I gape. "Making part of a memory disappear is completely different from conjuring something out of nothing."

"You can do this, Izzy," Cyril says warmly, straightening and dropping his hands from my arms. "You need only apply yourself."

"But—"

"You are so much more powerful than you think you are. And whether or not you can do this will determine whether or not you'll be able to help me in a little task."

"What kind of task?"

His eyes glimmer. "A task *outside the opera house*."

I blink several times. My mouth goes bone-dry.

He settles a hand on my shoulder. "I'm not certain yet if it's even a possibility, and I'm still working the kinks out, but I think you're ready for big things, Izzy. I just need to make sure before I take any unnecessary risks."

I swallow the knot of fear in my throat and nod.

Outside. Under the great, big, star-studded sky. Like any other normal girl. "I'll try," I say, my voice thick.

"Good girl." He smiles. "Now, there's a young boy in my office. His name is Amadou. I need you to go into his memories to find the one in which we met. It occurred only a few hours ago, so it shouldn't be too hard. Once you locate that memory, I'd like you to change it. I've been going over and over in my mind how we'll be able to tell if you've really succeeded, and the only thing I can think of is if you give the boy a reason to fear me. Something that will cause him to react to me in the present."

I force myself to nod though my whole body seems to have gone stiff with panic. I've never tried anything like this before. What if I fail? What if Cyril decides I'm not powerful enough for whatever task he's planning?

"Perfect." Cyril almost bounces as he twirls back to the door and turns the knob. "Amadou, I've brought someone to meet you!"

I pause with my hand braced against the doorframe, trying to breathe in and out slowly the way Cyril taught me. He has never asked me to do anything with my power that I was incapable of doing. I think of those long afternoons back when I was nine or ten, all those hours I spent trying to manipulate the emotions in his clients' memories. It had seemed such an impossible task then, and now it comes effortlessly. Like I've always known how to do it.

Perhaps this will be like that. A challenge. Cyril thinks I can do it, so I must be able to.

Imagining the satisfaction and pride that will fill his eyes when I succeed, I step into the office behind him and close the door.

A small boy barely the age of five sits on my wooden chair gnawing on a baguette. Crumbs litter his arms and the floor around him. Dirt smudges his cheeks in layers so thick I'm not even sure what color his skin is underneath. His hair hangs in clumps around his head, and his filthy, tattered clothes drape from bony shoulders.

He's obviously a Forgotten Child, one of the homeless children who wander the streets. The children whose parents got so poor they had to sell their memory elixir—and then had so much extracted that they forgot they ever had children to begin with. Twenty-six hours after elixir is taken, memory loss becomes permanent. Even if those parents purchase elixir again once they've come upon good fortune, they'll never be able to recover the experiences they lost. Forgotten Children are forgotten forever.

My first instinct is to reach out to the boy and wipe the muck away, but when he sees my face and takes in my mask, his body goes rigid. "It's a fendoir!" he cries, throwing his arms across his face to hide. "Please don't let it take my elixir, monsieur!"

Cyril tousles the boy's mop of hair and crouches down to tug his arms away from his face. "She'll not touch a drop of your elixir," Cyril murmurs with warmth. "She's simply going to take a look at how much you have. I promise I won't let her remove any."

The boy eyes me around Cyril's white head. "Why does it need to look at how much I have?"

"Because I heard stories about a fendoir sneaking around stealing elixir from people without them knowing." Cyril nods in my direction. "This fendoir here is named Colette, and she's helping me catch the bad fendoir."

The story is preposterous. Fendoirs cannot extract elixir unless people are singing, and it's not like elixir extraction is a sneaky affair—what with the golden ribbons of glowing liquid streaming out of people's ears and all. Though I've never witnessed it myself, I have seen it in many memories. The only way it could be done without a person's knowledge is if they had their eyes closed while they were singing.

The boy seems to be considering. After a moment he swallows and nods.

"Good lad." Cyril tousles Amadou's hair once again before straightening. "Now, I'll need you to sing so Colette here can check your elixir levels. Go ahead."

Amadou stares down at the half baguette clenched in his grimy hands and begins to sing. His voice is quiet. High-pitched and lovely like the trilling of a flute.

Immediately, the tug to view his memories pulls at my

power through the place where the Manipulation Mark was on my ankle. I release myself to it, sinking into the gentle trickle of black-and-white images. Wading upstream past the last few minutes to the memories of a few hours ago, I dip into each scene, looking for Cyril. It takes me a moment or two, but finally I find it.

Amadou was scrounging in an old rubbish bin in an alleyway when Cyril approached him with an offering of baguettes and several chunks of cheese. The boy snatched the food from Cyril's hands and shoved a fistful down his throat.

Hope, though wary, stirred in the boy's gut as he blinked up at Cyril between bites. I'll start with that—manipulating emotions is something I do well. Gritting my teeth, I feather a brittle slice of fear into the scene until the memory trembles with an edge of panic.

Squinting an eye open, I glance at Amadou and Cyril both. Amadou hasn't changed position, hasn't even paused in his song. Cyril is watching me, the confident grin he was wearing a few minutes before fading slightly.

Obviously manipulating the emotions isn't enough. Gritting my teeth, I cast about for what to try next. When I've erased moments in other memories, all I did was focus intently on the parts I wanted to take out and sucked them away as though sucking through a straw. So maybe if I want to put something in, I should reverse that process?

But what should I put in Amadou's memory to make him scared enough of Cyril to have a reaction that Cyril can see? I frown, thinking of the people whose memories I know best: the opera performers. What are they afraid of?

My gaze strays to a small red book poised on the end of Cyril's desk. I recognize it instantly; it's the book he used when he began teaching me about my powers back when I was a child. I haven't seen it in ages. I chew on my lower lip, thinking back to those days.

The performers have come and gone over the years, but they all have come to fear the same thing. Shadows in the corners. Creaking staircases. Sudden rushes of wind through empty practice rooms.

The Opera Ghost.

It started out as an explanation Cyril made when I was little to keep the performers from becoming too curious when things moved or disappeared from their places during the night. I was careless back then, utterly unable to comprehend the danger I put myself in by risking being seen, and Cyril needed to be creative in order to keep me from discovery. At first his little ghost story had been a joke, but soon the performers' imaginations had run away with the tale.

Now, I'm careful never to leave a trace of my presence. Other than Emeric, no one has glimpsed me in years, but the story of the Opera Ghost has lived on in the quirky noises and odd drafts of the building as it has gotten older.

Perhaps I could send some kind of ghost like that into Amadou's memory? A terrifying beast made of shadow and fear?

I conjure up an image of Cyril cloaked in darkness with a pale face, unseeing eyes, and sharp, pointed teeth. Concentrating everything I have on the vision I've created, I blow it out into the memory over the sight of Cyril in Amadou's mind.

Nothing happens. Memory-Cyril's gray shape does not change. His smile does not waver.

The craving for Cyril's pride and satisfaction washes through me. My whole life, he has been my confidant, my family, the closest thing to a father I've ever known. The idea of disappointing him now when he's on the verge of asking me to help him with something huge makes my soul ache.

Screwing up every ounce of power I can muster, I shove the ghoulish image into Amadou's mind. At first, memory-Cyril's face barely flickers. I grit my teeth so hard my jaw pops. A fire ignites in my chest, and I stoke it until it blazes through every limb, every bone.

Memory-Cyril sputters into shadow. His eyes transform into yawning, depthless caverns. His skin pales. His mouth snaps with a flash of teeth.

The edges are fuzzy, and Cyril's white hair pokes through in places, but I've done it. It's still him—recognizably so—but the new details I've added have transformed him into a terrifying demon spun of nightmares.

I back up in the memory and watch it play anew. This time when Cyril approaches with the baguettes, the fear I breathed into the scene earlier comes to life. I infuse the rest of the memories leading up to the present with the same imagery. Soon, what was once a recollection of a kind gentleman offering a Forgotten Child a meal has become a vision of a villain luring a helpless boy into his lair.

Amadou's song cuts into a scream that pulls on my power in a way that makes me feel as though it's wrenching my stomach out through my navel.

My eyes fly open as Amadou crashes away from Cyril. He scrambles over the desk, shrieks as tears turn the muck on his cheeks to mud, and dives out of sight, knocking several elixir vials askew with his foot. The vials drop to the ground and shatter, spattering gold onto Cyril's pant leg.

Wiping my sweating palms on my skirts, I turn to Cyril, trying to get the sight of Amadou's wide-eyed terror out of my mind.

Cyril is beaming. "You've done it," he whispers, clapping his hands once before crossing to me in two strides of his long, wiry legs and wrapping me in a rib-breaking embrace. "I knew you could."

I sag against him, suddenly aware of how weak using that much power has made me. "I did it," I hear myself say.

"You did, chérie." He pulls back to look me full in the face. "You brilliant girl. I knew you were ready for more."

I can't keep the smile from spreading across my face, the warmth from flowing down my arms and into my toes.

Whimpers gurgle out from underneath Cyril's desk. I glance back toward the sound. I should feel a bit more remorse for causing the child so much trauma, but I'm so high on the pride in Cyril's expression and the satisfaction in my gut that I can barely hear the sobs.

"You'd better go over there and get him to sing so you can set things right again," Cyril says, releasing me. "While you're at it, erase the memory of him meeting you, too. He may be a child, but we really can't afford the risk of him saying anything about you to anyone."

Nodding, I make my way around the desk and crouch. "Amadou?"

He peeks at me between his hands, then shrinks even deeper into the shadow of the desk.

"It's all right," I say, picking up the baguette from where it dropped on the floor nearby. "Would you like some more bread?"

"Is that man still here?" Amadou shies away from me.

"No," I tell the child. "He's gone."

He blinks up at me with wide, glassy eyes, and I nod at the bread. "Don't worry. I'll protect you. You're going to be okay."

Amadou gulps, considering my words. After a long moment, he finally accepts the baguette from my outstretched hand and, with a whimper of relief, crawls onto my lap to wrap his arms around my neck and bury his face into my chest.

I pat his back, not quite sure what else to do with my hands.

As his tears soak into the fabric of my dress, a gnawing ache fills my gut.

What have I done to this poor child?

A lump rises in my throat, and I brace my arms more firmly around Amadou's small frame, pressing my cheek against his hair. "It's all right," I murmur. "Nothing is going to hurt you."

Sobs continue to shudder through his body, so I do the one thing I can think of.

I sing.

The only lullaby I know is the one Emeric taught me last night, so I sing that one in a voice barely above a whisper as I comb soft fingers through the clumps in his hair.

I meet Cyril's gaze over the top of his desk. He nods at me to continue.

When the child's sobs finally slow, I pull back to wipe the tears from his cheeks with my thumb. "See? All better. Nothing to be afraid of."

"Was that man the bad fendoir?" the child asks, lower lip quivering. "The one who steals people's elixir?"

I shake my head. "No. I don't think the bad fendoir has gotten to you. But why don't I check your elixir again just to make sure? Would you sing a bit more?"

Mopping the rest of his tears with the back of his hands, he nods and begins to warble out a quaky tune.

I slip back into the memory and suck away the monster image until all that is left is a kind-eyed, baguette-bearing Cyril. Then I ease the feelings of fear back into the wary hopefulness they were before. Finally, I retrace my way to the most recent memories to draw my existence away from them.

By the time I've finished, my body is shaking with exhaustion, and the well of my power gnaws like a fragile animal in my gut. I shift the boy onto the floor against Cyril's desk and back away from him on trembling legs. He continues to sing, the horrified expression on his face transformed into one of well-fed contentment. I back around the desk and, just as Amadou finishes his song, erase the last seconds of myself from his mind.

Cyril places his hand on my shoulder. I try to steady myself so he doesn't see how weakened I've become.

"Well done," he says.

A swell of joy gives me the strength to respond with a clear, confident voice. "Merci."

"Where did you learn that lullaby?"

I stiffen, but Cyril's expression is thoughtful. "I overheard the opera performers singing it the other day," I mumble.

The doorknob rattles, and Cyril's smile vanishes. He gestures at me to hide behind the door. Panic jolts through me, but I leap to where he indicates.

Giving me a warning look, he reaches out with a steady hand and unlocks the door. He eases it open slowly, and I hold my breath.

"Hello?" He ducks his head out into the hallway.

No one responds.

Cyril signals for me to wait and disappears through the door.

Several moments slide past. The silence is broken only by the distinct crunch of crisp baguette crusts coming from under Cyril's desk.

After what feels like hours, Cyril finally returns.

"There is no one there," he whispers, glancing toward the smacking sounds coming from the other side of his office. "But be careful on your way down. Wouldn't want you to run into the Opera Ghost." He smiles, but the lines around his eyes are still tight with suspicion.

I nod, gulp, and move toward the hallway. I pause and glance back. "Was that enough? Will I be able to go outside the opera house with you?"

Cyril smiles and tucks my unruly curls behind my ear with a slow, quiet gentleness. "We'll practice once or twice more.

And I'll have to figure out the technicalities of everything before I can say for sure, but…" He gives one of my curls a loving tug. "I think we could make it work."

My breath rushes out, and my chest feels as though it might explode into a cloud of butterflies. "Thank you," I whisper.

He leans in and plants a kiss on the crown of my head. "Good night, Izzy."

The door clicks shut behind me. I lean back against it for one long moment, breathing deeply, willing my knees to stop quaking with fatigue and my heart to stop its erratic beat before setting off in the dark.

As I make my way down to my crypt, I have to remind myself to watch every statue, every shadow, every candelabra for any hint of movement. So focused am I on the prospect of leaving the opera house that I almost forget Cyril's warning to be careful.

But still, I see nothing. Perhaps it was only an errant gust of wind that rattled the doorknob.

My nerves dissipate when I pass through the mirror and into the catacombs. As my pace slows and my heart rate returns to normal, something stirs in the ashes left behind by that blazing fire of power in my chest.

I inserted a new image into Amadou's mind—something that was not there before. Something so vivid and real it sent him screaming across a desk to hide. And though my stomach still knots with guilt over the boy's tears, that stirring in the ashes fills me with a quiet sort of satisfaction.

Cyril's words echo in my mind: *You are so much more powerful than you think you are.*

I *feel* powerful. I feel solid. I feel real. And tonight, I wasn't hiding behind a statue, glaring down at masses of people who hate me. Tonight, I was powerful, just like Cyril said.

As I limp into my crypt to prepare for my lesson with Emeric, the ashes in my chest reignite into a small, flickering flame that grows and grows until a quiet laugh breaks forth from my lips.

For once, I did not let society cage me. For once, I was more than a phantom in the rafters. I was even more than a performer.

I was the director, the maestro, the creator.

So this is what it feels like to affect others. To be in control instead of cowering away in the dark.

I love it.

CHAPTER
EIGHT

Emeric chatters nonstop the whole way from the front lobby to my crypt. He muses about the statues we pass and how he could probably best them all at arm-wrestling matches. He points out all the oddest costumes downstairs to ask if I've ever tried them on and even proceeds to tug a curly-haired wig over his head. Finally, as we make our way through the catacombs, he pauses to peer deep into the eye sockets of the skulls to see if he can last longer than they can without blinking.

By the time we reach my crypt, I've nearly forgotten my fatigue from using my powers on the Forgotten Child upstairs. I'm too focused on not snorting at Emeric's intense expression of concentration as he challenges the skull to the left of my doorway to his little contest.

"Ah, Albert." He shakes his fist at the grayish bit of bone and its wide, toothy smile. "You scoundrel. I don't know how you did it, but I am certain you cheated."

"Albert? Really?" I tease, leaning against the stone.

"You mean you've lived next door to him all this time and never bothered to make his acquaintance?" He clucks his tongue. "How devastatingly rude of you."

"It seems I am a complete dolt. Please give Albert my apologies."

He turns back to the skull. "You really ought to forgive the poor girl. Seems no one taught her any manners." He cocks an ear and nods. "I know, I know, but she's not so bad. You should give her another chance." He pauses, then murmurs, "I see…" and turns to me. "Isda, Albert here says he'll only forgive you on one condition."

"What's that?"

"A kiss."

I plant my fists on my hips. "What a charming devil Monsieur Albert has turned out to be."

Emeric nods. "Quite debonair."

"Well, Albert," I say, moving next to Emeric to face the skull head-on, "I commend you for your attempts at romance, but I'm afraid I really prefer my men alive."

Emeric winces. "Oooh, ouch." He pats the skull's cheekbone. "Take heart, my man. Even the most well-bred of gentlemen fall prey to the foils of love from time to time."

A chortle blurts from my mouth. "You are ridiculous."

"And you," he says, jabbing a finger in my face, "are really good at assigning me adjectives."

"Adjectives?"

"Oui. Let's see. First there was 'incorrigible,' I believe. 'Irritating' was another. Oh, and then there's my personal favorite, 'impossible.'"

I cross my arms and give him a thoughtful look. "Would you say my descriptions have been inaccurate?"

"Oh no. In fact, I've been rather impressed by your keen attention to detail. It usually takes people a few weeks to surmise what you've come up with in only a day. Brava."

"I am rather remarkable, aren't I?"

He grins, pulls his cap from his head, and sweeps into a mock bow. "Undoubtedly so."

"You know, as observant as I am, I'm beginning to wonder if my initial assessment of you was incorrect."

"How do you mean?"

"Lately I've been thinking that you'd be more suited to a circus than an opera stage."

"World's most dashing lion master?"

"Hmm…" I tap my chin. "I was thinking something along the lines of 'Human Ape—Looks like a man, behaves like a monkey!' You'd be the talk of all Vaureille."

He mock-scowls at me. "Apes are very intelligent creatures, you know."

"Oh, I didn't mean to mock your intelligence."

"Just my looks? I mean, I know I keep the hair a little shaggier than most, but I was always under the impression that it wasn't too bad." His voice softens, and I meet his gaze over the dancing flame on the cigar lighter in his hand.

My eyes trail upward to the dark hair sweeping across his brow, and I am suddenly overwhelmed with a desire to reach out and touch it.

"Your hair is…fine," I say, the jovial, teasing feeling suddenly gone. In its place, a timidity makes the words stick like paste to the roof of my mouth. "It's not apelike at all, actually. It…suits you."

He holds my gaze for a long moment, and it's as though he's stolen every bit of oxygen from the tunnel, leaving my hands sweating, my heart hammering, and my lungs tight. "Then what did you mean?"

"I meant…" I swallow. "I meant that I…it's just that, well… I've spent a lot of time observing people, and you're…different."

He cocks his head and wets his lips. "The people you've spent all this time observing are the type who frequent the opera. I didn't grow up in their world."

"No?"

"Those who can afford to spend their money on music, dancing, and fancy clothing are usually born into a world of influence. I suppose I'm not unlike you in that I grew up pretty isolated."

I stare as the words fall from those mesmerizingly perfect lips, as his flawless cheeks dimple with every syllable. What would it be like to be so beautiful and unmarked?

He settles the cap back on top of his head and crosses his arms, leaning against my crypt door. "It was just my mother, my sister, and me. My father died when I was very young in a mining accident. After my sister was born, we moved into a tiny little cottage practically in the middle of nowhere. Not another house in sight, and the nearest town was a few miles away. I didn't get much social interaction."

"Why so secluded?"

A shadow passes across his face, but then he shrugs. "I guess you could say my mother was a bit afraid of people."

"Where is she now?"

His eyes turn somber, and I'm struck once again by how deep and dark they are—as though he stole a piece of the night sky. Drawn as I am to darkness and the things it hides, I imagine myself slipping into those eyes and falling and falling and never ever stopping.

"She passed away when I was fifteen." His Adam's apple bobs as he drops my gaze. "Almost three years ago."

"Oh." My hands suddenly feel awkward where they are at my sides, so I snatch nervously at the chain around my neck. What do people say in situations like this? "I—I'm terribly sorry."

"Thank you," he says. "At least she is free from the fear that plagued her in life."

"Have you been in Channe for the past three years then?" I ask, eager to steer the subject away from mothers and death, not liking the way it's drawing my thoughts to the few memories I have of my own mother before she sent me to be drowned.

He shakes his head. "No. I went to live with an uncle in a little village called Luscan in northern Vaureille for a time. Which reminds me…" He shoves a fist into his pocket and produces a handful of small, rock-shaped mounds wrapped in white parchment. "Would you like one?"

"What are they?"

"Caramels." He holds out his hand, but I don't take one.

"Candy is terrible for the voice," I say.

"Ah, but Isda, it does wonders for the soul."

I study the candies. Cyril has brought me peppermints before, and chocolates on holidays, but I've never tried caramels. My mouth waters at the prospect of finally tasting one.

Sighing dramatically, Emeric tugs my wrist upward. His hand is warm, and I stifle a gasp when it brushes against my skin. He places one of the little wrapped mounds into my palm and curls my fingers over the top of it.

My whole arm is shaking, every nerve zinging with an awareness of his touch on my knuckles.

He meets my gaze and smiles softly. "Go on. Try it." Releasing me, he unwraps one for himself, popping it into his mouth and closing his eyes. "Ahhh…my soul feels better already."

My hand tightens around the caramel as he swallows and unwraps a second.

"Come on." He points at my clenched fist. "I made them myself. I promise they're not poisoned or made with goat's blood or anything like that."

"You made them? I thought you were a janitor."

"I hate to be the one to tell you this, but sometimes janitors do *other things*." He feigns a dramatic gasp. "Shocking, I know."

"Oh fine." I unwrap the caramel and put it into my mouth. "Are you happy now?"

He grins. "Quite."

It melts quickly, warm and sweet on my tongue, even more decadent than I imagined it would be. "You made that?"

"Don't ask for the secret ingredient. I won't tell you."

"I wasn't going—"

"It's sugar." He winks. "Don't tell anyone."

I snort in spite of myself, then make the sign of the God of Memory. "Your secret is safe with me."

He drops the rest of the caramels back into his pocket.

"All right, if you're ready," I say, pushing against the crypt door. "I think it's best we get started." Tonight, I plan to dip into his memories to look for the gravoir girl. At the prospect of hearing him sing again, of finally getting a chance to plunge into a world so very different from my own, my magic prickles, eager, waiting, ready. But my body is still weak from the expense of power during my encounter with the Forgotten Child upstairs, and I can't seem to muster the strength to open the crypt. I struggle with the door. It doesn't budge.

Emeric's smile fades. "You all right? I've been thinking you seem a little…drained tonight. Is everything okay?"

"It's been a long day." I shove my shoulder against the stone.

"Would you prefer if I let you sleep? I could come back tomorrow instea—"

"No!" I almost shout. Easing the panicked edge out of my voice, I murmur, "I mean, no. I'm fine. The music will make me feel better."

"Allow me," he says, never taking his eyes from my face as he steps in so close I can almost taste the burnt sugar and vanilla scent of him. He places a strong hand on the door and eases it inward.

"Merci," I manage before darting under his arm and into my room to light the candles.

He trails in behind me and sets his stack of music books on my organ's bench. "I went through the practice drills you sent me home with. Several of them proved rather difficult."

"Perfect. I'd like to hear your progress." I finish lighting the candles and toss the cigar lighter onto the collection on my shelf before sliding his books aside and taking my place at my organ. "First let's warm up."

We run through a few scales and simple tunes to get his vocal cords warm, and then spend half an hour going through some of the drills in the books I gave him.

"No, no, no." I stop him midarpeggio. "You're still breathing into your shoulders. You're going to give me an ulcer."

"I'm sorry." He gives me an apologetic smile. "Wouldn't want to curse a poor ulcer to the likes of your temper."

"Very funny," I huff and hop from my seat. "Place your hands on your abdomen and inhale like you've got a balloon inside that you're trying to fill. You should feel your stomach expand into your palms with each breath."

He obeys, holding my gaze as he breathes in slowly.

"No. Your stupid shoulders. I'm going to cut them off." I place my hands on both shoulders and press them down. "Now breathe in and don't move my hands."

He sucks in a breath, and I push firmly on his shoulders to keep them in place.

"Again," I order.

He inhales. Exhales. Inhales. Exhales.

The room fills with the slow, steady sound of his breathing. He blinks, and his eyelashes feather for a brief second against his cheeks. I stare. I feel like I'm plummeting, spinning into some oblivion, but somehow the sensation doesn't fill me with terror the way it should. It's not like tumbling from a great height into the unknown… It's a fall like in that moment when I close my eyes and surrender myself to slumber. Cocooned in warmth, with the reassurance that I will reawaken to a world bathed in gold and light.

It isn't until my knees bump against his that I realize we've moved closer together. So close our breaths twist the air between us into a vapor of caramel-scented warmth.

I drop my hands and turn away, trying to ignore the way I can still feel the dip of his collarbones on my thumbs and the broad curve of his shoulder blades on my fingertips.

"I'd like you to try singing the opening number to *Le Berger*," I say through a mouth thick with cotton, crossing to pull the new sheet music Cyril gave me from my shelf and handing it to him without meeting his gaze.

I need to stay focused. If I'm going to find out anything about the gravoir in his memories, it is imperative that I spend more time rifling through his past and less time getting distracted by his dimples and his shoulder blades.

Settling in at the organ, I ease my hands into place. The opening number of *Le Berger* is an old favorite of mine, one I could perform flawlessly in my sleep if I wanted to. It'll be the perfect song for me to play as I dive into Emeric's memories—I won't need to focus on the music at all.

I plunge into the familiar prelude lines, and then, when Emeric begins to sing, instead of barring myself against the flood like I did last night, I open my soul wide and let the flow overtake me. The tide rips me under, the emotions filling me so deeply and so wholly that I almost cry out with joy. Biting down on my tongue, I swim backward. Further and further until the images of a small village are replaced with glimpses of golden sunlight, rolling hills, and a tiny cottage nestled at the edge of an apple orchard. My heart leaps when the gravoir's face flashes by, but I kick my way even deeper into the past.

I need to get to the beginning, to see where this girl started, where her story began.

After several long moments of swimming against the tide, I settle into one memory that, though the images show it oc-

curred in the gloom of midnight, sparks as though charged
with lightning.

Emeric is a child—maybe five or six. The night is dark, lit
only by a pale, yellow moon in the window and a sputtering
lantern on the bedside table. Emeric's mother lies half upright
in her bed, her face red with effort and her hair dripping with
sweat. He clutches her hand. "It's okay, Maman," he says in
his high-pitched voice. "You're almost there."

A tremor of fear, an urge to run, to hide, courses through
his tiny body, but he holds firm against her bed and squeezes
her knuckles, trying not to look down at her swollen belly
or the bloodied sheets at her legs.

A midwife bustles about at the foot of the bed, setting out
a pot of hot water and a pile of rags as she murmurs comforting things to Maman about breathing and letting the labor
surges roll through her.

When the next surge hits, Emeric screws his eyes shut,
wishing he could clap his hands over his ears to keep away
the sound of his mother's howls.

"That's it, Danielle," the midwife urges. "The baby's almost here. One more push!"

With a final cry loud enough to crack the cottage in half,
it's all over. The baby's wet little body topples out into the
midwife's hands, and Maman collapses back against her pile
of pillows, sobbing and clinging so tightly to Emeric's hand
he's lost feeling in all of his fingers.

"You've done it, Maman," Emeric says, holding back tears
of fright and relief.

"How is the baby?" Maman asks the midwife.

The woman does not respond.

Maman sits up in her bed, her voice ringing with a slice
of panic. "Is it okay?"

"She's fine," the midwife manages, but her back is turned,
and the baby has not cried.

"Is she…alive?" Maman's voice breaks on the last word. "Please don't tell me she's…"

"She's alive," the midwife says after a moment.

"What's wrong?"

The midwife clears her throat.

"Give her to me." Maman releases her grip on Emeric's hand and holds out her arms, eyes blazing. When the midwife still does not turn, Maman shouts, "Give me my baby!"

Emeric's gaze darts back and forth from his mother to the midwife, that urge to run making a sudden return and filling his body with hot adrenaline.

The midwife takes a slow step around until she's facing his mother. "The child," she says, her tone impossibly quiet, "is a gravoir."

"Bring her to me."

"It's best if I take her away now." The midwife tucks a white blanket over the baby to hide it from view. "Holding her will only make what needs to be done more difficult."

With a screech, Maman dives at the midwife. They wrestle over the child, who lets out a tragic wail.

Emeric clings to the bedpost as his mother lands a slap straight across the midwife's cheek. The midwife gasps as Maman rips the bundle from her arms and pulls it securely against her chest.

The midwife stares at Maman, one hand reaching up to touch the bright pink mark on her cheekbone. "I must take the gravoir. It's the law."

Maman tightens her arms around the infant. "Are you sure she's a gravoir? She could just be a fendoir…"

"Even if it was, you would not get to keep the child. Fendoirs are raised at the Institution." She inhales a staggering breath, pressing a palm to her chest. "But there is no doubt in my mind. That child is no fendoir. It doesn't have the spiral birthmark on its sternum."

Maman turns her attention to the bundle in her arms and pulls the bit of blanket away from the baby's face. The determination in the set of her jaw twitches only for a moment when a spasm of shock flits through her eyes, but then she smiles, trailing a thumb along the baby's brow.

"Maman?" Emeric's fright is a sharp slice of ice in my chest.

"Arlette," Maman breathes, turning toward Emeric and lowering the bundle so he can see. "Isn't that a lovely name? Arlette. Yes, I think that will do quite nicely."

Emeric peers into the face of his tiny sister, his gaze tracing the hills and valleys of her gnarled features. The purplish, mottled skin, the knot where the nose should be.

He reaches out a tentative hand to pat her belly.

"I'm—I'm so sorry, Danielle," the midwife says to Maman, laying a hand on her shoulder. "But I really must—"

"Look at her ears," Maman says, her tone gentle.

"I—"

"Look at them."

The midwife obeys, her gaze darting to the baby and then back to Maman. "They're nice."

"They are, aren't they? Sort of round, right? And a bit too big. Exactly like her father's were." Maman stares down at Arlette, tears trembling like dewdrops on her eyelashes. "You know he died before I found out I was pregnant?"

The midwife wrings her hands. "I'm so sorry for your loss."

"He always wanted a daughter, my Richard." Her voice breaks. "I wonder what he would say if he were here now." She squeezes her eyes shut, sniffing.

Emeric stands up on his tiptoes to get another look. His new sister's arms flail jerkily in the air.

The midwife lays her palm against Maman's shoulder. "I know this is hard, but I really do need to take the baby. It's the law."

"No." Maman's voice is like the edge of a serrated blade,

and when she opens her eyes, they blaze like an inferno. "You're not taking her from me."

"If I don't and it is discovered, we'll all be beheaded." The midwife watches Maman with caution, as though afraid she might strike her again.

"She won't be discovered." Maman crosses to the bedside table and, holding the baby in one arm, yanks open a drawer to reveal a bulging bag. When she heaves it out, it clinks with the sound of hundreds of glass vials. She turns to the midwife and holds it out. "For your silence."

The midwife frowns but takes the bag and peers inside. The glow of the elixir within shines on the planes of her face. "How many?"

"Two thousand three hundred and forty-two," Maman says with finality. "It was all they were able to extract from my husband before he died, and it is everything I can offer you. It should fetch more than enough money to earn your discretion. Please." She approaches the midwife with tear-filled eyes. "Please."

The midwife meets Emeric's mother's gaze with a furrowed brow, her lips pulling down into a wrinkled frown. Emeric clings to his mother's bloody nightdress with sweaty fists, his heart pounding in his ears.

After a long moment, the midwife finally sighs and nods. "Fine. But I won't be putting my neck on the line for you. If the child is found, you must tell everyone you gave birth without the aid of a midwife."

Maman's face flushes with joy as she darts forward to clasp the woman in a loose hug. "No one will ever know you were here. Merci!"

I drag myself out of the memory as the midwife gathers her things and leaves. Emeric's fear, his relief, his confusion all pull on me as I do, but the song is nearing its end, and there's more—much more—I want to see.

I skip forward, dipping in here and there, catching glimpses of the little gravoir child as she grows. The cottage from the earlier memory is gone, replaced by a tiny house on the edge of the apple orchard. Emeric's mother must have whisked her children away to prevent Arlette from being discovered. Which is why Emeric grew up so isolated from the world, why he sang to toy animals instead of other people, why he never had the funds nor means to have any sort of vocal training.

Emeric's voice softens as it nears the end of the song, and I am filled with a longing so strong my heart might burst. I'm not ready to be done living and seeing and breathing in his past yet. I could remain here, swirling in the lights and colors of his memories until the end of time, and it still would not be long enough.

As he hits the last note, I glimpse Arlette facing an eleven-year-old Emeric in a small bedroom. He is singing, and golden strands of elixir are pouring out of his ears.

My hands jam sideways into the keys, sending a shock wave of noise blaring through the organ's pipes.

"Isda!" Emeric rushes to my side. "Are you all right?"

I lurch away from him, my mind reeling. "I'm—I'm fine..." I say, but my hearing has gone fuzzy, and his voice sounds as though I'm hearing it from underwater.

Arlette is not a fendoir. Yet there she was, extracting elixir straight from Emeric's ears just like one. Are gravoirs capable of that?

Am I?

I'm stumbling back and forth from one end of my room to the other, hands knotted in my hair. Emeric follows me a pace or two behind, begging me to tell him what's happened.

I whirl to look at him. He stands there in his dusty, patched jacket and gray trousers, his cap tied into a knot between white-knuckled fists.

"Isda," he says quietly. "Please talk to me."

I release my hair and smooth my skirts. "I'm sorry. I think the exhaustion of the day has finally gotten to me. That's all. I'm fine."

His brow furrows. "Are you sure?"

"I am." I lead the way back to the door and escort him into the catacombs. "I just need some rest."

He frowns, but then, finally, nods. "All right. I'll see you tomorrow." He puts the cap back into its place and turns to leave, pauses, then reaches out to brush my shoulder. "Take care. Please."

His touch shocks through me. I freeze as he strides off into the dark.

His footsteps fade, and I am left in silence.

It takes every bit of energy I have left to snap my jaw shut and turn back toward my room.

I catch sight of the skull right next to the crypt's entrance, grinning at me like it sees right through my mask to my stupefied expression.

"What are you laughing at, Albert?" I huff past and heave the door shut.

CHAPTER
NINE

I face my room. Books are strewn about from our lesson, and pages lie scattered on the floor where I must have knocked them down in my dazed state. The candles burn low, and the clock on the nearest shelf reads nearly 2:00 a.m. Though my body is more exhausted than it's been in as long as I can remember, my mind is abuzz and my heart is wild.

From projecting that demon into the Forgotten Child's mind to discovering that gravoirs might be capable of fendoir power, tonight has sent my world spinning.

Of course I've known that there is more to my power than the manipulation I do every night. But elixir extraction is a fendoir ability, not a gravoir one. And gravoirs are born without the fendoir birthmark that seems to be what allows fendoirs to do their magic. I suppose a gravoir could carve the symbol into their skin, but I've inspected every rune in that painting of Les Trois upstairs, and the fendoir symbol—the spiral in the space between collarbones—is decidedly absent.

I ease into my bed and pull the duvet up to my chin, not even bothering to change out of my clothes or take my boots off.

But try as I might to sleep, all I see behind my closed eyelids is the trail of golden elixir in Emeric's mind. All I feel is the tingle of curiosity that shivered through Emeric's chest at the sight of his baby sister at her birth. All I hear is the echo of his heartrendingly beautiful voice, soft as velvet in my ears.

My thoughts stray to Cyril, to the years of learning I spent at his knee as he struggled to teach me the intricacies of a magic he didn't have from that small red book on his desk. It's possible he didn't know the extent of my power.

He always told me we kept away from the other gravoir symbols because he wasn't sure what they did, wasn't sure which ones might set me on a path of madness from which he would be unable to retrieve me. He wanted to keep me from becoming volatile and treacherous like Les Trois.

Perhaps there is something to elixir extraction that I do not understand. Maybe it affects gravoirs differently. If he knew I was capable of it, then he kept it from me for a purpose, and I should leave it alone.

But...

My body shivers with curiosity. With excitement.

Reason tells me to wait and ask Cyril about it tomorrow night, but the zing in my blood won't let me think of anything else. Cyril would likely tell me it's not safe for me to try it, and he would probably be right. Besides, he might get to asking how I found out it was possible, and I've never been good at lying to him.

Which means if I want to see what extraction is like, I'll have to betray his trust for the second time.

The thought of sneaking around behind his back even more when he's already risked so much for me makes my stomach churn, but now that I know elixir extraction is possible, I cannot ignore it. I have to know more.

I think of all the hours he spent honing my ability, reading about my magic from that leather-bound tome in his office and teaching me the things he found there.

As a child, I was never curious about the book, never took it upon myself to try to read it—I had better things to do, like hiding in the dressing rooms to steal trinkets from the dancers. Now I wish I had cared more.

What exactly is written in it? What more could I learn about myself from it?

I have to know.

So in spite of the tremor in my limbs and the heaving of my lungs, I toss the duvet aside and make my way through the catacombs up into the opera house.

As I prowl through the deserted black hallways, shadows of great angel statues watch me, spreading their wings to guide me in the dark. Starlight glimmers on the floor. I brush my fingers against windows as I pass, and their panes send a chill up my arm like ice filming over a lake in midwinter.

When I reach the corridor where Cyril's office is, I slow my pace and creep closer to the wall. Though it is after two o'clock in the morning and Cyril is likely long gone for the night, I keep my footsteps silent. He's been known on occasion to work later than usual, and I'd prefer to not be caught tonight. Plus there's still the disturbing possibility that someone tried to enter his office earlier, and if that was the case, whoever it was might still be hidden in this hallway somewhere.

I slide against the oak door and press my ear to its surface, holding my breath.

No sound comes from within—not the creaking of the leather in his chair nor the clink of glass vials nor the shuffle of papers. I press my palm to the doorknob and twist.

It is locked.

I curse. Of course it is locked. It always is.

Sighing, I lean my cheek against the door once more, as though the wood's grain might whisper the answer to me. The distant scratching of the branches against his office window bristles through my ear, and I pause.

The tree.

Whirling, I sprint up the hallway, down several flights of

stairs, and through half a dozen corridors until I reach the back exit where the janitors and other employees leave during the night. I prop it open with a nearby rock and duck into the shadows of the trees that line the building.

And stop.

Blink.

I'm *outside*.

The blood drains to my feet.

The sky is so big. I stare, the breath whisked clean from my chest, the beat stolen from my heart. Gaping at wispy clouds drifting across diamond stars, I tip my head against the stone wall and inhale deeply.

The air is chilly and tastes of crisp leaves and chimney smoke. Though I've smelled these scents from the windows a thousand times, there's something entirely new and different about having them tickle through my nose and into my lungs out here in the open.

I reach out tentative fingers to the tree in front of me and stroke the nearest golden-edged leaf. It trembles beneath my touch. Its edge is not unlike the tips of the raven feathers that adorn my mask.

The tree rustles in the autumn breeze. Somewhere far away, a cab's wheels clatter across cobblestones. A horn blares. Crickets strum a harmony.

It is more beautiful than any symphony I've ever heard.

The city is quiet, as though listening to the same music. I imagine its people asleep in their beds, their faces soft and unblemished, their hearts untroubled.

There are no gunshots, no angry shouts. No one to condemn me.

They may have forced me into the dark, but I am not as powerless as they would have me be.

I grind my heels in the dirt.

It must be nice for them to live in a world that welcomes

them. That lets them walk, unafraid under the stars, free to experience the world's symphonies, its musks, its tastes. That grants them the liberty to harness their own destinies, whether that be on a stage or anywhere else.

One day, somehow, they will pay for their laws, for all the gravoirs they've murdered, for the years their disgust has imprisoned me underground. I don't know how, and I don't know where, but when that day comes, I will be free, and they will be the ones who will live in fear.

But first I need to find that book. Whirling, I creep around the side of the building, keeping behind the shrubbery. I find the wall where Cyril's office is and count the windows across. It should be the twelfth window from the end of the hallway, which would put it somewhere around...

There. The familiar scratching sound of branch against glass is louder out here. I inspect the tree leading to his window and rub my hands together, willing them to warm up in spite of the cold wind.

I gather my skirts in one arm to free my legs and hoist myself into the tree. Luckily, the branches are low and evenly spaced enough for me to make it most of the way up without much trouble. By the time I reach his window, however, I am gasping for breath, and my arms and legs are burning. It probably would have been a better idea to come back and do this when my body was not quite so spent, but even as the thought crosses my mind, I know I wouldn't have waited for anything. My need for answers would not have allowed me to.

Shimmying across the branch, I drop my skirts so I can hold on to the tree with one hand and reach for the window's latch with the other. It pops open, and I clamber over the sill to land in a heap on the floor next to Cyril's map of Channe.

Air burns in my lungs, and my corset feels suddenly too tight, like my ribs might burst through its boning. Gasping, I pull myself upright and light one of the lanterns.

I glance at the corner of the desk where the book was earlier this evening, but I find only a stack of psychology reference books.

Turning, I scan the titles on the shelves, searching for the red cover and the distinct cursive scrawl of its title. Hundreds of record books from the King's Council of Channe stand in tidy black rows, uniform and rigid as soldiers. Then there are the atlases and the encyclopedias, the music scores and the folders filled with Cyril's opera house dealings.

Rapping my knuckles against their spines, I whirl and dive for the shelves on the other side of the room. Here live the books he likes to read for entertainment. Literary magazines and lengthy tomes by ancient philosophers.

I search every single shelf. Even the children's books on the back wall that Cyril used to read to me when I was young. Nowhere in the room is a single book about gravoirs or fendoirs. Not even the history books, which are sure to discuss how fendoirs affect the economy, seem promising enough for me to pull them from their places and flip through.

Grinding my teeth, I fling myself into Cyril's chair.

What did he do with that old red book? Where could it be?

I pick up one of his elixir vials and roll it around my palm, chewing on my lip. The amber liquid sparkles, and I lean it closer to the lantern's light to inspect it. The elixir glows as though it's made of stardust, glittering motes suspended in molten gold. I think of how that elixir looked in Emeric's memory as it spilled from his ears toward his sister's outstretched hands, tiny ribbons of light pulled from somewhere deep in his soul, shining in the afternoon sun.

I lean back against the chair's armrest and gaze absently at the books on the wall, trailing the tip of the tiny vial along my jaw at the edge of my mask.

If I were Cyril, what would I have done with that book?

The vial slips from my sweaty fingers and shatters against

the tile, spraying the hem of my gown with liquid sunlight. I curse and rummage through Cyril's drawers for a handkerchief.

But when I turn to mop up the elixir, I pause, frowning. Is the puddle…shrinking?

I drop to my knees to get a better look.

The glowing pool of liquid is definitely getting smaller.

I crouch lower until my nose brushes the floor and run my fingertips along the smooth gloss of the marble. My hands pause on a small, almost imperceptible groove in the tile. I follow the line of it to where the elixir has almost disappeared completely.

"What on earth?" I mutter, tracing the crease all the way to where it meets up with a gap between the shelving on the walls.

The nearly invisible crack in the floor forms a perfect semicircle outward from one of the bookshelves.

Pinning my lower lip between my teeth, I approach the bookshelf and, keeping my feet just outside the semicircle, shove on one end of it. At first nothing happens, so I dig in my heels and throw all of my weight into it. The tile groans, then finally gives way, and the bookshelf swivels to reveal another set of shelves mounted on its other side.

"Sweet Memory's song," I breathe.

The hidden bookshelf is nearly empty. Only a few small tomes rest on the middle ledge: A pile of tattered, black journals, and the book with the faded, red cover I saw on Cyril's desk earlier tonight.

I pluck it from its place and angle it toward the light so I can see its title.

An Exploration of Fendoir Magic.

Footsteps click in the hallway outside the door.

Panic slices through me. I swing the bookshelf back around

and jam the book into my pocket just as a key scrapes in the lock and the doorknob turns.

"Isda?" Cyril stares at me, shock written in every wrinkle on his face. "What in Memory's holy name are you doing here?"

"I—I was looking for a book," I blurt.

"At three in the morning?"

"I couldn't sleep, and I remembered all those fairy tales you used to read to me before bed…" I step in front of where I spilled the elixir. Though the golden liquid has all disappeared into the crack in the floor, I'm afraid he might notice the broken glass, and I discreetly kick it under his desk.

He pulls his key from the lock and crosses toward me, mopping his face with a long-fingered hand. He clutches a torn envelope in his fist. "How did you get in here? I keep it locked."

I shrug, hating myself for every lie as it slips from my lips. "You must have forgotten."

He holds up his key and frowns. "It was locked just now."

My cheeks burn. Why am I so terrible at this? "Oui, I—I locked it behind me. I was afraid that whoever it was that tried to open the door earlier might come back."

Though the excuse rings obviously false, he doesn't seem to hear the quaver in my words. He simply nods and makes his way to the stack of children's books. His implicit, unquestioning faith in me makes my heart ache.

"These are the fairy tales," he says. "Was there one in particular you were looking for?"

"Oh, I'm sure any of them will do." I knot my fingers together so he won't see them shake.

He slides one out of its place. "Ah, *Charlotte and the Mirror of Forgotten Things*. This one was always a favorite of mine." He holds it out.

I take it and tuck it under my arm. "Me, too."

"Do you remember the poem at the end?"

I nod, every nerve in my body buzzing. "Of course I do."

"'When Charlotte looked in the mirror, she saw a great many things...'" He whispers the words with the same lilt he used to when I was a child.

The familiarity of the poem eases the spike of adrenaline in my body. When I join him to recite it, he smiles.

A bone, a bauble, a book, a barrel
Of berries picked last spring.

All the images she'd forgotten
As her mind grew old and gray
Little details, bigger ones too,
A thousand nights and days.

But her favorite thing to see
When she looked into its depths:
A four-layer cake, fourteen roses,
And sixty strands of baby's breath.

The lace on her sleeves and veil,
And the ringing of bells up above.
The thud of her heart, the strum of the strings,
As she gave her soul to her love.

For a moment, I am six years old again, tucked into a small cot in the corner of a practice room down the hall from here, clinging to the dregs of consciousness. Cyril is brushing the hair from my face and pulling a comforter to my chin. "Good night, chérie," he's saying.

I snap myself back to the present. "Thank you for the book," I say.

Cyril's smile is lined and tired. "I hope it helps you sleep."

"Merci." I shuffle toward the door.

"Oh, Isda. One more thing before you go." He crosses around to the front of his desk and leans back against it. A smile crinkles his eyes, and he fiddles excitedly with the envelope. "I have fantastic news. I've been promoted."

"On the Council?"

"Yes!" He jumps up and bounds toward me, as joyous as a child on the anniversary of its naming day, brandishing the envelope to the sky like a holy scepter. "I found this letter on my doorstep as soon as I got home. It seems the King has decided to take notice of all that I have done for Channe over the past decades. He's promoted me to the position of first advisor to Channe's Council Head!"

"Congratulations!" I say. "Finally, you're being rewarded for all of your hard work."

"And all these late nights," he agrees.

"Speaking of which…why did you come back? Surely you're exhausted."

"I am. But once I discovered the King's message, I realized I left my Council notebook here, which I'll need in order to write my acceptance letter. I tried to sleep, figuring I could do it tomorrow, but…"

"You couldn't?"

"I haven't been this excited in years." He beams. "So I decided to come back and retrieve the notebook." He slings an arm around my shoulders and pulls me in to plant a kiss on the top of my head. "I couldn't have done it without you. My star, my gem, my lucky vial of magic. And, after what you accomplished earlier tonight, I daresay our luck will continue."

I smile back and wrap my arms around his torso. "I'm so proud of you."

We embrace for another moment longer before he releases me and nods toward the hallway. "Now, off to bed with you. I really can't afford to have you falling asleep on the job tonight. The Council Head himself is coming to see the show, so you'll need to take special care with his memories. I want him astounded and amazed."

"Of course," I murmur. "Bonne nuit. Thank you for the book."

"De rien, my child."

But my smile fades as soon as I shut the door. The book weighs heavy in my skirt, like an anchor of iron set to pin me to the floor and wrap me in chains.

If Cyril knew what I planned to do…if he knew all of the ways in which I'd already betrayed his trust and risked discovery…

I shake my head and force myself to trek downstairs with my chin held high.

"I will be careful, Cyril." I whisper the promise over my shoulder as I walk. "And no matter what I do, I'll make sure no harm ever comes to you. I swear it."

CHAPTER
TEN

I untie my boots and rip off my stockings, stretching my toes for the first time in what feels like years. Then I undo the buttons on my dress, pull the entire mess of fabric over my head, and unlace my corset.

Dressed in nothing but my undergarments, I flop onto my bed and pull the red book in front of me. Its spine crackles like grease spitting into a fire as I ease it open. The pages inside are yellowed and brittle, and I handle them with care.

The title page indicates that this book is the primary text used by the Institution des Fendoirs de Vaureille to teach the instructors there the basics of fendoir powers and how best to train their students.

I fan through the pages to the first chapter. It begins with a description of a typical fendoir face. The purplish skin and the twisted nose crop up in the several illustrations that follow, with small variations for race or skull structure depicted.

I trace my finger along the profile of one of the fendoirs. I've never seen a maskless one before. Law demands that they wear their silver masks at all times. A part of me has always wondered how much like my own face theirs might look.

I tear my gaze away from the drawing and turn the page.

I could almost be beautiful if my face were only as misshapen as a fendoir's.

The following chapter describes how fendoirs are an uncommon mutation in an otherwise healthy human child.

Fendoirs have been recorded as part of the human race since the world's oldest discernible records. Even prehistoric markings on rock walls include depictions of people with unusual faces and curious marks on their sternums. However, it seems that the discovery of the fendoir ability to extract memory elixir was not well-known or understood until later. Once fendoir magic was discovered and formally analyzed in the early tenth century, elixir started to be sold, bought, and traded in various capacities, finally becoming standardized and regulated in 1201.

I try to imagine a world without vials of memory elixir. The thought of Channe's streets empty of the ambling, muttering Memoryless and the sobbing Forgotten Children is an entirely foreign idea to me.

The memory market has become a huge influence in the world's economy—so inherent in our system that it's difficult to fathom what it would be like without it. Selling one's own memory elixir is mostly a last-resort course of action for those desperate enough to make the sacrifice.

Yet I've noticed in the memories I've watched from my perch in the theater that the memory market seems to have grown drastically in the last few years. Is it because there are more poor people in Channe now whose finances are so precarious that the risk has become more worth taking? Or has the allure of what ingesting memory elixir does to a person driven the price so high that selling the elixir has become an attractive option even to those not on the brink of ruin?

It is a lucrative market. The more elixir one has, the better one is at remembering things. I've even heard of people who have purchased so much of it, they've developed photographic memories and become brilliant in their fields; after all, the more a person is able to remember from schools, books, and experiences, the wiser that person becomes.

Economics was never something Cyril spent much time teaching me, so I'm not quite sure what has changed.

I lean in closer to the page to read on.

Initially, we were not aware of what these disfigured children were capable of or how they would fundamentally change the way society functioned one day. We allowed them to grow up among their unmarked siblings as equals.

Fendoirs as equals? Nowadays, fendoirs are raised by the Institution and forced to work for Maisons des Souvenirs as little better than indentured servants until they die. While their existence is permitted and protected by the King, they are loathed by the general population. Shunned as though they carry a disease. Only tolerated because of their contribution to a thriving economy.

My eyes snag on the word *gravoirs* a bit farther down the page, but I force myself to continue reading where I left off.

However, as the market drive for memory elixir grew, so, also, did corrupt practices to "water down" the elixir in order to sell less of it for the same price. As use of tainted elixir became commonplace among the lower class, new fendoirs began to crop up—but these ones were different. Their faces were much more misshapen, and their chests lacked the extraction birthmark.

Initially, these new fendoirs were treated like the others, especially once it was discovered that carving the mark into their skin allowed them to perform the same magic.

I blink down at the text. There it is, in black and white. If I carve the fendoir symbol into my skin, I'll be able to extract elixir.

My nerves buzz, but I force myself to concentrate on the next passages.

In the late 1500s, three of these new fendoirs discovered that slicing different symbols into their skin gave them unprecedented control over others' memories and, therefore, others' lives. These three young women renamed their kind gravoirs to differentiate themselves from the fendoirs, whom they considered inferior due to the fact that carving symbols on a fendoir's body did not result in further powers.

The three gravoirs rose quickly to dominion, and thus we entered the period of time now referred to as l'Age de l'Oubli—The Age of Oblivion.

"Les Trois," as they soon became known, commenced a reign of terror. Fendoirs and gravoirs were recruited and trained as soldiers to enforce gravoir control. Any who resisted were put to death.

Their reign lasted for only two years, but during that time, tens of thousands of people were tortured and killed.

Rose's fierce glare shimmers in my vision as though the painting upstairs lies before me now.

Of course I know about their reign—it would be impossible to not know of it. Not with the way I've had to hide from a society that fears and loathes me because of what Les Trois did during their time.

Part of me hates them for using their power in such a manner, for plunging the world into darkness, blood, and pain.

Yet another small, damnable part of me wonders what controlling all of creation in that way would feel like. Marguerite, Éloise, and Rose never wore masks, never hid what they were. Cowering in the shadows was not a behavior they would have known.

What would it be like to stand before the world, unashamed and unafraid like they did? They commanded a stage of their own making just like I do in my dreams.

> There are dozens of variations in historical records regarding what happened with Saint Claudin, but the general consensus is that he was a lowly, unmarked servant working in the queens' residence. Details surrounding the affair are vague and difficult to prove, but what we do know is that he and Rose were somehow romantically involved.
>
> Rose's weakness for him soon proved the downfall of Les Trois, however. One night, after sharing her bed, Claudin slaughtered Rose and her two fellow monarchs, who slept in neighboring rooms, in their sleep. When dawn broke over Vaureille and the three women were found dead, the unmarked humans and the fendoirs, the majority of whom had been working for the queens against their will, banded together to take the rest of the gravoirs by surprise, effectively slaughtering them all.
>
> Once the unmarked humans had gained their victory, they set up an institution to train the fendoirs to use their powers solely for the good of the public and its market, and the King's Imperial Council established protocols to monitor fendoir activity.
>
> From then on, gravoirs were deemed too dangerous to continue to exist. To prevent anything like l'Age de l'Oubli from happening again, laws have been strictly upheld that a midwife attend each and every birth, and that those midwives see to it that if a gravoir child is born, it is immediately disposed of before it can become a threat. Additionally, in order to reduce the occurrence of such births in the first place, the King's Council in each city keeps careful logs of the dealings of the fendoirs residing in their jurisdiction to ensure elixir remains pure. While illicit activities

are impossible to entirely contain, the enforcement of this law
has drastically reduced the number of gravoirs born each year.

I stare at the page. At the words, "immediately disposed of."

The memory of my own birth is still as vivid as though I lived it moments ago. I close my eyes, and the emotions roiling in my chest pull me back seventeen years to a cold night in a dark cottage somewhere in the North.

My life began with pain and a white shock of light, but what haunts me to this day is the gasping sound my mother made when she saw my face for the first time.

Her gasp wasn't one of relief or joy or surprise. It was one of horror. Of pain. Of soul-crushing despair.

The midwife's words were garbled, as though caught away on a current of water. "I'm sorry, madame. Your daughter appears to be a—a gravoir."

Mother's gasps became sobs. "Take it away."

I never knew her touch. Only saw her blurry outline for an instant before I was whisked out into the night.

And then I was falling. Falling. Falling.

A splash of cold water engulfed me, and then all was torture and all was pain until a strong pair of hands pulled me from the darkness.

"Disposed of" indeed.

I tug the pendant from my shift and twirl it around and around. The glass reflects slivers of light as it spins, projecting sparkling squares on the wall that dart back and forth. Its light reminds me of memory elixir, so brilliant and shining and pure.

Rolling onto my back, I drop the pendant and hold the book above me, flipping to the following page. The next chapter contains a short section on what is known about gravoirs, which isn't much. There are a lot of phrases like, "extremely dangerous," and "deceitful," and "kill immediately," but not a lot of explanation as to why.

But it is clear that gravoirs are not a separate type of being from fendoirs; they are a further mutation of them. Apparently we are able to do the elixir extraction that fendoirs do, as well as view people's memories, manipulate them, and erase them from existence. My gaze pauses on one particular section:

> *If a gravoir is in possession of a catalyseur, as Les Trois were, the results for mankind would once again be catastrophic. When coupled with the correct symbols carved into the palms, catalyseurs augment the reach of a gravoir's power, which would allow that gravoir to view or manipulate memories and extract elixir from anyone in the immediate vicinity, whether they are singing or not.*

I flip through to the next page, but there is nothing further on catalyseurs. It does not specify what they are or how to find one.

The rest of the book describes the function of fendoirs in the economy, with pages and pages of dull explanations on the flow of vials and the necessity of each city's King's Council to keep detailed records of fendoir dealings.

The final section's title makes me sit up and pull the hair away from my face so I can see it clearer. *Fendoir Power: Methods.*

I spend the next several hours poring through the instructions, a thrumming like a distant drumbeat buzzing in my veins. Louder and louder it grows, until the clock on the mantel strikes seven o'clock, and I reach the end of the book.

Flipping back to the page with the detailed depiction of the fendoirs' Extraction Mark, I leap from my bed to retrieve the dagger on my bookshelf.

The book says that in order for the mark to work for a

gravoir, it must be carved in the skin at the top of the chest, just below the place where the collarbones meet. If I were to cut the symbol there, Cyril would see it and know I'm up to something immediately. Turning the dagger over and over in my hands, I grimace down at the book.

Rose's fierce glare in the painting upstairs comes to my mind, and I imagine the bloodied symbols etched into every inch of her exposed skin. The Extraction Mark was nowhere to be found.

Is it possible that a gravoir might be able to inscribe the mark in another location? Maybe one that is less visible?

It's worth a shot.

I hike up the skirt of my slip and shove aside my under-garments to reveal the smooth skin of my thigh. Gritting my teeth, I ease the tip of the knife into my skin. Blood pools, hot and dark, dribbling down my leg and dropping like a stream of shining garnets to the stone floor as I etch the spiral into my flesh. The pain is sharp, but my hand remains steady.

Cyril has always erred on the side of caution when it comes to allowing me to use my powers, but with the words from his book and the images from Emeric's memories flooding my mind, I'm not so sure anymore that caution has been for the best. If I am to ever find my way out of the shadows, I'll need to know for sure exactly what my power can do.

So I'm going to try my hand at elixir extraction.

Tonight.

On Emeric Rodin.

CHAPTER ELEVEN

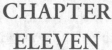

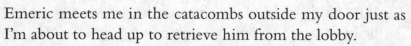

Emeric meets me in the catacombs outside my door just as I'm about to head up to retrieve him from the lobby.

"I'm sorry," he says when I run into him. "I was up there waiting, and I... I was worried. I wanted to make sure you were all right. I was a fool to leave you like that last night."

I shake my head. "Don't. I asked you to."

He licks his lips, scanning the planes of my mask as though he might be able to peer through it to assess my health. "So... are you all right?"

"Yes. I needed rest, like I said." I gesture into my crypt. "Ready to begin?"

He nods and steps forward, pausing to tip his hat to the skull on his way in. "Evening, Albert."

Biting down a laugh, I follow him inside, making sure not to wince when the new symbol carved into my leg stings from the movement.

"So... I kind of left all of the books you lent me here last night. I tried to practice without them—the breathing with my diaphragm and all that."

"Perfect." I cross to the organ, trying not to let him see the way my eagerness to get him singing again has me twitchy. "After we warm up, you can show me your progress."

We begin. Hearing his voice again is like drinking cool water after a long, hot, arduous day. The tension in my shoulders eases. Even the excitement in my belly slows to a gentle simmer.

As he runs through warm-ups and then sings an aria for me to watch his breathing technique, I consider what would be the best way to extract his elixir.

An empty glass vial I lifted from Cyril's office an hour ago is jammed into the sash of my dress, uncorked and ready to be filled. Its presence weighs heavy against my hip bone, a constant reminder of my potential. Of my power. Of what I plan to do.

I need to make sure his eyes are closed when I do it. Even then, I'm taking a risk. If he sees the elixir coming out of him, he might report me to the authorities. No matter what, he'll at least not want to continue working with me. Which means I'd lose my chance to learn more from Arlette. And, though I tell myself I don't care, the idea that the kindness I see in his eyes when he looks at me might fade makes my stomach twist.

He finishes the aria and looks at me expectantly. "So? How did I do?"

"Very well. I don't think I saw your shoulders move once."

He punches the air in victory.

"But you do need to work on not sliding up to the notes," I continue, fiddling nervously with the chain on my necklace. "Hit each one right from the top—imagine dropping onto it from above instead of rising up to meet it."

He nods. "All right."

"Why don't you sing…" I glance down at the pendant. An idea strikes me, and I grin. "The necklace's song? Your mother's lullaby?" Last time the song had been enough to take us both over. He'd closed his eyes then, and if he'd been anything like me, he'd gotten completely lost in the music—lost enough that he probably wouldn't have noticed the glow of extracted elixir drifting away from him.

"Sure."

I twist the locket open, and the tiny ballerina begins her dance. The bells tinkle. Emeric sings.

He cocks his head to one side as the lyrics knot the air between us, somehow pulling us closer even though neither of us has moved. For a moment I can almost imagine my mask is gone. That he's seeing me—all of me. Monster. Manipulator. Girl.

The momentum of the song's crescendo builds, and his eyes flutter closed. His lashes send spidery shadows over his cheeks that slip in and out of his dimples, and I'm struck with the impulse to trace those creases with my fingertips.

I keep my hands on my pendant, but my eyes follow the places where I wish my fingers could go. Into those dimples, up over his cheekbones, across his brow, into his hair...

No. Now is not the time for distraction. My time has come.

Concentrating on the tug of his memory river and the way the undertow of it has ignited both the skin on my ankle where the symbol once was as well as the new rune on my thigh, I reach into the place where the moments of his past swirl.

The book described that for fendoirs, a person's song brings up a view of a shining pool of elixir. Fendoirs simply reach into that pool and pull portions of it out through the person's ears.

However, as the visions and emotions and sounds churn past me, I see no golden pool of liquid light. How did Les Trois manage to extract elixir if they could not see it? How did Arlette?

Maybe the symbol on my thigh isn't working. It's possible I was wrong about being able to use it in spite of its being carved on my leg instead of my chest. Perhaps the artist who did the depiction of Les Trois upstairs wasn't entirely accurate when he painted the three gravoirs' wounds.

Yet the thrill of Emeric's voice pulses in that symbol exactly the way it does in the place where the Manipulation Mark used to be on my ankle.

It has to be working. I just need to figure out how to use it.

Gritting my teeth, I sink into a random memory. Maybe I'll be able to locate the elixir somewhere inside the scene.

The recollection I find myself in is a simple one of him making his way home from the opera house. The air is cool, and the cobblestones are wet with autumn rain. His feet splash through puddles reflecting the grayish gaslights overhead, and his lips purse into a buoyant whistle. He tips his cap as he passes a Forgotten Child, digs in his pocket, and tosses the boy a gold piece. The child dives for it, and Emeric smiles as he turns the corner.

The shimmer of gold pulls my gaze, and I push back in the memory to the moment the coin hits the ground. Freezing the scene, I focus on the gold, begging it to give me a hint, a clue, some idea how to find the golden elixir that keeps it bright in Emeric's mind.

I find nothing.

The memory fades; Emeric has reached the end of the lullaby. I nod absently at him to sing through it again. He closes his eyes once more and starts back up.

I return to the gold piece, staring and staring at it, frustration growing like embers in my chest. The longer I glare at the coin, the hotter my blood roils.

This was supposed to work. Why is it not working?

The gold piece gives off a sudden, bright flash of yellow and then fades back to its dull, brass color.

Grinding my teeth together, I focus every inch of power vibrating through the symbol on my leg on that coin.

The image of it quivers, and then the whole scene ripples

as though it has liquefied. Gaslights and stars and cobble-stoned streets swim before me. Beneath the waves, I catch glimmers of gold.

Excitement floods my limbs. I push forward, clawing *through* the fluid of the memory to whatever lies below. It's like digging my way through sludge, and I strain my mind, force the fire in me to feed my power and make it stronger.

Then, finally, I burst through.

I stifle a gasp so as not to startle Emeric from his song.

Beneath the tide of his memories runs another river made of gold.

His elixir.

I stare, sparks dancing under my skin, a victorious smile threatening to take over my whole body.

Determined, I get to work. Much in the way I was able to erase pieces of people's memories before, I suck in my breath as though I'm drinking through a straw, focusing every bit of my concentration on that golden glimmer. It resists at first, but I tug as fiercely as I can, and soon it comes loose, flowing out toward me.

I open my eyes. A soft, amber glow has gathered around Emeric's ears. My power purrs, sending delicious warmth through my body as it surges outward, beckoning the elixir my way. The glow brightens, and a long, slender ribbon of liquid sunlight twirls lazily into the air.

The elixir sparkles as though it's made of human soul, which, now that I consider it, maybe it is. I lick my lips as it flows toward me, and I'm seized with a sudden, unruly desire to send it straight into my own mouth just so I can taste it. I've never cared to try elixir before, but now I quiver with a thirst so strong my mind spins. Swallowing the saliva that has collected on my tongue, I direct the elixir down into the open vial in my belt and shove the cork in.

I dart a glance at Emeric, but he doesn't seem to have noticed anything has happened. He's still singing, his voice harmonizing perfectly with the music of my pendant.

The warmth and pleasure of my power shrinks back into my chest, leaving my hands and arms and the mark on my thigh suddenly cold in its absence.

I want more.

Whipping my head around, I scan the room for another vial, an empty container, a vase…anything. But I find nothing. I turn back to Emeric. The pull of his memories is a slow, tantalizing torture. My power reaches toward it, aching to drag more and more and more of it out.

Oh, how I *want* it.

All of it.

My mouth waters.

I plunge once again into the memory river. Deeper, deeper, deeper until I find the gold again, and I yank it out. My whole body is trembling with desire, with hunger, with *need*.

This time, I direct it straight into my mouth.

Ecstasy tingles through my soul when the elixir hits my tongue. I sip at it, wishing I could pull more of it out at a time, that I could swallow mouthfuls instead of sucking at such a thin stream. Maybe with more practice I could siphon it out faster. I've never tasted anything so exquisite in my life.

It tastes like honey and life and…caramel.

My body warms, brightens. My hearing grows clearer. My vision sharpens. I feel as though I could run miles without tiring—and I want to. I want to make my way aboveground and sprint into the horizon and never, ever stop. I want to fling my arms out wide, let the wind lift me up into the skies, and soar.

The textbook last night mentioned something like this occurring. Apparently for unmarked people, the elixir only augments memory and mental capacity. But part of what makes fendoirs and gravoirs so dangerous is how consuming elixir expands their bodies' abilities. Senses, strength, speed.

It's a tremulous, delicious high.

The music halts, and I gasp as my supply of Emeric's elixir cuts off abruptly.

I blink around at my room, realizing I'm not actually airborne among the stars, but still leaning against my organ bench a few feet from Emeric. I meet his gaze.

His eyes are dark coals. "You promised me you wouldn't extract." His voice is so quiet I might not have heard it were it not for his elixir pumping in my veins making my hearing so vibrantly clear.

"I—I was just practicing." I yank the vial from my sash and hold it out for him. "I wasn't stealing. I meant to give it back."

He glares daggers at me, a vein pulsing purple in his jaw. He rips the vial from my palm, shoves it into his pocket, and strides toward the door. "We're done."

"Emeric, wait!" I dive after him and tug on the back of his jacket. "Please, don't go. The memory loss isn't permanent yet—not for another twenty-six hours. As long as you drink that vial, it'll all come back." My claim isn't strictly true, considering I ingested a few vials' worth, but I'm hoping he didn't notice that part.

He growls and jerks his jacket out of my grip.

"I swear I won't do it again," I plead.

He whirls to face me. "How could I possibly trust you after that?"

"I know." My stomach sinks. "It was stupid of me. I made a mistake." If he leaves now, he won't come back. The thought of not hearing him sing anymore, of never swimming through his memories again, turns my bones to ice.

"You're a fendoir, so you don't understand—you can't possibly understand—what a violation it was for you to take my elixir without permission." Though his words are still quiet, they ring in my ears as though he's shouting. "Elixir is not just some…*thing*. It's my *life*. There are people in my memories that I—" His voice breaks, and he turns away to take a calming breath. "There are people that I've lost, Isda. Every drop of elixir taken from me is a part of them that disappears."

Guilt surges in my gut, hotter and more acute than I've ever known it. Does its severity have something to do with the way his elixir has made every sensation in my body stronger? Or is it just that I've never lived enough of a life to ever have a reason to feel this guilty for something before?

"You're right." I knot the pendant's chain around my fist. "I didn't realize that, and I didn't consider what it would mean to you."

He glances back at me, and I meet his gaze, searching for any hint that his anger may be softening. But where he's always seemed warm and open to me before, now his stare is closed off and cold.

"Please," I whisper. "You're the first person I've ever—I mean, besides Cyril, I've never known anyone." My words tangle around each other, weak and useless and stupid. "If you leave, I don't know if I… I don't know what I'll… Please…"

He considers me for a long moment, his fists clenching and unclenching at his sides.

I wait, my heart gurgling in my throat. I can't go back to my old life, the one without his voice or his memories. Not with what I've already learned in the few moments I've seen of his sister. Not with how dipping into his past has made me feel like a whole, complete person who's lived a life worth having. Not with the way his voice soothes my soul and makes me forget, even for a moment, what I am.

But it's not only the loss of his memories, his elixir, or his voice that would crush me. It's him, too. In only a few short days, I've become accustomed to the idea of having him here. Of him joking with the skulls in my catacombs and snooping around in my collections and making me laugh in spite of my better judgment.

I'd miss him, too.

So I wait, hardly daring to breathe.

Finally, he speaks. "I'll make you a deal. I will continue to take voice lessons from you on two conditions. One." He holds up a finger. "No more extracting elixir. Ever."

I bob my head, swallowing. "Of course. I swear."

"And two." He holds up a second finger and meets my gaze directly. "You get me a key to Monsieur Bardin's office."

"What?" I step back. "Why?"

"Those are my terms." He crosses his arms. "I have no idea why you want me to take these lessons so badly, but I won't do it unless you promise me those two things."

"What do you want from Cyril?"

"Does it matter?"

"Yes, I'd say it matters a great deal."

"Why? He's not your father."

"He's—he's—" My hackles rise.

"Why does he keep you locked up down here, Isda?" Emeric's voice is almost soft but for the sharp blade around its edge. "What's in it for him?"

"I told you, he's a very good friend. Like family. He…he cares about me."

Emeric barks a laugh.

My anger flares. "What do you know of it? You don't know me. You don't know him. You don't know anything of the situation at all."

His eyes trail all over my mask and finally rest on my glare. His brow furrows. "I do know that it's cruel of him to keep you locked away like this. Living in the sewers like an animal, surrounded by rats and darkness and rot."

"What other choice do I have?" My voice comes out shrill. "I'm not like you. I cannot just *live* out there. Not with my face. Not with what I am. He's at least given me a better life than what the world would have offered."

"I don't claim to understand his motives, but I do know that someone like you—with talent and spirit and fire—does not deserve to be treated this way. And—" He pauses to draw a long breath. "I also know that whatever Cyril Bardin has been to you in your life, whatever he has given you, whatever he claims to be, he does not care for you."

My body quivers. Rage boils, hot and ravenous, and it sears away everything in its path. "Get. Out."

"I wanted to warn you. He's—"

"I said *GET OUT!*" I scream.

"I was just—"

I raise a hand as though to strike him, and he flinches away from me.

The fire in my chest roars to life, coalescing into a great beast with snapping teeth as the elixir in my system throws every detail of Emeric's trembling fear into sharp relief. My laugh slices the night and watches it bleed with satisfaction.

"Please, Isda. At least consider that Cyril—"

I hiss through my teeth. "I thought I told you to leave."

"But—"

With a roar, I whirl, snatch up a candlestick, and hurl it at his face. He ducks, and the candle smashes into a lantern on the wall. Glass shatters. Oil spatters down the stone and all over the floor.

My body burns from the inside out. Fire carves its way through my veins, sets my heart thundering, fills my mouth with venom. I glare down at Emeric's cowering form and step forward.

He scrambles out of my path, wrenches the crypt door open, and disappears.

I growl, slamming the stone shut behind him so hard the

wall cracks. Emeric's elixir tears through my body, making my hands quiver with power.

I twist to face the room, and my gaze catches on my mirror in the corner.

Crossing to it, I scrutinize my reflection and force myself to breathe. In and out. In and out. Find my center. Settle into the silence.

The fire inside of me recedes.

Shrinks.

Cools.

I reach up to touch the edge of my mask, pause, then pull it away from my head.

I meet my own gaze in the mirror as my mask drops from my grasp and hits the floor with a soft thud. With a shaking hand, I trace along my rigid, gnarled brow, over my disfigured knot of a nose, across the sunken hollows where high cheekbones should be. My skin is rough and bubbled, a patchwork of purple and dark gray with vivid splotches of crimson. My mangled lips pull back as I suck in a breath.

I shudder.

Who am I fooling? I put on pretty dresses, sew glitter into a mask, and pretend to myself that I deserve to live in this world. But I stole a piece of Emeric's soul, drank it in like a rabid animal, and then screamed at him for being upset about it. Shame creeps hot down the back of my neck and raises the hairs on my arms.

I pretend to be human, but the mirror does not lie. This face marks me as a gravoir, and as much as I want to believe that still means I'm human, deep down I'm not so sure anymore.

Even now, the elixir thrumming in my veins calls to me, makes me tremble with thirst for more. More. *More.*

But on the edges of that hunger, Emeric's words eat away at my thoughts. *I wanted to warn you,* he said.

How proud. How self-righteous of him to presume he knows what's best for me when he understands so little of what it means to be what I am. How dare he suggest that the one person who has ever been able to bear the sight of me might not care?

Emeric was wrong about Cyril, about me, about everything. Even so, the image of the anger and fear I saw on his face fills me with humiliation.

Emeric's claim was ungrounded and unfair, but I behaved like the demon they say I am.

And now he's gone.

A strangled sound chokes out through my throat. I turn away from the glass. Pressing my palms to my eyes, I sink to my knees and sob.

CHAPTER
TWELVE

Emeric does not return the next night. Or the night after that. Or the night after that.

Watching the operas has lost all promise and excitement. Now that I've heard Emeric's voice, even the lead soprano's performance is lackluster, her tone sounding more nasally than I remember it, her vibrato warbling and uneven. And after having seen Emeric's memories, the performers' pasts leave much to be desired. They're too colorless, too drab, their emotions too dull and distant to be worth perusing.

My nights are lonely, and I find myself talking to Albert on my way in every evening.

"No, he's not coming tonight," I tell the crumbling skull. "He's probably never coming back. Quit holding your breath."

And every night as I curl up in my bed, I keep my ears alert for the sounds of a police force storming through the catacombs to come and cart me away. Surely, if nothing else, Emeric reported my existence. He seemed angry enough, and Memory knows I would deserve it for behaving the way I did.

As I await my doom, I whisper silent prayers that no matter what they may do to me, Cyril will be all right. In trying to extract Emeric's elixir, I broke the promise I made to Cyril in my heart that I would keep him safe. The idea that he might suffer because of my foolishness fills my bones with an icy dread.

But no one comes for me, and the only sounds in the catacombs are the scrabbling of rat claws and the scuttle of beetles over the stone floor.

Emeric's words about Cyril burn in my mind, hot as wildfire. *He does not care for you. He does not care for you. He does not care for you.* Over and over like a terrible chant that never stops.

But it isn't true. Would a man who didn't care for me raise me as his own? Bring me everything I asked for? Read me fairy tales in the night?

On the third day without Emeric, Cyril brings in another Forgotten Child. This one is a girl dressed in rags with hair the color of dishwater. When I transform her memory of Cyril, she bursts into tears and is inconsolable for nearly a half hour.

Guilt stings in my chest until I notice Cyril's eyes gleaming with pride.

He wouldn't look at me like that if he didn't care for me. Would he?

So I shove the guilt away, letting my anger consume it until I'm numb.

The fifth night without Emeric, I cannot sleep. The instant I drift into slumber, his voice echoes in my ears as though he is in the room with me. Haunting me. Singing to me. I sit bolt upright in bed and scan every inch of my crypt for him.

He's not there.

I stuff my face into my pillow and wrench it over my ears.

But I see his dimples in the dark, smell his caramels in the fabric, and hear his laughter in the silence.

All this remembering will drive me to madness.

He's truly gone.

I squeeze my eyes shut as my power wilts along with my

heart. An animal hanging its hungry head, its empty belly growling, echoing, pleading.

More music, it whispers to me. *More elixir.*

On my way out to the evening performance on the seventh night, I glance at Albert as I pull the door shut. "No." I sigh. "Not tonight, either, Albert. You'd best stop asking."

The skull's empty eye sockets seem to follow me as I move to depart.

I pause but do not turn back. "Do you really think there's a chance?" I whisper. "Do you think he'd ever return?"

I lift my gaze to the black, bone-lined corridor in front of me as the cold air feathers soft against my throat.

"I miss him."

I wait for Albert to respond, but of course he never does.

Is this truly my fate? To live alone down here for the rest of my days? Talking to the dead because the living cannot bear my existence?

Before Emeric, that future didn't seem so bleak. Now I feel as though it might suffocate me.

I trudge to the theater to sulk in the shadows, an ugly, unwanted thing hiding behind glamor and gold.

Cyril meets me outside his office after the show holding a large, white costume box. A nervous smile twitches on his lips, and he glances back and forth down the hallway as though verifying that we are as alone as we always are this time of night.

"What's this?" I ask when he shoves the box into my hands.

"I need you to put it on. Tonight is the first part of that task I mentioned before. I think you're ready."

My grip tightens on the edges of the box, which crinkle slightly under my fingers. "We're leaving?"

He nods. "Quickly. We have an appointment at eleven."

"An appointment?"

"I'll explain on the way." He ushers me into his office and pulls the door closed to give me privacy while he waits in the hall.

My blood zings hot and cold at the same time. My stomach churns, suddenly bubbling with anxiety, excitement, and terror all at once.

With shaking hands, I settle the box on Cyril's desk and lift the lid. I gasp.

Inside sits a pool of deep, moss green, gauzy fabric that I can only assume is some kind of gown. Resting atop it is a cream-colored mask with blushing, freckled cheeks, perfectly crafted so that it looks like a normal, human face. The material is soft and pliable, as though it's made of real skin.

I pull off the black mask and set it down next to the box. Taking an extra moment to marvel at the perfect shape of the cheekbones on this new disguise, I slide it into place.

It fits perfectly, as closely as my black one does, but its flexible construction makes it move when I do. The mouth opens when I open mine, and the cheeks dimple when I smile. I glance into a small mirror on the wall and marvel at how lifelike the skin looks. While daylight and scrutiny would reveal it as false, the shadows of the night will serve to hide what I am completely.

With my heart thudding in my throat, I pull off my black gown and tug the green one over my head. It slides down my body, slipping easily over my curves. Its hem hits the floor with a quiet thud. Tying the sash around my waist, I notice a bit of cloth the same color as this dress sitting in the corner of the box.

The light fabric tumbles between my fingers, silky and slippery as water.

A veil.

I slide its comb into the knot of crimson curls at the crown of my head. The veil drapes across my face all the way down past my chin, and it puffs away with every exhale.

Cyril knocks, and I pull the door open. He surveys my appearance and nods. "Perfection."

This dress, this veil, this mask…while wearing them, I can nearly forget the image of my own face in the mirror. With these things on, I finally might resemble a normal girl. Almost like one of the ritzy, glamorous patrons at the opera with purses full of enough coins to purchase the world.

Cyril offers me his arm, and I take it, trying to keep my hand from pinching the inside of his elbow too tightly. He leads me downstairs and out the back exit. A cab waits on the street behind a broad-backed, black horse whose mane stirs slightly in the cold air.

The driver hops down and opens the door. I keep my face angled away as Cyril helps me inside.

Just like that, I am out in the city, riding in a real cab like one of the opera performers I've watched from the windows for so many years.

The seats are firm but comfortable, and though the windows are small, they are all I need. I watch the streets rattle by in silent rapture.

Though the shops are all closed and the sidewalks are mostly empty, the city teems with life. Journal shops pop out on every other corner, with bright displays of a hundred different bound books for the express purpose of remembering things that will one day be forgotten. Windows boasting professional photography to memorialize life's moments sparkle in the moonlight. Cafés advertising the perfect tea to improve the body's natural elixir capacity wink from iron-framed panes.

What draws my attention the most are the Maisons des Souvenirs with their flapping crimson flags proclaiming to the world that this is the place to go have memory elixir cleaved from the mind. Stitched into each flag with shining, golden threads is the spiral Extraction Mark. I think of the identical scabbed mark on my thigh and tighten my grip on the armrest.

I hold my breath as we pass it all, recognizing nearly every street from one memory or another. Somehow everything seems so different—so much more exquisite—in real life.

In the alleyways, hunched figures stumble listlessly in the dark. The Memoryless stare with glassy, empty eyes as we pass.

It is shocking how much like corpses they look, so drained of elixir they've forgotten how to live, how to function beyond basic survival instinct. A few more vials extracted from any one of them would leave them dead in the streets. When a person has that little elixir left in their systems, their bodies stop creating new memories in an effort to preserve what is left.

A shiver prickles down my neck that has nothing to do with the icy breeze leaking in through the cracks around the door. I back away from the window, unease making my hands clammy.

We round a corner and follow a slowly rising road to the wealthier neighborhoods built into the side of a hill.

"So." I tear myself away from the view to face Cyril. He's rustling through a stack of papers in his lap, his lips pursed as he scans the writing on each page. "Where are we going?"

"To pay a little visit to the Head of the King's Council of Channe. Monsieur Gaspard LeRoux. He so enjoyed coming to the opera last week, I offered him the privilege of a little private performance."

"A private performance?"

"Don't worry." He laughs. "I'm not asking you to do anything scandalous. Just go in there, act like you're one of my best divas, and sing for him. You're as accomplished a vocalist as any of my sopranos, anyway. He won't know the difference."

A thrill runs through me. I get to *perform*? "You want me to sing for him? Why?"

"Because it will give us the perfect opportunity to use a bit of your magic." His eyes gleam. "When you've finished your little selection of songs, I want you to invite him to sing 'La Chanson des Rêves' with you. While he's singing, you'll go into his memories and put things there like we've been practicing with the children back in my office."

"What kinds of things?" I chew on the inside of my cheek as my stomach sinks. Am I going to be able to pull this off? I may be wearing a particularly well-made mask, but if LeRoux looks too closely he'll be able to tell it's not real.

"The goal, dear Isda—" Cyril taps his papers against his knees to straighten them and meets my gaze "—is to make the man go mad."

"I—but… How?"

"This is going to be a gradual process. Thankfully, my promotion has given me the perfect excuse to bring you to his home. As thanks for the honor of being named his first advisor, I've promised him a nightly private performance from my best vocalist." He smiles, and I mirror the expression. "We'll be coming to visit him every evening for the next few weeks. I've already ironed out all the details and have a whole wardrobe for you to use to play the part. But tonight, I want you to start out small. Just put a whisper of something horrific here and there. It would probably be best to begin several years ago so that the tweaks aren't as noticeable. Each time you visit, you'll add a little more."

I listen, my grip on the armrests tightening with each word.

"Based on some research I've done," Cyril continues, "I believe that as the psychological trauma in his past increases, his behavior will become more erratic in the present. The hope is that once you've added enough hallucinations to his memories, his mind will begin to conjure up those images on its own going forward."

I lick my lips, which have gone suddenly dry. "But why

the Head of the Council? He's so well-known… If anyone finds out, we'll be—"

"No one is going to find out, are they? You are going to be careful. Don't let him get too close. Don't give him any reasons to suspect you." He pauses to set his papers into a black briefcase. "And why the Head of the Council? I should think my reasoning obvious. We discussed him not last week, didn't we? Channe is on the brink of ruin because he doesn't have the gall to do what needs to be done, and things are only going to get worse unless something changes."

"You want his job," I say quietly.

"If those fendoirs are siphoning elixir away for themselves as I suspect they are, they could stage an uprising. And with the number of them that live here, they pose a very real, very terrifying threat. Our police teams would not be able to stand against a group that large."

I dig a fingernail into a seam in the seat and tease out a loose thread.

What exactly would an uprising by the fendoirs look like? If they'd be fighting for the chance to live as they wish and take off their masks…could that liberate me, too?

Would giving them back their freedom be so bad?

Cyril pauses, leveling my gaze with his steady one. "I want to keep Channe from collapse, and, unlike LeRoux, I'm willing to do what's necessary, no matter how difficult, to rid our city of danger and make it a safe place once again."

He lifts his chin proudly as he speaks and bats at an invisible fleck of dust on his knee with more poise and confidence than I've ever witnessed in any other man.

Cyril would make a fine Council Head. Fearless and brilliant, careful and well-spoken, it's a marvel it's taken so long for the Council of Channe to name him First Advisor. But if the fendoirs feel about unmarked people the way Les Trois did, they'd come straight for the Council first. They'd blame Cyril for their troubles. Slaughter him while he dreamed.

Ice walks fingers down my spine.

I want to be free, but not at the expense of the only family I have.

Cyril's methods may be a bit extravagant at times, but it is only because he is so determined. Although giving a man hallucinations makes me a bit queasy, it does seem to be a solid plan. Cyril has been campaigning to be promoted for as long as I've been alive and was only just now given the role of First Advisor. There's no telling how long it would take to overrun the Council Head's rule using normal means. And it sounds like time is a luxury we no longer have.

"How can you tell the situation is getting worse?" I ask.

"The fendoirs are being given too much freedom," he continues. "Walking about without restraint in the streets, interacting with people without supervision." He sighs. "I know that might not sound like much, but fendoirs can be an unruly bunch. When they are given too much liberty, they begin to get ideas about what the world owes them. We don't want another Age de l'Oubli, do we?"

"Certainly not." I try to ignore the grimace that twists his lips when he talks about the fendoirs. As though he's not talking about me, too.

But even as that thought crosses my mind, I know I'm different to him. I'm sure Emeric's mother feared gravoirs as much as any other person before her daughter was born one, but she loved Arlette fiercely enough to risk her life to keep her from harm.

And Memory knows Cyril has risked his life for mine a thousand times over.

CHAPTER THIRTEEN

Monsieur LeRoux's mansion towers over Channe, an enormous castle of peaked roofs that pierce the cloudless sky. Its stone walls glow white as the moon, and its expansive lawn shimmers in the breeze.

Cyril leads me to the entrance. Our heels click on the tiled porch. A butler ushers us inside, and my gaze trails upward to the rounded, ornate ceiling several stories above our heads and the elegant chandelier that hangs from it.

I close my eyes and inhale slowly through my nose, pressing my palm to my stomach as my mind conjures up an image of another chandelier—the tremendous, sparkling masterpiece that hangs so close to my perch in the theater.

I may not be singing on the opera house stage tonight in front of thousands, but I will be performing in front of an audience for the first time in my life. My mind whirs, and I cling to Cyril's elbow to keep my balance.

"You all right?" Cyril whispers, nudging me gently.

I swallow down my nerves and smile up at him. The mask stretches with the movement. "Oui. Just a little nervous."

"You'll be splendid." Cyril winks as a maid in a black dress pressed to perfection comes around the corner to escort us up a grand marble staircase and down a long hallway with plush, red carpet.

"Monsieur LeRoux," she calls softly through a white door with gilded detailing. "Monsieur Bardin and his soprano are here."

"Oui, oui," comes the reply. "Entrez."

She opens the door for us, smiles, and curtsies out of our way.

This is it.

The room is dark but for a roaring, golden fire in a luxurious hearth. Monsieur LeRoux rises from an overstuffed chair and sets his half-empty wineglass on the nearest table.

"Welcome!" His voice is as squat as he is. He grins as he combs his fingers through a thick gray mustache. "I'm so glad you've come."

"Monsieur LeRoux," Cyril says with a slight bow of his head. "May I introduce one of Channe Opera House's best sopranos, Colette Dassault." He tugs me forward, and I curtsy deeply, keeping my face angled away from the fire and praying that doing so shrouds everything in shadow.

"So pleased to make your acquaintance," I murmur.

"The pleasure is mine," he says. "How delightful! Come, come! I've been dying to hear more of that wonderful music from the other night." He moves back toward his chair and plucks up the wineglass to take a nice, long swig.

"How about we have her stand near the window?" Cyril asks. "A fresh breeze does wonders for the vocal cords." He indicates a corner of the room lit only by starlight. It is dark and shadowy—perfect for keeping me mostly hidden.

"Whatever you think is best."

I make my way silently to the corner, hoping the trembling of my legs isn't apparent in my gait.

"Whenever you're ready, darling." Monsieur LeRoux plops back into his chair and slings one thick leg over the armrest.

The hem of his slacks rides up high enough for the chalky white flesh of his calf to peek out over the top of his sock.

Swallowing my nerves, I face him and try to let my arms hang loosely at my sides even though every inch of me is dying to reach into my dress to touch my pendant for comfort. I lick my lips, inhale, and sing.

The first few notes come out quiet and weak as my nerves choke up into my throat, but as the melody progresses, I settle into the ebb and flow of the musical line, let my body sink into the percussion of the staccato notes and the gentle feather of the largo ones.

LeRoux's eyebrows rise slowly as my song progresses. I feed on the way his eyes widen when I hit my high E's and the way his mouth drops open when my voice slides through a run without stumbling.

When I finish, he jumps to his feet, applauding like a madman. "Incroyable! Magnifique!" he cheers. "A voice like an angel!"

Pride heats my cheeks, and a small measure of relief settles my nerves. He's buying the act so far. "Merci, monsieur." I dip into another curtsy and wait for him to sit again before launching into my next piece.

As I sing, I hear the places where Emeric's voice would fit against mine. I let my memory of the sound of him twist through me, and as it does, the loss I feel for him grows, filling my chest with an ache that snakes its way into my song, too. The music surges, saturating everything until I'm afraid the fire in the grate might catch on the charge in the air and send the whole room up in a torrent of smoke.

When the song ends, I stand there, hands numb and chest heaving as though I've run miles.

Monsieur LeRoux wipes a sloppy tear from his cheek. "It's like music can reach inside of you and touch your soul, don't you think so, Monsieur Bardin?"

He has no idea how close to the truth he is.

"Oui, monsieur," Cyril says. "There's nothing else like it in the world."

LeRoux nods like they've had a profound discussion and turns his attention back to me.

For the next half hour, I entertain him with ballads and arias until his face has gone red with the wine and the excitement.

I was born to perform like this. To affect people with my music. To make them laugh and weep. But even as the joy of the song rushes through my blood, my chest aches for the missing harmony.

So I let my eyelids fall shut and imagine. As long as I keep my eyes closed, I can almost convince myself Emeric is there with me, that if I reached out my hand to the side, my knuckles would brush against his, that if I peeked through my lashes, I'd catch a glimpse of his dimples in the starlight.

But then each song ends, and all I am left with are the coals in the fireplace, Monsieur LeRoux's clumsy grin, and Cyril's willowy shadow near the door.

No scent of caramel. No brush of a callused hand. No dimples of stardust.

"Now, as part of the Channe Opera House's tradition," I say once Cyril nods that it's time to wrap things up, "I'd like you both to join me in a rendition of 'La Chanson des Rêves' before we finish for the night."

"My favorite part!" LeRoux claps his hands and sits up straighter, loosening his cravat.

I begin the familiar tune, and he sings along with me. Though I keep my eyes on LeRoux, I can feel Cyril's penetrating gaze. Watching. Waiting. Urging.

I glance at Cyril after a moment and frown. He's not singing with us.

With a start, I realize I've never actually heard him sing. I reach back for any memory where he might have serenaded me with a lullaby or demonstrated a musical phrase during my vocal lessons.

There are no such memories.

Emeric's words, *He does not care for you*, rush through my mind once more, this time dropping a weight in my chest that makes it difficult to breathe.

Cyril offers me an encouraging smile, and I force the thoughts away. I've got a job to do here. I need to focus.

LeRoux's flat, nasally song makes the mark on my thigh tingle, but I ignore that sensation and instead let the one on my ankle pull me into the lazy current of his memories. I move back a few years' time, considering silently where would be the best place to start implanting the hallucinations Cyril described. Perhaps something subtle, like a dream? I sift through the flow until I find one.

These are some of my favorite memories to peruse. It seems no matter what a person's face looks like, the world of dreams equalizes us in its unassuming, undiscriminating exploration of our deepest fears and grandest hopes.

Wading into one, I find LeRoux galloping bareback on a mighty stallion through whipping golden grass.

My voice slides along on the edge of my periphery, spouting out the lyrics of "La Chanson des Rêves" without effort as I conjure up a non-Cyril version of the pale-faced demon I placed in the Forgotten Children's memories.

This time will be a bit trickier, as I will need to create the whole body as well as its movement instead of simply pasting it over Cyril's form. I imagine the ghoul's face first, with the gaping holes where its eyes should be and the wide, snapping mouth. A dark cloak might be easier than a detailed form, I decide, so I drape the beast's head with a black hood and attach a fluttering form below that glides like a specter in the wind.

As dream-LeRoux rounds a copse of trees and urges his

steed toward an imperial city in the distance, I push the demon into the air in front of him. Concentrating on making the cloak whip in the breeze, I widen the specter's jaws as it lunges down from the sky toward the rider.

Once the vision is complete, I siphon away the euphoric emotion of the dream and feather the air with an unmistakable dread.

Perfection.

LeRoux is still singing, his words sluggish and slurred with drink. Perhaps I should find one more memory to alter.

During the final verse of the song, I implant my monster into another dream. Instead of riding a horse, this time LeRoux is sailing on the back of a great, winged beast with a lovely, black-haired woman in his lap. When I'm finished with the scene, the ghoul sails upward from below the giant bird and rips the woman from LeRoux's arms in a shower of shadow and blood. I put in an echoing, soul-rending scream for effect.

Satisfied, I release my grip on LeRoux's memories as "La Chanson des Rêves" ends.

LeRoux's jovial expression has faded just a tad. He watches me with glassy eyes.

I meet Cyril's gaze and incline my head slightly. He smiles and strides forward to take Monsieur LeRoux's hand. "Merci bien, Monsieur LeRoux. It has been such a privilege to come into your home."

"Oui, oui. The pleasure truly has been mine. I'm dying to hear more of her spellbinding voice tomorrow night." He smiles as he gets to his feet.

"You flatter me, monsieur," I murmur.

Cyril extends his arm. We exit the room, and it takes everything in me not to lean too heavily on him. My legs wobble, and as we climb into the cab and rattle back through

Channe toward the opera house, I grip the seat to keep from toppling right off it.

"So?" Cyril asks. "How did it go?"

"I altered two memories. Distant ones, like you said. I think I was successful."

"You played the part of opera diva very well," he says.

A thrill goes through me. "Merci."

"And? Was it fun?"

I grin in spite of my weariness. "Better than I ever dreamed."

Cyril smiles so wide his eyes crinkle up. "LeRoux seemed quite enchanted with your performance. I think our little arrangement will work out splendidly. Especially if he plans to continue drinking that much alcohol every time."

I nod and look out the window, watching as houses and trees clatter by. Maybe the reason Cyril doesn't sing in front of me has nothing to do with me. Maybe he's simply embarrassed by his voice, or maybe he just doesn't like to perform.

But I can't shake the way my insides gnaw at my heart, asking questions I'm not sure I want to know the answers to.

"Why did you save me?" I blurt, keeping my gaze away from Cyril's. I tell myself I'm not looking at him because I'm so enraptured by the sprawling mansions glittering from the window, but deep down I know it's because I'm afraid of what his reaction might be.

"What?"

"When you pulled me out of the well. The night I was born." My voice comes out squeaky. "Why did you do it?"

He sighs. "Haven't I told you this story about a thousand times? I was out walking nearby and heard you struggling alone in the water. I didn't know you were a gravoir at the time. It was too dark. All I knew was that a baby had been abandoned to drown."

"Yes, but why did you keep me once you saw what I was?

Why not dump me back into the well or turn me over to the authorities? They have rewards for things like that."

"Because of your eyes."

I stare at him, momentarily forgetting in my shock that I didn't want to look at his face. He hasn't told me this before. "What?"

His expression is soft. Warm. Fatherly. "Oui, your eyes, sweet Izzy. I looked into your little face and they were all I could see. I had no choice. I had to keep you. I swore to myself I would do everything I could to protect you—I would keep the world from hurting you and teach you to control your emotions and your powers so that you wouldn't be a danger to anyone."

I swallow the lump that has suddenly grown in my throat and wipe my hands on my dress, but the silk does little to soak up the dampness on my palms. Trying my best to blink away the moisture collecting on my lashes, I turn my gaze out the window again.

"You truly did splendidly tonight," he says, shuffling through his papers once more.

"Thank you." Though my body sinks lower with exhaustion, my heart roars its pride.

Because he's right. Tonight, I was not hiding in the shadows. Tonight, I was a terrifying phantom come to turn dreams into nightmares.

The only time I've ever felt more powerful was when I was wading through Emeric's memories, siphoning away his elixir. Even thinking of it now makes my power raise its hungry, tired head and lick its lips.

Arlette's face flashes across my mind. Does she know what people like us are capable of? Has she discovered any other secrets I don't yet know? Has she found a catalyseur—that mysterious object mentioned in the red book that is said to compound gravoir power?

I may have chased Emeric out of my crypt, but I'm not ready for him to be gone. Not while I still have so many questions. Not while my body craves his music like this. Not while I cannot sleep for fear of seeing him in my dreams.

I cannot steal his elixir again, no matter how much I want to. But his memories would give me the answers I need. He is sure to have more of Arlette, more clues about gravoirs I could use. And, even if there is nothing else to be learned of her, his music would at least soothe me, soften the edge of the weakness I feel now. What I wouldn't give to have his voice trail its caress through me one more time.

My eyes fall shut as the cab jolts over the cobblestones. As we make our way home, I see Emeric smile on the inside of my eyelids. A shadow of floppy, black hair traces his brow. A crooked grin quirks his lips. Dimples crease his smooth cheeks.

I cannot live the rest of my days wondering about the secrets his past holds and what those secrets might mean for my own life, and I surely cannot survive without his voice.

I refuse to.

CHAPTER FOURTEEN

The following evening after another successful performance at the Council Head's home, I retreat to my crypt to change the veil and silk for a simple, unremarkable black dress and a thick cloak. I keep the new mask on and pull the hood low over my brow.

"You'll be happy to know," I tell Albert as I pull the crypt door closed and tug on a pair of gloves, "that I am going to apologize."

The skull's grin mocks me, and I cluck my tongue.

"Unless you've got any better ideas, you can quit with the attitude." I whirl and stalk off.

This time when I duck out of the opera house's back exit, the tremor of fear has been replaced by a sudden calmness. I am the Channe Opera House Ghost. Bearer of nightmares. And just as worthy to walk under an open sky as anyone else.

I follow a trail of streets familiar from all the memories I've seen over the years, marveling at the way autumn leaves crunch under my heels and the chill, night air draws its fingers into my hood to stroke my neck. I relish the feel of the cobblestones and the uneven shuffle of my footsteps over them. Though I spent little time in Emeric's recent memory during our time together, I caught glimpses of his apartment, and with my knowledge of every street in Channe, I am able to navigate to the small flat without much trouble.

It isn't until I've entered the leaning building and climbed the creaking stairs to the top floor where he lives that my stomach sinks.

I threw a candlestick at his face. Screamed at him. Chased him off. No matter what he said or implied about Cyril, I cannot deny that my behavior was extreme. How is an apology going to help? I wouldn't forgive me, either.

My hand hovers over the wood for a moment. I steel my nerves and rap on the door.

There's a thud and a shuffle inside followed by footsteps. The door tugs open halfway, and Emeric pokes his head out.

Even in the dark, his appearance is striking. His hair sticks up in every direction as though he's spent the night running his hands through it.

"Hi." My eyes stray to the bit of bare collarbone peeking out where the top two buttons of his shirt are undone. The blue stone hangs from its leather cord, as usual, and it bobs as he swallows.

He squints, his brow furrowing as though he's trying to decide if he's supposed to know me. After a moment, the corners of his mouth turn down. He must have figured out who I am.

"I'm sorry to bother you in the middle of the night," I say in a rush. "Unfortunately, the middle of the night is really the only time I could come."

"Why are you here?"

My hands are already twisting my pendant's chain though I don't remember pulling it from my neckline. "I wanted to apologize. My behavior last week was unforgiveable. I should not have extracted your elixir without permission, and I should not have spoken to you that way."

He rolls up his sleeves to the elbows and crosses his arms. "Correct on all counts."

"I'm humiliated by my actions, and I'm terribly sorry."

"Good. Are you finished?"

"Yes."

He makes to close the door.

I brace my hand against it. "Wait. No."

He leans his forehead against the doorframe and raises an eyebrow.

"I…" I take a deep breath. "You were right. I didn't consider what taking that elixir would mean to you. I didn't recognize how violating it would be, how wrong I was to even think of it. I got too caught up in the prospect of what it would feel like… And, I'll be honest with you, it was the first time I'd ever extracted. I let my excitement and curiosity run away with me." I pause, searching his dark eyes. My voice lowers. "But it was wrong for me to even try it in the first place, and I…" I trail away and drop his gaze, cheeks heating.

"You…?" he prompts, his voice a touch softer than it was before.

I squeeze my eyes shut and let the words tumble out. "I swear I won't do it again. Please forgive me."

He is silent for an eternity, but I can't bear to open my eyes to check if his expression is thawing. Finally, he sighs. "Is that a new mask?"

"What?" I squint through my lashes. He is now bracing an elbow against the doorframe and leaning his head against the back of his forearm. My mouth goes dry at the sight of his bare skin. "Oh, yes. It is."

"It looks like a real face."

"I think that's the point."

He coughs in a way that almost sounds like a laugh and pushes the door open wider. "Fine. You can come in. I was about to make a new batch of caramels, so I guess that means you've earned yourself the much-coveted position as my assistant tonight. Don't let it go to your head."

Come into Emeric's apartment? I think of how exposed I
felt when I invited him into my home. Is he truly allowing
me into his?

My head spins, but I follow him inside.

As I ease the door shut behind me, Emeric rushes to a
spindly, three-legged table in the center of the room. Strewn
across it are what look like dozens of newspaper clippings.
He shoves them unceremoniously into a folder and tosses that
under his unmade bed.

I pull my hood back with quivering hands, letting my hair
spill out over my shoulders. Yanking off my gloves, I say, "I'm
afraid I won't be much help with the caramels. I've never set
foot in a kitchen in my life."

"Never?"

"Not once."

"Well, then, let me introduce you to my favorite room of
every apartment, home, and restaurant in the world. I think
you'll find it quite enchanting." He gestures to the far end of
his one-room flat where a cabinet and counter combination
piece of furniture stands near a fireplace. A warm fire crackles
merrily in the hearth. "Kitchen, Isda. Isda, meet the kitchen,
and may you never recover." Though he smiles as he says it,
his voice is still stiff.

I chuckle nervously. Does this mean I'm forgiven?

Emeric doesn't mention a word of my apology, however,
as he rustles about in the cabinets to retrieve a cast iron pot
with a long handle. Hanging it from a hook over the fire, he
scoops in a lump of butter and a measure of sugar and hands
me a wooden spoon.

"Your job is to stir that until the sugar melts and turns
golden."

I cross to the pot and jam the spoon into the mound of
sugar at the bottom.

"So that was your first time extracting elixir?" Emeric asks, pulling a jug of milk from the tiny icebox on the counter.

My stomach twists, but I force my voice to remain even. "It was."

"Why did you do it?"

"Memory, you really don't shy away from an awkward conversation, do you?"

"Not when I can help it."

I give a nervous laugh through my nose and dig at the sugar, gripping the spoon so my hand won't shake. "I did it because…" I lick my lips, searching for a lie as close to the truth as possible. "Because your voice is so different from any other I've ever heard. I was convinced your elixir had to be different, too. I half expected it to be as colorful and full of life as you are."

"Sorry to disappoint you," he says, rifling through a drawer for something.

"I wasn't disappointed," I whisper.

He pauses, his hand frozen on a measuring cup.

My cheeks warm. "I meant that your elixir was…nice. Not that I had any right to see it, I—"

"I get it, Isda," he says, and I swallow the rest of my clumsy excuses before I can make myself sound like even more of a fool.

"I'm sorry," I say again.

He opens his mouth to reply, then shakes his head as though changing his mind. "Let's talk about something else. What was it like growing up in the opera house?"

"It was…" I pause, searching for the right word as I drop my gaze back to the pot. "It was lovely. There was always so much color and light. I used to hide and watch the rehearsals, then teach myself some of the choreography on the stage after everyone had gone for the night."

"No wonder you sing the way you do. You've been sur-rounded by music your whole life."

I twirl the wooden spoon through the concoction, watch-ing as the sugar bubbles into a golden liquid. Emeric taps a bit of vanilla into the mixture and dumps some milk into the pot. I stir vigorously to incorporate it.

"You're a natural." Emeric's voice is close—right by my ear—and its nearness makes me jump.

"A—a natural?" I am a bumbling imbecile.

"At stirring. A born stirrer, if you ask me. It's rare to find such talent in someone so untrained."

I elbow him away, cheeks flushing under my mask. "Don't make fun. It's not my fault I've never cooked before."

"Fair enough." He laughs, turning to stack a few bowls. He hums under his breath as he works, and even with that small bit of song, my power perks up and reaches for him, begging to plunge into his memories.

As if on cue, he begins to sing quietly, wiping down the counters as he goes. He casts a glance my way, one full of questions and dares, as though this is a test he knows I will fail.

But even under his careful scrutiny, I exhale as a huge weight I hadn't even noticed I was carrying releases from my shoulders. I let the flow of his memories envelop me in warmth and contentment.

Emeric stops singing, and I'm ripped back to reality. The sharp scent of scorched sugar fills the air. He jumps to my side. "Is it burning?"

I blink down at my hands. The spoon dangles from my limp fingers, and the caramel mixture bubbles a thick, sticky, brownish black.

Emeric wraps a towel around the pot's handle and whisks it away to safety.

"I'm sorry," I mumble. "I must not have been paying at-tention."

"No, no, it's okay," he reassures me. "It's just a little over-done. It'll still taste fine."

"Are you sure?" I peer over the pot's rim at the foul-looking concoction. "It doesn't smell right…"

"Of course, of course. Trust me." He picks up a spoon and scoops out a bit. "I've overcooked it a thousand times. Just makes it a bit harder to chew, but it shouldn't be too bad." He blows on the mixture to cool it.

"I'm so sorry," I say again, fluttering around him feeling utterly useless.

He waves away my concern and asks, "What do you see when I sing?"

I search for horror or mistrust in his expression. Instead I find thoughtful curiosity. "Nothing," I lie. "I just feel the elixir calling out to me."

"Is that distracting?"

"You get used to ignoring it."

"Except when you don't ignore it, apparently." His lips draw into a line, but the anger in his expression has cooled a bit since I arrived.

"I'm so sorry. I—"

He raises a hand to silence me. "I know." Lifting his spoon to the sky as though making a toast, he says, "Bon appétit!"

"Are you actually going to eat that?" I grimace at the dol-lop of hardened sludge.

"Of course. It's your first time making caramels. I want to be able to say I was a witness to this moment."

"It's going to be bad."

"I'm the caramel expert here, not you. It's going to be de-licious." He puts the spoon into his mouth and chews. "See? It's…" He pauses, scrunches up his nose. "It's not very good." He swallows. "No, it's quite terrible, actually."

"I warned you."

"You did."

"In the future you should probably take my advice."

He puts his finger to the side of his nose. "Duly noted."

I snort. "Well, it seems we have a conundrum. We used the last of your milk in that pot of goo."

He tosses his spoon back into the pot. "I'm sure I've got some spare caramels around here somewhere that'll tide us over until I get some more." He roots around in a small pile of clothing in the corner, shoving his hands into the pockets one by one until— "Aha!"

I sit on the floor by the fireplace where it's warm. He settles next to me and hands me a caramel.

"Nothing like a little bit of sugar to make everything better, eh?" He chews for a moment, bending his knees up to his chest and resting those distracting forearms on top of them. His hair trails across his face as he tips his head against the wall.

Wiping my hands on my skirt, I angle myself toward the fire. The coals at its heart glow as gold as a memory.

"So," he says. "You said you used to teach yourself choreography in the middle of the night?"

I nod.

"I suppose we're not too different, you and I. I used to sing and dance for an audience of toys my mother made me. At least you had a stage."

I chuckle. "I never considered how lucky I was in that regard."

"Did anyone ever see you?"

"When I was little, I wasn't very careful. There were a few instances where I was almost caught. I would sneak into the dressing rooms during the day sometimes. Cyril used to get so mad at me for trying to steal jewelry from the dancers while they were busy onstage." I snort. "It took me forever to realize he didn't care so much about the theft as he did about my being noticed."

"Did Monsieur Bardin really raise you?" His voice is a little too quiet all of a sudden, as though he's afraid he might miss something I'm about to say.

His earlier words—*He does not care for you*—swirl in my ears, and I harden my jaw.

"He's the only father I've ever known. He taught me everything—mathematics, reading, science, music. He made me handwritten cards on holidays and brought me chocolates on my naming day anniversaries." My words rush out faster and faster as I speak, as though I can convince Emeric with the force of them that he was wrong about what he said. "He's the one who bought me my organ and all of my music."

"Really." He purses his lips like he's trying hard to marry his perception of Cyril with the reality I'm showing him.

"Yes. There was a special production we did the year I turned six where the score called for an organ. He had one brought in, and I fell in love with it. I begged him for weeks to let me have it when the show finished. It was a rental, and he kept telling me he had to return it, but on the night of the final performance, he had it brought into that crypt downstairs and set up for me there."

A lump of tears rises in my throat as I remember the way Cyril beamed down at me when he told me I would get to keep the instrument. I flung my arms around his neck so tight he had to pry me off to breathe.

"I'm sure it was extraordinarily expensive," I continue, my voice thick. "But you don't understand the significance of a gift like that for someone like me."

"What do you mean?"

I pause, swallowing. "I don't have friends, Emeric. Outside of you and Cyril, I've never interacted with a soul, never had a conversation." I stare at my hands as I speak, hoping the heat flushing into my ears isn't turning them red, praying he can't see how embarrassed I am to admit this to him. "But that organ makes me feel less alone. It speaks my language. Every time I play it, it's like I'm sharing a part of myself with it, and it's giving me something in return." I press my hands flat on my thighs. "I know it probably sounds stupid—"

"It doesn't," he whispers.

"But that organ has become my friend. In a world where people like me are afforded very few of those, that means more than you can possibly imagine." I pause, close my eyes, and let the fire's glow trace its sparkling light on the inside of my eyelids. "Cyril gave me that."

I shift back to face Emeric, and the afterimage of the fire lines his face with flares of gold and red.

"The organ is why I live in the catacombs. It's the only place Cyril could find where it wouldn't be heard if I played during the day. He didn't banish me to the sewers. I used to have a bed up in one of the practice rooms." I smooth my skirt with my palms. "I *chose* to build a life down there underground. Because in the dark, my beauty is as unlimited as the music I create. In the dark, I can be anyone, go anywhere, do anything. That crypt you think a prison is the one place in this world that offers me the freedom you get just by breathing."

He ponders that and raises his eyes to meet mine. "It seems I owe you an apology as well, then. I'm sorry for what I said. You were right. I didn't know what I was talking about, and it was wrong of me to speak that way about him."

I turn away from the intensity of his gaze. "Thank you."

Emeric is silent for a long time. He stares at his hands, opening and closing them.

The silence makes the thudding of my heart seem so impossibly loud I'm sure Emeric can hear it.

"So…" I search for something, anything, to fill the quiet. "Where'd you learn to make caramels?"

His face instantly relaxes. "My uncle is a candymaker. The

best in Luscan. After my mother died, he became like a father to me. He taught me how to make all kinds of things, but caramels are my favorite. They remind me of my sister."

"Why?"

"You know how once the sugar melted, everything was oozy and golden and popping? She was like that. Bright, spunky, and sweeter than any sugar." He pulls another pair of caramels out for us to eat.

I unwrap mine enthusiastically, loving that of all the words he could have used to describe a gravoir, he chose those ones. "If the opera thing doesn't work out, do you think you'll become a candymaker, too?"

He shrugs. "It's a definite possibility. My uncle promised there'd always be a spot in his shop for me if I ever want a job."

"Why did you come to Channe, then?"

"I actually came to audition for *Le Berger*, if you can believe it." He chuckles, shaking his head. "But you were right about no one wanting to even consider me without training."

"You'll be on that stage, Emeric," I say with certainty. "You were meant to sing, trained or not, and the world needs to hear you. If you let me, I will get you there. I will force them to listen. I will make you the thing you were born to be."

He scrubs a hand over his face. "I hope you're right."

If anyone deserves to have his dreams, it's Emeric. This kind, accepting, honest boy with a heart full of hope and pockets full of caramels.

"Tell me," he interrupts my train of thought. "What is one thing you've always wished you could do but haven't because you've been stuck in an opera house your whole life?"

I laugh sheepishly. "Play *Chasseur et Chassé*, actually." I've seen it played a few times in people's minds, but since most of the memories of the game are from their childhoods, the details have always been too foggy for me to make out the exact rules. All I've gleaned is the intense joy they all seem to experience when they play it—that and the camaraderie of sharing those moments with people they love.

"You've never played?"

"Games aren't really Cyril's thing."

"Well, as it turns out, you've come to the right janitor." He hops to his feet and crosses to his bed. Crouching, he reaches underneath and slides out a wooden box. The game pieces rattle inside as he carries it over to the table. "Come on. I'll teach you."

"Are you sure?" Excitement dances through me. "It is three o'clock in the morning."

"I can't think of a better time." He grins in that devastatingly lopsided way of his and pulls out one of the chairs for me to take. "Please play *Chasseur et Chassé* with me."

A giggle bubbles out of me before I can tamp it down, and I take the offered seat.

He pulls the game board out of the box and settles the different pieces in their proper places. As he describes the rules of the game, he waves his hands around with enthusiasm, and I catch myself watching the way his shirt opens and closes over that blue stone and the bare skin at his collarbones.

Once I'm pretty sure I've got the rules of the game down, he takes his place in the chair across from me, and we begin to play. I'm slow to remember where each piece is allowed to move, and with so many new thoughts swirling in my head, it's hard to come up with an effective strategy. But after his first win, he offers to play again. And again.

By the fourth game, I'm getting the hang of it, and on the fifth time through, I actually manage to win.

It isn't until the grayish blush of dawn feathers through his window that I realize how much time has passed. Sunrise is when many merchants begin to make their way to their shops. The streets will no longer be deserted. I might be seen on my way home.

I leap to my feet. "I need to go."

He follows me to the door as I pull my hood back on and stuff my hair inside. "When will I see you again?"

The soft, hopeful tone in his voice makes me pause. He watches me with an expression I can't quite read.

"Do you mean you'd like to start lessons again?"

He chuckles and tousles his hair so it sticks out in even more directions. I'm overwhelmed by how untidy and yet how perfect it is.

"Sure, I guess that's what I mean," he says.

"I'm not going to get that key for you," I remind him, pulling the door open and peeking into the hallway to make sure it's empty. "If you're willing to come back without that…"

He sighs, the upturned corners of his lips dropping slightly. "I'll figure something else out."

"What do you want from his office?"

He reaches out to tuck a tuft of my hair behind my neck. I freeze at the rough brush of his fingers against my skin. "We all have our secrets, Is," he whispers. "You keep yours. I'll keep mine."

With a simple touch, he has stolen every bit of air from my lungs, every word from my mouth, and every thought from my mind. There is nothing but those dark eyes and his fingertips on my neck.

"Midnight?" His voice is but a breath.

"Actually…" I clear my throat. "Would two o'clock be too unholy an hour? I have another obligation at midnight now."

"Two o'clock should be fine. It seems you have made me nocturnal these last few weeks." He glances back at the golden light brimming over his windowsill. "You'd better go."

I turn, then pause. "Sorry about the candy, by the way."

He grins. "That was just about the worst caramel I've ever eaten."

I snort. When he chuckles, a bubble releases in my chest,

and suddenly I am laughing, and we are laughing together, and it doesn't matter that the sun is cresting the horizon because I've lost myself in this tiny, tattered room and the scent of smoking sugar.

Our laughter fades as we hold each other's gaze a moment longer. The fire is low behind Emeric, and silvery sunlight shines across his cheekbones and the bridge of his nose.

A small bit of burnt caramel clings to Emeric's cheek near his left dimple. Before I realize what I'm doing, I've reached up to brush it away. Just as my fingertips graze his skin, I freeze and pull back, cheeks heating.

He catches my hand in his. I stifle a gasp as he presses his lips against my palm. "See you tonight." His breath tickles goose bumps up my wrist.

"See you then," I echo, stumbling backward, my whole body vibrating with light. Forcing myself to appear calm, I nod in his direction and retreat into the hallway.

As I make my way down the stairs and out into Channe, I duck my head away from the view of passersby and keep my pace brisk. Even with the incriminating sun climbing its way into the sky and the pulse of fear in my limbs, I cannot help but trace the lines in my palm where the ghost of Emeric's lips still tingles.

CHAPTER
FIFTEEN

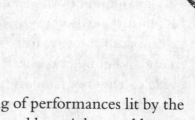

My nights blend together, a string of performances lit by the fire in Monsieur LeRoux's parlor and late night vocal lessons spent drowning in the ecstasy of Emeric's music.

The more I meddle in LeRoux's past, the better at it I become. Soon, I am not simply flashing images into his dreams but reworking entire waking memories, complete with the demon chasing him through streets in broad daylight, interrupting his meetings with the Council, and awakening him in his bed at night to whisper treachery through fanged teeth. As the weeks pass, LeRoux's mannerisms begin to change. He becomes twitchy and paranoid, jumping at the tiniest of noises. The only thing that seems to relax him is my voice, which simultaneously pleases me and makes me feel like someone is kneading my insides with something acidic.

But I remind myself that in doing this, I'm keeping Cyril safe. The fendoirs out there may be dangerous to him now, but I have no doubt once he takes charge, they'll grow to appreciate him the way I do. He raised me to be better than the monster society would have made of me, and I know he will do the same for them.

And one day, maybe, Cyril can make this city a place where fendoirs and gravoirs are not only welcome but also are no longer viewed as threats to those around them. So I stuff away my remorse, grit my teeth, and do what needs to be done.

Besides, LeRoux would have me "disposed of" if he knew what I was. I should not pity him.

Meeting with Emeric after each session soothes the trepidation and helps me forget that twist of guilt in my gut. He's learning at a remarkable rate, picking up techniques that took me years to master, blossoming under my care. That first night back, he brought *Chasseur et Chassé* with him, and it has become a nightly routine for us to play a round or two once we're done with lessons. He supplies the caramels, of course, and a healthy dose of laughter.

Things are too good. Everything is progressing too well. I find myself dodging glances over my shoulder, waiting for the illusion to shatter, for this tiny bubble of contentment I've found to burst. Performing every night for a captive (albeit small) audience, and then making music and laughing with Emeric until dawn? My life was never supposed to feel this comfortable or this joyous. How long will it last?

No matter how many times I ride through Channe, I can't seem to pull myself away from the window. Tonight, I watch the shops pass in the same fashion they have every night for the last two months since I started meeting with Monsieur LeRoux. Though the midnight hour means the shops are always closed and the lights are always out, when I look at them, I see new details of the world I once only knew through faded memories.

"I brought you a little surprise." Cyril hands me a brown paper bag with its top folded over.

"What's this for?"

He flashes me a knowing smile as I take the bag. "The effects of our little visits are beginning to take their toll on Monsieur LeRoux. There were murmurs among the members of the Council today that the Head might be hitting a spot of 'emotional trouble.' They were discussing whether or not to contact King Charles."

"Really? It's working?"

"You, Izzy, are a marvel. In only a matter of weeks, I'll be able to take over and make Channe a better, safer place, and it'll all be because of you."

I lean back in my seat, faint with a thrilling rush of shock. "Because of me."

He nods at the bag. "Open it, chérie."

When I unfold the top, the distinct scent of sugar and butter makes my mouth water. I peer into the opening and gasp. "Pastries!"

Nestled inside is an array of little bundles wrapped in parchment. I pull one out and tug the paper off to reveal a flaky croissant oozing red jelly. I lift my mask up past my mouth, take a hearty bite, and moan when the sweetness squeezes onto every corner of my tongue.

Cyril chuckles and pulls a notebook from his briefcase.

I finish off the pastry, and, though I'm dying to tear into the religieuse or one of the pains au chocolat peeking out from their wrappings, I wipe my lips, pull my mask back into place, and fold the bag closed. I'll keep the rest of these to share with Emeric later.

The thought of him with crème pâtissière caught on his lower lip makes my smile widen even further. He's nearly ready now—ready to take on the Channe stage, ready to take on the world. The more time we've spent together, the more I want to be with him. Listening to his music. Drowning in his memories. Laughing at his jokes. Finally sharing my dark little corner of the world with someone who wants to be part of it.

True to my word, I have not stolen any more of Emeric's elixir, though I have watched more memories of Arlette. None of them hinted at any further powers. But even if those memories teach me nothing else about my gravoir abilities, simply living in them is enough. While I am in his past, I'm no longer Isda, the shadow in the dark. I am Emeric, and I am loved. I eat at a rickety table with a teapot ring burned into its wood. I fall asleep listening to my mother's lullabies. I spend summer evenings chasing fireflies in the apple orchard with my sister.

The more I live in Emeric's past, the more I want him on that opera stage. Every moment of every memory is enlivened by his passionate dream.

So over the last few days I've been mulling over an idea.

I turn to face Cyril. "How are things going for *Le Berger*? Opening weekend is coming up quickly."

He scribbles something down in his notebook. "Splendid, splendid."

"I've been watching rehearsals. Seems like a good cast."

Cyril sighs. "It's passable. I had high hopes for the man I cast as the lead, but he doesn't quite live up to his reputation."

I grimace. I've heard that tenor sing. He'll be an absolute embarrassment to our opera house. Emeric is four times the vocalist he is.

"That's too bad," I muse, trailing a finger along the glass as the landscape outside changes from businesses to residential buildings. "Do you remember that new janitor you hired not too long ago?"

Cyril's gaze snaps to mine, but I keep my expression soft, uninterested. "Oui," he says slowly. "I remember him."

"I overheard a few of the dancers talking about him backstage. They say he's been getting lessons from a very accomplished tutor."

"What tutor?"

I shrug. "They didn't say, but they did mention that the boy's become quite good."

Cyril purses his lips.

"I think their exact words were, 'Whoever snatches him up stands to make the largest fortune Vaureille has ever seen.'" I let that sink in.

Cyril leans back, his hands settling in his lap. "The dancers know very little about what it takes to make a star." But his tone is curious. Intrigued.

I nod, turning my gaze back out the window as though I don't care a single bit about it. "You're probably right."

Neither of us speaks for the rest of the ride to the Council Head's house, but the scent of the pastries under my seat permeates the cabin, and I can't help but think of how in the last few weeks I've been able to control so many more things than I ever thought possible, like a master puppeteer twitching her marionettes until they dance exactly the way I want them to.

Once, I would have balked at the idea of manipulating Cyril like this, of lying to him to get my way. But now as a tiny twinge of guilt needles into my chest, I think of the secrets he kept from me about my powers, and I let that twinge sizzle and fade.

It's just a small lie. And Cyril will thank me for it later.

My breath steams a cloud on the glass, obscuring the reflection of the satisfied glimmer in my eyes.

Shafts of golden light dance across the gilded designs on the walls in the grand theater. The plush, velvet seats are empty, and the stage is quiet but for the ear-gnawing sound of one tenor's voice.

I slink from shadow to shadow in the rafters, clad all in black. My feet are light as I struggle to keep every movement silent.

My stomach twists into a knot of fluttering wings and dancing things. I force a slow inhale and then an even slower exhale, find my center, and settle in the silence for a moment.

Ropes twitch nearby as I climb onto the upper railings of

a massive set piece—a magnificent palace. I crouch behind its turrets and move to where there's enough of a gap between the wooden pillars to peer out through knots of fake vines.

The man stands on the stage below. He's singing the finale, a piece that should leave any listener's soul in pieces. With a voice like the sawing of a blade against metal, this man's version will be more likely to leave listeners' eardrums in pieces than anything else.

I reach into my neckline and pull out my pendant. Pressing it to my lips, I wait.

The tenor grips his libretto loosely in his hands, waving it about as though it's a lacy handkerchief, and moves stiffly through a set of choreographed strides across the stage to a staircase in the corner.

Once he reaches the top of the stairs, he belts out several warbling syllables.

Squeezing the pendant, I give in to the tug of the man's memories on the scarred skin at my ankle.

This had better work.

Instead of going back minutes or hours or even days, I skip along in the place just seconds ago, where the memories are flowing out as though from a gurgling spigot. The slow, practiced mounting of the stairs only a measure or two earlier in his song.

I push the image of my eyeless, fanged monster into his mind. It swoops down toward him from the chandelier like a bat, blasting through his body.

The man's singing chokes into a shout, and I open my eyes to see his face pale and his arms flail. He careens backward, crashes down the stairs, and lands with a sickening crunch on his right leg.

He cries out in agony, wrapping his hands around the place where a jab of white bone protrudes bloodily from his thigh.

My stomach knots at the sight of the twisted limb—I didn't

mean to hurt him that badly—but something deeper and darker inside of me, that quiet, smoldering beast in my chest, raises its head and smacks its lips.

Yes, a broken femur will keep this tenor out of my way for good.

With a small smile, I fade into the darkness, nothing but a phantom in the rafters.

CHAPTER
SIXTEEN

"Isda!" Emeric's shout sends a thrill through me. I tuck tonight's veil and dress away under my bed as he comes career-
ing into my crypt waving his arms. "It happened!"

"What happened?"

He skids to a halt when he reaches me and huffs and puffs
for a moment to catch his breath. His eyes dance, and his face
is flushed. The dimples in his cheeks crinkle.

"Cyril has given me the lead role in *Le Berger*."

Relief, pride, and satisfaction roll through me. "What?
Why? When?"

"Apparently the man who had the role fell off a set piece
during rehearsal and broke his leg. Monsieur Bardin asked
me to come to his office and audition for him tonight. Only
listened to a few bars before he offered me the job." Emeric
wraps his arms around me and swings me in a lopsided circle.

"That's fantastic!" I squeal as he lowers me to the ground,
keeping his arms around me.

"I can't believe it," he murmurs into my hair, and the feeling of his breath on my nape makes the skin on my back tingle. "You did it."

A spark of panic zaps the tingle away. "What do you mean?"

He pulls back to look at me. "Your lessons, Is. There's no

way he would have chosen me if not for the things you've taught me the last two months."

"Oh." I let the flare of anxiety fade. No one knows what I did. "My lessons may have helped, but it was you he chose. Your voice, your talent."

"My looks." He releases our embrace and winks.

I roll my eyes. The underground chill swirls around me in the absence of his touch, and it leaves me wanting to reach for him again. "You deserve this, Emeric. If anyone in the world does, it's you."

"This calls for caramels," he declares, punching the air.

"You're absolutely right."

We settle onto the ground with our backs to the side of my bed, and he digs into his pocket to produce a small mountain of the little wrapped candies. Dumping them on the floor between us, he unwraps three and pops them all into his mouth at once.

I wolf down six in as many seconds, barely pausing to chew.

He nudges me. "Don't you know candies are terrible for your voice?"

"You keep your mouth shut."

"I'll make no promises on that count."

"Fair enough." I snort. "I don't think you could keep quiet if you tried."

He nods gravely. "Silence is not one of my talents, I'm afraid."

"Most assuredly not," I say around a mouthful of caramels. "Doesn't *Le Berger* open next weekend?"

He nods. "I've got a lot of practicing and memorizing to do. I'm enlisting your help."

"Do I get a say in the matter?"

He flashes me a smile. "Not at all."

I laugh and toss in another caramel. "What can I do?"

"You know the play, right?"

"By heart."

"That's what I thought. I was hoping you'd walk me through some of the choreography and help me prepare. Monsieur Bardin has called special rehearsals next week to make sure I'm on track, but I really don't want to mess this up."

"Of course I'll help."

Emeric grins and pulls a libretto out of the inner pocket of his jacket. "I was thinking we could go through the finale scene. The one on the grand staircase at the end."

"The duet," I say dreamily.

It's the biggest, most emotional scene in the whole opera. The final love declaration between the lead tenor and the princess he has spent the whole play searching for. It is my favorite piece from this particular show—maybe from any show, ever.

Wiping his mouth, Emeric gets to his feet and pulls the organ bench out into the middle of the floor. "Why don't we use this as the staircase for now?"

"If that's the staircase, it needs to be farther to the side. Stage left."

He obeys, and the memory of how I hated him touching my organ the first night he came here flashes through my mind. The idea that I feared him is almost laughable now.

"All right, where do I start?"

I stand, wipe dust from my skirt, and steer him to the other corner of the room close to my music books. "Stage right."

"Where do you go?"

"I don't enter until the middle of your verse. When I do, I come from the palace up here at the back." I move into place.

I spend the next half hour teaching him the movements and the blocking for the entire scene. He catches on quickly, and soon is moving fluidly across my room as though he's been rehearsing for months and not moments.

"Now let's try it singing a cappella," I say, returning to the back of the room.

He nods, flipping through his libretto to the beginning of the song.

When he opens his mouth and floods the crypt with the duet's opening bars, I know. It doesn't matter the sacrifices or the risks I took to get him here. Even if Cyril finds out what I've done. Even if the world somehow unearths the truth about the Channe Opera House Ghost. Everything will all be worth it the moment the audience hears this sound, feels it in their bones. It's a sound like magic, tender and seductive and full of sparks, sliding and spreading through space and time, filling everything with gold and light.

And it is mine forever.

For as soon as people hear him sing, they won't want him to stop. He'll have a job at the opera house for the rest of his life.

Which means that no matter what else happens, no matter if I never find out what a catalyseur is or if I never find a way to live outside the walls of the opera house, I will have a life through Emeric.

In that way, I will finally be free.

I step forward, letting my voice roll out to meet his.

He turns and sees me. I know he's acting, playing the role of a lowly shepherd finding his princess, but the way his face lights up and the way his smile opens the tremor of his voice in a new, vulnerable way makes my knees weak.

We approach each other, our voices quieting into the soft, andante lull before the song's chorus. He reaches for me, and I lift my hand to meet his, as the choreography dictates. Just before our fingers touch and shatter the air with electricity, I twirl away from him, imagining myself to be that little dancer in my music box. Lovely and perfect. Meant to be seen. Heard.

Emeric follows, and we circle to center stage as the chorus of our voices crashes bright and clear.

He glances quickly at the notes he wrote down in his libretto before charging toward me, determination and fire in his gaze. I waver a step back, stunned by his sudden ferocity.

He pulls me against him as our voices reach the highest notes in the melody. Trembles shake through me, and I know he can feel each one of them.

Then, silence.

We stare into each other's eyes, chests heaving against each other, his grip strong and hot on my waist.

As his hands move to mine, he pulls me backward up to the organ bench. We climb atop it, and I imagine myself trailing him up the stone steps on the stage, a brilliant, cream-colored dress with a bustle and train flowing around my legs. Lights shine on my bare, clear, unblemished face. My hair tumbles in waves over my shoulders, glowing fire red.

The duet reaches its climax, but instead of crescendos and crashes, it is pianissimo. Our voices are barely more than breaths, like the shivering of a crimson leaf on the autumn breeze just before a final wind spirits it away to the night.

We fade in unison.

I hear the orchestra's last notes in my mind, and then all is quiet.

Emeric's eyes dart back and forth between mine, his cheeks flushed, his hair swept away from his forehead. His fingers are warm against my palms.

My body vibrates, more alive than it would be if I drowned myself in elixir. My heartbeat is everywhere. In my chest and in my throat and in the air.

"And then…" Emeric releases one of my hands, and his fingers press against the mouth of my mask. "We kiss."

I feel the pressure on my lips through the material, and my head spins.

He leans closer. So close the heat of his body sends tingles across my skin. I taste the caramel on his breath.

His fingers trail over my mask, and I wish I could feel the brush of that caress. He reaches my chin, and then his thumb strokes against the skin of my bare throat.

Letting go of my other hand, he reaches up to cup my jaw on both sides. I'm sure he can feel the rush of my blood in the veins of my neck.

I want him to kiss me. With every part of my trembling, weak body, I want him to pull me closer. I want to touch those dimples and feel his eyelashes against my cheek and knot my hands in his hair.

My eyes flutter closed as I imagine how it might be. Him and me, breath tangled in our mouths, hearts crushed against each other, bodies as entwined as our voices were moments ago.

But then the edge of my mask begins to lift away.

I jolt back, crushing it into place. My feet skid off the edge of the organ bench, and I topple to the ground. A shriek bursts from my lips as my elbows ram into the stone.

"Isda!" Emeric leaps down beside me. "Are you okay?"

I scramble away from him, wetness filming across my vision. The image of Saint Claudin's sword slashing for Rose's heart flashes through my mind.

I can never let Emeric see what is beneath my mask.

Because even Emeric—beautiful, kind Emeric—is unmarked. And the unmarked are taught to fear me. To hate me. To kill me.

"Just go." My voice comes out a strangled sob, and I turn my face away from him so he won't see my tears.

His hand rests on my shoulder. "I'm so sorry, Is. I didn't mean—"

"Emeric, please."

He pauses, and then the weight on my shoulder disappears as his footsteps shuffle slowly toward the door.

I push to my feet, hugging my arms across my chest as though that could keep my heart from cracking.

Emeric's footsteps stop.

"You sing like a goddess." His words are quiet but strong.

I steal a glance at him. He stands facing away from me, his hand braced against the doorframe.

"You could shatter the sky with a voice like that. If only our world would let you."

I open my mouth to reply, but he disappears into the catacombs before the words come.

CHAPTER
SEVENTEEN

Every time we practice after the night he tried to take off my mask, I make sure to keep my distance. Inhale. Exhale. Find my center. Settle in the silence. Don't let the feeling of his hands on mine or his voice sliding its way along my skin distract me from the task at hand.

We don't speak of what happened between us. Instead, we focus entirely on practicing every song and every moment of Emeric's part in *Le Berger* until I'm sure he could perform the whole show in his sleep.

I sneak up to watch his rehearsals with the cast during the day. Cyril surveys from the audience, his attention never straying from Emeric. To everyone else, Cyril's face likely seems smooth, impassive, impartial, but I know him better than that. I see the slight arch of his eyebrow, the gentle upward curve of the corners of his mouth, the slow blink of a man afraid to miss a moment. He is impressed. Pleased.

As he should be.

Opening night comes quickly, and the gentle murmur of distant crowds becomes a roar as I hide in my place behind the cherub. People trickle in and take their seats, tugging off shawls and pulling gloves away from dainty, soft hands. Their gowns and their shoes gleam in the chandelier's light.

I watch, silent and still. I don't fiddle with my necklace or adjust my mask. I survey the audience with a wry smile. *Just wait*, I think to them, imagining myself whispering the words into their bejeweled ears. *Just wait until you hear him.*

Excitement makes my whole body tingle. Because once the show ends and Emeric meets me in my crypt tonight, I'll be able to experience the joys of the performance through his memories, as real and vivid as though I lived them myself.

Cyril strides onto the stage. A spotlight illuminates his benevolent smile.

"Welcome to this year's production of *Le Berger*," he booms. "I'm pleased to say we have a full house tonight! Now if you'll direct your attention to your playbills, I'd like to point out a small change. The role of Arnault is being played by Emeric Rodin, as our original tenor, Guillaume, sustained an injury last week. I assure you, you are in for a treat. This is Monsieur Rodin's debut performance. Remember, you saw him here first!"

The crowd cheers as Cyril takes a bow and exits the stage. With a cue from the maestro, the symphony starts its overture. The audience hushes, and the curtains billow for a moment before rising.

I lean forward, ducking between the cherub's calves to get a better look.

Emeric stands, solitary in the light. Even with the makeup and the costume and the wig, he is my Emeric.

The music mounts. I tighten my grip on the cherub's leg.

Then Emeric begins to sing.

His voice is pristine and perfect, and every patron in the seats below stills as it rolls over them. Their eyes widen. Their jaws go slack. One woman freezes with her hand halfway to her face. A man pauses in the middle of whispering something to his wife, his gaze riveted on the stage.

I find Cyril. He sits in his premium box seat, grinning like a fool.

When the first number ends, the air stills for a moment as the echoes of Emeric's final notes fade away. Then the audience roars to life, applauding like they're ready to bring down the chandelier with their noise.

I sit back on my haunches, pleased.

I did this. Emeric may have had the voice and the talent, but I honed it. I made him what he has become. Through his song, they hear me. They are enraptured by my spell, entranced by my music. I am no longer hiding in the shadows, powerless and meaningless.

I control this theater. They all belong to me.

As the performance continues, I settle against the wall. There will be no need to modify any memories tonight. This run of *Le Berger* will be the most successful show in Channe Opera House history, thanks to me.

I relax into Emeric's memories, letting the weight of them pull me under and trickle over every part of me. Instead of searching for Arlette and signs of her power, as has become my habit, I simply allow the images to swirl past in shocks of gold and crimson, of light and music.

As I drift through, places and faces flash past. Emeric's mother. Arlette. His uncle. Cyril. Me.

I sit up, churn back to the image of myself, and drop into the memory.

Emeric is speaking, and I feel the thrum of his voice in my throat, the rumble of his speech in my chest as I experience the moment from his perspective. "I also know that whatever Cyril Bardin has been to you in your life," he is saying, "whatever he has given you, whatever he claims to be, he does not care for you."

Past-Isda is turned away from him. Her hands clench at the pendant at her throat. Her body quivers. She circles slowly, lowering her arms to her sides. Her hair quakes around the sparkling black planes of her mask, a crown of crimson. But her eyes are what draw Emeric's gaze. They blaze, icy fire whipping in their depths.

A tremor of fear slices through Emeric. His hands begin to sweat.

"Get. Out," Past-Isda spits.

"I wanted to warn you. He's—"

"I said *GET OUT!*" Her scream reverberates in Emeric's chest.

"I was just—" he stammers.

She raises her hand as though to strike him, and he flinches away.

Past-Isda laughs, an eerie sound that splits the night open wide and drags claws through all its darkest parts.

"Please, Isda. At least consider that Cyril—"

She hisses. "I thought I told you to leave."

"But—"

Growling, she twists, wrenches a candlestick from her organ, and flings it at him. He dives out of the way, and it whizzes past his face. The sound of shattering glass splinters the air as the lantern on the wall behind him explodes.

Emeric cowers as past-Isda prowls forward.

He scrambles out of her path, wrenches the crypt door open, and flees into a tunnel lined with bones.

I resurface from the memory and peer down at Emeric on the stage, his fear still jolting in my gut. My cheeks burn hot, and my breaths come out shallow and shaky. How could I have behaved like that? It's a wonder Emeric ever came back to me at all after a tantrum like that.

But as my mind replays the memory, the beast of flame and shadow that lives in my chest purrs. A tiny tingle of pleasure seeps into my blood. A grin steals across my face, pulling my mangled lips tight.

I've never seen myself in a memory before. Clothed in shadows and wreathed in a halo of blood-red curls, I was a sight to behold.

Chills jolt straight through my bones and into my soul.

It's as though I was one of Les Trois, someone with authority. Someone with power. The fear—the absolute terror—that shook through Emeric during that memory was real and raw and rabid, and *I* was the cause of it.

Perhaps this is why society has put a mask on me and locked me away. Why my mother was so horrified by what I was that she banished me to a cold, icy death.

Because they fear us. Because we are powerful.

Because we are meant to be their masters.

As the lead soprano twirls onto the stage, her bell-like voice joins with Emeric's and sets my teeth on edge. I should be on that stage. I should be singing duets with him and dancing across the floor on his arm. I should be the one he kisses in the final act.

The beast inside me turns its hungry stare to the audience below, the people who have banished me to the dark. It imagines the golden elixir shimmering beneath their memories and licks its lips.

I stroke it, calm it. Now is not the time. One day, perhaps, I will have power like that. The kind of power described in the red book where a gravoir could extract elixir from everyone in proximity simultaneously, regardless of whether they're singing. But I am not there.

Yet.

So I sit forward to watch Emeric and try to ignore the way my skin prickles every time the lead soprano playing opposite him touches his hand.

The audience sits spellbound throughout the entirety of the performance. It isn't until the finale, when Emeric's mouth comes down on the princess's, that the people roar to life. They burst from their chairs, clapping, whistling, and crying.

"Bravo!" they shout as one. "Encore!"

When Emeric steps forward to take his final bow, their screams make the glass in the chandelier rattle.

Emeric bows once more, then raises his head in my direction. Pressing his fingers to his lips, he blows a kiss to where I hide.

I freeze, dodging a look at the main box seats. Cyril's gaze snaps to mine. His smile twitches. His eyes narrow.

An icy barb of fear lodges itself in my chest.

CHAPTER
EIGHTEEN

Once the people have gone and the lights are out, I drop into the hallway. A hand wraps tight around my arm, and I shriek as it pulls me into a shaft of moonlight. Cyril's face shines silver, his expression hard.

"What did you do?" His voice is something caught between a whisper and a snarl. His fingers are tense as wire on my elbow.

My anger flares. "What are you talking about?"

"You know precisely what I'm talking about." He drags me up the hall toward his office.

I yank backward, hissing when his fingernails dig into the inside of my arm. "No. I don't. Please enlighten me."

He wrenches open his office door and shoves me inside, glancing behind us once before he slams it shut. I stumble forward and catch myself on my chair.

"You're the boy's tutor, aren't you?" He glares, arms crossed across his chest.

The way he's looking at me, with distaste knotting his mouth, makes my body quiver with rage. Haven't I been nothing but obedient to him for years? Haven't I done everything he's asked of me? Hidden in the shadows, altered people's memories, singlehandedly made every coin of the Memory-damned fortune he's so proud of?

Yet, at the first sign I didn't adhere to his every whim, he's jumped to the worst conclusion. No matter that his suspicions are correct, the fact that he's already decided that they are makes me want to scream.

I try to keep the blaze out of my expression and the acid out of my tone. "Even I'm not that stupid."

"Then would you care to explain why he blew you a kiss? No one—*no one*—knows about that little perch up there. Why would he look directly at it unless he was looking for you?"

I shrug. "I don't think he was looking at my hiding place. Even if he was, I was out of sight. He could have been blowing a kiss to the God of Memory for all I know."

Cyril moves closer, forcing me to tip my head back to maintain eye contact. "You do realize what would happen if you fraternized with him, right?"

"He'd call the authorities. I'd be killed."

"Not just you." Cyril's voice slices like a blade. "I would be executed, as well. Then everything I've built, everything I've worked for since before you were born, would come crumbling down. The Council. The Opera House. All of Channe."

"He doesn't know I exist," I hiss.

Cyril's eyes search mine for answers, for lies, for truth.

I give him nothing but a glare.

"Do you swear it?" he whispers, brow knit tight and low. "On the name of Saint Claudin, do you swear he does not know you?"

I draw two fingers across my brow. "I swear on anything you like."

He considers me for a long moment, then sighs and rubs the back of his neck.

"That kiss was a coincidence," I say. "He blew a lot of them in every direction. Or didn't you notice the young ladies fainting in the audience?"

Cyril's anger flickers. "There were quite a few episodes like that tonight, weren't there?"

"I didn't have to alter a single memory."

He crosses to the desk and eases into his chair. Though his expression has begun to relax, the tension in his shoulders, the hard angles of his arms, and the rigidity of his movements tell me he still doesn't believe me.

I grit my teeth.

Perhaps Emeric was right about Cyril after all. Perhaps he doesn't care about me. Perhaps he only keeps me around because of my power.

If he cared for me as if I were his own daughter, he wouldn't automatically assume the worst. He'd trust me. Take me at my word.

I hide my clenched fists behind my skirt.

"You should have seen the bags of coins I had to have carted to the bank." Cyril pulls out one of his many notebooks to scribble in tonight's figures. "Hundreds of repeat tickets and season passes were purchased. People were practically throwing money at us."

"The new tenor was remarkable."

Cyril glances at me, but I keep my gaze steady, and he returns his attention to his notebook. "Indeed he was. I asked him who his tutor is, but he would not say."

"I'm sure as news of the boy's success spreads, the tutor will speak up. Only a fool would let fame and fortune like that pass by."

"Only a fool. Or someone with something to hide." Cyril's tone is light, but its edge is sharp.

He stoops to rifle through the briefcase propped against the nearest bookshelf. After a moment, his rifling becomes more frantic. His frown deepens. His fingers fly through the pages inside, tearing through file after file.

"Is something the matter?" I ask, my thoughts snapping to the stolen red book under my bed. If Cyril has noticed it is missing…if he realizes it was me who took it… My mouth goes dry.

He yanks the whole briefcase onto his lap and opens it properly, his hands whirring so quickly through the papers they become a blur. His cheeks take on a greenish hue. "Just… missing something important."

"A book?"

"No, a folder…"

I breathe easier. "For the Council?"

"What?" he snaps. "Oh, no. It was…personal."

"I see. Should I help you look for it?"

He slams the briefcase shut. "No. Merci. I probably left it at home." He pauses, then nods. "Yes, of course that's where it is. My office at home." He shoves the briefcase onto the desk in one tense motion, knocking a bulky envelope onto the floor.

I pick it up. It is embossed with the King's seal. "You heard from the King?"

"Hmm?" Cyril is still glaring daggers at his briefcase, as though it's the one at fault for the missing folder. He drums his long fingers on the edge of his desk.

I wave the envelope. "King Charles sent you a letter?"

"Oh, yes. That. He's named me Head of the Council of Channe. Monsieur LeRoux has been deemed mentally unstable."

I drop the envelope. "It worked?"

Cyril smiles in spite of himself and flattens his hands on the desk. "Yes. You did it, child."

I squeal. "Congratulations! Finally, the King is starting to recognize you for the work you've done. You can fix things here. Set the Council straight!"

Cyril leans back in his chair. "It took him a few decades,

but I'll give the man the benefit of the doubt, considering the other issues he's had to deal with during his reign." He interlaces his fingers over his chest and considers me. "You know, with the success of *Le Berger* and my new appointment, I should throw a party. It has been far too long since my last."

"You are known for your parties."

But it's as though he's entirely forgotten that I'm here. "I should do a masquerade ball," he murmurs, tapping his chin. "Yes, that would do splendidly. The only night we could really do it is Sunday, since we have performances every other night of the week. I do have that meeting in Chanterre, but I suppose I could arrive late to the ball."

I clear my throat. "A—a masquerade?" A little bubble of hope inflates in my chest. A masquerade is a party I could go to. No one would know that my mask is any different in purpose than anyone else's. I could blend in.

"Oui, isn't it brilliant? Because there's that masked scene in *Le Berger*..." He sits forward and scrawls into his notebook. "Though I'll need to post security personnel at the opera house entrance to check people's faces before they come in. Wouldn't want any fendoirs to get any ideas." He taps his chin with the back end of his pen. "I'll have to hire a decorator, too, and someone for the food. Perhaps that place down on the corner of Rue de la Gare would do it. Their pastries are to die for..."

I shuffle, waiting for him to look at me. Waiting for him to invite me to attend.

Instead, he scribbles down a few more notes, muttering to himself about champagnes and tablecloths.

Of all people, I should be invited to this ball. I am the reason behind every success worth celebrating.

Squaring my shoulders, I ask, "Can I come?"

He stops writing to laugh. "Of course not, chérie. Don't be ridiculous."

My heart pummels against the inside of my rib cage, but I

manage to keep myself from snapping something childish in response. Instead, I straighten my corset. "Fine. Of course." I turn to leave, then pause. "I'm assuming we aren't going to visit Monsieur LeRoux anymore?"

"What?" Cyril squints. "Oh, him. No, of course not. I think we're all done there." He waves me away as though I am nothing more than a nuisance now that I've completed his little task.

"Bonne nuit," I say through gritted teeth.

Cyril grunts in response, bending over his notebook to jot down another list.

I stalk to the door and yank it open. The cold air in the hallway brushes along my collarbones, and I wish more than anything I weren't wearing this stupid mask. My cheeks are boiling, and with the warmth trapped between my skin and the material, hot air steams into my mouth and nose in a way that makes me want to growl.

Inhale. Exhale. Find my center. Settle in the silence.

It would not do for Cyril to see how much his lack of regard for my feelings affects me. I've already given him too much power over my emotions and my life.

My eyes snag on a shining brass key jutting from the door handle. Cyril must have left it there when he was busy throwing me inside like a misbehaving animal.

Emeric's request for access to Cyril's office surfaces in my mind.

Letting a rush of air out through clenched teeth, I jerk the key from its place and jam it into my pocket.

Turning, I sweep away in a rustle of skirts. The statues watch my progress downward, and I spit curses at them as I go.

Damn them for their flawless faces, their perfect marble hair, their knowing smiles.

Damn this whole Memory-forsaken place.

And damn Cyril. I don't need his permission to go to a ball.

Not anymore.

CHAPTER
NINETEEN

I'm stitching the finishing touches into the mask I plan to wear to the masquerade tomorrow night when Emeric shows up. The shows are taxing on his voice, so we've taken to spending the evenings playing *Chasseur et Chassé* and laughing about the ridiculous things some of the dancers have said to him backstage instead of continuing the vocal instruction. Tonight, he enters my crypt talking animatedly about something one of the papers printed about him when he sees the white, lacy mask in my hands and stops short.

"What is that?"

I set aside my needle and thread and the crystals I was sewing into the lace. "A mask."

"Well, yes, but what is it for?" He dodges past me to inspect it, but I shove in front of him.

"The masquerade ball."

He laughs. "You can't possibly be—" When his eyes meet mine, his mirth fades. "You're going?"

"Of course I'm going," I snap. "They may be celebrating *your* performance, but who taught you? I deserve to go to that party as much as any of those dolts you share the stage with."

"It's not about 'deserving' to go."

I cross my arms. "Then, pray tell, what is it about?"

"It's about the fact that you're—" His voice cuts off as his gaze trails over the curves of my mask.

"Oh, so this is about my face, is it?" I know I'm being petty, but I don't care.

"Of course not."

"I'll be wearing a mask just like everyone else. No one will look twice at me."

"It's too dangerous."

I turn away to tidy the sheet music scattered around my room. The paper crinkles as I slam the stack against the top of my organ to straighten it. "It's only dangerous if I'm not careful."

Emeric doesn't respond right away. When he does, his voice is measured and quiet. "Why, Is? It's only a party."

I whirl, accidentally knocking my stack onto the floor. The sheets of paper flutter around my skirt like dead leaves. "I've lived my life in the shadows, Emeric. I've watched their parties, envied their pretty hair and their pretty dresses and their pretty faces. I've imagined what it would feel like to dance on the arm of a handsome man in a tuxedo." I pause, voice quavering. "Is that my fate? To always watch and envy and imagine?"

His Adam's apple bobs.

"When is it my turn?" I ask. "When do I get to step out of the shadows and live?"

When he still says nothing, I sigh and drop to my knees to gather the fallen pages. After a moment, he joins me on the floor, pulling the loose papers into a bundle in his arms. I reach for them, and he holds them out toward me but does not let go when I try to take them.

I glance up to his face and meet a passionate, wild-eyed stare. "You're not a fendoir," he says quietly.

"What?" My stomach spasms. I yank the stack from him and arrange it atop my own pile. "Of course I am."

He continues as though I did not speak. "You're right, though. You do deserve to dance, wear pretty dresses, and eat fine foods. You are worth celebrating."

Words have stuck in my throat. My body has gone completely numb.

"But they'll kill you if they find out the truth." He pushes a lock of hair back over my shoulder. "And a world without you in it? That's not a world I want to even imagine."

I draw in a slow, shaky breath. "How long have you known?"

"A while. I wondered about it that first night when I met you in the hallway. The way you reacted to my singing, as though your mind had been transported somewhere else. Fendoirs don't see memories when people sing, but I know gravoirs do. And…" He pauses and reaches out to brush my collarbones. "You don't have the mark here, but you extracted my elixir. Which means you must have carved the spiral somewhere else on your body. That only works for gravoirs."

I clutch my stomach, feeling suddenly dizzy. Why hadn't I thought of the fact that he'd notice the spiral mark was missing? Of course he would suspect. "If you knew what I was, why didn't you report me to the authorities? Why did you agree to come down here with me?"

He opens his mouth to respond, then mops the back of his hand over his face and sits down on the edge of my bed.

My ears buzz as they wait for his response. My hands and feet tingle as though all the blood has drained from my body and I'm nothing but bone and dying nerve endings.

"You've seen Arlette." It is not a question.

I swallow the dryness in my mouth and nod. "Yes."

"Then you already know why I didn't report you."

"Fair enough. But why did you agree to the voice lessons? You knew I'd go rooting around in your memories. You knew what I was capable of."

"Because you reminded me of her, and I…" His voice cracks, and he shakes his head. "I failed her in so many ways. And you had that same wild, desperate hope in your eyes." He pauses. "You seem to think I should have been afraid of you, but I grew up with a gravoir. Fearing you never crossed my mind. I figured I'd be able to handle anything you might throw at me." He turns away from my gaze and shrugs. "I don't know. I guess I decided I had nothing to lose."

"Nothing to lose," I repeat faintly.

It's too much, standing here as all of our secrets unravel. I don't know how to have conversations like this. I haven't a clue how to listen when someone bares their soul or what I'm supposed to do when it comes time to speak my truth with words instead of songs. I turn to my stack of papers and lug it over to my bookshelf as though hiding from him might shelter me from the fear. And the hope.

"That was just at first, though," he continues. "Once I heard you play, heard you sing… Everything changed. I never knew music could be like that."

"Like what?"

"Like it's taking over my soul. Like it's changing me from the inside out. Like it's filling the world with color and light."

He approaches me, but I don't turn. I feel him behind me, the warmth of his body just inches away. I want to lean back and let that warmth enfold me, let it cocoon me in a place where there are no questions and no answers, only quiet.

Instead, I don't move at all. I don't even breathe.

"Before you, music was just music. But not anymore. Where everything was dull and mute before, you've brought brightness and life. I don't want to lose that." He grasps my arms and pulls me around to face him. "Please don't go to that ball, Isda."

I tremble under the tenderness in his touch and the intensity in his gaze. I want to nod, to give him my word I won't go, to promise him I'll stay away.

But something in my chest flickers hot and smoking.

"I—I am going to go."

He releases my arms. "Why?"

"Because I want to." My voice rises in pitch. "I'm sorry if my wanting to spend one harmless night as a normal person jeopardizes your *music*, but I don't exist only to improve things for you."

He rears back as though I slapped him.

"All my life I've been doing Cyril's bidding. Hiding away and serving him so that he can reap the benefits of what I am and what I can do. I'm sorry if I don't feel like doing the same for you, too."

"That's not what I—"

"What did you mean then, Emeric?" My voice is edging toward hysteria. "I make your world brighter? I make music better for you? What about me? What about what makes my world brighter and better?"

"How about not dying?" he snaps. "Seems like that would be a good start."

I glare. "I don't understand you. You come barging into my life flinging caramels everywhere and spouting off platitudes about how it's unfair of Cyril to keep me locked up down here, and yet that seems to be exactly what you'd have me do, too."

"Not wanting you to die is not the same as keeping you locked up."

"And what your mother did for Arlette is so much better?"

His eyes flash. "Yes. She gave her sunshine and a family who loved her."

"Sorry to be the one to break this to you, but not all of us are so lucky. My mother had me dumped in a well before I was five minutes old. I take what I can get."

"It's not a choice between hiding down here and throwing yourself to the wolves," Emeric says, his tone softening. "There are other options."

"Enlighten me."

He gestures at himself. "Living somewhere safe, out in the open where you could breathe fresh air. I could take you there."

"And throw away everything we've worked for? Throw away the career you just launched?" I bark a laugh. "Do not make light of what we've accomplished by tossing it aside like it means nothing."

He clenches his jaw and shakes his head. "Why do you have to make everything difficult?"

"*I* make things difficult?" Now I'm the one reeling back as though I've been slapped. "Feel free to leave if you'd like. I wouldn't want to trouble Channe's new favorite tenor."

Emeric turns and stalks past me to the door. "Funny, Isda, because to me, it seems like that's exactly what you want."

I slam the door shut behind him.

CHAPTER TWENTY

For all of my confidence and determination last night when I told Emeric I was going to the masquerade, I feel awfully tiny and terrified now that I'm staring at my reflection in the mirror.

I'm wearing an old wedding dress I found in the basement storage area. I noticed it years ago and have always wondered why such a lovely gown had been banished from the costume gallery upstairs. Though I'm sure it was once white, it has now faded to ivory. It is low-cut in the front and features off-the-shoulder sleeves that make me feel elegant and exposed all at the same time. Lovely lace has been stitched over every bit of it, from the fitted bodice to the wide skirt, bustle, and train. I've made it my own by sewing tiny beaded crystals every-where that sparkle when they catch the light.

Reaching up with sweaty hands, I adjust my mask. It doesn't fit as well as my others—it's the old white one I used to wear—but I've covered it in spare lace from the dress and stitched in beads so that it matches.

I let my hair fall over my bare shoulders, the red coils a stark contrast to my ivory dress, and take one last look in the mirror.

I hardly recognize myself. Even Cyril probably wouldn't

realize it was me. Not that I'm going to risk letting him. I'll make sure to leave before he finishes his meeting in Chan-terre. He'll never know I was there.

Clutching my stomach as though I can somehow push my anxiety away with my hands, I take as deep a breath as my corset will allow, turn, and venture out of my room.

As I ease the crypt door back into its place, I catch the near-est skull's eye. "Don't look at me like that, Albert. I'm going to be careful."

I feel the skull's gaze on my back as I make my way up the corridor and have to force myself not to glance over my shoulder.

Goose bumps erupt on my arms, which are not used to being uncovered here in the underground air. Shivering, I quicken my pace, pulling my skirts away from my feet so the lace doesn't drag on the dirty floor.

Though quiet and far away, the ball's music trickles down to me when I emerge into the basement storage room. The sound of it knots the breath in my throat, making it difficult to breathe.

I'm going to a masquerade ball.

Trying to keep my shaking hands under control, I climb the stairs until I reach the main level. Following the symphony's song, I make my way toward the south end of the opera house and the grand ballroom there.

I pause in the shadows near the side entrance. The doors have been propped open, and golden light floods into the hallway.

So long I have hidden just outside the line of light. All my life I have ached to step into it and let it bathe me in its warmth. But now that I stand here on the edge of it, I cannot seem to move. My limbs feel as though they've been turned to stone—too heavy, too cold.

People pass without even noticing me, their faces obscured

by fashionable masks in every shape and color. Gowns glitter under the light of glowing candelabras. Laughter punctuates the symphony's music, and glasses of champagne clink. The scent of butter and roasted duck makes my mouth water.

I catch sight of Emeric and nearly choke.

He stands off to one side clad in a fitted tuxedo that makes him look supremely important and wickedly handsome. His hair has been swept away from his face into a low ponytail. A simple black mask accentuates the perfect arch of his brow. In his hand is a glass of some kind of sparkling drink, but he makes no move to taste it. His eyes flick from person to person as though he's looking for something.

Or someone, perhaps?

Steeling my nerves, I plunge into the light. My heart hammers, and I squeeze my eyes shut, certain someone is going to see me and know instantly what I am hiding beneath my mask.

I take another step forward and chance a peek. No one seems to have noticed me.

No one but Emeric.

His eyes meet mine. A myriad of emotions tumble across his face. Confusion. Recognition. Shock. Relief.

Setting his untouched glass on the nearest table, he makes his way straight for me.

"Bonsoir, mademoiselle," he says, taking my hand and bowing to brush his lips along my knuckles.

My whole body quivers, and heat rushes up my neck. I manage a stiff curtsy, the echoes of his harsh words last night still repeating in my head. "Bonsoir."

"You look—" He pauses, stepping back to take in the full effect of my dress. "Different."

"Different how?"

"You usually wear black."

"So?"

"I don't know. It's just that the white of that dress makes you look like…"

"Like what?"

"Like an angel?" He pauses, his cheeks dimpling as he smiles. "Oui, an angel of music."

His words rock through me, crystalline and bright and real. I stumble for a response, but my mind has gone completely blank.

"I'm sorry for what I said last night," he says. "I was not very kind."

I nod, brushing imaginary dust from my dress.

"Don't get me wrong—I still think it's unwise for you to be here." I open my mouth to make a retort, but he holds up his hand. "But I recognize that you're fully capable of deciding where you go and what you do. I've made my point clear, and you've made yours. Now it's time for me to respect your decision."

"Thank you."

He grins. "Are you hungry?"

"Yes, actually."

"Good. Because I think they piled every morsel of food in Vaureille onto that table over there."

He holds out his arm, and I take it. As he leads me through the crowd, I try not to focus on the curve of his bicep under my fingertips.

Whispers follow us as we approach the table.

"I thought you said you were going to be careful," Emeric murmurs under his breath as he hands me a plate.

"What do you mean? I've barely been here two minutes. I haven't—"

"I mean showing up looking like that. No one can take their eyes off you."

I glance around. People watch me from behind their masks and whisper excitedly to one another.

My stomach lurches. I turn away from their stares.

"Easy. They're only curious." He grins sideways at me. "And I don't blame them."

I try to ease the jumpiness in my limbs and turn my attention to the food. My mouth waters.

Cyril has always kept me stocked with a supply of baguettes, cheese, dried meat, and the like. Every now and then he's treated me to finer cakes, pastries, and wines. But never in my life have I seen food like this.

Trays of steaming vegetables, platters of roasted pheasant, and plates piled high with croissants feathered with powdered sugar weigh so heavily on the table it's a wonder the whole thing doesn't collapse.

I fill my plate to overflowing. Pastries stuffed with cream. Succulent meats smothered in buttery sauces. Plump grapes and soft cheeses. Hearty breads with hard, golden crusts.

"Easy there. You don't want to make yourself sick."

"Speak for yourself." Stuffing a bite of foie gras under my mask and into my mouth, I moan as its savory flavor dissolves over my tongue. "For food like this, I'm willing to take the risk."

He chuckles. "Fine. Just don't blame me later when you vomit all over that dress."

"Monsieur Rodin!" I scold. "It is not polite to talk about such things in proper company."

"Apologies, mademoiselle." He grabs us a pair of drinks and steers me past a marble statue of a centaur to a bench in the corner.

It takes everything in me not to wolf down my whole plate at once. I focus on eating like the dainty lady I'm pretending to be. The boning in my corset creaks as I swallow more and more food. Finally, when only crumbs remain, I set my dish on the nearest table and sigh contentedly.

"Good?" Emeric asks as he polishes off an éclair.

"Utterly divine."

The orchestra finishes its piece and launches into a Vaureillean valse. Emeric catches my eye. "Dance with me?"

A wave of nervousness washes through me. "I have never danced before. Not with a partner, anyway."

"You danced with me when we were practicing the *Le Berger* finale."

"That's not the same. That was choreographed."

"You've seen nonchoreographed dancing, though, oui?"

"I've watched enough other, both of us blushing as applause fills the room"

"Perfect. All you need to do is follow me, anyway. Come on." He grabs my wrist and tugs me onto the dance floor.

"If I injure you, you cannot say I didn't warn you."

"I promise if I end up maimed I won't press charges."

When we reach the center of the room, he grasps my right hand in his left and curves his other around my upper waist. I wipe my palm on my skirt and rest it on his shoulder.

"See? You're already a natural." He grins.

"We haven't even started yet."

"Oh, curses. You're right."

All at once, he sweeps me into the dance. I stumble, but his steady grip keeps me upright. I study his feet and try to mirror his movements.

As the beat picks up, he pulls me in so close his breath tickles against my ear. "Relax," he whispers. "Stop trying so hard. Let me lead."

Feeling suddenly faint, I manage a nod.

He guides me across the floor as though he was born in a ballroom. The hand braced on my back is warm and comforting, and with it he moves me easily around in slow, arcing circles.

"Where did you learn to dance like this?" I ask.

"My mother taught me."

I think of the woman I know so well from his memories, with her messy brown braid and tired smile. "Where did she learn?"

"She was a dancer long ago. It's how she and my father met." He shakes our entwined hands a bit. "Stop squeezing. You're going to break my fingers."

"Sorry," I mumble, loosening my grip.

"Don't concentrate so much on what your feet are doing. You're a musician—your soul will respond to the music even if your body doesn't know how."

I force myself to relax and follow his lead.

The beat escalates, and soon the room is nothing but a blur of color and light. I tip my head to look up into Emeric's face. He's watching me with a flush in his cheeks and a confident quirk to his brow.

"That's better," he murmurs in a way that makes me tremble, and he tightens his hand on my waist.

There is nothing but him and me and the music. Our movements become a duet: his body calls, and mine answers.

For so many nights, our voices have been the ones dancing, but now our bodies are wrapped around each other, my skirts swishing against his legs as he pulls me across the tile. As perfectly as our voices fit together, our bodies seem to fit even better.

We surge and retreat, twist and flow. Closer and closer we whirl, until my skin is alight with the feel of him everywhere and my soul is on fire with the look in his eyes.

The music rises, and every muscle in my body tenses.

The orchestra strikes its final chord. Emeric pulls us to a sudden stop.

We stare hungrily at each other. My hair is everywhere around us, red as blood, wicked as fire. Our chests press together, our hearts thudding madly in the same torturous, syncopated beat. Our breaths heave in and out. I'm drunk on the taste of caramel in the air. His thumb caresses my knuckle, light as butterfly wings.

Someone begins to clap.

We let go of each other, both of us blushing as applause fills the room.

A group of women breaks free from the sidelines and rushes to encircle Emeric.

"Monsieur Rodin, you dance as well as you sing!" one cries, pulling a swan-esque mask away to reveal smooth skin and perfectly pink cheeks.

"An absolute pleasure to watch," a woman in a tiger costume agrees.

"Perhaps you should give the rest of the men here lessons," a third teases from behind a bejeweled crimson disguise, twirling black hair around her pinky finger.

"Might I steal you for the next one?" a tall woman asks in a voice as smooth as one of the cream sauces over on the table. Her mask and dress ruffle with bright green and purple peacock feathers that shimmer with every movement.

Emeric raises a brow at me over her shoulder.

Though every bit of me wants to claw past them and claim him as my own, I force myself to nod. *It's all right*, I tell him with my eyes, hoping he'll understand my message. *Go. I'll be fine.*

He purses his lips, then turns his gaze back to the woman in the peacock dress and gives her a polite nod. "It would be my pleasure."

Ignoring the sinking feeling that squeezes my chest when she takes his arm, I make my way to the corner to watch, putting some distance between myself and the prying stares that seem to follow me everywhere I turn.

But as Emeric takes the woman's hand and twirls her onto the dance floor, my blood boils. I turn away and rush to the nearest door. It opens out onto a balcony, and I stumble over to the railing, gulping at the frosty, starlit air.

Gaslights illuminate flurries of snow twisting on the breeze. Winter is fast approaching, and its icy chill strokes soothing fingers along my bare skin, cooling the jealousy simmering beneath it.

It's better this way. Emeric is, after all, one of the main reasons for the ball in the first place. With all the revenue and popularity he's brought to the opera house, it's best if I don't draw any more attention to myself by dancing with him again. People have already been watching me more than I'd like.

My fingers curl on the railing as the music behind me swells, and I force myself not to glance back to see whether Emeric is smiling at his partner or if she fits as well in his arms as I do.

I wait for the song to end. And then another. And another. I know I have only so much time before I'll need to leave—Cyril will likely show up soon, and I've barely spent any of my evening actually at the party. Yet the idea of seeing Emeric dancing with any of those other girls makes my stomach turn, so I stay right where I am in spite of the way the winter air has frozen the skin on my arms.

A shout echoes in the ballroom behind me, and the symphony creaks to a stop in the middle of a melodic line. I turn, frowning, and make my way back into the room to see what the commotion is about.

"The phantom! It's come to kill us all!" a familiar voice shouts from the middle of the ballroom, his cries bouncing off the marble floors and walls.

My stomach wrenches into my throat.

It is Monsieur Gaspard LeRoux, the former Head of the King's Council of Channe.

I need to leave now.

I keep my head bowed as I weave through the crowd, aiming for the nearest door.

"There!" LeRoux screams, and several people nearby gasp. I dodge a look back at LeRoux, who is staggering closer to me, flailing his arms at the ceiling. "See its teeth? And its eyes!"

Hoisting my skirts higher, I quicken my pace until I am almost jogging. "Pardonnez-moi," I murmur as I shove past people.

The crowds around me titter and shuffle their feet. LeRoux's voice grows in volume until it sounds as though he is everywhere at once.

"Colette!" he cries.

Panic seizes my gut.

How did he recognize me?

I dive in the opposite direction. His tone becomes more belligerent. "Colette, you've seen the phantom, haven't you? Tell them!"

I elbow past a group of men, chancing a look over my shoulder. Monsieur LeRoux is reaching for me, his hands inches from my face. His cheeks are ruddy and purple, and spittle trails white over his chin. I lurch away from him. I'm nearly to the door now. If I can make it out—

"Colette, stop!" He yanks on the back of my dress, and I stumble sideways, knocking into a waiter holding a platter of drinks. Glass flutes tumble to the ground, shattering and spraying champagne everywhere. "Mademoiselle Dassault, please!"

I scramble to my feet, my shoes sliding in the alcohol on the ground.

Before I've made it three strides, LeRoux grabs a fistful of my hair and jerks my head back. The string of my mask snaps with a sound like a crack of lightning.

CHAPTER
TWENTY-ONE

My mask is gone.

I fling my arms up to cover my face as I make a break for the door. Panic courses through my every limb as I skid through shattered glass, twist an ankle, and come down hard on my side, dropping my hands to break my fall.

A man shudders away from me and roars, "It's a gravoir!"

The ballroom erupts into chaos.

LeRoux's gaze registers on mine, and his face goes gray. His eyes roll back into his head, and he topples.

I scramble for the nearest exit.

An arm catches me around the middle and drags me away from the door. My feet twist in my skirt, and I hit the floor again.

Someone screams.

I try to shield my face as I fumble back upright, but hands tear at me from every side.

"Someone alert the police!"

"Shoot the gravoir!"

"Does anyone have a pistol?"

I barrel through the crowd, but I make it only a few paces before a fist knocks into my cheekbone and sends me sprawling to the glistening white tile for the third time.

I wrench myself upright, ducking to miss another fist, and anger boils in my stomach. These people don't know anything about me. Even if I opened my mouth and sang just like all the opera stars they love so much, it would not matter. They would still hate me.

Someone spits at my feet, and I seethe.

I hate them, too. They taught me how.

"Hurry, before it drains us all!" a panicked voice shouts.

All at once, they are on me. Jeering, horrified faces. Fingers ripping at my gown, nails dragging across my skin. A man twists my arms behind me, jerking my head back with a fist in my hair.

"How did it get in?" The man's shout is so close to my ear it makes me wince. "Who let this monster in here?"

A woman nearby catches sight of my face and shrieks.

As she does, my ankle prickles in the same way it usually does when people sing. Her memories pull at me through her cry.

Desperate, I latch on to her scream and send LeRoux's ghoul blazing into her most recent recollections. The woman careens backward, knocking into one of her friends, and hits the ground. Her head cracks on the tile. Blood spreads, dyeing her pretty blond hair crimson black.

The screams begin, one after the other. I fling my monster into every memory I can find, filling the guests' minds with shadows, pale faces, and fangs gleaming the color of the girl's blood.

"It's the gravoir!" someone roars. "Kill it!"

"Don't shoot! You'll hit me!" the man holding me cries.

A gunshot rips through the air, and the man shoves me away, bolting for the door.

All is chaos. Shouts. Cries. Flashes of gilded masks. Faces twisted with disgust.

My power blooms in my chest, hot and ready to burn. I

reach out for cry after cry, raining terror on their minds one by one as the beast inside of me fills with rage.

Someone shoves me from behind, and I fall, smacking my head against the tile. I push to my hands and knees, but the world tips dangerously around me. A terrible, high-pitched ringing noise fills my ears, drowning out every other sound.

Including their screams.

The ballroom tilts, and vomit spews from my mouth. I scrabble on hands and knees through the muck to the nearest pillar and pull myself up, only to be dragged backward by my hair and rammed against the wall. A man with a sleek, black mask jams the cold barrel of a pistol into the hollow of my throat.

His face distorts in and out of focus, and the rest of my dinner threatens to come up. The man's mouth is moving as though he's shouting, but all I hear is a faraway, garbled mash of syllables.

He yanks my hair harder, and I let out a shout.

"I'll shoot!" His words finally break through the ringing in my eardrums. The cacophony of the ballroom roars suddenly loud in its absence.

He shoves the pistol deeper into my neck.

This is it. Emeric was right. I will die here because I wanted a moment in the light.

A gun fires.

I flinch, but there is no pain. No death. Only sudden quiet.

Someone shouts, "What in Memory's name is going on?"

My legs buckle at the sound of Cyril's voice, and when the man's grip on me slackens, I wrench away and sprint blindly for the door.

Don't let Cyril see me, I plead. I can't bear the thought of him witnessing me like this, defeated, disobedient, and destroying everything we've worked for.

"It's a gravoir!" someone cries.

"Bring it here." Cyril's voice is ice.

Hands wrap around my arms and haul me backward. I squirm, but they drag me across the room and toss me like a rag doll against Cyril's shoes.

I scramble away from him, ashamed of the tattered remains of the dress I wear, ashamed of my missing mask, ashamed of my face.

"I'm sorry," I whimper from behind my arms. "I didn't mean for—"

"Look at me."

I blink up between clumps of limp, red curls.

His eyes meet mine. Ice-blue and impassive as stone with pupils hard as flint.

"Please." My lips are slow and thick, as though they've forgotten how to form words. My cheek stings where I was struck, and the side of my head aches.

"Why are you here?" His words are crisp and cut and cold.

"I wanted to—I thought I could—"

Boots pound on the floor behind me.

"Channe City Police," a voice barks. "We were informed you have a gravoir on your premises."

"Please," I whisper again.

Cyril stares at me a long moment, and then his mouth twists with disgust. "I want this vile creature removed immediately."

His words bludgeon through my chest.

I stare at him, and all I can see is the man who brought home raspberry jam to smother on baguette slices. The man who read stacks of fairy tales to me. The man who gave me the gift of music.

Who is this stranger?

He dusts his jacket as though ridding himself of a nuisance. Two pairs of gloved hands yank me unceremoniously out of his sight.

The vomit I've been struggling to keep down erupts, and gasps of horror and revulsion ripple around me.

Someone spits as we pass, and the mucus slaps against my left cheek.

With tears burning in my eyes, I let the police drag me away.

The world has won.

We're nearly to the door when a great groaning sound echoes through the ballroom. Someone shouts, and I glance over my shoulder in time to see the centaur statue fall. It smashes into the refreshment tables.

Food explodes. Chunks of marble hurtle. Glass shatters.

The hands on my arms disappear as the policemen dive to cover their heads.

Something sharp knocks me across my temple. White stars spasm across my vision.

And then all is black.

CHAPTER
TWENTY-TWO

I awaken to a hot cloth dabbing gently at my cheekbone. Hissing, I lurch away from the shock of pain.

"Sorry. I didn't mean to hurt you."

I sit bolt upright, and then promptly collapse back against a pile of pillows when the world rocks violently to the side.

"Easy." Emeric's whispers feather at the periphery of my pain. "Don't move too much."

I squint through white flares in my vision. I'm lying on a bed, but it's not my own. And there's a window across the room. "Where are we?"

"My apartment, but we can't stay here. I doubt it'll take them long to realize we know each other."

Pressing my palm to my stomach as the pain in my head triggers another wave of nausea, I wheeze. "What happened?"

"I went looking for you after the dance with the peacock girl. I thought you'd gone into the hallway or something. When I couldn't find you, I wondered if maybe you'd gone downstairs. You'd seemed kind of upset. But on my way down there, I heard screams and gunshots. I got back in time to see the police."

"You knocked over the statue?"

He nods.

I exhale slowly. The relief that I'm still free—still *alive*—makes me weak. "Thank you."

He peers into my face, his expression full of concern. "How did they find you?"

A lump rises in my throat. Tears blaze hot, boiling trails down my cheeks.

"Someone ripped off my mask. It was all over after that." My stupid, perfect gravoir memory plays back every jeer, every horrified look, every scream. Humiliation scalds through me. Maybe if I let it burn its course, it'll empty me out until there's nothing left but an empty shell. One that cannot feel pain. "Cy-Cyril, he—" A sob chokes out, and I reach a quaking hand into my neckline for my pendant.

Only it's not there. I left it in my crypt.

I turn my face into the pillows as the tide of pain and betrayal crash over me. My body convulses with the strength of my tears. I cry until I feel as though my soul is coming apart, its seams unraveling one by one until I'm nothing but a crumpled corpse left to be swept away into a tomb.

No matter how hard I try, I can't seem to push away the image of Cyril's face, callous and impassive and so very *disgusted*, regarding me as if I were nothing to him.

As if I were worse than nothing to him.

Emeric's hand rests warm on my back. He does not try to shush me or explain away the hurt. He simply strokes my spine with his thumb and hums softly. The song from my pendant.

After what feels like days but must only be moments, my sobs begin to recede. His voice soothes the ache, dulls the memories for just a breath.

"You were right," I say. "I shouldn't have gone. It was too much of a risk."

He continues tracing lines on my back. The sensation ripples through me, and I try to banish away every thought so

I can lie here and focus on how his touch feels instead of re-membering what I am and what I've done.

"How's your head?" he asks when the shaking of my shoul-ders has subsided.

"It feels like I've been trampled by a horse."

"Oh. So not too bad, then?"

I snort and shake my head, then wince when the move-ment shoots pain through my skull. "Can I have something to drink? My mouth tastes awful."

He crosses to the sink, fills a cup, and brings it to me. I gargle away the sourness of vomit, spitting it into an empty bowl Emeric provides. Then I drain the rest of the water in a series of sloppy gulps.

Wiping my lips on the back of my hand, I ask, "Do you have any caramels?"

"Do I have any caramels? Honestly, Isda. What do you take me for?" He shoves a hand into his pocket and produces a fistful for me.

I take one and place it into my mouth, letting the warm, buttery sweetness roll through me. Emeric sits on the edge of the bed and props his head against one of his hands. His fingers knot in his hair, and his other hand grips a dripping, brown rag that soaks through the knee of his pant leg. Mar-ble dust and debris cover every bit of him, turning his once-shining black tuxedo a faded, drab gray. His cravat is undone. His shirt is ripped so that the blue stone on its leather cord is visible. Cuts on his cheeks and forehead leave nicks of blood. His black mask is gone.

But it's his face that makes me forget the throb in my head and the ache in my limbs. That carefree expression he always wears is gone. He stares at the floor, but his eyes are far away and ringed with pain.

"Emeric?" I push myself into a sitting position. "Are you hurt?"

"Me?" He laughs, but it's forced. "I'm fine."

I slide next to him and pull the wet cloth from his hand. It has gone cold, but I reach up to wipe the flecks of blood from his cheeks with it anyway.

"Talk to me," I say softly when he meets my gaze.

"What am I supposed to say?"

"I don't know. Something. Anything."

He pushes to his feet and tromps across the room to shove open the window. I wring the dripping rag between my fingers, letting the water splatter onto the floorboards next to the bed, and wait as he ducks his head out into the night air and gulps in several deep breaths.

I can't take the silence for another moment. I rise, gripping the edge of the bed until my head stops spinning.

"I am so sorry," I say. "I've put you in danger, and I've risked your career."

"You're standing there bleeding, and you think I'm upset about my *career*?" He whirls to face me. "Isda, they were dragging you away to execute you! You nearly died!"

"I know."

"Why didn't you stay hidden? Why did you have to be so—"

"Foolish? Irresponsible? Pig-headed?"

"—trusting?" He mops a palm over his face. "They're so quick to call you dangerous, but the only one I saw in any kind of danger at that stupid party was you."

I knot my hands tighter in the rag.

As he moves toward me, his voice lowers. "They scream and rail that you're the monster, but you don't want to hurt anyone. You simply want to *live*."

"That's not true." My voice is raspy and weak. "I do want to hurt them."

"All right, if I'm being honest, I'd like to hurt them right now, too."

He stops in front of me. Only inches away.

He reaches up to gingerly tuck the hair behind my ear. "Let me take you away from here, like I said before...to somewhere you don't have to wear a mask, somewhere you can live out in the open—somewhere you can be free."

"Like where your mother took you and Arlette?"

Visions of dashing across green, rolling hills dotted with marigolds the color of butter flash across my mind. I imagine catching fireflies with Emeric in the dark, singing under a bright expanse of stars, parading through the burbling streams I've seen only through other people's eyes.

I want that.

"Yes," he says, then pauses and shakes his head. "No. Better than where Maman took Arlette. Because we'll go someplace where you can't be found."

His voice cracks on that last word, and I frown. "You mean... Arlette was caught?"

"She was."

How did I not know this? All this time I've been focusing on her earlier years as she discovered her power. I never took the time to press forward to more recent memories. I always assumed she was still hiding out in that little house among the apple blossoms and rippling grass.

I sink onto the edge of the bed. "How did they find her?"

"I'd tell you the story, but... It's not something I much like to talk about. Why don't you see for yourself?"

He begins to sing his mother's lullaby again, quietly, as though he's afraid of what I might find in his music.

I sink into his tide and press slowly through the memories there, searching for Arlette in each until I find the most recent one of her.

Arlette appears to be around nine years old. She wears a brown dress and has her hair done up in a pair of pigtail braids. Without a mask to hide her face, her gnarled cheeks are almost rosy in the sunshine. Emeric tugs her through the underbrush of some kind of forest.

"All right. Here it is," Emeric whispers, pulling her to a stop next to him. He releases her hand and pushes aside the branches of a bush to reveal a view of a small village.

Dappled sunlight shines across Arlette's face as she beams. "Marvault," she breathes. "It's exactly how you remember it."

"Beautiful, right?"

She ducks her head into the leaves to get a better look. The village is still a mile away, down a sloping hill and across a bubbling spring, but its bright red roofs are as brilliant as ever.

"Do they really sell candies in the town square?" Arlette asks.

"The best candies in the world." He pauses, then says, "All right, second-best. No one beats Uncle Gérald's caramels."

She giggles, and the sound of it settles something deep in his heart.

As he takes in the wonder in her expression, the joy in her smile, he presses a comforting hand to her back. This is the first time he's seen her happy in weeks. All she's done lately is stare out the window, her eyes blank, her mouth drawn. Barely eating, barely talking.

Their maman has sensed the change, too, Emeric can tell. She's always had meetings with the other parents who are hiding gravoir children, but she's been sneaking off to speak with them more and more the past few months, coming home with secret books and trinkets—a leather cord with a blue stone for Emeric to wear "for Arlette's protection," a set of symbols to carve into Arlette's palms that were meant to compound Arlette's power "just in case."

None of it has seemed to give Arlette hope. If anything, it has made her quieter, more withdrawn.

What Maman doesn't understand is that Arlette doesn't wish for more power or protection or for Maman's group of gravoir sympathizers to fight for her. What she wants is a friend. A life. A childhood.

But now as she looks down at the village, she's laughing, and Emeric finally feels like he can breathe again. If he can give her small moments like this—moments where she can forget what she is—perhaps she'll hang on long enough for Maman's group to figure something out that could free her.

"Tell you what," he says. "You stay here, and I'll go get us some of those candies. I'll be back in a half hour."

She turns to him, face as bright as the village's colors behind her. "Really?"

He tugs one of her braids. "Really. Don't move from this spot."

She nods eagerly, and he plants a kiss on her forehead before jogging out of the forest.

Moments later, he's dropping a few coins into the candy merchant's palm in exchange for a bag of assorted bonbons. "Merci," he says, turning to make his way back through the throng of people. He whistles as he walks, nodding hello to a weaver beating the dust out of a rug.

As he angles toward one of the side streets, movement drags his attention to the other end of the square. A shadow hunches behind a cart of potatoes. A child. He squints and shades his eyes to get a better look.

The figure shifts, and a flash of sunlight slants across her face.

The blood drains to Emeric's feet.

His bag of candy hits the ground as he bolts across the square to his sister, panic slamming through his chest.

CHAPTER
TWENTY-THREE

Panic floods me as surely as it floods Emeric's body in the memory.

"I told you to stay behind!" he whispers when he reaches Arlette, pulling her deep into an alleyway and away from the crowd.

She tugs her arm out of his grasp and drifts back toward the sunlit square.

"Arlette?"

She stops at the edge of the shadows. "There are so many of them…" She pauses, eyes flicking from person to person as they bustle past. "Are people this colorful in all the cities? And this loud?"

"Arlette, we have to go."

If she hears him, she does not acknowledge his words. She watches the salespeople shouting their wares and the buyers scurrying about, a soft, curious grin softening the corners of her mouth.

"Look at their faces," she says distantly. "They're so pretty."

He follows her gaze to a small group of children sitting in a circle playing with marbles. Their freckles stand out against pink cheeks under sun-kissed eyelashes.

"You are as pretty as they are," he says.

She cocks her head. "Have you ever played that game before?"

He glances back at the children, impatience and fear making his vision hazy. "What? Yes. Of course."

"Why haven't you taught it to me?"

"I'll teach it to you right now. At home. Let's *go*."

One of the boys squeals a victory, and Arlette smiles. "They seem nice."

"We've got to get out of here." Emeric tugs on her sleeve, but still she does not move. With a glance over his shoulder to make sure no one's looking their way, he leans down to scoop her up. As soon as he does, she goes rigid.

"No!" Her voice is too loud. Too noticeable. "Don't touch me!"

"Shhh!" Emeric soothes, releasing her, shielding her from the view of the few passersby who have turned their way. "It's all right. Shhh."

"You always ruin everything." She smacks him away with her hands, which are still bandaged from when Maman carved those symbols into her palms the other night. "I want to play."

"Well, you can't." The words come out harsher than he means them, and she blinks up at him, eyes wide and fresh with tears. He sighs. "I'm sorry. But we really need to go. It's not safe for you here." His whole body is quivering, his arms and legs buzzing and ready to bolt.

Tears dribble down her cheeks. She wrings her hands so hard the knuckles peeking out of the bandages bulge white as she darts another look past Emeric's elbow.

He grabs her wrist, but her sobs escalate quickly, and she shoves him away. "Stop it, Emeric!" she snaps. "Leave me alone!"

Her shrieking draws more attention from the square. Sweat trickles cold down Emeric's back.

A thousand plans for escape fly through his mind at once,

and all of them hinge on one thing: He needs to calm Arlette down before she draws too much more attention.

So he does the one thing he can think of to soothe her.

He sings.

As his voice fills the shadows between the buildings, she quiets, and her fingers cease their twisting. He reaches for her hand, ushers her deeper into the alleyway.

At first she lets him lead her away, ducking her chin into the collar of her jacket and letting her braids drop over the sides of her face. But then she stops.

Emeric sings on, a little more urgently, tugging as insistently on her hand as he dares, praying his grip doesn't hurt the wound on her palm.

She raises her gaze to his, and he takes a step back.

Her eyes are glassy, distant. Her pupils have dilated, nearly consuming her irises. They stare at the necklace at his throat— the blue stone Maman gave him the other night "for Arlette's protection."

She licks her lips and grins a predator's grin, all teeth and angles and nothing like Arlette.

Terror unfurls in Emeric's veins, and he presses on with his song, pleading with his eyes and his insistent yanking on her hand to come away from all of the people.

Arlette whips out of his grasp and bolts into the town square.

"Arlette, no!" He dives after her.

The world erupts into blinding, golden light. A force stronger than stone knocks Emeric and everyone else in the square to their knees. Emeric tries to shake it off, struggles to push forward, but it's as though his limbs have been bound. Elixir streams out of his ears, bright as sunlight, hot as stars. It pours toward Arlette's tiny frame, twirling and winding alongside the elixir of every other person in the square. She drinks it all in, gulping like a starving Forgotten Child. Bright light blazes through the bandages on her hands as she raises them to the sky.

Emeric's heart might have stopped. Something inside of him feels as though it's been cleaved in two. Still he keeps singing, as though some part of him hopes she might hear the lullaby and come back to herself.

There is a gunshot. Blood appears on Arlette's right shoulder, and she slams to the cobblestones. The elixir in the air spatters against the street like rain.

Relinquished from whatever power dropped them to their knees and drained away portions of their memories, people scream. Run. Shout.

Emeric sprints toward his sister, fear making his movements jerky. His shoes soak with elixir.

Before he reaches her, a herd of police swarm and hoist her tiny frame onto their shoulders.

Emeric chases after them, trying not to look at the scarlet trail shining in their wake through the golden puddles.

But they are too quick. They toss Arlette into a black, barred cart before Emeric makes it halfway across the square. His agony and despair are as sharp as though they are my own, his thoughts as immediate as though they have come from my own mind.

This is my fault.

I should never have brought her here.

"This might be the gravoir Bardin's been looking for," one of the policemen says to the other as they climb onto the cart and crack a whip. The horses lurch forward. "Let's get her to him as quickly as possible. Might get a few extra coins if we're right."

"Oui. It'd be nice to get a break from combing the stupid wilderness looking for her," another one responds.

Then they wheel around a corner, and Emeric is alone in a sea of chaos. He slows to a stop, staring blankly at the place where the carriage disappeared. His mind whips from one half-formed thought to another until it lands on one word.

Maman.

He whirls and dashes for home, pounding through the stream, crashing through the forest. Panic surges through his legs, pushing him faster, faster, faster.

He has to get to his mother. Arlette is not dead, so she could still incriminate their family and Maman's resistance group if questioned.

Maman is sweeping the porch when he comes pelting up the front walk. "Honey, would you go get your sister? I need her to—"

"We have to get out of here, now. They got Arlette."

Maman's brow furrows. Then understanding dawns in her eyes. Her jaw goes slack, and her cheeks turn green. She steps back, clutching her chest. "My baby girl… Where? How?"

"There's no time. They'll come for you, too, Maman. They'll kill you." The words tumble out as he grips her arms. "We need to move now!"

She gasps out a choked sob, then nods and charges for the door. "You get us some food. I'll gather clothes. Quickly, son."

They dive inside the house. The door swings shut behind them with a bang so similar to a gunshot that it makes Emeric's heart stop. Forcing himself to breathe, he sprints to the kitchen and jams anything he can find into a burlap sack.

He is just tying its top when someone raps on the front door. He freezes.

"Danielle Bernard!" a gruff voice shouts through the wood. "Open up!"

"Into the floor." Maman comes around the corner.

"What? No, Maman—"

She doesn't listen to his protests, only wraps her wiry fingers around his wrist and drags him into the living room.

Shoving away the threadbare rug on the floor, she hoists up the trapdoor underneath and ushers Emeric into the darkness.

"Maman!"

"Stay silent. I cannot lose you, too." She shuts and locks the door before Emeric can say another word.

He crouches in the dark, hugging the bag of food to his chest and praying harder than he's ever prayed in his life. In the dim light slanting through the floorboards, Maman's emergency supply of elixir glitters in stacks of tiny bottles lining the walls. Every time he looks at them, all he can see is Arlette sucking gold into her mouth like water.

The door creaks overhead.

"Madame Bernard?" the gruff voice asks.

"Oui, monsieur. What can I do for you this afternoon?"

"You are under arrest for harboring a gravoir, falsifying records, lying to authorities, and for the organization of an illicit, traitorous movement." The man pauses, then says, "Our notes indicate you have a son. He'll need to come with us, too."

"Where is my daughter?" Maman's voice is cold. "What have you done with her?"

"Where is your son?" There is a rustle of paper. "Alexandre Emeric Bernard?"

"He's dead," Maman says flatly, and the words send a chill down Emeric's spine.

"When did he die?" the policeman asks. "We have no record of that."

"Tell me where you've taken my daughter."

"Do not make this any more difficult than it needs to be."

"Where is she?" Maman's coolness breaks into hysteria. "You tell me where she is right now!"

Emeric pushes against the trapdoor, but it doesn't budge. He works his fingers around its edge, searching for something—anything—that could get it open.

Footsteps pound above. There is a scuffle. A shout. The sound of breaking bone. His mother's scream.

Emeric bites down on his tongue to keep from crying out.

The second gunshot of the day blasts into Emeric's eardrums.

Maman's cry cuts off. Something heavy thuds on the floor overhead.

"Blast," the gruff voice mutters. "I hate when they go for my gun."

"She was going to die for her crimes anyway," another man says.

"True, but I still don't like when they force my hand like that."

Emeric stuffs his fist against his mouth as tears stream down his cheeks.

Maman... Maman... Maman...

The policemen leave, and all is quiet.

Still, Emeric cannot get the trapdoor open, no matter how he bangs on it, no matter how he screams and wails. Finally, after what seems like hours of trying, he gives up, curls in on himself in the dark, and sobs.

CHAPTER
TWENTY-FOUR

When I pull out of the memory, tears are blurring across my vision again. "I'm so sorry," I whisper.

He sniffs and attempts a smile, but it wavers, tight and forced, before he gives up and drops his head into his hands.

Gunshots ring in my mind—the ones from the masquerade ball alongside the ones from Emeric's memory.

"How long ago was this?" I ask, reaching out to nudge his wrist with my knuckles in what I hope is a comforting gesture. He seizes my hand, weaves his fingers through mine, and holds tight.

"Nearly three years." He doesn't meet my gaze. Instead he stares at the dusty tops of his once-shiny new shoes.

"How long were you under the floor?"

His thumb strokes along the edge of mine as he considers. "Three days, I think. I sort of lost track. It was really dark down there. I was lucky I'd taken the sack of supplies with me, because that was my only source of food and drink. That trapdoor had to be the most poorly constructed piece of junk in the world. Built to only open from the outside—how ridiculous is that?" His chuckle is weak and humorless. "But it kept me hidden when the police searched the house. I spent that time drinking my mother's stash of elixir to replace what

Arlette had taken and trying to break out. Finally, my uncle Gérald came looking for me. He knew about the trapdoor, thank Memory, and he brought me back to Luscan with him."

I consider that for a moment, then pause when I remember something the police had said. "Is your name really Alexandre?"

He gives a quiet laugh. "It was my father's name, but I always went by Emeric. Once Maman died, the police were looking for the missing son on her record for a while, so I ditched my first name completely. My uncle had a friend in the Luscan records office who put together an account for me as my uncle's son, so I took Uncle Gérald's last name, Rodin. Once I came of age, I left Luscan and have been on the road ever since."

I stare down at our intertwined hands. "I wish things had turned out differently for you."

He nods. "I'd do anything to go back to that day, to stop myself from taking Arlette to see the village." He lifts his chin to meet my gaze. "But I suppose if I hadn't done so, I wouldn't be here with you, and I don't like the idea of that very much, either."

My heart flops, lurching into my throat. "Funny how things turn out, isn't it?" My voice comes out slightly higher in pitch than normal.

"It is." His eyes don't leave mine.

I clear my throat and look back down at our hands, desperate for a change in subject to get my pulse back under control. "So, uh…what was the 'illicit, traitorous movement' your mother organized?"

"A group of other parents of gravoirs all over the country. I think, ultimately, they wanted to build up a resistance to the King's Imperial Council. She believed that eventually, if they were able to gather enough support around Vaureille, they could march on the capital and demand that gravoirs be granted freedom and rights."

I gnaw on my thumbnail. "How many families were part of the group?"

He shrugs. "She didn't tell me much about it. In fact, I don't think she would have told me anything at all if she didn't have to leave me in charge of Arlette so frequently to meet with the others. She said the less I knew, the better."

"There was something in your memory about your mother finding books and carving marks into Arlette's hands. Do you know what those were?"

"She always came home from her trips with new information about gravoir power and history. I believe she spent some of her time digging through old libraries looking for ways to make Arlette and the other gravoir kids powerful enough to fight, if it came to that. She didn't tell us anything she discovered—I think she was afraid of making Arlette dangerous—but there at the end she was really worried about Arlette running off and doing something stupid. I walked in on her carving these marks into Arlette's hands a day or two before the incident in Marvault. She promised the marks would help Arlette 'compound her power' if Arlette ever came into trouble."

"I'd say her power was certainly 'compounded.'" Cyril's red book mentioned palm markings when it talked about catalyseurs. Arlette had to have had one that day.

Emeric flinches but then nods. "I guess the marks worked."

My thumbnail has begun to bleed with how much I'm chewing on it, so I force myself to stop. "Do you think those books and trinkets your mother brought back from her trips are still out in your old house?" If Arlette was in possession of a catalyseur, maybe there are more hidden somewhere in their cottage.

He shakes his head. "It's gone. I read about the people of Marvault burning my house down in the paper a few days after my uncle found me. Some kind of protest for what my sister had done to them."

I deflate. "Emeric, I—" I fumble for something to say, but nothing comes.

"Arlette's not dead."

I blink at him. "What?"

"The policemen said they were taking her to Bardin." Emeric is talking too quickly, as though he's afraid I might interrupt and tell him he's wrong. "He was looking for her. Why would he be looking for her just so he could kill her?"

"Because... Emeric...someone probably found out about her and told the authorities. They give huge rewards for things like that. It could have been one of your mother's allies, even. Whoever was looking for her likely wanted to get rid of the threat."

He goes rigid. "My sister was not a threat."

"Of course not," I say, but his memory of her draining the elixir from an entire market full of people is too fresh in my mind for me to fill the words with enough confidence to sound like I mean it.

"They shot her in the shoulder. They missed her vital organs on purpose. He wanted her alive."

"Right. They were probably hoping to find out about your mother's resistance movement." I try to keep my tone soft, aware of how raw the subject is for him. "I'm sure once they got the information they were looking for, they executed her. Like they always do."

"No." His face reddens. "Bardin wanted her for something else. She's alive. I'm sure of it. I just have to find her."

I stare at him, realization dawning on me. "You think the Bardin the police mentioned is *my* Bardin, don't you? Cyril?" My mind whirs. "*That's* why you came to our opera house? Why you agreed to work with me? Why you asked me to steal his key?"

"Cyril Bardin is known throughout Vaureille for his dis-
like for fendoirs and gravoirs alike. He has a reputation—"

"No. That's not possible. Bardin is a really common name,
and Cyril has always been kind to me. He wouldn't..." I stop,
the image of the disgusted indifference on his face when he
called me a "vile creature" filling me with a soul-cleaving
ache.

"I've been gathering information on him for weeks," Emeric
says. "He seems to have a personal vendetta against fendoirs
and gravoirs. In addition to his clerk work for Channe's Council, he's been conducting investigations for other cities' coun-
cils, as well."

"Investigations?"

Emeric crouches and pulls a folder from underneath his
bed. I recognize it as the one he hastily stowed away last time
I came to his apartment. He opens it, flips through the thick
stack of papers within, and hands me a fistful of newspaper
articles. "I was able to nick this from him a few weeks ago."

I think of Cyril tearing through his briefcase, searching for
a missing file. The throb in my head intensifies. My hands
quake as I flip through the pages, but my vision is too splotchy
for me to be able to read.

"What are these stories about?"

"Mysterious disappearances," Emeric says. "Sometimes one
person, sometimes a whole family. They all have one thing
in common—they involve a pregnant woman who vanishes
once her baby is born. I'm assuming a lot of them were involved in the resistance group." He pulls one out of the stack.
"This one is about my mother."

"So all of these articles are about different women who gave
birth to gravoirs and went into hiding? Like your family?"

"Seems likely. And it appears Cyril was looking for them."
He pulls the papers out of my hands and shoves them back
into his file.

I stare blankly at the wall across the room. It warps and churns to the beat in my head.

Cyril is hunting gravoirs down, but for what purpose? It can't be to kill them all, can it? The only other logical explanation is that he would want them for their magic. Then again, if gravoir power is all he's been looking for, he's had me for seventeen years and never asked me to do more than a few small tasks. What would he want from the others?

"Isda…" Emeric's voice is suddenly quiet. Uneasy. He shuffles the file from hand to hand. "I've been meaning to ask… That is…uh…do you know if…are there any other gravoirs? Down in the catacombs or somewhere else?"

"What?" I shake my head. "No, it's always been only me."

He nods. "I assumed as much." But the hope in his expression fades a bit as he slides the file back under his bed.

All this time I thought I knew Cyril. Now I'm beginning to realize how little he's let me see.

I think of how careful he's always been around me, how he's made sure never to sing in my presence, even when giving me vocal instruction. Not once have I been able to step into the tide of his memories. Not once have I been allowed into his head.

He's been keeping things from me.

I think of his words weeks ago in the cab. *Fendoirs can be an unruly bunch. When they are given too much liberty, they begin to get ideas about what the world owes them.*

Could that be the answer? Is he looking for gravoirs as part of some plot to control the fendoirs? Or is it to use gravoir power to get himself crowned King of Vaureille? He always has been ambitious…

I close my eyes. Inhale. Exhale. Find my center. Settle into the silence.

But, as always, nothing is silent. My blood rushes too loud. Bells ring in my ears. As does Arlette's giggle. Emeric's song.

Gunshots. *Vile creature.* Spittle smacking into my cheekbone. All of it roars too loud for me to settle. Too loud for me to be calm the way Cyril always taught me to be.

"I have to save Arlette," Emeric says softly. "I know she's out there somewhere. Tonight, we'll get you someplace safe. Then, once I find her, we can leave for good and go where you can both be free."

I shake my head. "There's nowhere like that, Emeric. I'm a gravoir, hated by everyone in the world. There is no place we could go where that won't be true. I'd be trading my crypt for something prettier, maybe, but it'd still be just as much of a prison."

He is quiet for a long time. When he finally speaks again, his tone is somber. "So, what? We give up? Let them capture you?" His voice grows stronger. "Right now, finding a new place to hide is your only option." He strokes a thumb against my cheek, soft and tender. "Please let me try."

My eyes fly open, and I lurch away from him, flinging an arm up to shield my face from view.

My mask. It's still gone.

"Isda—" The bed creaks, and the mattress shifts as Emeric leans toward me.

"Don't!" I cry, keeping my hands in front of my face so he cannot see what my mask usually keeps hidden.

Emeric's palm settles on my shoulder. His touch is warm. Calming. Right.

"You may have to hide from everyone else," he says softly, "but you don't have to hide from me."

He wraps his fingers around mine and pulls them slowly, ever so slowly, away from my face.

I shrink back, letting my damp, blood-soaked hair droop to cover my features.

Moving to kneel next to the bed in front of me, he reaches out to touch my chin.

I don't want to face him without my mask, but his hand is so sure in mine, his fingertips on my chin so light, so careful. I let him turn my head.

When I meet his gaze, all of the fright and panic fades. Because his eyes are open and warm and dark and endless. They don't shrink away from me. They don't even flinch. They trail over every feature of my face as though drinking me in. As though they want more.

He leans in. His forehead brushes against mine as the hand that was on my chin slides up to cup my cheek.

I tremble, my body suddenly acutely aware of every part of him that's touching me. His hips digging into my knees as he leans over them, his other hand entwined with mine, his callused palm against my face.

His thumb grazes along my mouth.

I breathe him in. Caramel and the faint scent of marble from the dust on his jacket.

Every bit of me wants to sink into the lips that are centimeters from my own. To finally kiss him the way I've craved for so long. To knot my fingers in that thick, dark hair and lose myself in his touch the way I've already lost myself in his song.

But.

"We can't do this," I say, putting my hand to his chest and pushing him back. My body aches with the movement, begging me to wrap my fist in the lapel under my palm and yank him close instead.

His breathing is ragged. "Why not?"

"Because." The words hurt as they come out, as though I'm digging them from my soul with a dull spoon. "It can't work between us. If we tried, it would be the death of your singing career, the death of your freedom." I take a deep breath. "Life with me is a life of hiding in the dark. I won't take you away from that stage or that spotlight. I won't be the reason you don't get to live your dreams. You were right about everything—it's too dangerous for me to be a part of the same world as you."

"That's not what I meant—"

"But it's true. People like you…" I trace the creases his dimples have left in his cheeks, swallowing the way my heart feels like it might burst as I do. "Unmarked, lovely, perfect people would only be corrupted by my darkness." I think of how I made the Council Head lose his mind, of the horrible images I planted into his memory, of the pleasure I took in having such an effect on him. I think of the lead tenor whose femur I snapped. I think of the woman in the ballroom whose blood I spilled.

And I think of how I don't regret a single one of those actions.

My fingers feather across Emeric's cheekbones, and he watches me, a tempest in his eyes.

He's too good.

He deserves more. Better.

"Isda." His voice is gravelly as he presses his mouth to the center of my palm. "You've seen my past. You know I'm not perfect."

"That's not the point."

His jaw hardens. "That's exactly the point. We're *all* monsters. Every single person in this Memory-damned world." He places his hands on either side of my face. "What someone looks like isn't what determines their humanity."

He ducks close—so close I can see every fleck of amber in his eyes, every lash trembling against his cheeks. My heart might have stopped beating. I cannot breathe. Cannot think.

"I may not be able to see your memories," he murmurs, "but I have heard you sing. I've felt the vibratos and crescendos of your soul in every part of mine. You are no more a monster than I. You are a song." His fingers trace along my gnarled cheeks, around my twisted nose, across the jagged edges of my brow. "One composed of a thousand different instruments all perfectly harmonizing into the melody they were crafted to create. A masterpiece."

He smiles, and I'm undone.

Those dimples. Those stupid, stupid dimples.

I knot my fingers in his collar, pulling him against me, and his lips come down hard on mine. I taste sunshine and summer and burnt sugar. His hands weave into my hair and drag me deeper into him.

My resistance vanishes. I wrap my arms around his neck, easing him back onto the bed with me.

We are the music that wove the world. The soft buzz roll of sticks pitter-pattering across a snare drum like rain. The laughter of violin strings like grass billowing in the wind. The birdcalls of twin piccolos. Every piece of earth and sky harmonizing as one master symphony, one venture into the expansive realm outside my tiny sphere of safety.

I rise like the swell of the sea, a crescendo of movement; he falls like rapids over a cliff, a diminuendo of emotion.

My whole body is alive in a way it never has been before. It's as though I am full of elixir, vividly aware of every touch, every caress, every brush of his lips against my trembling ones.

He has ignited me.

It isn't until he pulls back with concern in his eyes that I realize I'm crying.

"Did I hurt your head?" he asks.

"No," I say, drawing him back against me, even as my chest aches with the motion.

Because I've been waiting my whole life to have someone care for me in this way. And I feel how much he cares for me as deeply as I feel his kisses burning their way along my jaw. I've longed for this forever. Hungered for it. Craved it.

Now that I have it, I know I shouldn't keep it.

For all his words, he has not seen the corruption of my

soul. The beast who burns me from the inside out. The fury that lives deep in my veins.

This boy, with his caramels and his dimples and his lullabies, is too good for the things that lurk below my skin.

I blink the tears away and crush myself against him, drowning out the doubts with the surge and tide of our kiss, and I pretend for just this moment that I could be the girl that belongs in his world.

I pretend that I could be worthy of someone like Emeric Rodin.

Just when I'm beginning to believe my own lies, a door bangs open somewhere downstairs.

Emeric and I rip apart and bolt upright, panting. We stare at each other, wild-eyed and panicked, for a split second before Emeric darts on silent feet for the door. "Stay here," he whispers.

"Emeric!" I reach for him, but he's already slipped out onto the landing. I sink back onto the bed, reaching for the pendant that is not at my throat. "Be careful…"

I wait for what feels like an eternity listening to the *thud-thud-thud* of my heart. I strain my ears for a crash or a shout from below, but nothing ever comes.

I'm about to sneak out to go look for him when a quiet footstep creaks on the landing. Relief floods through me. Emeric has come back.

But when the door eases open, it's not Emeric's broad shoulders and dusty tuxedo that fill the doorway, but the tall, willowy frame of Cyril Bardin.

CHAPTER
TWENTY-FIVE

Cyril's eyes find mine. "Isda!" He leaps across the room and enfolds me in his arms, pressing my face into his chest. "Thank Memory... I was afraid I was too late, that someone might have found you..."

I stand there, still. Not returning the embrace, but not resisting either. "I'm all right," I say. "More or less."

He holds me at arm's length and surveys the grime on my face and gown. His expression breaks. "Look what they've done to you."

I stare at him woodenly, a thousand words battling behind my lips, words of accusation, of betrayal, of hurt. But none of them are strong enough to capture what I feel, so I keep my mouth shut.

He reaches out to brush something off my chin with his thumb, and his voice drops to a broken whisper. "I'm so sorry for what I said. I had no choice. I was just instated as Head of the Council." He pauses, wringing his hands. "If they knew I'd been keeping you alive, they would have arrested me, too, and then we wouldn't have a chance."

I want to believe his words, to believe there was a reason for everything that happened.

But that's the problem with believing. It doesn't guarantee truth.

A horn blares outside, and I jump. Cyril nudges me toward the door. "That'll be my cab. We have to get you out of here before anyone discovers where you've gone."

"But Emeric—" I begin.

"We'll worry about the boy later," he says, pulling me out onto the landing and down the stairs. His hand is like a vise around my arm, and his footsteps thud on the steps so loudly I wince.

I look around frantically for Emeric as we descend. "You didn't see him when you came in?" I whisper, craning my neck to search one of the hallways before we round the corner.

"No. I'm sure he's fine," Cyril responds, his words clipped.

His grip is so stiff I'm starting to lose feeling in my fingers. "Cyril, you're hurting me." I yank on my arm.

His hand softens a bit, but he does not release me. I stumble after him, my legs clumsy and slow.

"We have to find Emeric," I say, dragging back on my arm and planting my feet with every ounce of strength I have. "I won't leave without him."

Cyril heaves an impatient sigh. "Emeric will be fine. No one is after him. The sooner I get you away, the safer he'll be. Now come on. We don't have much time."

"For what?" I ask as he pulls me down another flight of stairs. I wish my head would stop spinning so I could think clearly. "And wouldn't it be safer to go out the back, bring the cab around there?"

Cyril ignores me, charging for the front door and pulling me out into the frigid night.

The frozen air drives barbs into my exposed skin, sending me into a round of violent shivers that makes my aching skull throb. I shake my head to clear my vision. A black carriage stands waiting in front of us, and behind it is another horse with some kind of cart—

"Isda, run!" Emeric's shout breaks the night from my right.

I whip around in time to see a policeman shove a gag into Emeric's mouth. Emeric's eyes are wide, and he struggles against ropes wrapped around his wrists and ankles. A pair of men hoist his writhing form into the carriage. Panic spasms through me.

"Cyril! Do something!" I yank on his arm.

But Cyril isn't looking at me or Emeric. His eyes are on the cart parked behind the carriage. "Here's the gravoir," he says to a second policeman, who hops down from the cart and strides our way.

I blink from Cyril to the policeman, my mind still swirling with pain and confusion. But when the policeman gets near enough, Cyril shoves me into his grasp.

"Wait. No. Cyril!" The policeman drags me to the cart, which is nothing more than a glorified cage on wheels.

Cyril wipes at a smudge on his jacket and frowns. "Damn it, Isda, you got blood on my best suit." He turns toward the carriage.

"Cyril!" I scream as the policeman lifts and tosses me into the cart as though I weigh nothing. I land hard on my side as the door slams shut. The whole thing shudders when the lock slides home.

Pausing with his hand on the carriage door, Cyril glances back my way. He smiles, and it's unlike any smile I've seen on him in my life.

And yet…it's not. I've seen glimmers of that cold calculation in his eyes before. When Emeric nearly caught me that night I knocked over the candelabra. When he told me his plans to drive LeRoux to madness. When Emeric blew that kiss to my perch.

"Don't make a scene," he says.

And then he climbs into the carriage where they've stowed Emeric and pulls the door closed behind him.

Frost slaps my cheeks as the cart lurches forward. I scramble to the side and cling to the bars, shivering madly in my tattered gown as my fingers turn blue. Every time the cart slams against the uneven stone streets, my head feels as though it's being smashed into the opera house's tile all over again, and I grit my teeth to keep from crying out.

The pain in my skull makes it difficult to think. All I can see is the glimmer in Cyril's eyes when he looked at me. The way his nose wrinkled ever so slightly as though I were something foul he'd stepped in.

Is this all part of some act? Is he trying to show Channe he's a Council Head they can trust?

Is he willing to sacrifice me to keep his image unblemished?

I want to believe that is the only explanation—that he has chosen ambition over me. That would hurt less than the other possibility…the one lurking in the back of my mind that I desperately wish I could push out.

No one was in Emeric's apartment with us. Cyril could have taken me out the back door and sent the police off in the opposite direction. The Cyril I've known since birth would have done that.

He had the chance to save both me and his reputation, and he chose not to.

As we rattle through the streets, a terrible dread fills me, and it hurts so much more than the cold.

Perhaps I've been wrong this whole time. Perhaps Cyril is not who I thought he was.

Maybe Emeric was right. About everything.

All of the nights I spent modifying memories at the opera house for Cyril, all the times I manipulated LeRoux on his orders…

What was it for?

He once called me his "lucky vial of elixir." Maybe that's all I was.

I wrap my arms around my knees and press my fists to my temples.

I've seen him paste on winning smiles and schmooze with politicians and businessmen for years. He always knew what to say to get people to play into his hands, and I admired him for it.

Turns out he had been doing the same to me all along.

My eyes burn, but I refuse to cry for him.

He doesn't deserve my tears.

I let my mind go numb as I stare out between the bars of my cart. Faces flash in windows as we clatter by and then disappear quickly behind anxiously drawn curtains.

If only I could use my power without needing to hear my victims sing or scream. Despite the fear the policemen hide behind cruel grimaces, I pose little threat to them as long as they don't sing.

What I wouldn't give to get my hands on a catalyseur.

By the time we reach the entrance of Channe Prison, my body is convulsing in the cold. I can't move my legs, and it takes every bit of strength I have to pry my fingers from their frozen hold on the bars. The police yank me down from the cart, banging my knees on the stone walkway in the process. I bite down a yelp.

"Shut up," one of the men barks, hauling me through the front gate. I crane my neck to see where Cyril's carriage has gone, but it has disappeared. I'm towed past a dozen guards and into a dark stairwell that must lead to the prison cells.

"Wh-what ab-b-bout Emeric-c-c?" I manage through chattering teeth.

The nearest guard backhands me across the face, and another cry chokes out before I can clamp it back. "I thought I told you to shut up."

I press my lips tight and focus on trying to get my legs to cooperate so that the police don't have to drag me.

Inhale. Exhale. Find my center. Settle in the silence. Don't think about where they might be taking Emeric. Don't consider what is going to become of me. Don't allow Cyril's betrayal to break me.

The air grows darker and colder the farther we descend. When the stairs finally level out, a long, black corridor lined on both sides by iron-barred doors stretches in front of us. The only sound that breaks the thick silence as the police jerk me forward is the solemn, ragged breathing of prisoners as we pass their cells. Yellow eyes peer out from the darkness. Smudged hands grip the bars on their doors.

I shudder away from their gazes and focus on keeping my head high and my back straight.

One of our company stops and pulls open a door, and the policemen holding me kick me across the threshold. My feet catch on an uneven lip of rock, and I crash against the ground as the door grinds closed behind me. A key scrapes in the lock.

I shoot a scathing glare back at them, but they are already gone.

Nursing my aching head and ignoring the white flashes of light that jolt across my vision with every movement, I push myself upright and scrabble around the cell looking for some way out. My search does not take long. The space is small and carved entirely out of frigid stone. All I find is a chunk of rock dislodged from the corner, but the crevice it left in the wall when it fell out is barely big enough to fit my fist.

I sink to the floor and lie with my back to the wall, wrapping my arms around my knees to warm the chill in my bones. My dress still reeks of blood and vomit, and the boning in my corset digs into my ribs as though someone is pressing a knife to my side.

But I do not cry. I do not pray or sing or plead.

They think they can keep me here. That the iron and stone will intimidate me. That the darkness will break me.

They forget I was raised in the darkness, that I've been imprisoned my whole life.

They can threaten me with blade or poison or death, but they cannot make me afraid.

Not anymore.

I close my eyes and wait.

CHAPTER TWENTY-SIX

The whine of my prison cell door's hinges jolts through my awareness hours later. Adrenaline courses through my body and makes my head feel as though it's been split through with an axe. I bolt upright and move back into the farthest corner from the door.

A pair of guards drag a tall, struggling form into my cell. My heart stops. "Emeric?"

He lifts his head. "Isda!" He hurtles forward, but the guards yank him back by a set of iron shackles.

As I dive for him, another pair of guards jerk me sideways, wrenching my arms behind my back so forcefully my shoulder pops. I hiss.

"Ah, what a happy reunion." Cyril strides into the room, his face lit eerily by a small lantern in his hand. I find it suddenly difficult to breathe.

"What do you want?" My voice rings sharply in the small space.

"As Head of the King's Council of Channe, I have come to discuss your sentences."

"As though anything about our sentences is up for discussion," I spit, wishing there was something I could say, something I could do that would hurt him as much as he's hurt me.

"Well, Isda dear, it is true that *your* fate is unchangeable. We simply cannot allow a gravoir to live. Your execution will take place tomorrow morning." He pauses, eyes glinting. "However, it seems your scheming has yielded results that may benefit young Emeric here."

"What do you mean?" Emeric's jaw clenches as he speaks, as though he's working very hard to keep from shouting.

"As it turns out, the new lead tenor in this season's production of *Le Berger* has caused a significant stir among the citizens of Channe. Word has spread throughout the city and surrounding areas about this young prodigy." Cyril sneers down his nose at Emeric. "It seems people are willing to pay quite the sum to hear you sing, boy."

Emeric's nostrils flare.

"The promise of a substantial income like this is an unmistakable opportunity. Beginning my time as Channe's Council Head with such a surge in profits could bring the city together under my rule. It would be a fantastic way to inspire trust and confidence in my appointment."

"I won't do the show if you kill her," Emeric cuts in. "Behead me if you like, Monsieur Bardin."

Cyril laughs. "It's really charming of you to think you have a choice."

"You can't force me to sing."

"Ah, by the time we're done with you, boy, 'convincing' shouldn't be necessary."

"What are you saying?" I ask.

"The King's Council has agreed that a fine will be sufficient enough of a punishment for Monsieur Rodin. But not of money. We'll require a hundred thousand vials of memory elixir." He lets that sink in, his mouth twisting in a sick smile that makes his teeth glitter.

My jaw drops. "A hundred *thousand*? How is that better

than execution? There won't be anything left of him in there if you take that much."

"True. He'll be void of all of his memories except the ones we want to remain."

"The ones you want?" Emeric's face has gone sickly pale in spite of the orange glow of Cyril's lantern.

"Unlike fendoirs, who can only pull from the general well of elixir, gravoirs have the ability to remove elixir tied to specific memories. We'll have Isda extract all of your memories, save for the ones you need to be able to do the show." Cyril's sharp eyes flick to me. "You'll leave vocal experience, specific training, recollections of the show's rehearsals—things like that, but only the barest minimum. Don't even leave the whole memories of him learning these things—I want just the knowledge and skill acquired in them left. Everything else must be gone. I'll have a fendoir check his elixir levels once you are finished. If there is any more than twenty vials' worth left in his mind, we'll know."

I spit at his feet.

Eyes flashing, he rams me against the wall by my throat, jamming his elbow into my windpipe as he holds the lantern in his other hand so close to my cheek it almost burns. I squirm in the guards' grip as Cyril's breath gropes wet fingers across my face. "This is mercy, Isda," he growls. "You would do well to thank me for my generosity."

My arms quiver. "You can't do this."

"I'm the Head of the King's Council of Channe. I can do whatever I want." He pulls back, and my knees buckle, but the guards who hold both my arms keep me from toppling to the ground. Cyril whistles as he hangs his lantern on a hook by the door, and several young men enter carrying massive crates full of empty glass vials.

The clank of glass on glass echoes louder and louder until it's all I hear. All I know. The bottles shimmer in the orange firelight, warping as my eyes glaze. My hands curl into fists, and my fingernails cut deep into my palms.

Cyril is serious. He's going to force me to ruin the only friend I've ever had.

I stare at the man in front of me, searching his storm-blue eyes, wilted wrinkles, and smug smile for the Cyril I knew. The one I pretended was my father. The one who protected, provided for, and loved me.

But that Cyril is gone.

He never existed.

The family I thought I had with him, the life he built for me…it wasn't real.

I force myself to breathe.

None of it was real.

"Even a gravoir cannot remove my elixir if I'm not singing. You can't make me do that," Emeric says.

"Can't I?" Cyril grins, then nods at the guard holding my left arm, who shoves my hand against the wall.

"What—" I begin, but Cyril moves quickly, detaching a small hammer from his belt and swinging it with such force it whistles through the air. It slams into my hand with the soul-curdling sound of crunching bone. Pain jolts through me. I see nothing but stars and agony. My scream scrapes my throat raw. Blood spatters the floor.

The guard releases my wrist, and I collapse. The other guard still holding my right hand yanks me up and wrenches both arms behind me.

I buck away from him, pain shooting bullets through my body, but his grip on me is solid. Immovable.

Emeric roars, diving for me, but the guards on either side of him drag him back, too.

The world tips, spins, dances in sparks. Tears stream down my cheeks.

My left hand…

The one that commands the lower notes in my music.
The one that drives the bassline.
The one that builds the foundations of my songs.
How dare Cyril take that from me?

I whip around, tears scalding tracks down my cheeks. He's watching me, a pleased smile tugging at the corners of his lips like he finds this all wildly entertaining.

The beast in my chest rears its ugly head and bares its fangs.

I tear out of the guard's grasp and launch myself at Cyril, knocking him into the stone floor and going for his eyes with the fingernails of my remaining hand. I manage to gouge red marks into his cheeks before the guards haul me off him.

Cyril gets to his feet, straightens his vest and cravat, and gives me that cold smile. "Oh, you *are* going to make this fun, aren't you, chérie?"

I make an inhuman noise somewhere between a snarl and a hiss. The guards squeeze my arms, and my injured hand sends a jolt of pain through me that makes my eyes sting.

I bite the insides of my cheeks to keep from crying out. All I can see is the broken, crumpled remains of what were once long, slender fingers perfect for spanning octaves.

Fury bubbles hotter than the tears on my face.

The clink of the vials in their crates clangs high and hard in my head as the servants stack more and more inside my cell. Emeric stares at them, his expression unreadable.

"The gravoir's execution is set for tomorrow." Cyril's voice is quiet as he speaks to Emeric, but each word is iron. "She can either spend her last day whole or in pieces. It's up to you."

Emeric's brow shines with sweat. He looks at me, the veins in his neck bulging as he strains against the guards who hold him. I know what he sees: blood, vomit, trembling legs, shaky breaths, tears streaking to the floor. He squeezes his eyes shut. "I'll sing," he grinds out through his teeth. "You filthy son of a—"

Cyril's nostrils flare. "We *could* cut the whole hand off…"

Emeric's jaw twitches, but he snaps it shut.

"I won't do it." I heave, choking on the stench of vomit and blood. "I don't care what you do to me. I don't care if you take every finger, every toe, both eyes, my tongue…"

"All very good ideas." Cyril's hand drops to his belt and strokes the handle of his weapon. "I suppose I could use this on Emeric instead. He doesn't need fingers to sing. Would that be enough motivation for you to cooperate?"

I swallow, trying desperately to mask the flinch of panic that surges through my body at his words.

He smirks. "That's what I thought."

Firelight dances across the slick surface of the vials, which are crammed in crates stacked nearly to the ceiling and trailing out into the hallway. The sheer amount of elixir it will take to fill them… I shudder.

If I do this, they will allow Emeric to walk free. He won't be Emeric anymore—I've seen enough of the Memoryless to know that a man without memories is not much of a man at all—but he'll be alive. If I can find a way to escape, I might have a chance to get him some elixir to restore everything. As long as I can do it in the twenty-six hours before his memory loss becomes permanent.

If I can get myself out of this prison in time, I might be able to save us both.

"Fine." My whisper is so quiet even I can barely hear it, but Cyril grins so wide it looks as though his teeth might devour his own face.

"That's a good girl."

"What have you done with Arlette?" The words burst from Emeric. "Where is she?"

"Arlette?" Cyril furrows his brow. "Who in Memory's name is that?"

"As if you don't know." Emeric's voice rises in pitch, cracks like he's coming undone from the inside out. "She's the gravoir you captured in the town square of Marvault nearly three years ago."

Cyril considers him for several moments before his lips purse. "The one who tried to drain the whole village of its elixir?"

Emeric's jaw clenches.

"She's dead." Cyril shrugs. "Killed her myself." But his mouth twitches when he says it.

"Liar." Spittle flies from Emeric's lips. "What have you done with her?"

Cyril merely motions with a finger to the young men with the crates to bring one closer, impatience tugging at the wrinkles around his mouth.

Emeric struggles against the guards. With each grunt and shout, I shudder. Though the pain radiating from my hand streaks up my arm in white hot waves, I cannot tear my eyes from Emeric's face, from the brokenness, the rage, the disbelief, the fear. His expression contorts into a mask of madness.

Cyril slams a hand across Emeric's cheek, and I buck against my captors. "Stop your sniveling, boy. Her fate can't be that much of a surprise. She was dangerous."

Emeric deflates, collapsing so that the only thing holding him up are the gloved hands wrapped around his arms and torso. His head droops, and his shoulders shake with sobs.

Cyril whirls on me. He draws a knife from his belt and crosses the cell.

"If you're planning to carve the Extraction Mark, save yourself the effort," I say, tugging the hem of my dress upward to bare the scar on my thigh.

Cyril's mouth thins into a white line. "It looks like you should already know what you're doing then. And I was worried you'd be too stupid to figure it out. What luck." He jams the knife back into its sheath. He's all elbows and harsh movements and jagged corners. "Drain him."

232 JESSICA S. OLSON

I glare at Cyril, wishing with every piece of my trembling body that I could become the phantom I've created in so many minds, that I could swoop at him and snap his head from his body in a flash of teeth and a rush of shadow.

"Isda," Cyril barks, lifting his hammer and angling it toward Emeric. "Don't make me ask you again. I don't want to have to hurt the boy, considering how much money he's worth, but I will if you force me to."

Emeric lifts his head to meet my gaze. Tears glimmer on his cheeks, but his jaw is set. He nods once. "It's all right, Is."

Anger and pain battle through me so hard I can barely stand. "I'm sorry," I whisper.

"Don't be. With Arlette and you both gone, there will be nothing left in this world for me anyway."

We hold each other's gaze for one long moment. With every second that passes, the fibers of my heart stretch and snap one by one.

The memories that brought me to life, the music that gave me hope, the rainbow of emotions and light… I'm going to have to take it all from him.

Of all people, Emeric deserves this the least.

I blink back tears.

He gives me a broken smile.

This time when he sings, his voice is thick and hoarse. It breaks over the notes, clinging for life at their edges.

The memories take me slowly, sweeping me in beautiful, heart-rending arcs of color and joy. Tears of rage burn trails into my skin as I dip into the tide, sift through the flow to the place where it glows at the bottom, and draw the elixir out of his ears. It shimmers, gold and glowing, innocent and beautiful, as it ribbons into the vials.

I watch each memory as it goes with tears streaming down my cheeks.

His mother's fierce smile. Arlette's laugh. A squat little cottage nestled against an apple orchard.

The smell of chocolate in his uncle's candy shop. Bubbling caramel syrup over a blazing hearth.

Star-strewn skies. Rain-spattered streets.

My hand in his, my name on his tongue. Our bodies entwined. Our lips crashing and breaking over one another.

As each memory disappears one by one, the splash of Emeric's elixir echoes against the cell walls. Louder and louder it roars, an ocean of golden memories come to slam over me and rip me out to sea.

Emeric sinks to his knees, clutching his head between his shackled hands. His arms quiver. Sweat pours down his arms, but if he is in pain, he does not cry out.

His parents, his sister, his life drains from him in one steady amber stream, snaking out into the air and twirling into the vials.

I try to leave glimpses of his family, of his home, of me, but Cyril's warning that he'll have a fendoir check to make sure there are only twenty vials of elixir left clashes with the tide of Emeric's music in my mind.

Twenty vials will be barely enough for the instinct for music, the rote memory of how to sing, and the ability to function. Nothing more.

Cyril watches the elixir, his eyes shining and hungry.

My body quivers with an anger and hatred I have never known. It threads through me, sharp and fast as the pain in my hand even as my body weakens with the expense of so much power.

When everything that made Emeric who he was has been extracted, I collapse, shivering. The servant boys who have been corking and uncorking the vials as I worked settle the last few glass jars in their places. The crates stand full, glowing like hot suns, bright as the caramels Emeric once made.

Caramels that, if I fail to replenish his elixir in the next twenty-six hours, he will never make again.

"Very good." Cyril approaches Emeric and unlocks his shackles. "Come," he says. "The evening performance begins in an hour and a half."

Emeric allows the guards to hoist him to his feet. His face is drawn, his hair wet with sweat. He looks at the elixir vials stacked all over the room and cocks his head.

Cyril gestures to the door as he retrieves his lantern. "Shall we?"

Emeric shuffles past the crates.

"Emeric," I call weakly after him.

He stops and glances over his shoulder with empty eyes. His gaze settles on me, and he pauses. Surely he recognizes me. The memories of our vocal lessons may be gone, but I left the technical ability he learned from them there. Surely there's a trace of me somewhere in it all.

But he turns and exits without a word.

The servants and guards stoop to lift the crates and carry them out after him.

And then they are gone, and I am alone. Weakened, bleeding, and filthy, but still standing.

My whole life I've hidden underground, a monster fearing the day someone would glimpse my face and discover what I was. I found refuge in music, in darkness, and in solitude. The people who would have killed me at birth were never able to break me.

But now they have taken the only thing that truly meant something to me in this world.

I rise to my feet.

Blood drips from my hand.

My body turns to ice.

I throw back my head and scream.

CHAPTER
TWENTY-SEVEN

The scream fills every part of me, as though the crevices of my soul are roaring with it. It rams against the prison walls, pounds against the stone, wraps claws around the iron bars of my door. It reverberates down the hall, snaps teeth at the sputtering lanterns in the stairwells, climbs its way to the ceiling.

I imagine my scream ripping the foundation of the building from the earth. Cracking the stone. Toppling it all and crushing everyone within.

"Stop!" a guard shouts from somewhere far up the corridor.

I do not stop.

Until my heart stops beating, I will not stop. I will not bow to them. I will not surrender.

"I said shut it!" The voice is closer, and the pounding of boots on stone marks a hungering beat to my scream.

Tomorrow, I may die. But tonight, the world will hear me, finally hear me, and it will know what it has done.

"Gravoir!" The man's bark grows angrier. He'll reach my door soon. "Quiet!"

His shouts make the beast inside of me purr, sniff the air for his scent. My mind swims back to when, through people's shrieks at the masquerade, I was able to force my will upon their memories, flooding them with images of ghouls and creatures made of night.

Perhaps there is more than one way to sing.

I stoop and heft the loose rock I found earlier into my good hand. Facing the doorway, I slide it behind my skirt and wait.

The guard's face appears. I glower at him and scream louder than ever, wishing the sound of my fury could lash his face to bits. There are tales of Les Trois using music to do things like that to people. And worse.

Perhaps one day soon, I will learn how to do it, and the whole world will see what it has forced me to become.

He grips the bars with both hands to spit at me, and I charge forward, slamming the rock against his knuckles. Bone crunches. The man howls.

My beast pounces onto the beautiful sound of his pain, blazes straight through to the river of elixir in his mind, and wrenches the liquid out of his ears.

The cell walls glisten amber as the elixir floods toward me. I greet it hungrily, pulling it straight into my mouth. Its honey taste flows across my tongue and down my throat.

He tries to cut off his cries, but I suck harder on his elixir, pulling the sound from him against his will. It's like all I had to do was undam the flow, and now I own it. I control the sounds of his agony far more than I ever controlled anyone's singing.

I drink in that scream with relish, savoring every last drop.

It is a serenade. A sonata. A song.

I let it fill me with gold. As the elixir slides into my veins, my vision sharpens. The exhaustion in my limbs fades. The gnawing in my stomach subsides. The pain in my hand and my head dulls.

The sinews in my muscles, the pumping of my heart, and the breath of life in my chest compound as though I've been turned into the God of Memory himself.

I laugh.

Ecstasy and hatred dance a Vaureillean valse through me, and I revel in the exquisite way they complement each other.

I imagine myself at the top of the world, surrounded by the golden elixir of a million souls. I am as fearsome as Rose, as all three of Les Trois.

Elixir spatters my cheeks as I slurp more and more of it down.

The guard's eyes grow emptier and emptier.

His face pales. His jaw slackens. His skin sags.

Still I drink.

More. More. *More.*

His beautiful scream chokes off into a gurgle, and his body slumps, skull clanging against the bars of my cell door before he hits the ground with a sickening crunch.

I gulp down the last shining droplets in the air and wipe my mouth on the back of my hand.

Sliding my arms between the bars, I tug the ring of keys from his belt.

Shouts echo from above. Footsteps crash somewhere in the stairwell.

But I hum as I locate the right key and unlock the door to my cell. Fire burns through me, consumes me in its wicked, wild heat.

Every moment of my life, this world has told me I'm a nightmare. So let them come for me. I will burn them up until nothing remains but ashes and smoke.

I step over the corpse and sweep down the hall.

If they want me to be a nightmare, then a nightmare I shall be.

CHAPTER
TWENTY-EIGHT

With the guard's elixir making my body faster, stronger, and more agile, I reach the end of the corridor, rip the iron bars from a window, and scale the window well before anyone catches up to me. I sprint into the night, blood-soaked lace streaming behind me in the icy, whipping wind.

Shadows trail me across the prison grounds, but I am faster. I make it to the outer wall and climb it in moments, leaping down to the frostbitten grass on the other side without even breaking my stride.

Channe's lights blink on the horizon, and I focus on them as I hurtle over shrubs dying in winter's cold grasp. I know my bare arms and face should be frozen, but with the elixir burning away all pain and all weakness, the wind feels more like a soft, spring breeze. I spread my arms as I run, letting my fingers trail in and out of the air's current, and for a moment, I am flying.

I push my legs even faster and imagine myself soaring up to the skies. To somewhere far away from this world that would crush my music and carve my body and stop my heart.

But even flying like this pales in comparison to the flying I've done in the tide of Emeric's memories. The rush of emotions that buoyed me straight into the heavens. The thrill of his music enveloping me.

The image of his empty, glassy stare fuels my fire, and I grind my teeth as I barrel up the last hill before the grass gives way to outlying, scraggly homes.

Emeric has fewer than twenty-six hours left until his memories are lost forever. There's little room for error.

The dead man's elixir in my system thrums to the wild beat of my heart, but I know I will need more than this to be able to take down Cyril. To face an entire city of people who would capture or kill me on sight. If I show up at the opera house during a performance as I am, there is no way I'll make it out of there alive, let alone with a mindless Emeric in tow. Cyril will be watching his lead tenor like a hawk to make sure I did my extraction correctly. The entrances and exits are always manned by guards during events, a precaution to protect all of the important members of the Council who attend. And I have no idea where they'll be keeping Emeric when he's not performing, so looking for him outside of performance hours would be a waste of the precious little time we have.

Which leaves me with only tomorrow night's show to save him.

If I'm going to return to the opera house, I need to be able to do so in a way that will ensure my success. Getting locked up again when I have minutes remaining to restore Emeric's memory would be catastrophic for the both of us.

I think of Arlette standing like a tiny goddess in the middle of Marvault's town square, strands of liquid elixir wrapping around her, bathing her in light and power. An entire village of people on its knees in spite of the fact that not one of them was singing.

She had to have found a catalyseur. I search my memory for any glimpse Emeric might have gotten of something she could have been holding, maybe a lump of some kind of rock in her pocket or a trinket she was wearing, but I find nothing.

My mind drifts back to that moment when the town square was full of the gold of stolen memories. Arlette was so powerful, a true force in braids.

The ground beneath my feet changes from dirt to gravel to cobblestones as I tear into the city. From far behind me come the shouts of angry guards and the thunder of galloping hooves. Somewhere back there, Cyril must sit astride a horse, his silvery blue eyes shining with an emotion I know all too well on him—determination.

Cyril would not have let Arlette die, not after what she'd shown she was capable of. He likes power too much to quash it without at least trying to harness it the way he did with me.

His words to Emeric earlier, his declaration that Arlette was dead, were lies. I knew the truth the moment I saw his jaw twitch.

Arlette is alive. She has to be.

And she either has a catalyseur or knows where I'll be able to find one. If I can compound my power like she did in Marvault's town square, it won't matter where Cyril is or how many guards he has posted at the opera house. I will be unstoppable.

It's the only way to ensure that Emeric makes it out of this with his memory intact.

I need to find her, and quickly.

I aim straight for the nearest manhole, wrench the cover from the ground, and drop into the blackness below.

Coughing on the acrid stench of ripe feces, I wade through the muck as quickly as I can.

As the hours pass, the elixir in my system slowly dulls. My hand begins to throb again, and my head swims every time I make a sudden movement. The ache in my limbs returns, and exhaustion fills my body with lead. The filthy water swirling around my calves sends chills straight to my bones.

I press on, twisting through the tunnels, winding my way deeper into the heart of Channe, turning back when I feel I've gone too far. Every now and then I pause to listen. I don't know if I would be able to hear a horse's hooves on the streets far above my head or if the shouts of policemen would carry through the ground, but still I check.

At least one thing is certain so far: no one has followed me into the sewers yet.

My teeth are clattering and my knees are knocking violently against each other when the water begins to slink lower. Soon, I am squelching across damp ground.

The air feels familiar in this tunnel. Quiet, waiting, comforting. I swear I almost hear music in its breath.

I trail my fingers along the wall. After several minutes of trudging, they slide over the unmistakable curve of a skull.

Relief surges through me almost as wild and warm as the dead guard's elixir did. I pick up the pace, dragging my palm over femurs and ribs, vertebrae and kneecaps, until all at once, I stop. Inhale. Exhale. Inhale again.

The scent of home.

I've found my crypt.

I rush forward until I reach the door, jam it open, and hightail it inside. With frozen, clumsy hands, I locate a cigar lighter. It takes several tries before my numb fingers get it to ignite, but then the flickering yellow light illuminates the room.

My bed. My things. My music.

My organ.

Pausing only to light enough candles to see by, I rip the ruined dress from my body, yank my stinking shoes and stockings from my feet, and dive for the washbasin I keep in the corner. With feverish, jerking movements, I scrub myself from head to toe with my good hand. Even though I know I will regret having wet hair when I venture back out into the cold, I dump the clear water over my head and scrub out the blood, vomit, and muck tangled in my curls.

When I feel sufficiently clean, I towel off and rush, shivering, to my wardrobe. I drag underthings on, tug a thick, warm, black dress over my head without even bothering to put on a corset first, and fumble through the buttons, trying my best to manage it with only the thumb of my left hand to help.

Cyril won't take long to come looking down here. I need to be quick.

Once I'm dressed, I knot my hair on top of my head and pull on a cloak. Biting down on my tongue to keep from crying out, I wrap the bulging, purple mass of my shattered fingers in clean linens. Using my teeth, I tug a glove onto my right hand. I snatch one of the pocket watches from my collection of knickknacks, trying to dispel the wave of dread that fills me when I catch sight of how many hours have passed.

It is nearly three in the morning. Which means it's been roughly nine hours since I drained Emeric of his elixir.

Seventeen hours left until his memories are gone. Less than that until the show begins and I need to be in place, ready to strike.

As I stuff the watch into my dress, my gaze snags on the sheet music from *Le Berger* propped open on my organ, and my heart flops. I approach it slowly and brush my fingertips over Forbin's signature and the lovely cursive title.

I lift the score and press my lips to the front cover.

Then I crush it in my fist, ignoring the way my chest seems to crumple along with it. The booklet drops from my fingers and hits the stone floor with barely a thud.

Forcing myself to breathe, I turn for the nearest bookcase

and retrieve my pendant from the shelf where I left it. It glimmers, and I catch the gaze of the ballerina inside.

All my life I've imagined what it would be like to be her, a beauty destined for the stage. For greatness.

All I see now is a girl trapped in a pretty little prison.

Stuffing the pendant into my dress, I tug on a simple black mask, make my way across the room to my bed, and fish under my pillow until my fingers brush against the cold brass of the key to Cyril's office.

When I took it, I imagined handing it over to Emeric. Yet every time I thought about actually giving the key to him, a part of me held back. *What if Cyril loves me?* I wondered. *I've already betrayed him too much.*

Now I know Emeric was right all along. Cyril never loved me. He kept me around only because of what I could do for him. Because I made him rich. Yes, he read me fairy tales and bought me an organ and rewarded me with pastries, but I'm beginning to realize that all of that was just part of his plan to keep me here, trusting him, willing to carry out whatever task he asked, blindly believing every lie he told me.

And he did it all so well. He orchestrated a relationship I cherished. I would have done anything for him. I would have walked to the ends of the earth to make him happy.

So I tuck the key into my pocket.

I don't know where Arlette is, but I'm sure Cyril does. And if he knows where she is, odds are I'll find a clue in his office.

CHAPTER
TWENTY-NINE

The opera house is as dark and grand as ever, but somehow it no longer seems beautiful to me. Its angels and winged creatures stare hollowly out from the walls as I creep past. This place once felt like my kingdom, my home.

Now I wish it would burn.

I steal along the corridors. The air is quiet and still in the way it only is a few hours before dawn—as though it is watching the horizon. Waiting for those gray tendrils of smoky light to curl over the edge of the earth and pull the sun into the sky. Thankfully, it seems as though the police and prison guards searching for me did not think I would be stupid enough to return here.

I slip down the hallway until I find the stairs and mount to the fourth floor.

The key to Cyril's door slides quietly into the lock. The mechanisms within give a satisfying *click* as I turn it, and the door opens. Shutting and locking the door behind me, I cross to Cyril's desk and light the lantern.

I have very little time. Soon the sun will rise, and the city will be crawling with people—people who will see my black mask. Though they might think I am only a fendoir, it is likely that the story of my capture, arrest, and escape have made it through the rumor mill already. The citizens of Channe will be watching for a fleeing gravoir with a damaged hand. I will not make it far once the city awakens.

I immediately shove against the hidden bookshelf until it swings around. I gather the small pile of notebooks there and rifle through them for any mention of Arlette. Inside, Cyril's loose cursive print fills the pages with notes about me. They date from over a decade ago. He describes my progress, the things he taught me, the questions he had about my potential.

One entry at the end of the most recent journal stands out to me, stark black and white I will never be able to erase from my memory:

Sometimes I wonder if I have chosen the right one. I have discovered so many gravoir children over the last couple of years, and I can't help but think about how much more powerful some of them might have been. What could I have discovered in them if I had chosen them instead? What might they have been able to offer me?

Isda is a good choice in many ways. She trusts me implicitly and never questions anything I tell her. She has a great deal of control over her emotions, and she works hard. But does she have power like Les Trois did? The strength to rule an entire nation—an entire world? I have no doubts in my ability to keep her under control as her power grows. I just pray that I've invested my time and money in the gravoir that is capable of doing what I need her to.

Perhaps she is too young for me to be sure yet, but she seems too soft. Too wrapped up in the music and finery of the opera. She doesn't seem passionate enough for that kind of dominion.

So, I wonder, have I chosen the wrong gravoir for my plans?

I tear the page from the journal and turn to the lantern, letting the crimson and black of curling flame eat through the words until all that is left is a pile of scraps. I stare at the ash for a long moment, trying to push the words out of my head. Instead, it's as though Cyril himself is whispering them to me, his voice quiet and soft the way it used to be when he would tuck me into bed.

He must have been amused by how much I adored him. By how I squealed when he brought me sweets and how I drew pictures for him of us on picnics when I was small. How I begged him to read me stories and asked him to kiss my wounds when I skinned my knees.

All along, he was manipulating me more precisely than I've ever done to any memory.

I reach for my pendant, crushing it in my palm until the pain of it makes me hiss. I press my fist against my mouth, forcing back the tears that are filming across my vision all over again.

I cannot give him any more of myself.

I breathe deeply through my nose, and as I do, my veins ignite with the hungry, furious, delicious power that burns away all sorrow and all pain until there is nothing but hate.

I drop the pendant. It hits my chest with a thud.

"Not powerful enough for you, Cyril?" I spit, whirling to yank book after book from his wall. "Not passionate enough?" I shove the vials from his desk and listen to the sweet song of glass shattering against the floor. "Wait until I usher in a new oblivion. Wait until I stand over you, powerful and wicked and *beautiful*. Wait until I burn you from the inside out."

I kick over the globe—his gift from the King—and laugh when it crashes to bits against the wall.

I know I don't have time for this, but blood rushes in my ears and the beast screams its fury in my chest. I knock Cyril's folders from their neat, tidy rows and tear papers to shreds with my teeth.

Destruction is a music all its own. One composed of drumbeats and a percussion of passion and pain.

Growling, I swing around and knock a statue from his shelf onto the floor. It cracks loud as a gunshot, and the sudden sound punches through the pounding in my head. I blink down at the rubble remains of Cyril's miniature figure of Les Trois. Rose's face stares up at me in two pieces.

I crouch to pick them up.

I think of what Emeric said when he came across that depiction of Les Trois in the hallway. *I've never seen a painting of them before. Most people don't even like to speak of them.*

The signs were there all along. Cyril's obsession with Les Trois and their powers, the way he glorified them as gods when everyone else was terrified to even whisper their names, should have been the most obvious one.

I scrutinize Rose's face. It's as though every artist who ever tried to render her was able to imbue her with that same sadness, that same ferocity in the face of death.

I know something of what she felt in that moment.

But Rose's emotions got the better of her and resulted in her ruin. I cannot allow myself to be overcome by rage. Not when so much is at stake.

I set the marble bits carefully on Cyril's desk.

My gaze strays to the fairy tale book Cyril lent me two months ago when he caught me in his office, the book he used to read to me from when I was a child. *Charlotte and the Mirror of Forgotten Things* lies half-open atop a pile of torn Council records.

A shard lodges itself in my chest.

Where that book was so long a comfort to me, its poem a promise of safety and love, in less than a day it has become a symbol of Cyril's lies.

I cannot let him win.

I check the pocket watch in my dress and blanch when I

realize it's already four in the morning. Whipping back to the piles of books around my feet, I focus on the task at hand. For the next hour, I comb through every volume in his office with my teeth ground together.

I find no sign of Arlette. No hint of any other gravoir besides me. Perhaps Emeric found everything there was to find in that folder full of newspaper clippings under his bed. If there were any clue about Arlette's whereabouts in there, Emeric surely would have gone after her by now, so there's no use risking my life returning to his apartment to look through it.

After I've pulled the drawers out of Cyril's desk and dumped their contents on the floor, I glare at the mess around me with my good hand perched on my hip.

"Where is she?" I scan the loose papers and books jumbled in piles so thick the floor is no longer visible. "Where have you hidden her?"

Something shuffles in the hallway.

I slow my breathing, straining to hear.

Yes.

Footsteps.

I whirl and sprint for the window, heart hammering in my throat. As I clamber onto the sill, my gaze snags on the envelope Cyril received last week—the one bearing the glad tidings of his promotion to Head of the Council. Cyril's home address is printed in distinct lettering.

There are no clues about Arlette's whereabouts here in Cyril's office, but maybe I could find something at his home.

The footsteps grow louder and then stop outside the door. The doorknob rattles as a key slides into the lock.

I fling myself out the window and onto the tree branch just as the door clicks open behind me.

Swallowing a cry of pain from accidentally using my bad

hand, I shimmy quickly to the trunk and climb the rest of the way down to the ground.

Cyril's gasp of shock echoes out the window, followed by a string of curses and crunching footsteps over broken glass as he pounds his way to the window. I leap into the bushes and pull my feet out of sight an instant before his head ducks into the wind.

"Who's there?" he shouts.

I cover my mouth with my good hand to stifle the heaving of my breaths.

"Isda." My name sounds like poison in his mouth. "Where are you?"

Still I do not move. I squeeze my eyes shut, waiting for him to leave the window so I can flee.

"You can't hide from me forever, chérie. Creatures like you don't last long in our world."

My bad hand is pinned underneath me, and the longer I wait, the more it aches. It pulses blades up my wrist, which slice through my arm.

Go, Cyril, I plead silently. *Please go.*

Though I do not open my eyes, I hear the rustle of his suit jacket as he leans out over the window's ledge. The steady in and out of his breath through his nose. The wet *snick* of his tongue sliding over his teeth as he waits.

I grit my teeth as the agony in my hand explodes sparks across the inside of my eyelids.

I chance a peek through the brambles. Cyril is looking at the street a few yards away.

Maybe if I move very, very slowly... I inch my pelvis upward into the air as carefully as I can. The bare branches of the bush brace against me, and I beg them not to crackle.

That's it. A little more.

The pressure on my hand lessens as I arch my back. I ease my arm gradually out from underneath my weight.

All the while, I keep one eye pinned on Cyril.

My body trembles with the exertion of keeping my spine arched away from the ground.

Easy. Easy, I tell myself.

The muscles in my back spasm, and my heels skid on the dirt.

I thud against the ground. The branches I was pushing against rustle back into place.

My breath catches in my throat.

Cyril's gaze snaps down onto my face.

"Bonjour, chérie," he says.

I wrench myself out from under the bush and run.

CHAPTER
THIRTY

My lungs burn and my sides ache as I dash through Channe. It seems Cyril has already managed to alert the police, as the slumbering streets of Channe echo with shouts so loud I cannot gauge how far away they are. But I no longer have elixir pumping through my veins, and my body is weak with fatigue. The pain in my hand and my head are blinding, and my body is still trembling from how much power it took to drain Emeric. Channe's police force will catch me.

Unless I find some elixir.

Grasping to that thought, I search the storefronts as I pass. Bookstores, cafés, banks, churches. Where are the Maisons des Souvenirs? And why did I smash all those vials in Cyril's office instead of stealing them?

I swing around a corner and catch sight of the familiar, whipping crimson flag with its golden stitched Extraction Mark. Gasping with relief, I make a beeline for it. When I reach the door, I yank on the handle, but of course it's locked. I peer through the glass, cupping my good hand around my face to see if I can glimpse anything inside.

A grand desk looms in the dark, bleached pale by the silver glow slanting in from the gaslight behind me, but there is no one there. Likely the fendoir who runs this place is home asleep in his bed.

A clatter of hooves reaches my ears from somewhere nearby, and my stomach lurches to my throat. I need a way into this Maison now.

I whirl as adrenaline jolts through me, making my head spin so painfully I gag. Catching sight of a loose cobblestone, I skid toward it, pry it free, and hurl it as hard as I can at the window.

The crash splits through my eardrums as shards scatter across the tile in front of the reception desk. I glance over my shoulder to check if I've been seen, but every shopfront on the street is as silent and still as before. I launch inside.

In all the memories I've seen of people visiting Maisons des Souvenirs, there's always a grand receiving desk like this one in the front room for some kind of receptionist. The elixir extraction usually takes place inside one of an array of private rooms adorned with cushy pillows and dimmed lights. As soon as the elixir is extracted, the vials are whisked away. So there's got to be some kind of safe or vault somewhere in the back where the fendoirs keep their supply until it is picked up by government officials for sale and distribution.

As I dash for the dark hallway on the other side of the desk, someone grabs me from behind and yanks me back.

"No!" I shout, trying to disentangle myself from the stranger's grip.

"Easy there, child."

I stop and stare up into a pair of iron-gray eyes framed by a silver fendoir mask.

"You don't look like a thief." He cocks his head and surveys my black mask, the thick knot of still-dripping hair atop my head, and the bandaged lump of flesh on the end of my left arm.

"Please. I need elixir. They'll catch me, and I—"

"Why the mask? If you were a fendoir, you'd have the symbol there." He nods at the place where my collarbones meet. My gaze darts to his collar. The top of his own spiral mark peeks out above it. "So what are you?"

"I—I—" I glance past him through the broken window to the street. The shouts are getting closer.

I meet his gaze with my chin held high. I may be a gravoir and he a fendoir, but we are not too different from each other. Both of us hide our appearance from the world. Both of us don't quite fit into the society we were born in. We are two sides of the same coin, he and I. Perhaps trusting him is the only way for me to make it through tonight alive.

So I hold my breath, slide my fingers under the edge of my mask, and lift it away from my face. It clatters to the floor between our feet.

"You're a—" He steps back, his face going pale and his eyes widening.

"Please," I whisper as the shouts outside grow ever louder. "They'll kill me."

His Adam's apple bobs as he takes in the full effect of my face.

Then he turns. "Hey!" he bellows, stomping toward the window. "She's in here!"

Acid ripples through me.

Even a fendoir?

The beast in my chest growls.

As a fendoir, this man's elixir is untouchable for me. But he can still bleed.

I grasp a shining shard of glass from the ground and leap for him, plunging it deep into the side of his neck. He stumbles backward, groping at his collar. Blood spatters his mask and soaks his shirt. He topples.

Leaping over the reception desk, I careen down the hall, ramming open door after door, searching for the elixir.

"Come on, come on, come on," I growl each time the room is filled with only pillows and overstuffed chairs.

Finally, at the far end of the hallway, one of the doors is locked. Mustering up every ounce of life left in me, I jam my foot through the feeble wood. It splinters, opening a hole wide enough for my arm to fit through. Sliding my hand into the darkness, I unlock the door and duck inside.

A glass case stands in the corner, full to the brim with glowing vials.

My mouth waters. My knees go weak.

I stumble to the case. Wrenching it open, I uncork vial after vial, guzzling down the contents as though I've never drunk a thing in my life. Elixir splashes down my front in my haste, and my fingers quiver with each new glass bottle.

The more I drink, the more alive I feel. Once again, my exhaustion fades, my vision sharpens, my hands steady, and the pain dissipates.

A crash and a shout come from the reception area.

I throw back one last swallow, wipe my mouth on my sleeve, and turn toward the door. Shadows twitch on the wall across the hall. Footsteps crackle on broken glass.

Body thrumming with power, I prowl forward. I pause at the doorway, and the toe of my boot nudges against something propped against the doorframe, knocking it sideways. I crouch and catch the object before it hits the floor.

An umbrella.

I hold it aloft.

A guard strides into my view and points a pistol at my head.

"Bonsoir," I purr, grinning when he catches sight of my unmasked face and blanches. I ram forward, jamming the umbrella's sharp tip into his gut. He grunts, and the gun drops from his fingers. It goes off when it hits the floor, filling the air with the bite of gunpowder.

Boots pound in our direction. The guard in front of me

gags, reaching for his gun, but blood is pooling on his lips, and his fingers shake. Kicking his arm aside, I pick up the weapon, face the shadow hurtling toward me in the dark, and fire.

The bullet takes the second policeman in the forehead, and he drops without another sound.

Shoving the pistol into the sash of my dress, I stride down the hall and into the reception area. Cold wind bites through the room. Pausing only to retrieve my mask from where it lies a few feet from the fallen fendoir, I fasten it around my head and duck outside.

A pair of sturdy, dark brown horses saddled in police garb paw at the ground where they stand tied to the nearest gaslight pole. Sifting through a hundred memories of how to handle horses, I make my way cautiously to the bigger one.

I unknot his reins, hoist myself one-handed into the saddle, and pause. I think back to the moment I found Cyril's letter in his office earlier and try to remember the address scrawled across the envelope. *12 Rue de l'Orchidée*. I purse my lips. It is not a street name I recognize. How am I going to find it? Tapping my knuckles against my knee, I quickly think of all the addresses and street signs I've glimpsed in my years sneaking through the corners of people's minds.

I imagine the soft, bright petals of the orchid for which Cyril's street is named. A small collection of flashes of street signs from other memories pop up. Rue de la Tulipe. Rue du Lis. Rue de la Violette. Tulip. Lily. Violet.

There must be a neighborhood with street names that all come from flowers.

I latch on to the memory of Rue de la Violette—the one with the clearest glimpse of the area. In the memory, the sun is setting to the left. I glance at the sky and take note of the grayish glow on the horizon. Yanking on the reins, I pull the horse around in the right direction and, mimicking the behavior of riders in memories I've witnessed, urge him into a gallop.

As I lean low over the saddle, I remind myself of the things I must do before Emeric's performance.

I need to track down Arlette, get her somewhere safe, and ask her where I can find a catalyseur. I need to locate one, retrieve it, and make it back to the opera house in time for the show.

And I need to do it all within the next fourteen hours without being caught.

"Hang on, Emeric," I mutter through my teeth as the wind whips my hood back. "Once I get my hands on that catalyseur, nothing will be able to stop us."

It takes me the better part of half an hour, courtesy of a few loops and backtracks, before I finally arrive at Rue de la Violette. I continue more slowly, scanning each street sign as I pass, searching for Rue de l'Orchidée. The boxes hanging on every lamppost and public wall are draped with the shriveled remains of lilies, chrysanthemums, and roses. Dead petals rustle in the wind.

I slow the horse to a walk and urge him along each street, straining to see past grand, sky-high fences to the palatial homes beyond.

There it is. Rue de l'Orchidée. Though dark, purple-black clouds are gathering in the sky and obscuring the approach of dawn, a gilded sign on a nearby gate bearing the number 12 still glimmers in the faded light.

Dismounting, I tie the horse to a tree around the corner near a birdbath. He ducks his muzzle into the half-frozen water and gulps noisily. I stroke his mane once in thanks before slipping around the back corner of the brick wall at the perimeter of Cyril's yard, ducking to hide behind icy bushes whenever a cab or carriage passes on the street. Cold air puffs silver in front of my face as I make my way forward. With every step, the sky grows thicker and darker, and the wind picks up its ferocious howl.

Though I know from the memories I've seen from people

at the opera that my legs will be sore from riding later, the elixir coursing through my system keeps away all pain, and I walk proudly in spite of the icy air that has frozen my wet hair solid.

When I've reached a small alley between Cyril's back wall and that of the nearest neighbor, I wedge my feet and good hand into the bricks and climb up and over. Even with a useless arm, the elixir makes the feat easy, and before I know it, I'm skirting the lawn of his backyard, watching the pale gray house for any sign of movement within.

For the most part, all of the windows are dark. It isn't until I round the corner on the south side that I see yellow light shining through gauzy white curtains.

I crouch behind a massive trash bin and peek around its edge, squinting to see if Cyril has come back home or if it is someone else who is moving about inside.

A shadow passes one of the windows, and the curtain ruffles enough for me to see the customary white uniform of a chef. How many servants does Cyril have? What time do they arrive? If I'm going to be able to search for clues about Arlette, I'll need to get in and out quickly and with as little of a ruckus as possible.

Chewing on my lip, I wait for a sign that anyone else is home, but I see only the chef bustling his way back and forth in what must be Cyril's kitchen.

Steeling my nerves, I creep out from my hiding place and scuttle along the walkway and onto the back porch. I slide my hand onto the brass handle of the back door and give it a slow twist. It pops open silently on well-oiled hinges.

The air inside is warm, and the scent of freshly baked baguettes makes my mouth water. I pull the door closed behind me, taking care to turn the handle so it doesn't click when the mechanism slips back into place. I pause a moment with my back to the door, inhaling the fragrance of bread and tea.

Pots and pans clang from the kitchen's entrance a few yards ahead. I creep forward, pressing my back to the wall until my fingers curl around the lip of the doorway. Sneaking a quick peek around the corner and finding the chef's back turned my way, I take a deep breath and leap into the darkened hallway beyond.

The clamor of dishes pauses for a moment, and I freeze, flattening myself in the shadow of a bookcase and holding my breath. Once the noises from the kitchen resume, I steal forward, taking care to tread softly on the polished floors. As well-kept and lovely as this house is, the wood could still creak if I step on it wrong.

I poke my head into room after room. When I come across a parlor filled with plush, red seats and marble statues of winged beasts, I pause. The glass pieces of a gilded chandelier glitter in the dark. Even the scent of the place is that of burning candelabras with the faint hint of expensive cologne, just like the opera house. I turn away, unease rippling the hairs on my arms.

Moving into the next room, I find a smaller version of Cyril's office. A beautiful mahogany desk with a high-backed black chair is surrounded by more floor-to-ceiling bookshelves. A life-size statue of Les Trois stands in the corner, and I stifle a gasp at how fierce and lifelike the three gravoirs are. How many more depictions of Rose, Éloise, and Marguerite are there in this house? Chills that have nothing to do with the cold snake under my skin. Why exactly is Cyril so obsessed with gravoirs? Obviously he wants to use us for our power, but to what end? Is it simply to control Channe? Or does he hope to one day rule over all of Vaureille the way Les Trois once did?

Darting a glance toward the kitchen, I pull the door closed and light the lantern, avoiding the women's gazes, and get to work. My body still thrums with the remaining elixir in my system, though as the minutes tick by its power trickles slowly away.

I start with the drawers, pulling each one out and rifling through its contents. Stationery, extra wax, stamps, fountain pens, and paperweights. Nothing out of the ordinary, and certainly nothing to do with gravoirs or Arlette. With a huff, I cross to the nearest wall and run my fingers along the spines of the books, scanning the titles embossed on them as quickly as I can.

How long do I have before Cyril returns home? How many servants does he employ? Will one of them come into the office to clean out the trash can before I'm finished? I can almost feel time crackling away around me, setting my teeth on edge, making my heart beat faster.

I scour every title in the room, and though I find whole shelves devoted to gravoir history and the rise, reign, and death of Les Trois, there are no notebooks or logs that might give me Arlette's location. Despair sinks its cold teeth into my chest.

Was this a waste of the precious little time Emeric has left?

Maybe I was wrong about Arlette. Maybe I imagined Cyril's mouth twitching, and he wasn't lying to Emeric when he said he had killed her. Maybe I'm on a fool's errand, and I'll never discover what a catalyseur is or how to find and use one.

Maybe I wasn't meant to save Emeric.

Maybe I was meant to die.

No. There has to be something here. Somewhere else to look. Maybe in a bedroom or a storage cupboard or a cellar.

Even if there is nothing, I will not lie down and let them take me. Not when fire snaps in my veins and music roars in my soul.

Extinguishing the lantern, I stride across the room to unlatch the office door. I prowl out into the hallway and come face-to-face with the chef.

CHAPTER
THIRTY-ONE

I freeze with my hand still clutching the doorknob to Cyril's office. The chef's thick unibrow furrows as he takes in my black mask and cloak. Clutched in his hands is a gleaming silver tray piled with slices of baguettes and steaming tea.

"Who are you?" He takes a step back.

"An—an employee of the opera house," I say, releasing the knob. It is not a lie. Not exactly. "Is Cyril home?"

"He didn't mention he would be expecting anyone this early." He glances past me to the foyer and the front door. "May I have your name?"

"Colette." I keep my voice even and casual.

"Do you have an elixir delivery?" His gaze travels over my mask and drops to my wrapped fist.

I shove both hands into my cloak, and my fingers brush the pistol I stuffed into my belt earlier. "No, it's nothing like that. I've come to discuss a classified matter with him."

"I see." His brow lowers even farther so that his eyelashes seem to tangle in its coarse hairs. He takes another step back and lowers the tray of food onto an antique decorative table to his right. "Why don't you take a seat in his parlor? I'll go on up and let him know you've arrived." He gestures toward the room that looks so much like the opera house.

There's no way Cyril has made it home yet. He's likely still out in the city, searching for me in all of the wrong places.

I give a slow nod and turn, slipping the pistol from my belt.

As soon as I do, the chef slams me to the floor. He yanks my arms behind my back, pulling the gun from my grasp. I stifle a yelp when he jerks my injured hand.

"You're the gravoir they're all looking for, aren't you?" The man digs a solid knee into my back. I arch my spine as pain spasms down through my tailbone and bite my tongue to keep from shouting. "Monsieur Bardin is going to be so very pleased I found you."

Struggling against the thick swell of his fingers around my wrist, I buck and squirm. But he's too heavy, and the last of the elixir in my veins has gone.

He wrenches me to my feet facing away from him and jams the pistol's barrel into the side of my neck. I rear forward and slam my head back into his face. Pain flashes white and yellow across my vision, and my ears ring, but the man grunts and his grip loosens just enough. Swinging around, I drive the heel of my boot straight into his groin.

He yowls, doubling over.

His cry pulls at my power, and I let the river of his memories flood my mind. I sink easily to the place where his elixir lies, and I drag it out of him in one glowing, delicious stream, smacking my lips with each swallow. Every time he tries to silence himself, I strengthen my power's grip and force him to continue until the whole house quakes with the sound of his screams.

In moments, he is dead.

I laugh, reveling in the way the world has grown sharper and more alive around me, at the way the blood dances through me to the sweet music of a lifetime's worth of elixir.

As I retrieve my gun and scarf down all of the tea and bread on the tray, I listen for anyone else. I hear not a footstep. Not a creak of a floorboard. Not an intake of breath. Only the wind ravaging against the house outside.

Stepping directly on the chef's sternum, I make my way down the hall to another door and tug it open. A set of stairs trails down into the dark.

Resting my hand lightly on the smooth, polished banister, I glide downward, not even bothering to light a lantern or search for a candle. My elixir-enhanced vision will do perfectly, and besides, darkness is my home.

The cellar hosts a well-stocked store of wines and other alcoholic beverages in smooth, wooden racks. Where I expected to find the musty smell of dust, the place is as clean as any other part of the house I glimpsed upstairs. I lift the lid of one of several dozen crates in the corner and find what looks like files of every purchase Cyril has made in his life stacked in folders and organized by date.

Frowning, I turn, and a hulking black mass in the corner pulls my gaze. I approach it and run my hands along its smooth, glossy surface. It's a vault, complete with a complex-looking lock on its handle. My mind goes fuzzy at the thought of how many coins and valuables might be able to fit in a thing like that. As I shuffle along it, my foot nudges a slightly glowing bag near the vault's door.

I heft the bag between my hands, surprised by its weight, and undo the knot at its top. Golden light pours from the opening, shining off the vault and sparkling on the wine bottles. Saliva pools in my mouth as I stare in at the vials of elixir nestled snugly within. There has to be at least a hundred memories' worth in there.

My body quivers with desire, and I reach in to pull one of the tiny bottles out. As my fingers brush the glass, a sound stops me cold.

Has Cyril returned home? Has someone found the chef's body?

The sound comes again. It's a quiet, wet sound, somewhere between a cough and a breath.

And it's close.

I scan the area for anything out of the ordinary. The room is much too clean and organized for anyone to be able to hide.

When it happens again, my eyes snap to the vault. Is there someone *inside*? I drop the bag and press my ear to the door.

There it is. That choking noise. It's definitely coming from within. I wrap my hands around the combination dial on the front and let a breath out through my teeth.

I may be a musician, a manipulator, and a monster, but I am no lock pick.

I spin the dial this way and that, clicking through one pattern of numbers and then another. Anything that might be important to Cyril. His date of birth. The date of the opera house's grand opening so many years ago. The more combinations I try, the more frustration begins to buzz under my skin.

I run out of ideas. Grinding my teeth, I kick the vault and then, when my elixir-infused foot doesn't even hurt, I mutter every curse word I can think of at it.

The sound happens again, only this time I'm sure it's a sob. Someone is crying inside that vault, and I'm willing to bet every drop of gold in my veins that it's Arlette.

Squeezing my eyes shut, I force myself to focus. I sift back through my own memory, pretending it's like a tide of liquid time the way it is when I look into others' minds.

I trickle in and out of old moments. As flickers of Cyril's face grow younger and softer and as he seems to grow taller with the shrinking of my perspective to a child's height, something gnaws at my stomach. An achy longing.

If only I could return to that time. Back when it didn't matter what was outside the opera house because all the reds and golds, the fine silks and shining pearls filled me with such wonder. Back when I could look in the mirror without wincing, before I recognized that my face was different from everyone else's.

Mostly, I long for the time when Cyril held me on his lap to read me stories, when I had a little bed in that practice room near his office and I slept there with the window open to let in the starlight. Back before I knew what he was. Back when I was sure he loved me.

Glimpsing him again through the adoring gaze of a child brings a lump to my throat. Hissing, I swallow it down to where the monster can burn it to a crisp.

But it does not go down easy. No, every time I try to push it down, it rises back up, like a hopeful little bubble checking to see if I've changed my mind.

With tears stinging my eyes, I drop into one of the memories. My tiny frame is wrapped in a coarse wool blanket, and fatigue pulls my eyelids downward, but I force them to stay open so I can hear the end of *Charlotte and the Mirror of Forgotten Things*. The tale always ended with that little nursery rhyme, and I loved to hear Cyril recite it in his whispery, tired way.

> *When Charlotte looked in the mirror*
> *She saw a great many things*
> *A bone, a bauble, a book, a barrel*
> *Of berries picked last spring.*
>
> *All the images she'd forgotten*
> *As her mind grew old and gray*
> *Little details, bigger ones too,*
> *A thousand nights and days.*
>
> *But her favorite thing to see*
> *When she looked into its depths:*
> *A four-layer cake, fourteen roses,*
> *And sixty strands of baby's breath.*

The lace on her sleeves and veil,
And the ringing of bells up above.
The thud of her heart, the strum of the strings,
As she gave her soul to her love.

As memory-Cyril snaps the book shut, I open my eyes in the present. The echo of his voice drifts in and out of my mind.

What a silly story it was. A girl who gave up all of her memories in exchange for piles and piles of gold to travel the world. She didn't believe it would be possible to forget *everything*. But when she did and set sail across the sea, she left behind a husband and children and a whole lifetime without so much as a backward glance. Then one day when young Lottie had grown into an old, wrinkled woman, she came across a magical mirror that showed her the life she'd abandoned, and she finally realized that for all the gold and all the sights and all the experiences she'd gained, she'd given up the only thing that had meant anything at all.

When she returned to her home, her husband was dead and her children long gone. So she kept the mirror, became so obsessed with the things she saw there that she abandoned the present completely. She lived the rest of her life staring into the glass, longing for what she'd lost.

As a child who could never forget a moment of her life— including my mother's attempt to have me killed—the idea of valuing one's memories was a thrilling concept.

Now, standing here in the warm cellar of Cyril's home, I wish I could forget. If I could forget the sound of my mother's gasp when she saw my face for the first time, or those moments when Cyril seemed to care for me, perhaps I would be stronger. Perhaps I would have recognized his lies earlier. Perhaps I might have had the strength to break free of the opera house long before I finally did.

I grip the combination lock and swallow down that lump once and for all, squeezing away the tears that threaten to spill down my cheeks.

I don't have time for all of these memories and all of these feelings. I need to get into this vault, and quickly.

What could the combination be?

Cyril's voice is still trailing along the inside of my skull. *A four-layer cake, fourteen roses, and sixty strands of baby's breath.*

I twist the dial. Four. Fourteen. Sixty.

The lock clicks. The mechanism inside turns. Scarcely daring to breathe, I grip the handle and pull the door open.

Golden vials shine from inside, draped with jewelry and jammed next to bulging bags of coins.

But there is no one there. I stomp inside and whirl, scrutinizing every corner and every shadow.

Where has he put her?

The sob chokes out again, and I drop my gaze to my feet. The sound came from *below*. I crouch, dig my fingers into the corner of the carpet on the vault's floor, and rip it up.

The only thing I find is a waxy cement.

I pound my fists against the nearest shelf, and coins clatter.

Growling, I dive out through the door and brace myself against the side of the vault. I push all of my body weight into the cold stone, pulling on every ounce of the chef's elixir in me.

Perhaps I really have gone mad.

Perhaps I don't care.

I push harder than I've ever pushed anything in my life. My jaw pops as I clench my teeth against the strain, and my head pounds as blood rushes through the injured places in my skull.

It's as though the pocket watch in my dress is ticking in my blood, a constant *whoosh-whoosh-whoosh* of Emeric's time slipping out of my fingers.

I squeeze my eyes shut, digging my feet against the wall.

Finally, the vault begins to move. It groans slowly across the floor, revealing first a small crack in the stone, then the edge of a trapdoor, then an inlaid handle.

I do not stop, do not even breathe, until the vault is free of the door completely, and then I collapse, my whole body quivering as I gasp for breath.

The sobbing sound is louder now, and it is unmistakably high-pitched. A little girl's voice.

I wheeze, noticing a lever on the wall connecting to a trail of mechanisms in the floor that attach to the vault. "Well *that* would have been easier than pushing the cursed thing," I growl at myself, as I scramble off the trapdoor and wrench it open. A small rope ladder descends into blackness. Swinging my legs over the edge, I climb down quickly. When my feet reach the ground, I squint through the dark.

It is a small room, lit only by what looks like a lantern full of elixir. A girl with a dark nest of hair sits cross-legged on a cot, a white nightgown draped from her jutting collarbones and sharp shoulders. Her eyes are so black they seem to swallow the night as she stares past me at nothing. She is sobbing, but her face is expressionless, her skin as pale as the clothing on her body.

If not for her weeping, she might be a corpse.

A clammy, slick hand wraps around my heart.

"Arlette?" I whisper.

She does not acknowledge my presence.

I move slowly, cautiously, as though she's a small animal who might spook.

"Arlette, I'm a friend of your brother Emeric's," I say, hoping the mention of his name might jog her into reality.

Her expression remains blank.

"I'm a gravoir like you," I try.

At the sound of the word *gravoir*, she jolts back against the wall, shielding her face with her arms. Her sobs grow louder as she presses farther away. "Please. No more," she whimpers.

The eerie light illuminates jagged brown scars carved into her palms—the catalyseur marks. Even with elixir still making my vision sharp, it's too dark to tell exactly what they look like. Scars in varying degrees of healing trail all over her arms, which are accentuated by dark bruises and lashes. Her jaw swells purple on one side.

I feel as though a hole has opened up beneath me, and I am falling into nothing and nowhere. My stomach jolts into my throat. Blood rushes in my ears.

"What has he done to you?" I whisper.

Her sobs continue. She shakes away from me, a tiny, starving thing. Only eleven years old.

What would Emeric do if he were here? I can almost see him climbing down the rope ladder and taking her in his arms. He would sob into her hair, kiss her cheeks, and tell her he's sorry he let them capture her, sorry he took her to see the village that day. He'd run his hands along the marks on her arms, and as she continued to weep into his shirt, he'd stroke her hair and sing to her.

So I pull my pendant out of my neckline, tug it open with my teeth, and sing.

Arlette does not seem to hear me at first, but after a moment, her hands inch slowly downward, revealing red, swollen, tearstained cheeks. The purplish gravoir splotches in her skin have darkened from crying.

I sit down carefully on the bed next to her and hold out my hand.

She peers at my outstretched palm, her lower lip still trembling.

As I sing the last of the lyrics, she places her hand in mine. Her fingers are colder than ice, and her fingernails have all been chewed down to bloody stumps. I try to meet her gaze, but she refuses, so I say, "I've come to get you out of here. To take you somewhere safe, somewhere far, far away."

I wait for some kind of reaction, some kind of acknowledgment that she has heard me and understands what I'm saying, but her face is as unresponsive as ever.

How different this Arlette is from the vibrant, inquisitive child I know from Emeric's memories.

Gently squeezing her hand, I stand, hoping she'll follow suit.

She does not.

"Arlette? You can trust me."

A shout bursts from somewhere upstairs, followed by a thud and some banging footsteps.

Panic slams through me.

"Please, Arlette. Come on. We have to go now."

Nothing.

More cries from upstairs. The other servants must have arrived and found the chef's body.

My heart beats in my throat as I duck toward Arlette. "Here, I'll carry you."

But as soon as my arms wrap around her, she screams and claws at me, elbows and shoulders jamming every which way. "Shhh!" I lurch back, but she barrels into me, knocking me to the floor as she knots her tiny fists in my hair and yanks. "Arlette!" I whisper as forcefully as I can, gripping both her wrists with my good hand. My fingers wrap all the way around her forearms, and I shudder at how I can feel every bone and tendon through her starved flesh.

She cries out again as a stomp and a shriek echo from upstairs.

"I swear I won't hurt you," I plead, shoving her as gently and yet as firmly as I can off of me so I can push myself upright. "I've come to help."

Her eyes are wide with terror and hate.

Cyril did this to her. All while I sat eating sweets and playing my organ and dressing up in costumes. It could easily have been me who was shoved down here into the dark. As I glimpse a world of pain in her expression, I wish it had been.

Arlette wrenches backward and jams her heel into my stomach. When I stumble, she leaps for my throat, but her foot catches on the corner of her cot and she crashes to the floor, knocking her head against the stone wall.

She goes still.

"Arlette?" I push the hair out of her face so I can press my fingers to her neck. Her pulse beats, timid and quiet, under my touch.

A door slams upstairs.

I hoist her limp form over my shoulder. Her body flops as I swing around and climb the ladder. Pressing my bad hand around her waist to keep her in place, I pull us both upward into the cellar, thanking Memory that I didn't use all of the chef's elixir moving that vault—otherwise the pain in my hand would be unbearable.

I scan the room for an opening and locate a small window up near the ceiling. As I make my way toward it, I stumble over the bag of vials. A few topple out of the opening, drawing my gaze with their glow.

Darting a glance up the stairs to the door, I consider.

Carrying this bag and Arlette will be difficult, but I might need that elixir. I can't count on being able to find someone to drain every time I need the strength. And maybe I could get these vials to Emeric somehow. Restore some of what I took away. It wouldn't come close to replacing it all, but it would be a start.

Boots stomp closer to the cellar door, and I crouch to set Arlette down, grasp the bag, and tie it to my belt. With elixir still pumping in my veins, it's not difficult for me to lift, but I know that when I run out, it'll be extraordinarily heavy.

Once it's secure, I stack a few crates on top of each other, then I lift Arlette again and climb to the window. It takes a few tries to get it open, but eventually the rusted latch breaks free and the pane swings outward into a small window well. Gritting my teeth against the icy bite of the outside air, I clamber out as the cellar door clicks open and footsteps creak on the stairs.

Clutching Arlette's waist, I snake my way up the wall of the window well and push her over the edge before pulling myself the rest of the way up.

Wind claws at us from every direction. All is white and cold. Snow stings against my face, into my cloak, up my sleeves.

With a grunt of frustration, I yank my cloak off and wrap it around Arlette's shivering, tiny form, pull her back into my arms, and run.

I cannot see, cannot even think through the cold and the scream of the wind. My ears ache with numbness. The last of the chef's elixir is slowly pumping away as I make out the hulking form of Cyril's back wall and stagger toward it. With every step, the bag of vials drags me back, my hand's throbbing returns, and the quaking in my legs increases.

"No," I growl through gritted teeth. "Not again."

I reach the base of the wall. Lead drops in my stomach.

There is no way I'll be able to climb it, even if I weren't carrying a girl and a bag of elixir. The wind is too strong, my left hand too injured, and my right one too numb.

I dig into the bag at my hip and pull out a vial, uncork it with my teeth, and down the contents. My blood sings to life, and warmth floods my body. It's only a fraction of what I got from the chef earlier, but hopefully it'll be enough to get me over this wall.

Adjusting my grip on Arlette, I begin to climb. My progress is slow, and the bag sways against my leg with every movement, threatening to make me lose my balance and topple backward into the snow.

I focus on Emeric. On his laugh, on his smile, on his voice.

I have found Arlette. Once we make it out of here, I'll finally be able to ask her where to get a catalyseur and how to use it. After I've acquired one for myself, I'll take the opera house by storm. I'll drain every soul in this Memory-forsaken city and fill Emeric up. I *will* make him whole again.

But I need to get over this wall first.

For Emeric. For Arlette. For me.

I climb until my fingers curl over the top of the fence. Maneuvering myself and the girl over it, I grit my teeth and jump. We tumble into the snow, and I lose my grip on Arlette. She thuds into the white powder next to me, still unconscious.

"Sorry," I gasp as the last of that vial of elixir drains away and my body turns frigid once again. "I've got you." Arms straining, I struggle to get her over my shoulder, and then I stumble blindly through the wind until I find the horse near the birdbath where I left him.

I use one more vial of elixir to get Arlette onto his back and climb up behind her. Then I kick the gelding into a run and spend the rest of the gold in my veins keeping us both in the saddle as the wind and the snow threaten to tear us away and drag us both into the hungry, violent sky.

CHAPTER
THIRTY-TWO

I push the horse to gallop as fast as it can until we reach the outskirts of Channe. A little church sits on a hill, its humble spires reaching toward the snow-blown sky. I might have continued on past it had I not noticed the windows all boarded up. An abandoned chapel seems as good a place as any to wait out this storm.

We ride up its front path, and I slide from the saddle, cringing when I hit the ground and the force of the impact jars through my frozen limbs. I run my good hand along the boards nailed across the main entrance. They're soft with rot. I wrench them off one by one, wincing when my shoulder starts to ache.

Once the doorway is clear, I ease the still-unconscious Arlette out of the saddle and shoulder her inside, leading the horse along.

The howl of the wind cuts away to near silence when I kick the door shut behind us. I half drag the tiny girl down a row of pews, dropping the horse's reins to let him rest in the chapel as I heave Arlette into a back room that looks like it might have once been the residence of a priest of some sort. A threadbare, worn couch slumps in the corner, and I lay Arlette on its lumpy cushions. I scan the area for linens but only come up with a set of moth-eaten curtains, so I yank the fabric down and drape it over Arlette's shivering form. Her lips look terribly blue. I need to warm her up somehow.

The priest's quarters are small, but thankfully there's a fireplace with a stack of old, dried wood next to it, so I set about building a fire. Once a crackling lick of flame is burning on the hearth, I rummage through the cupboards at the other end of the room.

The only bit of food I find is a stale, inedible hunk of bread so hard that it sounds like a rock when I knock it against the counter. I toss it aside.

"Water. We need water," I mutter, scanning the area. A small, cracked pot sits on the counter in the corner, and I carry it outside to fill it with snow, then return to set it near the fire.

As the pot's contents begin to melt, Arlette bucks against the couch, screaming.

"Don't! Please don't hurt me! I promise I'll try harder!" She thrashes as though the curtains are trying to strangle her.

I move to her side. "Arlette." I try to make my tone as soothing as possible. "You're okay. You're safe. He's not here."

Her shrieking intensifies, and she flails at me, digging her fingernails so deeply into my neck that I cry out.

"Arlette!" I try a bit firmer. "Shhh! It's okay!"

Her cries echo in the room, sharp and scared.

Thinking back to how Emeric's lullaby calmed her in Cyril's cellar, I begin singing again, as loudly as I can while still attempting to sound calm and gentle.

Her sobs slow, and she stares at me, her brows furrowed and her eyes sparking with fear.

Then her expression breaks, and she buries her face in her hands. "I can't see this one's memories either, monsieur," she whimpers. "I'm so sorry…" She curls in on herself as though awaiting a blow.

"Of course you can't see my memories," I whisper. "That's not your fault."

She lowers her hands. Her glassy, tear-filled eyes register on mine for the first time.

I offer her the pot of water, and she accepts it, bringing it cautiously to her lips before eagerly gulping the liquid down.

Once the water is gone, she lowers the pot and wipes her mouth on the back of her bony hand.

"You sing like my brother," she says after a long moment, her voice high-pitched and not quite steady. "He loves that song."

I clear my throat, trying to calm the jumpy feeling zinging through my body.

"Are you a fendoir?" she asks.

"Me? No. I'm like you." I reach behind my head with my good hand to untie the mask and let it fall from my face.

She sucks in a breath. "What's your name?"

"I'm Isda."

Her calm expression cracks into a look of wild fear. She jerks away from me, tumbling to the floor in a knot of fabric and limbs. With a screech, she yanks herself out from the curtains and bolts for the door.

"Arlette!" I shout, dashing after her.

My cloak slips off her shoulders as she flees, and her threadbare nightgown whips between her spindly legs.

The horse stamps its feet in the corner.

Arlette halts, staring at the beast. Her whole body begins to tremble.

"Arlette," I say as softly as I can. "You're going to catch your death. Please come back by the fire and warm up."

She turns to look at me. Her whole body shivers.

"Please." I reach a hand out to her.

"I promise I'll try harder next time," she says, weeping, before stumbling back into the priest's quarters.

I follow her and pull the door closed. Arlette cowers behind the couch with the curtains pulled up to her chin. When our gazes meet, she ducks her face behind the fabric.

I sink back against the door and press my good hand to my forehead.

How am I supposed to get any sort of useful information about catalyseurs or how to compound my power out of her while she's in this state? I glance at her. She's still shivering. Her face is hidden, but her mass of oily hair hangs in clumps over the curtain.

"Here. This might help." I untie my bag, pull out a couple vials, and roll them across the floor to her. "Drink those."

With her eyes never leaving my face, she sneaks a trembling hand out to snatch them up. She gulps them down ravenously, and in moments her whole demeanor is transformed. Her cheeks pink up, her eyes lose some of their glassiness, and her shaking slows to a stop.

But she does not regard me with any less fear.

Her stomach growls so audibly it makes me wince, and she tucks the curtain closer around herself.

Maybe if I can get her some food, she won't see me as the enemy anymore. Maybe she'll be willing to talk.

I lift the pocket watch from my dress. Six thirty-seven. Barely more than thirteen hours left before Emeric's memories are gone for good.

I don't have time to come up with any other plans. If I'm going out to get Arlette some food, I'd better do it quickly. And if giving her a meal doesn't help things, then I'll have to head back to the opera house without a catalyseur and pray to Memory I'll be able to figure something out.

"I'll be back in a little while," I say as slowly and succinctly as I can. Arlette shrinks farther behind the couch. "I'm going to try to find food. Please stay here."

She does not nod or respond or give me any sort of indication that she has understood me, so I turn and duck out through the chapel, pausing only to untie the bag of elixir vials from my waist. As I do, I reach for the pistol at my belt, only to find it missing. I must have lost the gun at some point during the trek from Cyril's house. Cursing, I wrap my cloak around myself and slip out into the wind.

It takes me nearly an hour to drag my frigid legs through snow that is already to my knees to reach the nearest neighborhood. I take shelter for a moment from the wind in the shadow of a small cottage, and as I blow on my hand to thaw my fingers, a sound rides out to me—the first sound I've heard out here other than the wind. It's coming from the house on the other side of the road.

Pulling my hood down over my face, I sprint across the street and crouch under a window. Once I've caught my breath, I ease upward until I can see through the glass.

A woman is sawing through what looks like a freshly baked baguette on her counter. She's singing as she works, belting a song I recognize from one of the shows the opera house put on last year so loudly it can be heard easily through the windowpane. Her hips bob back and forth to the melody.

Both the skin on my ankle where the Manipulation Mark used to be and the Extraction Mark on my thigh prickle to life, reaching out to her music for the memories that ripple beneath.

I could drain this woman in a moment. It would be easier this time than it was with the chef or the prison guard because she's already singing. My mouth waters, and my limbs quake with longing.

I plunge into the woman's past, treading through the gray and white images to where her elixir streams pure and delicious as nectar. As I paw through, however, my attention snags on a flash of a little boy with mop-like brown hair clutching a stuffed animal. Though the boy's face is pale, his cheeks free of dimples, and his eyes a bright blue, my breath catches in my throat. Visions of Emeric as a child singing for a dozen toys in a kitchen much like this one flash across my mind.

With trembling hands, I pull my influence away from the golden elixir.

The woman continues her trilling, dropping slice after slice of bread into a brown paper bag with exaggerated flourishes that vaguely resemble the bowing of ballerinas onstage.

I tread through her memories to that place where the tide of thoughts burbles out of the present. Gripping the window-sill, I push in an echo of a child's voice.

"Maman!" I make him say. "Maman, come here!"

The lady stops singing, and my grasp on her memories vanishes. The beast in my chest protests, but I swallow it down and watch.

"Edouard? Was that you?" She sets the knife down next to the brown paper bag on the counter and makes her way out of the room. "Are you okay?"

Bracing my frozen fingers against the window, I push the pane upward. The wind roars into the room, blowing the curtains sideways and knocking papers from the kitchen table.

Not even bothering to make sure the woman didn't hear the ruckus, I bolt to the kitchen, snatch up the brown paper bag, and fling myself back into the snow. Clutching the bread close to my chest, I dash away from the cottage without closing the window behind me.

Time continues to trickle away, and as I push back against the onslaught of snow and wind toward the church, I can't help but imagine a giant hourglass pulling every moment away from me, one after the other, in a steady drumbeat. But instead of sand, this hourglass is full of elixir. Emeric's elixir. Each time a bead of it slides through the narrow tube in the middle, it drops to the bottom of the glass and sizzles, boiling away to nothing but a wisp of steam.

CHAPTER
THIRTY-THREE

When I try to open the church's front door, the wind rips it
from my hands and bangs it against the wall. I drag it closed,
praying the sound didn't startle Arlette.

She's sitting on the couch when I enter the priest's quarters,
the moth-eaten curtains still wrapped around her body, but
the elixir I gave her seems to have done its job because her
shivering has stopped completely and her lips have returned
to a much healthier pink.

As I pull my hood away from my face, she watches me
warily with eyes that seem much too pained, much too
haunted to belong to a girl of only eleven years.

"I brought you some food." I toss the bag to her.

She jerks away from it as though it might bite her.

"It's bread." I move close to the fire to let its warmth ease
some of the feeling back into my hands and feet.

She nudges the bag open with a finger. Once she glimpses
what's within, she plunges both fists inside and shoves slice
after slice into her mouth.

As she eats, I retrieve the pot from where she left it on the
floor and fill it with more snow. This time when I return, she
barely even glances at me, so intent is she on the bread. Once

the snow has liquefied, I hand it to her. She accepts it and guzzles noisily as crumbs flake away from her chin and hands.

I pull my pendant from my neckline and pop it open once more. The music is sweet and gentle as a kiss, and I close my eyes for a moment, imagining Emeric's voice along with it.

When I open my eyes again, Arlette is staring at me, the brown bag empty in her lap, chunks of crust littering the curtains and couch around her.

I reach up to push hair away from my face and remember I still haven't put my mask back on.

"I've never seen another one before," Arlette says quietly.

"Another what?"

She points to her face. "Someone like me."

"Me neither. Not in real life." I am afraid to breathe, terrified she might scream or attack me again.

"Have you come to kill me?" She asks it as though it is an ordinary question, as though that is the most logical reason I would be here.

"Of course not. Why on earth would I do that?"

"He used to talk about you." Her dark eyes—eyes so similar to Emeric's and yet still so different—bore straight through me as though they can pin me to the wall.

"Who did?"

"*Him.*"

"Cyril?"

She flinches, shrinking into the couch.

I soften my expression as much as I can and try to keep from making any sudden movements. "Sorry."

After a moment, she nods. "Yes. *Him.*"

I lick my lips. "What—what did he tell you about me?"

"Nothing." She pauses, considering me. "He used to mutter your name under his breath. I once heard him say something like, 'if the runt can't do it, then Isda definitely won't be able to.'"

It's as though the words are a blow to my gut, a sudden, stark reminder that I was nothing but a pawn to him.

"What was he trying to get you to do?" I ask.

The girl furrows her brow. "He tried to get me to do lots of things."

"Like what?"

"Extract elixir from fendoirs. Torture people with my power. Kill them. Confuse them."

"Did he ever say why?"

"No." Her eyes rove over my face, pausing on my mis-shapen lips, my twisted nose, my sunken cheeks. After a moment, she asks, "Why did you come?"

"Cyril—sorry, he—is looking for me. But I can't fight him unless..." I knot my hands together. "Unless I figure out how to use my powers better. I hoped you might be able to help me." I consider telling her about Emeric, but I'm not sure if she's stable enough to handle hearing about the danger he's in.

Arlette pushes the hair out of her face. "I can't."

"Did he do that to you?" I point to the marks on her arms. In the light from the fire, the bruises are darker than ever. Giant, purplish fingerprints around her wrists, and more trailing up to her elbow over all of the symbols carved into her flesh.

She runs her left thumb down the line of marks on her right forearm and nods. "He had a book of illustrations of Les Trois. He was trying to see if mimicking the marks they had would affect my power, as well."

"Did they?"

She purses her lips but does not respond right away. After a moment, she nods. "We never figured out what many of them did, but some of them..." She shudders and closes her eyes.

"What about the ones on your hands?"

"Oh, these?" She opens her palms. The symbols scarred

there are clumsier and older than the ones on her arms. "My maman did these."

Emeric told me as much. "When the police caught you that day in Marvault after the...incident, were you able to use those marks again?"

She shakes her head. "They made no difference. I didn't know how to do much of anything back then. I was little."

I ball my hands into fists. "Then how did you do it?"

"Do what?"

"When you sucked out the elixir of everyone in Marvault all at once. No one was singing. Did you have a catalyseur?"

She stares at me. "*He* kept asking me that, too."

"What did you tell him?" My heart is beating in my throat now, so hard I'm afraid I might choke.

"I told him I didn't know what that was."

My heart jolts to my feet. I press my hand to the wall to steady myself. "You—you don't know..."

"I don't know."

The world tips. My head pounds.

Tick-tick-tick goes the watch in my dress.

"Maman did mention catalyseurs when she carved the marks, though," Arlette offers, seeing the distress on my face.

"What did she say?"

"Maman said that the marks would make me stronger and the catalyseur would protect me."

"What does that mean?"

Arlette shakes her head, tugging the curtains up to her chin again. The brown paper bag and crumbs spill to the floor next to the couch. "I don't know."

I sigh and rub my knuckles over my eyes.

"I'm sorry, Emeric," I mutter under my breath.

"What did you say?" Arlette's voice is sharp.

"Nothing. It's not important."

"You said my brother's name. Do you know him? Where is he? Is he okay?"

"Yes. No. I'm not sure." I scrub a hand over my face. "Emeric is...a good friend of mine." Might as well tell her the truth. "He's been taken by Cy—by *him*. That's why I have to figure this out. I have to save Emeric."

"Do you know my maman, too?"

I bite my lip. "No." My voice sounds distant, as though it has been whisked away by the harsh winds outside. "I haven't met your mother."

Her expression breaks, and she buries her face into the curtains. This time when she weeps, her sobs aren't hollow or faint. They fill her whole body, shivering down her bony spine, jamming her limbs with each gulp. "She's gone, isn't she? It's my fault. I told them about her."

"None of this is your fault."

"I hate them," she sobs. "I hate them all."

My chest feels as though it might crack in half, and I move in to encircle the girl in my arms. "I'm sorry," I murmur as she presses her face into my collar, wraps both arms around my neck, and cries.

"Why didn't I listen?" she blubbers. "I shouldn't have followed Emeric into Marvault. I should have stayed put like he told me to."

I stroke her hair and stare into the fire until its crackling embers have branded their white-hot design on my eyes. "You didn't know what would happen. Not even Les Trois could see the future."

She sobs against me until her body grows limp with exhaustion. "Will you sing again?" she asks.

I tuck her in, stroke her forehead in the way I saw her maman do in Emeric's memories, and sing the lullaby until her limbs grow heavy with slumber and her breathing evens out.

I sit there, holding this tiny, starved eleven-year-old in my arms, staring at the fire as the wind continues to beat against the walls and Arlette's words continue to beat against my soul. Emeric may only have hours, but I know with certainty that he would want me to spare a moment or two to soothe his sister until she has slipped completely into the peace of slumber.

My thoughts whirl through our conversation, through all of the places in it where I hoped I would find answers and instead found nothing but more questions.

She doesn't know what a catalyseur is. I lean back against the couch and let out a slow, tired exhale.

That was it. She was my only chance at finding a catalyseur in time to save Emeric. The only other place I could find more about it is if I were to locate Emeric's mother's resistance group, but that will take far more time than I have. I dig my hand into my dress and pull out the pocket watch. Smoothing my thumb along its glassy surface, I watch the tiny second hand snap methodically around its circle. So unceasing, so relentless, so merciless.

It is nearly nine thirty, which means I have scarcely more than ten hours left. More than half of my time has been wasted on this fruitless chase. I drop the pocket watch back into place and wind my fingers into my necklace.

If nothing else, I got Arlette out of that hole in Cyril's cellar. If I cannot save Emeric, at least I will have saved his sister. That would have made him happy.

I think of Arlette's mention of catalyseurs. *Maman said the marks would make me stronger and the catalyseur would protect me.*

I frown down at the ballerina in my pendant. What else had Emeric's mother said? Hadn't she given them something else that was meant to protect them?

I twist my fingers through the chain. A sparkle of blue on a leather cord flashes through my mind.

The stone.

I gasp.

How did I not see before now? How did I not put the pieces together? For weeks I've been wishing for a catalyseur, and all along it was right there in my crypt with me, so close I could have reached out and snatched it right from Emeric's neck.

The marks in Arlette's palms have to be linked to the stone—when she extracted the elixir from the people in Marvault, those symbols had glowed bright with power. So I'll need the marks and the stone together in order to do what I need to do.

Gently, I pull her hands out from underneath the curtains to inspect the scars. They are two matching symbols. Serpentine marks from the base of the thumb to the bottom of the pinky.

I'll need to find a blade.

As I slide Arlette's hands back into the warmth of the curtains, my eyes catch on the bruises on her arms. I can almost see Cyril's wiry, slender hands pinching them until the blood pooled under her skin.

Fury ripples anew in my heart.

Cyril locked me up underground, imprisoned me in his opera house, and fooled me into loving him. He stole a girl from her family, killed her mother, and turned her brother into a puppet.

He will pay for the things he has done.

But not just him. No. This whole world, with its jeering laughs and its disgusted expressions, with its groping hands and its ice-filled wells.

The world will pay for how it has treated us.

My beast rears its horned head, fire hissing in its heart as I ease myself out from under Arlette's slumbering frame, collecting my cloak from where she dropped it before, and cinching it around my throat. I pull the hood over my head.

I will burn them.

I will burn them all to ash.

CHAPTER
THIRTY-FOUR

I spend the next two hours searching the entire chapel. Surely whatever priest once ran this place kept a knife somewhere for holy rituals, but all I find is dust and cobwebs and a set of old scriptural records of the God of Memory and his saints. With a growl of frustration, I shove the books back onto their dusty shelves.

Voices outside make me freeze. Adrenaline pumps through my limbs, and I creep past Arlette, who is still sound asleep. She stirs and rolls over, tugging the curtains closer around her as she snuggles into the couch.

I reach the window and peek between the boards. Several policemen seem to be surveying the perimeter of our hideout on horseback.

I curse, then grab Arlette's shoulder and shake her awake. "Arlette!" I whisper fiercely. "Arlette!"

She bucks upright, flinging an elbow at me, but I was expecting that, and I dodge it.

"Arlette. You've got to hide. Now."

Her eyes register on my face. She pushes the curtains away and swings her bony legs over the edge of the couch. "Is *he* here?" Panic rises in her voice.

I shake my head. "No, not him. The policemen that work

for him." I crouch so I can look her straight in the eye. "Listen to me. I need you to find somewhere to hide. A cupboard, a closet, anything. I'm going to go out there and draw them away from here, understand? I may be gone for several hours. Whatever you do, stay here and stay put. I will come back for you when I can."

"You promise?"

I pull her against me in a quick embrace. "I swear it."

She wraps her skinny arms around my waist, then turns and bolts across the room to the cupboards and climbs into one.

Once I'm sure she's hidden, I charge into the chapel where I left the horse. Footsteps creak on the church's front porch. I retrieve the bag of vials I stole from Cyril's basement and latch it once more to my belt. Downing two vials of elixir and chucking the empty bottles behind me, I knot my fist in the horse's reins and lead him to the front door, thanking Memory that the worn carpet underfoot masks the sound of its hooves.

With my heart hammering in my throat, I peer through the crack in the door at the policeman on the front porch. He's angled away from me toward a scraggly bush. I squint to catch a glimpse of what he's doing and hear the distinct spatter of urine against the ground.

I slide the door open, hoist myself into the saddle, and kick the horse into a gallop directly past him off the porch and down the walkway.

The policeman shouts. A gunshot fires from somewhere on my right followed by another one to my left.

Gritting my teeth, I duck low against the horse's mane and urge him faster.

The clouds have cleared and the sun on the snow blinds me, but at least the wind has calmed. Hoofbeats trail in my wake. Bullets whistle past. Barking cries punctuate the frigid air.

My hood whips away from my head, and the biting cold on my cheeks reminds me that I forgot to put my mask back on.

My expression breaks into a wicked grin.

Let them see my face. Let them gasp in horror. Let them feel the fear that I have lived with my whole life before they die.

Though the world is blanketed in a thick layer of fresh snow, I can tell when I've reached the cobblestoned streets by the way the horse's hooves pound harder and the way his limbs jolt with every step. I swing him to the right and barrel down one road and then another, winding and twisting through Channe, keeping my eyes on the sky to make sure that with every turn, I remember to correct my course west toward the opera house.

The city is crawling with police. They head me off in street after street. In spite of the elixir thrumming life through my limbs, fear trickles ice along with it.

When another group of policemen meets me in a marketplace, I spit a string of expletives, yank on the reins, and careen off in the opposite direction.

Hours tick by as I twist through the city, hiding in alleyways and behind buildings until the coast is clear, then galloping madly away when they catch sight of me again. I pause only a few times to give the horse a chance to gulp up some snow before taking off again, and by early afternoon he is beginning to show the wear. His stride is choppier and slower, his responses to my nudges on the reins clumsier.

"Come on, boy," I plead, rubbing his neck as another gunshot echoes on the buildings around us, making him flatten his ears back against his head. "I'll never make it to the opera house without you."

I've barely made it halfway across the city.

What has Cyril done—hired a whole infantry to track me?

I'm losing precious minutes. With each time I am forced to backtrack, my thoughts snap to that image of Emeric's hourglass of elixir, the gold liquid burning away to nothing drop by drop. It's nearly nightfall, which means I have only a handful of hours left.

I reach into my dress for the pocket watch, but before I can pull it out, another cohort of police clad in black comes around the corner. They raise their guns, shout, and kick their horses into a run.

I dig my heels into my own horse's ribs. "I'm sorry, boy. Just a bit more."

The gelding wheezes but gallops off the way I direct him.

Now that the storm has passed, people have begun to trickle out into the streets to shovel snow from their doorsteps. They raise their heads as I pass, but I am gone too quickly to see the fear flicker across their faces.

The police chasing me seem to be struggling with the crowds. Their voices grow more and more distant with each corner I turn. Their gunshots cease.

My horse's breaths come out heavy and winded. I don't know much about horses, but I do know that he won't be able to keep this up much longer.

I slow him to a trot and steer him into an inconspicuous alley. He huffs and puffs as I slide down from his back. "Good boy." I rub his nose, keeping my attention trained on the alleyway's opening and my ears perked for any sound of the police. "Easy there."

He shakes his head and paws at the ground as his belly balloons in and out.

I lean against his neck, inhaling his warm, animal scent, and clutch at my chest with my good hand. Though I've escaped capture for now, panic courses painfully through my system.

But with it comes relief.

At least Arlette is safe. For now.

I focus all of my energy on inhaling and exhaling until my heart rate slows back to normal and my hands stop shaking. I pull several vials of elixir out of the bag on my hip and gulp them down quickly.

I might have to leave the horse here and continue on foot. Though making the trek the rest of the way across the city will take more time than I want to even think about, I don't want to injure the horse. Besides, I might be able to hide from pursuers easier if it's just me.

I pull my pocket watch from my dress and nearly cry out.

It is six o'clock. Only two hours remain until Emeric's time is up.

Someone speaks nearby, and I freeze.

"Red hair, black mask, injured hand. On horseback. You seen her?" the voice says.

All the blood in my body drains to my feet.

Cyril.

Stashing the pocket watch, I creep slowly to the alley's opening and press my back to the cold brick of the wall on the left. Taking a deep breath, I chance a look around the corner.

Cyril is across the street, conversing with a young man carting a bushel of apples.

As I duck back into the shadows, he turns his head.

And meets my eye.

He grins.

Whirling, I yank myself into the saddle and goad the gelding into a run. Cyril yells, and a gunshot splits the sky.

The horse shudders beneath me and skids sideways to the ground with a scream. I shriek as I go careening off the beast and into the snow. Scrambling to his side, I press a hand to his flank. "I'm so sorry," I whisper before rolling up onto my feet, and breaking into a sprint.

"Stop!" Cyril barks.

I push the elixir in my body to its maximum, flooding my legs with power. Snow skids under my boots as I run. The sun slinks low to the horizon, staining the snow scarlet.

It's only me and Cyril and the bleeding sky.

"Isda!" Cyril's voice bounces against the walls around me. "It doesn't have to be like this!"

I grit my teeth so hard that even the elixir can't erase the pain in my head completely.

Of course it has to be like this. He ensured that it would be with every lie and false embrace he gave me since I was five minutes old.

The farther I run, the more the elixir in my body dissipates. The glow of it is fading from my limbs, from my raging heart, from my injured hand. My pace is lagging. Soon, I will have to stop to drink more. If I do, Cyril might catch me. But if I don't, he surely will.

As I sprint past a street, I glimpse a policeman on horseback. Whirling, I lunge down another alleyway before he sees me.

But Cyril shouts to him, and my body zings with panic. If he somehow calls the rest of his police force out here, I won't stand a chance no matter how much elixir I ingest.

I have to make it to the opera house. To Emeric.

Hoofbeats clatter behind me, and I swing around a corner and dive behind a trash bin. The policeman gallops past.

I wait only a moment to be sure he's out of sight before I take off running again. West toward where the tiniest sliver of gold emblazons the outline of the hills. Toward the opera house.

Always the opera house.

My plan is flawed and dangerous, but I don't have time to think of a better one. Somehow I'll sneak backstage as soon as the performance begins and locate a knife to carve the symbols into my hands. Once I get close enough to Emeric's stone, I should be able to channel its power.

Crunch-crunch-crunch. My boots churn snow in their wake.

Tick-tick-tick. Time disintegrates in my grasp.

Thud-thud-thud. My heart pounds out a drumbeat.

Streets whiz past. I elbow people aside and dodge cabs and carts at every turn.

Meet me in the darkness, meet me in the night, I chant in my head, as though Emeric might be able to hear it and heed my pleas.

I dart a look over my shoulder and catch sight of Cyril, also on foot, shoving a cart out of his way. He's far behind me now, but his legs are longer, his gait is quicker, and his body is uninjured. He'll catch up to me soon.

I jam my hand into my bag to retrieve another vial of elixir and try to dump some into my mouth without slowing my pace. Half of it spills down my front, but I manage to swallow some. A sudden burst of fire burns through my legs, and I channel that into a full-on sprint.

CHAPTER
THIRTY-FIVE

People gawk as I pass and dive out of my way, screaming.

I pay them no mind.

As the meager supply of elixir in my body starts to wane, my ears catch on the sound of voices nearby. Lots of them.

I am only a few blocks from the opera house.

With the sun now completely devoured by the horizon, I don't have to look at my pocket watch to know it is nearly time for tonight's performance. I have less than an hour left. If I can make it to the street in front of the entrance, perhaps I can lose Cyril in the crowd.

Gasping for breath, I speed around the last corner, yanking my hood up as I reach the swarm of fancy cloaks and well-pressed jackets. I duck among them, keeping my head bowed to hide my face. My heart thunders against the wheezing strain in my lungs, but I force myself to slow down so as not to draw anyone's attention, keeping my hands tucked carefully inside my cloak.

All around me, conversations bubble like the fizz at the top of a glass of champagne.

"I saw him the other night—he was absolutely spectacular!"

"They're saying he's the best voice Vaureille has ever heard."

"He's not bad to look at either."

Emeric's name follows me everywhere, in quiet, excited murmurs and bright, cheerful cries.

If they knew what he was like, if they knew about his caramels, gentle hands, and relentless teasing, they would love him all the more. But they will never know that Emeric. The singer on tonight's stage is nothing but a shell of that boy.

I glance over my shoulder to see where Cyril has gotten to. After a moment of searching, I find him in the crowd. He keeps his expression composed and comfortable in the company of so many of his patrons, but he peers into every face that passes, obviously scouring the area for any sign of me.

Slouching away, I weave among the sparkling gowns and pressed tuxedos. The elixir has depleted entirely from my veins, and my body is tingling for more. I reach the edge of the throng and shift around the corner of the opera house where I'm less likely to be noticed. Fumbling with the bag at my waist, I pull out another vial and raise it to my mouth to pull out the cork.

Someone shouts.

"It's the gravoir!" A woman points a finger in my direction. "From the papers!"

Jamming the vial back into my bag, I sprint away from the crowd, ignoring my cramping legs and the way it feels as though someone has plunged a knife into my side.

More shouting. More running footsteps. More gunshots.

Wheezing, I dash for the nearest street.

Half a dozen guards barrel toward me from the other end.

Wheeling around, I tear back the way I came, but Cyril is there, pulling a gun from his belt.

I am trapped.

Cyril squeezes off a shot. I dive for the opera house and barely dodge the bullet as it whizzes past my head. Wrapping my good hand around a drainpipe, I hoist myself upward, begging my legs to hold out for a moment longer, begging my heart to keep beating.

Gritting my teeth through the agony in my left hand, I climb. Each step is fire, and pain fills my vision with white smoke. I press on.

Emeric needs me. If I fail to restore his elixir within the next hour, he'll spend the rest of his life a puppet, good for nothing but an empty performance on Cyril's stage forevermore.

The beast in my chest growls.

I won't let Cyril or this Memory-forsaken city win. Not when I have the power to shatter the world.

The drainpipe clangs in my grasp. I glance down. Cyril has taken hold of it and is following me up the side of the building. One of the policemen in the street aims his pistol at me, and a bullet ricochets off the wall near my nose. Stifling a shriek, I pull myself higher, praying that they are all just as unlucky in their aim.

Another shot singes through the rim of my hood, and I choke down a gasp.

"Don't shoot!" Cyril bellows. "She's mine!"

I seethe.

Not anymore, Cyril.

I yank myself higher. My arms shake, and my body feels as though I've been run over by a cab, but still I keep climbing. With every movement, I think of Emeric's kiss, soft and fierce and full of passion. *You are a song.*

Finally, my hands reach the edge of the roof. As I muster the strength to pull myself upward, another gunshot splits the sky and slams me against the wall. My left shoulder explodes with pain, and a scream tears through my lips.

Hot blood pools in my sleeve, slides down my arm, drips from my fingertips.

Cyril laughs.

Spitting curses, I use my right arm to drag myself onto the roof. Once I'm over the edge, I roll away, sucking cold air through my teeth and blinking furious tears from my vision.

Gripping my ruined shoulder with my good hand, I scan the rooftop for a way in. I might be close enough now to access Emeric's stone, but I still don't have a knife to make the carvings in my palms.

A small entrance decorated with winged angels juts from the roof next to the domed ceiling of the theater. I stumble toward it, but my legs buckle, and I skid down into the snow.

"Come *on*, Isda!" I hiss, forcing myself upright and staggering forward once again.

But my legs seem to be made of jelly. I trip, landing so sharply on my left arm that I shriek.

I jam my good hand into the bag for some elixir, but my fingers are slick with blood, and the vials slip out of my grasp.

Cyril reaches the roof and hoists himself to his feet. I scramble backward away from him, leaving a trail of crimson in my wake, until I'm pressed against the door. I reach up to its handle and twist.

But, of course, it is locked.

"Valiant effort, chérie. I applaud you." Cyril dusts snow and dirt from the sleeves of his jacket. "I'll admit, I didn't expect you to be this clever. Brava. It made for quite an exciting afternoon."

Glaring through sparks of pain, I grip the door handle and try to stand.

If death is coming for me, I will meet it on my feet.

He strolls toward me, as leisurely as though he were taking an outing in one of Channe's city parks in the spring. He stops a few feet away and raises his pistol.

I meet his gaze and jut out my jaw.

"You were supposed to be it," he says softly. "All I taught you. All I sacrificed. All the money and time I spent on keeping you happy, alive, and safe. It was for a purpose, and now you've ruined everything we built."

The wind lifts the white hairs around his face, and for a moment I am reminded of how he used to look after a long night of recordkeeping for the Council. With exhausted circles around his eyes and his hair mussed out of its usual styled perfection. How he'd stop by to check on me before retiring to his home to sleep until the opera house's evening performances.

I always thought he made that extra trip to the opera house because he wanted to see me. Because he cared about me.

Now I know better.

"Why?" My voice is as weak as the skittering pulse in my veins. I sag against the door, but I hold his gaze. "Why me? Why am I still alive when you have hurt and killed so many others?"

His smile fades, and his nostrils flare. "How did you find out about that?"

"Does it matter?" I wheeze a laugh. "You're going to shoot me."

"I don't want to."

I laugh again. "Unfortunately, Cyril, I'm not so gullible as I once was."

His knuckles are white on the gun, but his gaze is steady. "I'm not lying."

Black stars eat away at the edge of my vision. My legs wobble. I inhale a slow, rackety breath. "What?"

"I don't want to do this any more than you want me to." He mops his face with his free hand but keeps his gaze steady on me. "You asked me why I chose you. I'll tell you why, Izzy. You were the first one I found. You were an ugly little thing. Skinny, bald, hideous…but your eyes were so trusting. They gave me an idea."

His words echo with the ones he said in the cab weeks ago.

Your eyes, sweet Izzy. I looked into your little face and they were all I could see. I had no choice.

"I suppose it was fate. Destiny. Kismet. You learned all that I taught you, and you believed all that I said. Everything was going according to plan except..."

"Except what?"

He grimaces. "Except I never planned to care."

My blood froths to a boil in an instant. "Save the breath and the lies for someone still deluded enough to believe them. You did not care for me. Buying me pastries and gifts is not the same thing as caring. You know what a person who cares about me wouldn't do?" I'm shouting now, and tears run down my cheeks, hot and furious and free, and though my body sways, my anger grounds me in this moment, here on the roof, with the man who gave me everything and then destroyed it all. "A person who cares about me would not call me *vile*. He would not hand me to the police and sentence me to death. He would not reduce the only person who actually *does* care about me to a walking corpse. And—" I raise my injured hand and shake it at him, my voice dropping to a deadly whisper. "He would not take away my music. Not when he knows what that would do to me."

Cyril swallows, his eyes never leaving my face.

"So pardon me, *monsieur*, but I'm done letting you pretend you know a thing about what it means to care for someone." A wave of dizziness overtakes me at the expense of so much emotion, and I lean back against the door to steady myself.

Cyril cocks his gun. "I suppose 'care' isn't quite the right word. I should have been more precise. You've proven yourself to be a blasted nuisance today, but in spite of that, shooting you still seems like such a waste."

"I was your weapon. An expensive, precious prize. One you spent a lifetime building. Of course you don't like throwing that work away."

He glowers at me for a long moment, and then, finally, nods. "You did always have a smart tongue." He steadies the pistol.

"I am still curious about one thing, though," I say, leaning heavily on the door handle. "Why did you do what you did to all of those other gravoirs? The torture and the symbols?"

He considers me for several breaths. Bells ring distantly, and I wonder for a moment where they're coming from until I realize that the sound is all in my own aching, whirling head.

"If I hurt you, you wouldn't have trusted me anymore," Cyril says quietly. "A dog who loves his master is much more obedient."

"They were your test subjects." My voice is so weak now it's barely a whisper. "I suppose I knew that. I just hoped it wasn't true."

His mouth twists. "You always did believe whatever you wanted to. Living your life in a fantasy world made of sparkles and feathers to cover up the hideousness of reality. Well, let me teach you one last thing, child. Life is ugly."

I do not blink. "I know enough of ugliness to recognize it when I see it."

He bares his teeth. And pulls the trigger.

Click.

We both stare at his gun for a split second before he tosses it aside, rips a knife from his belt, and rams me back against the door, pressing its edge to my throat.

"We were so close," he hisses into my face. "With you by my side, we could have had such power, could have rid the world of fendoir corruption. It would have been only a matter of time before the King would have been begging me to serve on his Imperial Council." His expression turns cold. "But then you had to go and get yourself seen, and now the whole city is begging for your head on a platter."

Tears sting the corners of my eyes, and I swing my fist

against his forearm, which loosens his grip enough to send his blade flying. It hits the ground and clatters away. With a grunt, he wraps his hands around my throat.

"But luckily, you are not so special. There are other gravoirs, other ways for me to get what I want."

I struggle against his grip, gasping for air.

"And," he continues, "thanks to you, I'll be Channe's savior, the slayer of the monster. With the Rodin boy singing on my stage, I'll begin my reign as Council Head with an influx of wealth and prosperity that will change the way Vaureille looks at Channe forever. And now that I control the Council, I'll be able to prove to King Charles how dangerous the fendoirs are. Finally, I'll be able to purge the world of them and their influence. You've orchestrated everything out so perfectly for me. Well done."

I buck against Cyril, and he tightens his hands around my windpipe. I gag, kicking at thin air.

As my vision flashes, I see Arlette's face from Emeric's memory. Wicked and wild in Marvault's town square, wrapped in the elixir of an entire marketplace. Dragging memories out of everyone in sight even though none of them were singing. All because of those marks on her hands and that stone at Emeric's throat.

I need to get to Cyril's knife.

I dig my fingernails into his eyes, and he throws me to the side. I slam against the dome of the theater's roof. Coughing, I scramble to the fallen blade and dig it through my bandaging and into my left palm. Pain jolts up my arm, but I tighten my grip and keep working. Once I've finished the first symbol, I position the hilt between my teeth and slice into my other hand. The runes are clumsily done, but I have no time to fix them.

Cyril barrels into me, pressing me into the opera house's roof, his fingers rigid around my windpipe once more, his eyes swollen and furious. Blood trickles from my nail marks on his right cheek.

The dome beneath us vibrates with the sound of the orchestra. The performance has begun. Emeric is directly below me, most likely waiting behind the curtain to come onstage. His stone should be close enough.

Yet I feel nothing. No thrum of power, no tingle in my hands, no tide of a thousand memory rivers come to whisk me to sea.

I swing the dagger at Cyril's face, but he jerks me sideways by the throat, knocking the weapon from my bloody fingers.

Shards of white slice through my vision.

I kick weakly, dragging slippery hands against Cyril's vise grip. My lungs scream for air. My body spasms uncontrollably.

I was wrong. The stone must not be a catalyseur. I am going to die here on the roof, and Emeric will spend the rest of his existence no better than dead.

My mind whirls with music that has nothing to do with the symphony below. Music that is faint at first, but soon grows. The tinkling of tiny bells in a pendant, the strum of organ chords against stone walls, Emeric's laugh.

The beast in my chest twitches as my vision fades.

Darkness welcomes me, drags comforting fingers along all the places where I hurt, dispelling the pain until there's nothing left but quiet and stillness.

I was not fast enough.

Cyril has won.

"Goodbye, chérie," Cyril whispers.

Then Emeric's voice fills the sky, and the world explodes into gold.

CHAPTER
THIRTY-SIX

The dome beneath me shudders. Cyril's grip loosens. Coughing and gasping, I shove away from him. The symbols I've carved into my flesh shine with a brilliant light to rival the stars.

Cyril gapes, eyes wide with wonder and fear. Sweat glistens on his brow. My blood streaks his white tuxedo shirt.

I push to my feet as Emeric's voice crescendos into my soul. Sweet, sweet music.

The melody caresses my arms, strokes down my spine, winds its fingers through my hair.

And it thrums like life in the marks on my hands.

At once, it dawns on me. I thought Arlette used her powers to drain everyone in the town square even though no one was singing. But someone *was*.

Emeric.

The stone wasn't the catalyseur; he was.

That's why my power was so drawn to him, why his music affected me physically. Why his memories were so different from everyone else's.

The roof's shaking increases until dust rises from the corners. Cracks spiderweb across the dome, and amber light swirls out from them, twinkling gold dust in the night.

There is a moment where the ceiling seems to billow outward, as though the opera house is inhaling.

And then the roof collapses.

The chandelier beneath my feet is a sparkling array of diamonds and light, and it falls as though in slow motion. Each shard of glass and each sculpture of crystal reflects the iridescent blaze in my palms as the air swoops upward, whipping my dress and hair.

Cyril and I plummet.

Two thousand faces turn upward, and, with Emeric's voice vibrating through the symbols in my hands, two thousand souls tug on my power at once. Instead of focusing on those memories, I swivel about as I fall, fixating on the stage and the lone figure standing at its center.

"Emeric!" I shout.

A crash shatters the air as the chandelier hits the stage. Crystal and glass smash across the wood. Fire erupts.

Cyril cries out as he slams next to it, splintering into the wood with an earsplitting crunch.

Somehow my power has already begun to grasp onto people's elixir, and it flows toward me in tiny, sparkling droplets that thicken the air and slow my fall. When my feet finally touch the edge of the stage, I break into a mad dash for Emeric.

Screams echo all around me. People stampede for the exits.

But all I see is Emeric.

He stares, his face blank, his eyes glassy. Though the symphony has long stopped playing, my power holds him bound to his music, and he continues to sing without pause.

As I leap over fractured wood and careen past broken glass and licks of flame, Cyril's voice cuts through the air.

"It's the gravoir! Stop it before it kills us all!"

I'm almost to Emeric now. If I can pull him away from the stage, get him somewhere safe, I can take all of this elixir gathering around me and push it into him to restore what was taken. And then we can run.

A pistol fires, and the bullet rips through my injured shoulder, throwing me headfirst into the stage. I clamp down on the scream in my throat and push myself up with my right hand.

My whole body quivers, and fuzzy spots take over my vision once more.

I've already lost too much blood.

I suck in the droplets of elixir hovering around my face. When the honey taste hits my tongue, I moan.

Why does it taste so *good*?

My limbs quiver with desire. I need more.

I need all of it.

As I gulp it down, my body fills with life and strength. The pain recedes. My vision clears.

Emeric is only yards away, still staring, still singing.

I charge for him, only to be knocked sideways by one of Cyril's opera house guards as he barrels in from the right.

Roaring, I channel the coursing elixir into my good arm and shove him violently off. But before I can get to my feet, another guard appears. And another. A dozen men in tuxedos rush forward, swinging umbrellas and baring their teeth.

A second gun fires.

One of my attackers yanks me by the hair, and another drags on my dress. A boot slams into my stomach.

I focus on the way Emeric's voice has brought the symbols on my palms to life, on how every person in the room's elixir is beckoning to me, taunting me, begging me to drink it all down.

A pistol is jammed into my face.

I grin down its barrel.

And undam every single memory river in the room at once.

Elixir floods toward me, wrapping me in light.

The gun drops. People collapse to their knees.

Pulling on Emeric's song, I turn to face my audience, raising my arms to the stars beyond the broken ceiling above.

After years of dreaming of performing on this stage, I am finally the finale of the performance. I inhale deeply and join in with Emeric's song, filling the world with the sound of me.

The rivulets of elixir trail up my body and into my mouth as I sing. Ecstasy rolls through my every nerve.

Thousands upon thousands of memories engulf me. Memories of love, laughter, sorrow, forgiveness...

I am surrounded, consumed.

The opera house glows, not with sparkling lights or candelabras, but with the blaze of a thousand memories.

I turn my gaze to the balconies and laugh as patrons topple from them, as eyes grow dim, as bodies go limp.

Now this stage belongs to me.

Now the music is mine.

Now the world pays for its cruelty.

This is what I'm capable of.

Fire roars nearby, and my dress ripples against my legs. My hair flies around my face.

The people who did not make it out of the theater crumple one after the other as I suck them dry.

The monster in my chest smacks its lips.

The more I drink, the more I want, and soon I stop my singing to gulp down whole mouthfuls at once. Faster and faster and faster I swallow. Elixir spatters down the front of my dress, dribbles down my chin, drips from the ends of my hair.

I never want to stop. I could drain the whole city and still it would not be enough.

I beckon the ribbons of light, twirl them around my fingers, devour them with relish.

All at once, my own memories are nothing but shadows in a world of light and sound. No longer am I the girl locked away in a crypt writing music that no one will ever hear. No longer am I the monster hiding among the dead, where none but the shadows love me.

As Emeric's music opens all of their minds, I become the girl playing with a doll at her mother's feet, the boy teaching his brother to play cards, the woman dancing at her wedding with flowers woven in her hair. I am the teacher, the baker, the musician, the jeweler.

I have lived a thousand lives, seen a thousand sights, sighed a thousand sighs.

I've done it. I am as powerful as Rose, as fearsome as Les Trois. I found the catalyseur, and I will keep him forever.

The catalyseur.

I pause midswallow.

Emeric.

His name snaps through the delighted roar of the beast in my chest, and my vision clears as worry floods me. How much time does he have? Minutes?

I whirl, peering through the haze of magic and smoke.

There, crumpled among the ashes, lies Emeric. His mouth is open with the trailing remains of the song I'm still pulling from him. His body is bent, and his eyes stare up, wide and somehow, impossibly, emptier than they were before. Empty as a Memoryless's.

Empty as a corpse's.

I've extracted the rest of his elixir with everyone else's.

I relinquish my hold on his music, and his voice creaks to a stop. He twitches and goes still.

"No," I breathe. "No!" I claw past the flames, leap over fallen bodies, and crash to his side. Smoke burns in my nose. Heat whips my clothes and sears my skin. I grasp his face between my hands.

Please, no.

"Emeric!" I shout. Somewhere nearby a beam collapses, and the fire roars.

But Emeric does not move.

I press my ear to his chest. Tears spill down my cheeks and soak into his shirt.

His heartbeat is a faint, pattering thing, nothing more than the wingbeats of a moth.

"Wake up," I plead.

Even in the smoke, I catch a whiff of caramel on his skin, and I cry harder, remembering the night I tried and failed at making a batch of it with him in his apartment. The time he opened my locket and taught me its song. The time his mouth burned across mine, so forbidden and so undeserved and so impossibly right.

The time he looked at my unmasked face and called me a masterpiece.

Each memory strikes me as though made of the same bullets that ripped through my shoulder.

I wrench the bag from my hip, yanking out cork after cork and dumping the vials' contents onto his tongue.

"Come on, Emeric. Swallow." My voice trembles in spite of the strength pounding in my veins. "This world needs you. Arlette needs you. I need you. Please."

Still his eyes do not open.

When we are surrounded by discarded vials and my bag is empty, I press my head to his chest once more.

His heartbeat has grown even fainter.

"No!" I scream, wrenching the nearest vial from the floor and hurling it into a corner where it shatters against a closet doorframe.

Something jolts away in the shadows of the closet. A sliver of white hair catches the firelight just before the door jerks shut.

I rise, fury boiling through every part of my body.

Incinerating me.

Igniting me.

"Cyril!" I scream, stomping across the stage and ripping

open the door—the flimsy bit of wood that must have been all that protected him from my power before.

He scuttles away from me, his broken legs twitching uselessly behind him as he squeezes behind piles of costumes and broken set pieces.

But there is nowhere he can go. Nowhere he can hide.

"Look what you've done!" I wrench him by the shoulder and shove him against the wall.

"Isda, I—" He trembles. Soot sticks to the sweat on his face, and his hair glistens with blood. "I'm sorry..."

"You're *sorry*?" I shout, spittle flying in his face. "You said I ruined what we built?" I shove my face so close to his that I can taste his fear. "*We* didn't build a thing together. *I* built this opera house. *I* built your success. *I* built this city. And I will burn it all down."

He gags on smoke, and I ram him so violently into the wall he mewls.

"All my life I've watched other people stand on this stage, playing music and performing roles that were meant for me. Now, it is finally my turn." I toss him to the ground and poise the heel of my boot over his throat. "Sing with me, chéri."

He licks his lips, eyes wide and bloodshot.

"I said *SING!*"

He whimpers, then begins to blubber through "La Chanson des Rêves."

And for the first time, Cyril's memories flood my mind.

I paw through the tide toward his earliest memories, my hands quivering with the desire to see every single thing he's kept from me all these years. When I drop in, the first thing I find is a kind-faced, golden-haired fawn of a woman with soft hands and a warm embrace. She has a tiny smile, one that makes her cheeks turn rosy when she laughs, and eyes that are as brilliant and blue as Cyril's.

His mother.

Moments swirl by. Cyril watches from corners, chewing his fingernails to bloody stubs as she scours the house for coins. He sifts flour while she bakes extra loaves of bread to sell for spare change. He helps her sort out which of her beloved trinkets could pay the rent.

Then one day she doesn't come home until very late, and when she does, she stumbles inside. The lights in her eyes have faded to stone.

She sees Cyril sitting curled up on her couch, and she freezes. "Who are you?" she asks, her voice uncertain. "How did you get into my house?"

"Maman?" Cyril's heart skips to double time.

The woman raises an eyebrow. "You'd better run along, dear. Your parents are probably worried sick."

But the longer he tries to explain that he's her son, the more frantic she becomes.

I cringe as Cyril slaps frozen hands against his own front door. "Maman! Maman, please!"

She yanks the door open a crack. "I said get off my porch, child, or I'll call the police!" Her blue eyes film wet, but they hold no love, no recognition. Only fear. She locks the door, leaving him alone and sobbing in the snow.

His tears steam in the winter air as he stumbles down the street begging for food. For shelter. For love.

And every time he passes a Maison des Souvenirs, he presses his nose against the glass, peering at the fendoir inside, wondering if that one was the monster who took his mother away from him.

Years whirl past, full of fear and betrayal and pain.

And then one night he fishes a baby from a well and gasps at the sight of its face.

He tortures a hundred gravoirs. Mutilates them. Executes them one by one.

Piles of gold grow in a bank vault.

Stacks of Council record books march two-by-two on his shelves, preparing to fight the war that's been battling in his heart since he was six.

A quiet cemetery with a pale marble gravestone appears. Cyril's gloved fingers brush snow away from a name. *Claire Bardin.*

I see him grapple with me on the roof, feel the snapping of his bones when he hit the stage, hear the chaos as he crawled away to hide. The shock of terror when I turned his way cleaves me to my core.

With tears streaming down my cheeks, I rip every drop of elixir from his soul and send it straight to Emeric's crumpled, dying form.

And then Cyril is nothing but a corpse, lying gray and cold on the stage.

I collapse to my knees next to him. He wears a quiet, gentle expression as he stares up at the stars.

Ash billows around us, fluttering tufts of white hair across his face.

"I'm sorry." The words are garbled, and they trip over each other on their way across my tongue. I push the hair away from his forehead and then press his eyes gently closed.

If it weren't for all the blood, he could be sleeping.

How many times have I seen him doze off at his desk, working late on records for the Council or tallying finances for the opera house? How many times did he nod off reading fairy tales to me when I was little?

"You may not have loved me," I whisper, my tears dropping onto his face and trailing down the smile lines around his mouth. "But I loved you, and my love was never a lie."

CHAPTER
THIRTY-SEVEN

It takes me longer than I'd like to pull away from Cyril.

I shouldn't care that he's dead. I should be happy he got what he deserved. I should feel powerful.

But his memories and his emotions slice through me, a torture of pain and hatred and regret.

Heaving a shaking breath and forcing myself upright, I turn and rush to Emeric's side. He coughs on the smoke, and relief surges through me.

He's alive.

The *Le Berger* set cracks and then crashes to the floor. Fire licks up the curtains to the ceiling. Shouts echo from the lobby.

I need to get Emeric out of here.

With hundreds of lifetimes' worth of elixir pulsing through my body, I pull him onto my uninjured shoulder and make my way out into the hallway, trying to ignore the glassy stares of all of the people I killed. Keeping away from the front lobby, I speed toward the back exit and into the night.

Channeling all of the power and elixir I have, I sprint through the snow, dodging past onlookers so consumed with watching the opera house burn they don't notice my face.

I head for the western boundary of Channe, and I keep

running until I've crested the hill that overlooks the city. When I reach the edge of a small copse of trees, I ease Emeric to the ground and check the pulse in his neck.

It beats, strong and warm, under my fingertips.

I collapse back against the trunk of a tree with a weak laugh.

"You're alive," I whisper, trailing my hands down the ruffled, soot-stained sleeves of his costume. "Thank Memory."

Emeric slumbers on, his lashes fluttering as his eyes twitch back and forth under his eyelids.

I wipe away the smudges of makeup and ash on his dimples, then grasp his hand in mine and turn to look out over Channe.

Black smoke balloons upward into the sky, spreading fat fingers to strangle the stars. The opera house burns red and orange and yellow.

A part of me aches as the only home I've ever known withers. I imagine my organ deep in the belly of the earth and wonder if it'll be safe from the flames. Glancing at my swollen, bloody hand, I blink away the ache in my eyes. Even if the instrument survives, I'll never be able to play it again. Not like before, anyway. Cyril made sure of that.

But the phantom inside of me thrills at the sight of its former prison crumpling to ash and soot.

No longer will I be locked away in the dark.

Emeric coughs again, and I turn my gaze on him.

The beautiful boy with the voice to shake the heavens. My catalyseur. I stroke the back of his hand with my thumb.

The smile slips from my lips.

No.

As though I've dipped myself into a river full of visions of the future, I see all too clearly what will happen if I keep Emeric the way I want to. This hunger of mine, this craving for his music and the way he compounds my magic will only grow stronger and stronger, until I am consumed by it.

He'll become my prize, my gem, my tool for revenge.

As much as I want to punish the entire world, as much as the phantom inside of me longs to drink the elixir of every person on earth, I know I cannot.

I cannot do to Emeric what Cyril did to me.

I won't.

Releasing Emeric's hand, I pull my knees against my chest and rest my arm across them. I trace his features with my gaze—the perfect point of his nose, the arch of his brow, the divot in his lower lip. The dark lashes and the dimples and the long, shaggy hair.

I think of him on that stage opening night when the world trembled to hear him. When the stars dimmed their light to listen. When the very sky quieted its breath to wonder at his music.

The way he glowed. Eyes shining, face pink with excitement.

I always knew he was meant to be there. Meant to perform. Meant to sing.

I cannot take that away from him, either.

My eyes dart to the city, burning under a blackened sky, flames glowing against the snow.

The Council and every police force in this country will hunt me for what I am and what I have done. I will be a fugitive for the rest of my life.

When Emeric wakes, he will try to stay with me. He will tell me that being an opera performer doesn't matter, that all he wants is to find somewhere where Arlette and I will be safe, happy, and loved.

But I know what it will cost him. His lifelong dream. His destiny. And, when I succumb to the demon inside of me, his freedom.

I press my palm to my forehead to quell the quaking of my heart and the trembling of my soul.

"Emeric?" I whisper, placing my hand on his shoulder and shaking him gently.

He stirs.

"Emeric, it's Isda."

"Is..." His smile is soft.

"Emeric, I—" My voice breaks, and I clear my throat as tears sting once again at the corners of my eyes. "I have a favor to ask of you."

"Any—anything," he croaks.

"Will you please sing with me?" The words come out quiet and strained, and I can barely see him through the film of wetness in my vision.

His eyes finally open, and he turns them on me, wondrous and beautiful.

My throat closes. I rub a fist across my face.

His hand settles on my knee. "What's wrong, Is?"

"I just need you to sing."

"Why?"

I give a weak laugh. "You ask too many questions."

"You keep too many secrets." He smiles, and I bury my face in my hands so that those dimples can't weaken my resolve any more than they already have.

The snow crunches as he moves, but I don't trust myself to look or speak.

His arms encircle me. His fingers ease into the knots of my hair. His lips press against my forehead. "What is it?"

"I have to go."

"Where?"

"Away. I've done something terrible."

"Then let's go. We'll head south. It'll be warmer there, and—"

I shake my head as a sob chokes through my teeth. "No, I have to go alone."

He is silent for a moment. His palms slide down to cup my cheeks and pull my face to look at him. "What are you talking about?"

I swallow, determined to keep my composure. His brow is furrowed, his expression confused.

"Did your mother ever say anything to you about catalyseurs?" I ask.

He frowns. "Not really. I think she mentioned they could protect Arlette."

"That's not entirely accurate. They actually compound gravoir power. Give us the ability to use our magic on people even when they aren't singing."

"All right…" He waits for me to explain the connection.

"For weeks I've been trying to figure out how to get my hands on one. Turns out it's not an object, it's a rare type of person."

"A person?"

"You, Emeric. You are a catalyseur."

He purses his lips, his thumbs stroking soot away from my cheeks. "So what does that mean?"

"It means—" I take a deep, quivering breath "—that I have to let you go."

"But why?"

"Do you remember what happened at the opera house tonight?"

He considers for a moment, then shakes his head. "The last memory I have is of you extracting my elixir in the prison."

"I used your voice to drain people," I whisper.

"'Drain'?"

I nod. "There are a couple hundred corpses lying in the theater."

He stares. I wait for his expression to sour, but instead he asks, "Why?"

"Because they were trying to kill me. Because they were keeping me from you." I pull myself out of his grip and turn away so he can't see my face. "Because I wanted to."

"Just like Marvault," he says faintly. "Like Arlette."

I nod.

He grips my shoulder. "It was not your fault. Not any more than what happened in Marvault was Arlette's fault. I was there. My sister was not a murderer or a thief. She was not mad or dangerous."

"I'm afraid I knew a bit more about what I was doing than Arlette did."

His jaw hardens. "You are *good*, Is."

"I wish I were the person you see when you look at me, but—"

"But nothing. My sister was not the one who hurt everyone that day in Marvault. It was like something *else* had taken over. She—"

"Exactly," I break in.

He blinks. "What?"

"This power inside of me is strong, and the more elixir it gets, the more it craves. My inability to extract from people unless they are singing keeps me sane, but with you around... with you affecting my abilities like that... I'm afraid it will take over. That it will destroy me."

"I won't let it." His voice is firm. "I'll help you keep it in check."

I shake my head. "I can't risk it. Every moment I'm here with you, that power is simmering beneath the surface, begging for me to use you again. Craving more elixir and more death." Even now, the beast reaches ravenous claws toward Emeric. *Sing again*, it hisses. *Sing for me, boy...* I swallow the saliva collecting on my tongue, the hunger gnawing in my gut, and meet his gaze. "If you come with me, I am certain that it will consume me completely."

His Adam's apple bobs. "So, what, you're expecting me to let you go by yourself? With a whole country after you? How does it help either of us if you end up dead?"

"Luckily, I have a whole life's worth of practice keeping out of sight. I'll be all right."

"What about me? I'm just supposed to go back to my life as though you never existed? That's not fair, Is."

"Please." I tremble. "Please don't make me fight this. I will lose."

He mops a hand across his face and sniffs, shoving to his feet and turning away to look down on the city. I stare at the hard lines of his back, at the way his broad shoulders are framed by the orange light of the flames.

"Why did you want me to sing?" he asks.

I move to his side and slide my right hand down his arm. His fingers interlace with mine and squeeze gently. He looks down at me.

"Why?" he repeats.

"You don't know how strong the...the *thing* inside of me has become. I'm afraid that just leaving you won't be enough. It'll know that I can always come back, that you'd accept me and care for me." I reach up and tuck a tuft of hair behind his ear, then trail my hand along his jaw. "I—I need you to forget me."

He drops my hand and backs away, expression darkening. "Why would you even ask me that?"

"You think I want to do it?" I say, balling my good hand into a fist. "Do you think I want the only person who has ever cared for me to forget I exist? Do you think I want to live the rest of my life running away from the one person I love?"

We both freeze, that final word striking between us and electrifying the air like a bolt of lightning.

My whole body is trembling again in spite of the elixir.

And I realize it's true. I do love him. I've loved him since those first nights in my crypt when he was rifling through my things and conversing with skulls on my walls. Since he saw my mask and chose to trust me anyway. Since he realized what I was and decided it didn't matter.

"You," I whisper. "With the caramels and that laugh and those damn dimples... How could I have stood a chance? From the moment I heard you sing, I was bound to love you."

He stares at me, an unreadable expression on his face. Then all at once he's stalking toward me, a sudden intensity in his gaze.

His lips meet mine as he wraps his arms around me and braces me tight against him. I gasp, and he kisses harder. The fingers of my good hand tangle in his hair.

His mouth is warm and soft and fills me with a fire hotter than the one blazing behind us in Channe.

He lifts me and presses me back against a tree, and suddenly there is nothing in this world but his lips and his hands and his heart thundering in time with mine. There is no beast inside of me. There is no police force hunting me. There is no death and no blood, no gravoirs or fendoirs. Only the two of us, locked away in this impossible moment where what is forbidden and what is right no longer matter, and all that exists is this feeling. Being loved. Being *wanted*.

When the heat in his kisses changes from a blazing inferno to the seductive smolder of glowing embers, I whisper, "This is why I have to do it, Emeric."

He pulls back to meet my gaze, his hands stilling against either side of my neck, his thumbs cradling the curve of my jaw. "This is why you *can't*, though," he says. "Because I love you, too, and that means I get a say in what happens."

I whimper as his words rock through me. *I love you.* Words said in fairy tales and dreams. Words I was never meant to hear. "It's *because* we love each other that I have to go. Do you know what it would do to me if I hurt you?" I press my forehead against his. "It. Would. Destroy. Me."

His thumbs caress my skin, leaving tracks of hot fire in their wake all up and down my neck. But he doesn't respond.

"I want to think I could keep the monster at bay," I whisper. "But when I was draining the elixir from those people in the opera house, I was not in control." I suck in a breath. "As much as I hate the world for what it's done to me, I don't want to imagine what I might do to it if that power overcomes me."

He leans in and presses a gentle, tentative kiss to the corner of my mouth. "But you're strong, Is. We're strong together. We can fight this."

I meet his gaze. Ferocity and fire, determination and resolve ripple one after the other in the expression on his face.

For a moment I let myself imagine it. Him, Arlette, and me, in hiding but happy. Far away. Maybe in a cottage like the one where he grew up.

But even as the scene plays out in my mind, I know it would never be like that. The beast inside me has tasted what Emeric can do to my power, and it wants more.

Do it, it whispers. *Take him back to the city and finish what you started.*

I shake my head. "I'll either succumb to it, or I'll go mad trying to resist." My voice trembles. "Do you want that for me? Because I wouldn't want that for you."

His thumbs slow their gentle movement. He releases me and interlaces his fingers behind his head with a grimace.

"The demon I would become...it wouldn't love you anymore. It would see you only as a pawn. I'm begging you, Emeric. Please don't force me down that path."

He mops his forearm across his face and considers me for several long, quiet moments. Then, finally, he nods.

"All right," he whispers.

My soul unravels, and the tears I've been keeping at bay spill out onto my cheeks.

He crushes me against him, and his own quiet weeping rocks through us both. I knot my hands in his shirt, press my face into his chest, and breathe him in. Caramel and burnt sugar tear me to pieces.

His hands move to my hair, weaving into the snarls until he's cupping both sides of my head behind my ears. He presses his lips against mine once more.

Our tears mingle and stain our tongues with salt. I cannot breathe through the lump in my throat or the pain in my chest. I brace my arms on his neck, and he hoists me from the ground. I wrap my legs around his waist. He pushes me harder against the tree.

"I would have loved you forever," he says, his breath hot on my mouth.

I meet his gaze. "And I *will*."

His mouth dips against mine once more, but this time it is soft and gentle, quiet and questioning, as though he is exploring every inch of my lips with his so that he might memorize them. They are gentle kisses. Kisses that know they cannot last. Kisses that beg for just a breath longer. Kisses that mean goodbye.

When I don't think my soul can bear it a moment more, I break away. I slide my legs back down until my feet touch the ground.

He unknots the leather cord from his neck, the one that holds the blue stone his mother gave him. He holds it out for me. "To remember me by."

I stare down at it, hiccupping. "I'm a gravoir. Remembering is just about the only thing I can be counted on to do."

"Please take it."

I lift my hair and turn so he can tie it around my neck. His hands settle on my shoulders, heavy and final, and his mouth presses against the hollow under my ear. I lean into the feel of him one last time and reach into the neckline of my dress to tug out the pendant. Pulling away, I lift it from my head and drape it around his neck. "Keep this for me, then."

He never takes his eyes from mine. "Always."

The pendant glimmers orange in the firelight. I dig the edge of my thumbnail into the crack, and it pops open, filling the night with our lullaby. The ballerina twirls. Her song fills the night with faraway tinkling bells.

Weakly, I sing, reaching up to trace his face.

Meet me in the darkness,

He joins in, his voice barely more than a whisper. But as always, his memories are strong, and they crash into me with their voracious current. My thumb trails along the contours of his nose, down into the crease of his upper lip. One last memory for me to keep.

Meet me in the night.

The beast inside of me raises its head at the sound of Emeric's voice. *More elixir.* It opens its mouth to drink.

But for now the pain in my heart is stronger than the beast's hunger. I push it down, down, down until its appetite is only an ache in my gut.

I drag my fingers over the dimple in Emeric's right cheek as his memories swirl, strong and beautiful, through my soul.

It's time.

I plunge into their depths. Back to the first night he glimpsed me in the opera house's hallway, dashing away from a toppled candelabra in the dark.

Meet me where the star-touched breeze
Whisks away the light.

The roughness of shaven stubble sandpapers along my palm as I follow the contours of his jaw and chin with my touch.

Gritting my teeth, I manipulate the image of myself on that first night we met, reworking the memory until I'm nothing but a shadow on the wall.

For there under the canopy
Of a tall and silent tree

I move forward to when he found me behind the chair the night I offered him voice lessons. I transform past-Isda into a regular-looking tutor. An older man with a crooked nose and dark hair swept away from his brow. No more fire-red curls, no more sparkling, feathered black mask.

Emeric watches my face as my fingertips trail over his mouth. He kisses them gently.

Midnight comes to life, my darling,
To guard our memories.

I am bleeding inside. Pieces of me break away, leaving gaping, empty crevices in my chest.

The shadows of yesteryear
Where dawn and afternoon fade

His memory of my crypt morphs into one of a music studio at the back of the opera house. My organ disappears. My music fades.

Keep our moments quiet waiting
In a whisper-worn glade.

Emeric's voice is thick. His eyes grow distant. His mouth twitches away from my caress.

As they rest in moonlight,
Angels sing them all to sleep.

I find past-Isda shining in white lace, red curls spilling over her shoulders. I feel Emeric's rush of warmth at the sight of her. I let myself fall into the dance we shared one last time, that moment before everything around us shattered. I revel in the heat between our bodies and the way the music drove us around and around and made the rest of the world vanish.

So meet me in the darkness, darling,

Our kiss in his apartment. Coming undone, carving out a piece of the march of time where we could pretend we belonged to each other for just a moment.

Until, finally, there's only one memory left to change.

Tonight.

I drop my hand to my side and back away from him. He does not protest, does not follow. He cocks his head, biting on his bottom lip like he thinks he should know me but can't quite place my face.

My body quakes, but I keep my head clear as I manipulate the last memory, as I transform the past hour into nothing more than him waking up alone and cold in the woods.

Where past and present meet.

The power growls its frustration, begs me to undo what I've done.

Emeric stares at me for a long moment as the song fades from his lips, his eyes tracing the hills and valleys of my face. "Do—do I know you?" he asks.

I shake my head, blinking away the tears still warping my vision. "I'm afraid not." I force the words through the thick knot in my throat, and they come out warbled and weak.

"Who are you?"

"Most people know me only as the Opera Ghost."

His eyes trail over my face—but he's not looking at my mottled visage. He's looking at the tears and the blood. He reaches out for me, tentatively, as though he's afraid I may run. "You're hurt." He glances at the bullet holes through my left shoulder and the bandage hanging in tatters from my hand. "Who did this to you?"

I shake my head. "Don't worry about me. I'll be all right. I've come to tell you where to find your sister."

His eyebrows shoot upward. "You know Arlette?"

I close my eyes and nod. A small part of me fears what sending him to her might mean for him. She could be even more dangerous than I am. There's no telling what she learned from Cyril.

But I could never keep him from her. She's the only family he has left. He's been searching for her since the day she disappeared, convinced that if he could find her, he might be able to make up for his mistakes.

It is my job only to love him, not to be his caretaker. Whether they learn to control her power is between the two of them.

And so I let a slow breath out through my teeth and say, "She's waiting for you in a small, boarded-up chapel on the northern outskirts of Channe. Rue des Morts."

"It's really her? She's alive?"

"It's really her. She's in bad shape, but she'll be okay."

He bounces on the balls of his feet.

"You'd better go now, though. She's hungry and cold."

He turns to leave but pauses. "Are you sure you're all right? I could at least help you clean your wounds."

I think of his soft, gentle hands working at my bandages,

brushing against my skin. A sob chokes through me. "No. Please. Just go."

"Are you sure?"

I nod. "I'll make it."

"At least let me give you this." He pats at his pockets until he finds what he's looking for. He pulls something out and presses it into my grip, shaking my hand as he does. "Thank you so much, mademoiselle." Then he turns and sprints down the hill.

"Adieu, mon amour," I whisper, glancing down at the caramel he left in the center of my palm. I curl my fingers around it. "I'll remember for both of us."

I watch him until he is out of sight, and then I slip into the shadows, tugging my cloak closer around my neck and pulling its hood up over my hair. Tears continue to fall as I stride into the night, but I do not wipe them away. Instead, I look upward at the open skies and the stars twinkling between the reaching branches. I breathe in the cool, night air. Let it soothe some of the pain in my heart.

I do not know where I will go. I do not know what will happen next or how I will survive. But I do know that wherever I go and whatever happens, I will meet it with both eyes open.

Because now not only am I the performer, I am the director and the maestro of my own life. And though I may spend the rest of that life cherishing the memories of what I have lost here, I won't let my past stop me from living.

I take one last look at the city that raised me. Imprisoned me. Set me free.

And then I am gone.

Disappeared.

Forgotten.

★ ★ ★ ★ ★

ACKNOWLEDGMENTS

I would never have made it to "the end" if it weren't for a whole lot of amazing people. So buckle up, friends, because I couldn't possibly let this book hit the shelves without shouting to the world about the following rock stars.

First off, Jon. This book simply would not exist without you. Thank you for being the man who inspired Emeric, the real-life boy who loves me always in spite of the madness within. I can never express my gratitude enough.

Next, Mom and Dad. You fostered in me a love of literature from the day I was born. Thank you for reading my childhood stories about princesses and sandwiches and assuring me they were genius. For never telling me how mediocre my poetry was in high school. For cheering me on through my decade of writing books that couldn't get me an agent, reassuring me that one day one would. You are the best parents I could have ever asked for, and I'll spend the rest of my life trying to be just like you.

To Carter, Derek, and Emily. Thanks to all three of you for being my best friends since day one. For supporting me through the setbacks and celebrating with me through my successes. I couldn't have asked for better siblings. And to

Hannah Johnson—thanks for the amazing website! It's even better than I hoped!

To Kim Chance and Megan LaCroix. You changed my life. Thank you for loving Isda's story even when it was a total mess. I'm seriously still pinching myself that I have you both as friends. Here's to more manuscript-swapping and video-chatting and all the shenanigans in the world. You're stuck with me now.

To Brenda Drake and the entire Pitch Wars team. Thank you for creating a space that helps so many writers like me find a place.

To Christa Heschke. I don't think I could have found a better agent to represent me or Isda's story. Thank you for plucking me out of your slush pile and making my dreams come true. And to Daniele Hunter. I seriously lucked out that I got you along with Christa. Thank you for your editorial insights, for keeping things running, and for laughing at my not-as-funny-as-I-wish-they-were jokes on Insta. You rock.

To Lauren Smulski, who read my book and loved it enough to make my publishing dreams a reality. Thanks for taking a chance on me.

To Connolly Bottum. You pushed me to make this book its absolute best, and I will be forever grateful for the hours and hours you've spent on Emeric and Isda with me. I don't think I could have found a better editor to work with if I'd tried. Thank you, thank you, thank you.

To Bess Braswell and the rest of the Inkyard team: Thank you for believing in Isda's story and in my ability to tell it. There aren't words to express my gratitude for all the work and all the time everyone has spent on me and my little book.

To Jessica Froberg. Thanks for not thinking I was too weird when I slipped into your Twitter DMs and demanded you be friends with me. You're the world's best friend and CP, and I wouldn't be here (at least not sane) without you.

To the Westsiders SCBWI critique group: Kelly LaFarge, Karen Ekstrom, Christine Kohler, Carl Watson, Sharon Van Zandt, and Chris Perry. Thank you for all of the advice, critique, and support. Y'all are the best!

To Tina Chan, for reading the embarrassing first draft of this book and giving me such insightful advice. To Mara Rutherford and Neicole Crepeau, who gave me query and chapter critiques in preparation for Pitch Wars—you both helped in more ways than you know! And to Adalyn Grace, who gave me feedback that sparked many of the ideas I incorporated into my Pitch Wars revision. You are a queen.

To my Pitch Wars buddies who let me into their DMs to share in all the wildness of this ride: Erin Bledsoe, Tiffany Liu, Lorelei Savaryn, Summer Rachel Short, Ava Reid, and Mindy Thompson. I couldn't have done it without y'all to vent to and celebrate with! And to Jess Elle, whose support via Marco Polo saved my sanity more times than I could ever count.

To all of the teachers who fostered my creativity during my childhood, especially Christine Coppinger Flatt, who took a particular interest in my writing. Teachers deserve so much more than an acknowledgment in the back of a book.

To my three munchkins. You make all of this worth it. I love you more than reading, more than writing, and more than Reese's Peanut Butter Cups. I hope that when you see me working on my stories, you know you can do anything you set your heart to. If you never read any of my books, please remember this: magic is real, and the love you show for others can change the world.

And, finally, to my readers. Thank you for giving up hours of your lives and space in your hearts for my characters and their stories. None of this would be possible without you.